WIT

CEREMONIAL MURDER

The late Roger Pettibon's body, I could see when the men had parted for Her Majesty, was sprawled before the Throne as if he had been engaged in some macabre Oriental form of supplication just before he had died. His lifeless white face was turned left in partial profile, one staring eye aimed toward a table displaying Garter regalia, one arm in a casual tattersall-checked shirt straining forward, the other sprawled in a small puddle of blood.

Even more disturbing than the blood was the sight of the weapon still lodged in Pettibon's lower back, the decorative hilt and part of the blade pointing to the ceiling like a beacon.

❖

Also by this author

DEATH AT BUCKINGHAM PALACE

❖

DEATH AT SANDRINGHAM HOUSE

HER MAJESTY INVESTIGATES

Death At Windsor Castle

C. C. Benison

BANTAM BOOKS

New York Toronto London Sydney Auckland

DEATH AT WINDSOR CASTLE
A Bantam Book / August 1998

Grateful acknowledgment for permission to reprint "To a Fat Lady Seen from a Train" by Frances Cornford, from *Collected Poems*. Copyright © 1954 by Frances Cornford. Reprinted by permission of Cresset Press in London, England.

ISBN 0-553-57478-7

Published simultaneously in the United States and Canada

Bantam Books are published by Bantam Books, a division of Random House, Inc. Its trademark, consisting of the words "Bantam Books" and the portrayal of a rooster, is Registered in U.S. Patent and Trademark Office and in other countries. Marca Registrada. Bantam Books, New York, New York.

PRINTED IN THE UNITED STATES OF AMERICA

OPM   15 14 13 12 11 10 9 8 7 6 5

For Jocelyn Hunter and for Janet Turnbull Irving, both of whom have a wonderful way of opening doors.

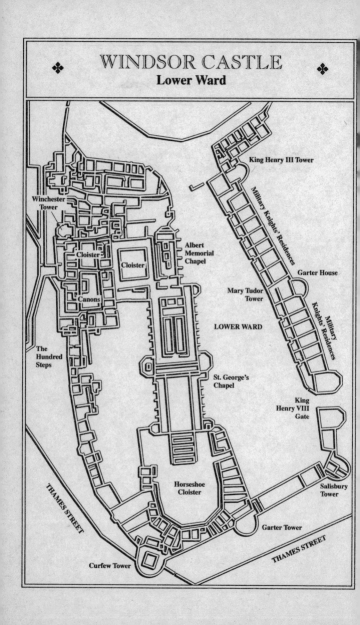

WINDSOR CASTLE
Lower Ward

King Henry III Tower

Military Knights Residences

Winchester Tower

Cloister

Cloister

Albert Memorial Chapel

Canons

Garter House

Mary Tudor Tower

LOWER WARD

Military Knights' Residences

The Hundred Steps

St. George's Chapel

King Henry VIII Gate

Horseshoe Cloister

Salisbury Tower

THAMES STREET

Garter Tower

THAMES STREET

Curfew Tower

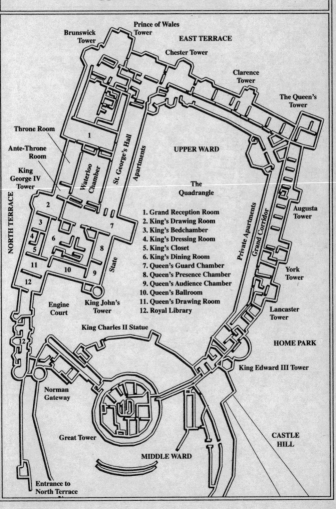

WINDSOR CASTLE
Upper and Middle Wards

Brunswick Tower

Prince of Wales Tower

EAST TERRACE

Chester Tower

Clarence Tower

The Queen's Tower

Throne Room

Ante-Throne Room

King George IV Tower

UPPER WARD

NORTH TERRACE

The Quadrangle

St. George's Hall

Waterloo Chamber

Apartments

1. Grand Reception Room
2. King's Drawing Room
3. King's Bedchamber
4. King's Dressing Room
5. King's Closet
6. King's Dining Room
7. Queen's Guard Chamber
8. Queen's Presence Chamber
9. Queen's Audience Chamber
10. Queen's Ballroom
11. Queen's Drawing Room
12. Royal Library

State

Private Apartments

Grand Corridor

Augusta Tower

York Tower

Lancaster Tower

Engine Court

King John's Tower

King Charles II Statue

HOME PARK

King Edward III Tower

Norman Gateway

Great Tower

MIDDLE WARD

CASTLE HILL

Entrance to North Terrace

AUTHOR'S NOTE

THOUGH THIS NOVEL is set at Windsor Castle and features the Queen and certain members of the Royal Family, it is nevertheless a work of fiction. With the exception of the Queen and other Royals, all of the characters, both central and peripheral and whether or not said to occupy certain positions in the Royal Household or official positions among the British aristocracy or in British law enforcement, are purely products of the author's imagination, as are the actions, motivations, thoughts and conversations of everyone in the novel, including the Queen and the members of her family. Moreover, neither the characters nor the situations which were invented for them are intended to depict real people, events or organizations.

Finally, it should be noted that this novel was written before August 31, 1997, and thus, the fictitious events portrayed in the novel are set at a time before the tragic and untimely death of Diana, Princess of Wales. Accordingly, the few passing references to the Princess are written in the present tense and presume that she is still living during the time of the story's fictitious events.

Introduction

I CAN SEE myself in my grandmother's kitchen back in Charlottetown, Prince Edward Island. I am somewhere in the middle of the terrible twos. My parents and my older sisters are in the next room, with my grandparents. Their conversation comes to me as a distant murmur. Somehow I've managed to slip their attention, and the unexpected taste of freedom, I think, has made me giddy and powerful. I am alone. Before me is a door, a big yellow door, only a cupboard door, really, one of several under the counter, but to me, height two and a half feet, it is as big as a door to a house. Behind this door my grandmother houses her cookies.

I do manage to pull open the door. My small arms encircle the first thing I see, a bright, round cookie tin on the lowest shelf which I draw forward, dropping myself onto my bottom and trying trying, with clumsy little fingers, to pry open the lid. It is hopeless, and I am on the verge of tears but my tantrum wavers before the image on the lid, a picture of a magical castle rising in the air, all turrets and towers. Who lives *there*? And then I stare at the figures on the side of the tin, of a woman in a glittering dress and a man in a navy blue uniform, grown-ups like my mother and father, and of two children not too much older than me, a boy and girl. Do *they* live there? And then I feel arms scoop me into the air. I only begin crying when my mother peels the tin from my furious fingers.

It is one of my earliest memories.

And like many an early memory it was submerged until one day it was prompted forth by a trick of the light, an evocative scent or a suggestive sound. My grandmother's kitchen, the cupboard, my cookie-lust came flooding back to me one hot summer weekend as the rowboat bearing me lazily down the Thames passed Windsor Castle and I happened to glance upward, toward the mighty Round Tower floating like a dream above a curtain of trees, the Royal Standard fluttering in the breeze over all. This was the magical castle on my grandmother's souvenir Coronation cookie tin, from the very perspective, the very angle. Indeed, the picture might have been taken from the very sun-dappled spot in the river on which I floated. I smiled at the memory of my childish wonder two decades ago. Who lives *there*?

I do, for one. (But then so do about three hundred and fifty other people.)

Do *they* live there?

Yes, they do. The woman in the pretty dress and the man in the uniform, the Queen and her consort, now in their winter years, spend most weekends at Windsor Castle. Midafternoon each Friday, a vintage maroon Rolls-Royce pulls up to the Privy Purse Gate entrance at Buckingham Palace, the Queen and a passel of corgis hop in, and she is sped to Windsor, a forty-minute journey west of the capital, glad to escape workaday Buck House, HQ of Monarchy, Inc., and relax inside the Castle's medieval stone walls with its magnificent views of parkland and the Berkshire countryside.

But twice a year the Court as a whole moves to Windsor, for Easter and, in June, for Royal Ascot. That's when I,

Jane Bee, housemaid, along with other members of the Household and Staff gratefully escape the routine of Palace life. For however grand Buckingham Palace may look to you on the outside, for those of us on the inside sometimes it's like living at the office or, to put it another way, working at home, day after day after royal day. A change is as good as a rest, and, at Windsor, the heart takes wing, for Windsor Castle is beautiful and romantic, steeped in nine hundred years of history, set like a jewel on the crown of a chalk hill overlooking the Thames and yet, curiously, at the same time, like a comfortable country village with its own houses and shops and gardens, its own church, post office, and library, its own distinctive residents, more august variations of the village constable, the vicar, the retired colonel. You might even say the Private Apartments in the Upper Ward of Windsor Castle constitute the manor house, around which village life once centred, and the lord of the manor none other than Her Majesty the Queen.

Of course Windsor Castle is no ordinary village. No other such small particular world could find itself the setting for Henry VIII to wait the news of Anne Boleyn's death, or for the young Elizabeth I to celebrate the first Christmas of her reign, or for Victoria and Albert to spend their honeymoon, or for the severed head of Charles I to find its final resting place. But, I think, the homelier passions and perils lurking beneath the surface of ordinary village life do prevail at Windsor Castle, nevertheless.

Or at least I think so now.

Royal Ascot may well be among the Queen's favourite weeks in the year (not that she is likely to tell you which is her favourite week, but you might presume; she *is* horse-mad after all). There are four straight days of superb racing in festive surroundings, a week-long house party with family and favoured guests, and a ceremony for the premier order of chivalry in the kingdom. For those of us below-stairs, Royal Ascot is busy—all those guests!—but something of the festive atmosphere rubs off and the week in flaming June often crowns the year for us as well.

But not, alas, this year . . .

1

IT ALL BEGAN—as it seems things have a habit of doing—the morning of the Garter Ceremony, Monday morning, the third Monday in June. Like many of my fellow housemaids that particular morning, I had sprinted through the usual chores—the bedmaking, the hoovering, the polishing (though I had had to undergo one extra and *un*usual chore)—in order to have time to relax, change, and prepare to join other members of Staff, guests, and lucky tourists lining the route through the Castle precincts down which the Queen and the other Knights of the Order of the Garter would later travel on foot. Quite a crowd gathers, as the procession is rather a splendid event. To get a good spot you must either have sharp elbows or arrive early. And if you arrive early, you must be ready to endure whatever the sky has in store. Since the Court had arrived at Windsor that Friday, the weather had been damp and cool—in other words, typically English. But through the lancet windows of my bolthole at the top of Clarence Tower late that morning I could see framed a sky of blazing blue, nearly cloudless, with barely a hint of the soft haze that normally brushes the vault over England's green and pleasant real estate.

Fair weather ahead, I thought hopefully as I opened the doors of my wardrobe on their shrieking hinges and stared disconsolately at what suddenly seemed an unsatisfying selection of attire. I had kicked off my regulation workaday black flats and absently nudged the top buttons of my dead boring white housemaid's uniform wondering whether I should go for the casualish blue jersey T-shirt dress or the ever so slightly dressier flower-patterned skirt with white and somewhat form-fitting tennis top. The occasion—the Garter procession—warranted something half-decent, I thought. At least this was the excuse I made myself, pushing from my mind the distinct recollection that I'd worn jeans at last year's event. Something else was driving me to do myself up a bit but for some reason I didn't care to acknowledge it. Or didn't want to. Or . . . oh, who knows. I felt hot suddenly. Heat had to be seeping through the Castle's thick walls. My uniform fell around my ankle and I lifted it impatiently with one foot. The skirt and top, I decided, tossing the uniform to the bed and unclipping the skirt from its hanger. Just then there was a knock against the door.

" 'M'on in," I called, assuming it was Heather Mac-Crimmon, or one of the other housemaids with rooms in Clarence Tower.

"Well, spare my blushes," gushed a male voice.

"Davey! Do you mind?!" I held the skirt against my chest as footman and corgi-minder Davey Pye stepped into my room.

"I've seen worse in Her Majesty's service, believe me. I'm sure my memoirs would fetch a commanding sum from *The Sun*, if I cared to write them."

"Worse? What do you mean, 'worse'?"

"Worse? . . . er, I meant more flesh. That's all. You know. Naked naughty bits. Gyrating . . . well, never mind, darling. That's a very fetching colour."

"Oh, do you think? What about this, then?" I pulled

the T-shirt dress from the wardrobe and quickly exchanged it for the skirt.

Davey pondered my second choice, two fingers pressed against a chubby cheek. "The other. Definitely. Absolutely. But if I was wearing it, I think I'd—"

"You'd never get the chance. I'm a size four. You're at least a women's eighteen and growing."

Davey pouted. "May I ask why you're getting all tarted up at this time of the morning?"

"I just thought it would be nice to look . . . nice. For the procession."

"I seem to recall you wearing trousers of some nature last year."

"Damn your selective memory."

"Ahh . . ." Davey purred. A Cheshire grin spread across his face. "Did you know that Windsor *is* the most roman*tique* castle that is in the world? Samuel Pepys wrote that. Or somebody like."

"Oh, sod off," I rejoindered wittily. "Shouldn't you be getting the corgis their elevenses? What *are* you doing here anyway?"

"Oh, my gosh and golly. I forgot." He paused and added dramatically: "You're *wanted*."

"Really! Wanted? Me?" I trilled, stepping backward to regard myself in a cloudy mirror still clutching the skirt to my bosom. "I knew someday my prince would come!" I would have spun around in a parody of girlish glee, but even Davey doesn't warrant a view of me in my knickers.

"No. You're wanted in a professional capacity—"

"Oh, hell. Why?"

"—in the Throne Room."

"The Throne Room?" I felt a trickle of dismay and alarm. The Throne Room, or more properly the Garter Throne Room, was where the Queen would shortly be investing two worthies—one a philanthropist businessman, the other the Duke of Cheshire—into The Most Noble Order of the Garter, the senior of the British orders of chivalry and probably the highest honour one could receive from the Sovereign. Then it would be luncheon next door in the Waterloo Chamber, then the leisurely trot down past the crowds to St. George's Chapel for the service of installation and thanksgiving.

"But why?" I repeated stubbornly.

"I'm sure I don't know. Did you forget to polish up the handles so care-ful-ly?" Davey sang G&S fashion, too obviously enjoying my discomfort.

"That room's as tidy as a nun's loo!"

I ought to know. Once the last of the tourists had been given the heave-ho from the State Apartments Friday, a team of Staff members, including some of us housemaids, had spent most of the weekend putting spit and polish to both the Throne Room and the Waterloo Chamber. The runners that protect the original carpets from a thousand tourist feet had been rolled up, chamois leather had been applied lovingly to the oak wainscotting, the brass handles had indeed been polished up so care-ful-ly, and the dust, which has an annoying habit of seeping in from the adjacent scaffolding-strewn Grand Reception Room and St. George's Hall (where restoration is underway from the terrible fire during Her Majesty's *annus horribilis*, 1992), was brushed away ever so delicately with a pony-hair brush from the gilded furniture and sucked up from the floor ever so *in*delicately with a industrial-strength Hoover. Even the gold chandeliers in the Throne Room were winched down for a brushing though the mighty crystal chandeliers in the Waterloo Chamber, a huge cleaning task, are left for dull days in the dead of winter when, mercifully, yours truly is skivvying at Buckingham Palace or Sandringham House.

My mind made a rapid reconnaissance of the rooms. Nope, clean as fresh snow on a Charlottetown, Prince Edward Island, morn. Even Mrs. Boozley, Windsor Castle's resident Housekeeper, a woman with a truly gimlet eye for grunge, had pronounced herself well satisfied when we had finished.

"Why me?" I groused. "There's a dozen other housemaids. Or they could get one of the daily ladies, for heaven's sake. I wanted to get a good spot in the Lower Ward to watch the procession."

"You were asked for specifically, m'dear," Davey drawled, inspecting his fingernails.

Oh, God. What had I done to deserve this? I recalled

once leaving my dust cloth draping the Negress Head clock
in the 1844 room at Buckingham Palace and racing back to
fetch it lest it startle Her Majesty and important guests. Had
I left my Hoover Dustette on the Throne? There would be a
nasty whir if HM sat on it. So much for the solemnity of the
Garter Investiture.

"Were you there? Is there something wrong with the
Throne Room?"

"Haven't been near the place all morning. Humphrey
told me to find you," he explained. Humphrey was one of
the Pages of the Backstairs who personally attend the
Queen. "We bumped into each other as I was dashing down
the Grand Corridor. Don't you think things would be easier
if they issued us mobile telephones? I do. Perhaps I should
bring it up with our shop steward." He paused and seemed
to recollect his mission. "Oh, anyway, Jane, you're wanted.
Now. At once. Sharpish, like. Hurry, hurry."

"Then get out of here and let me put my clothes back
on."

Davey's right about the mobiles. It's not simply that Windsor Castle is vast, it's terribly complex. Labyrinthine, I believe, is the word. The skyline of battlements and turrets
and towers may charm, but you should try navigating the
basement passageways. The first time I was at Windsor, for
the month-long Easter Court, I kept losing my way. I had to
pop up a few flights of stairs to find a window or a door and
try to get my bearings. Directional symbols want posting on
the walls. Or "You Are Here"-type signboards. Or perhaps a
book: *The Bewildered Staff Member's Guide to Windsor Castle.*
Although my orientation is better these days, there are times
I half expect to turn a corner in my subterranean wanderings
and come across the Minotaur calmly snacking on the flower
of British youth.

At any rate, the route from Clarence Tower to the Garter Throne Room isn't terribly long or complicated, though
the fire-damaged areas in the northeast section of the Upper
Ward do necessitate a few detours. I put on some speed
nonetheless, and soon darted up the Grand Staircase,
through the Grand Vestibule (funny, how rooms in royal pal-

aces are always Grand), and into the Waterloo Chamber, which seemed as quiet as a held breath—oddly so—though there was evidence of recent and painstaking human activity—Staff activity, that is. The great mahogany table stretching near the length of the room—set up the evening before—was laid for fifty or sixty guests. The silver gilt and Minton service glistened in sunlight filtered through skylights high in the lantern roof. Sprays of flowers were a river down the centre of the table, while splashes of floral colour relieved the gray chimneypieces under the portrait of George III on one side and Emperor Francis I of Austria on the other. There was a faint aroma of all that's fresh and clean, brought on by the blossoms, I supposed, by a tickle of spice from the new wood being used in the renovation of St. George's Hall next door, and, of course, by—dare I say it?— our superb cleaning job. The Waterloo Chamber appeared without fault, I concluded as I made my way past the gallery of guy portraits, each of whom had contributed to creaming Napoleon at . . . well, Waterloo of course. But what of the Throne Room? What could the problem possibly be?

The chandeliers had yet to be set ablaze. The two deep doorwells between Waterloo Chamber and Throne Room were cast in shadow, but I had espied the outline of a figure in the further doorwell who, it turned out when I screeched to a halt, was a largish man unfamiliar to me. There are, of course, heaps of people working within the Castle walls, and I can hardly know all of them. But this man radiated something foreign, and I don't mean foreign as in Calais and beyond. I mean foreign to the village atmosphere that is Windsor Castle. He was dressed in a dark boxy business suit; his expression contained more wood than the mahogany table, and his shoes—oh, his shoes: so big, so black, so polished. I'd grown up around such shoes. My heart did a little turn and settled toward my stomach.

"I'm Jane Bee," I said, rather wishing I wasn't. Kate Moss, perhaps. A clock on the mantel sounded the hour with a dainty tinkle. Eleven-thirty. The Investiture was scheduled for noon. "I've been sent for."

Expressionlessly, the stranger pushed the door open. "Don't touch anything," he growled as I slipped past into the Garter Throne Room. The door closed behind me with, I thought, an ominous *click*.

At first, nothing seemed terribly amiss. True, there was a knot of men at the far end of the room where a purple velvet and gold canopy marked the site of the Throne, but knots of men at Windsor Castle were not a rare sight. The Guard, the Military Knights, the canons of St. George's Chapel—men were always hanging about the place in knots. The gilded chairs were still where they'd been placed the day before in readiness for the Knights—in two tidy facing rows, one under the Winterhalter portraits of Queen Victoria and Prince Albert, the other under the gothic windows. And the view was, predictably, as pleasant and unremarkable as any warm day high summer in England might provide: a carpet of greenery tumbling down to the Thames, invisible below, the spires of Eton College a hazy apparition in the middle distance. My heart was almost buoyed by relief.

But for two things: a set of white feathers glimpsed in animation over the wall of men near the Throne and, much nearer, a puppyish sort of snuffle.

The latter, a sudden noise, made me jump. Damn! A corgi! was my first thought, worrying for my ankles. But no grinning teeth appeared from the shadows behind me. The sound came instead from a slight figure hunched on a gilded blue-velvet-covered stool near the door leading to the Grand Reception Room, where scaffolding was plainly visible behind the glass. All I could see of the figure was a length of scarlet coat and the top of a shaggy head of flaxen hair bent well over in apparent contemplation of a pair of shiny black shoes with buckles of equally shiny intensity. The life-form snuffled again and this time lifted its head. Oh, I thought, none too surprised when I saw the angelic face. It was Hugo FitzJames, Lord Lambourn, one of the Queen's Pages of Honour, grandson of the Duke of Cheshire.

Lord Lambourn glanced at me disinterestedly. His soft round features were pale—I had interpreted the snuffle as nasal hoovering in the wake of a jolly good cry and expected a wan complexion—but his expression was, contrarily, the one of exquisite naked boredom that only adolescents seem able to achieve, or at least try to get away with. (I could hear an echo of my father's command, "Wipe that look off your face," from my own not-so-distant adolescence.) He blinked at me through his flopping spaniel's mane of hair, protruded his lower lip sulkily, almost defensively, and returned to his footwear meditation, only this time with an impatient jiggling of his white-stockinged legs. Clearly, I wasn't anybody worth notice.

I was beginning to feel slightly awkward. Had there been a mistake? Ought I to make myself known? Would penetrating further into the Throne Room constitute the "touching" against which I had been warned? I glanced at my own feet. No, that was silly, I thought, and prepared to make a Bee-line for the wall of men, when the spray of white feathers, which I had noted earlier with some disquiet, pressed forward to part the wall of flesh and reveal its wearer.

It was—as I'd suspected—the Queen.

Perched on Her Majesty's head was a large soft black velvet cap garnished with ostrich plumes, the characteristic chapeau of the Order of the Garter. It was a rather jaunty-looking piece of millinery but, alas, the face of the Sovereign below the floppy brim failed to convey a corresponding lightheartedness. HM was swathed in the midnight-blue velvet mantle of the Order; she seemed almost to glide across the carpet, but one hand peeked forth as if to secure the heavy garment, the other clasped a pair of white gloves.

"Your Majesty," I said, curtsying, my eyes falling to the Garter Star pinned to her left breast, its rays of tiny diamonds surrounding a ruby cross of St. George, glistening in the light from the chandeliers.

"Jane. Good, I'm glad you're here—" the Queen began, although the grave tone of her voice contradicted any sense that this was a truly gladsome occasion. Her lips, reddened with lipstick, compressed into a pensive line. "There's been—"

She glanced at Lord Lambourn.

"Hugo . . . Hugo!" she addressed him in a loudish whisper.

Lord Lambourn shot off the stool. "Yes, Your Majesty," he said smartly, bowing and patting down the white lace jabot plumped about his neck.

"Hugo, how are you feeling?" Her Majesty continued gently.

"I'm fine, Ma'am."

"Are you quite sure?"

"Oh, absolutely. Yes."

"You've had a shock, I'm sure. We can get by with just one Page, you know. Nicholas can assist me at the Investiture," she added, referring to another of her four Pages of Honour.

"Oh, no, Ma'am," Lord Lambourn protested, affronted. He pushed back his thatch of hair. "My grandfather, I mean . . . He's so looking forward. And you'll need me for the walkdown. The train is much too heavy."

"Yes . . ." Her Majesty murmured, but there was reluctance in the tone. "Yes, of course. But I want you to come to me if you think you won't be able to carry out your duties."

"Yes, Ma'am." Lord Lambourn moved to leave. He seemed anxious to go.

"I think, Hugo, you'd better stay where you are for the time being." Her Majesty slipped her wrist through the opening of her mantle and glanced at her watch. She smiled at her page encouragingly. "Shouldn't be much longer. Come with me, Jane."

We walked a few feet to the dove-coloured fireplace over which hung the State Portrait of the Queen, a full-length of Her Majesty in the early years of her reign, young and slim in her white-and-gold Coronation dress and Robe of State. I regarded the more matronly rendering in front of me.

"There's been a death, I'm sorry to say, Jane."

"Oh, gosh, Ma'am. How awful. Who?" I added worriedly, trying to read her face. Not a family member, I hoped.

"Mr. Pettibon."

I didn't register the name for a moment, and then: "Roger Pettibon? From the Royal Library? But . . . ? He's not that old," I sputtered, feeling sad but oddly relieved at the same time. "Sudden . . . ? Was it?"

"Very, I should expect." Her Majesty blinked at me,

her china blue eyes unreadable. "I ought to be more specific, Jane: It appears Mr. Pettibon has been murdered."

A shiver went through me like a shard of ice, and I suppose I gasped. What hadn't been clear earlier—or what I had been unconsciously denying—came to me with full force. I looked over the Queen's shoulder toward the Throne and saw what should have been obvious before. There, to one side, was the Governor of the Castle, to be sure. And a couple of senior officers from the Royalty Protection Department, all recognizable. But the other figures were police detectives, plain as day even if they were in plainclothes. As the daughter of a Canadian police officer, I can make some claim to recognizing the type: sort of large and granite-faced. One man was packing up a photography kit, another closing the cover of a sketchbook. The man who'd ushered me into the Throne Room was probably a young detective constable. All courtesy the Metropolitan Police or Thames Valley Police—or both, given that people aren't murdered too often at Windsor Castle, at least since Plantagenet days.

"Oh, Ma'am, are they sure he was murdered?"

"I'm afraid there's no doubt. He's been stabbed, you see."

"Oh, poor Mr. Pettibon," I gasped again, trying to take it in. "He seemed like such a nice man." As if people who weren't quite nice deserved to be murdered. Really, these moments do find you babbling the most banal things.

"It was Hugo who found the body."

"Oh, I see." Suddenly Lord Lambourn's presence made sense, though I wasn't sure his sulky demeanour did.

"I'm sure he's had a shock," Her Majesty looked over my shoulder worriedly.

"Trying to be macho at that age, Ma'am," I supplied, wondering as I said it: *At what age did it end?*

Her Majesty glanced again at her watch.

"The Investiture is to begin shortly, Jane. The police have been most cooperative. They've done their work with great speed. And normally, this room would have to be sealed off as a crime scene, but given the circumstances—"

HM didn't need to explain. Two of the great and the good were scheduled to be invested into the Order of the

Garter in this very room in front of twenty-odd other Knights and members of the Royal Family. Fifty or more peckish people who were keen on lunch. And a thousand commonfolk were beginning to gather along the procession route even as we were speaking. Come rain, sleet, or snow, bright of day or dead of night, or inopportune corpse, the show had to go on. The Queen's responsibilities were to her guests. But what, I wondered, did this really have to do with me?

Of course, Her Majesty got quickly to the point.

"I asked for you specifically because . . . well, I know I can trust your discretion. One doesn't want one's guests' day spoiled by this tragic event. And there was a task I thought you might be able to help with—a rather ordinary task I'm afraid, though these are extraordinary circumstances. You see—" The Queen, rare for her, looked faintly discomfited. "You see," she began again, "there's a rather large stain on the carpet."

I blinked. Large stain? "Oh, I see," I said, finally seeing.

"I didn't wish to involve Mrs. Boozley. Time is short and I'm sure she has other duties occupying her this busy week."

"But, Ma'am, you'll never get a stain like . . . that out in time."

"Yes, I know. But I thought we might be able to cover it with something. It's precisely where one stands for the Investiture."

I thought for a second. You couldn't very well pull a rug out of the other State Rooms. They were not only huge and weighed down with other furniture but they were priceless antiques. They belong to the Nation, as Mrs. Harbottle, the deputy Housekeeper at Buckingham Palace, liked to lecture us girls in those moments of Nurembergian frenzy when Mrs. H thought we were being careless. There really wasn't time to whip down to the tourist shop in the Upper Ward and commandeer . . . commandeer what? A set of souvenir Windsor Castle tea towels?

"I know! Upstairs. There's some area rugs up there we can use." I looked down at the Throne Room carpet, royal blue with pale blue Tudor Roses and other heraldic motifs stamped on. "Should be something that will go with this colour."

Although I somewhat doubted it. Above the grand State Rooms, on the top floor of the Upper Ward, were a number of much more ordinary rooms used variously as guest suites, lodgings for members of Household or Staff, and the like. It was the sector of the Castle in which I had been toiling only a few hours earlier. I cast my mind over various floor coverings that I'd swept or hoovered and could only think of one that might be decent: a blue-and-burgundy thing with an Oriental motif that didn't look too tatty. The question was—would the rug be adequate cover?

"How big is the stain, Ma'am? Shall I look?" I added when she seemed to hesitate.

"I'm afraid the body has yet to be moved."

"Ooh." I grimaced. "Is it awful?"

"It's quite disagreeable. The poor man. Very shocking."

"It wouldn't be the first dead body I've seen, Ma'am."

"I daresay." Her Majesty regarded me critically. "You're much too young to have seen some of the things you've seen." She was referring to previous unpleasant deaths I'd become mixed up in at Buckingham Palace and Sandringham House. "But none of those ones in the past," she continued, "have had quite such a conspicuous degree of violence."

"I can take it, Ma'am," I assured her, feeling inordinately plucky at that moment, and somehow challenged.

"Come along, then."

The late Roger Pettibon's body, I could see when the men had parted for Her Majesty, was sprawled before the Throne as if he had been engaged in some macabre Oriental form of supplication just before he had died. His lifeless white face was turned left in partial profile, one staring eye aimed toward a table displaying Garter regalia, one arm in a casual tattersall-checked shirt straining forward, the other sprawled in a small puddle of blood that had almost been wholly absorbed into the carpet, turning the fibre a brownish-black. There was a faint but repellent odour of iron in the air. But, more disturbing, more even than the blood (which wasn't, I estimated, too bad in terms of coverability) was the sight of the weapon still lodged in Pettibon's lower back, somewhere around the left kidney, I adjudged. The decorative hilt and part of the blade pointed to the ceiling like a beacon.

I had but an instant to take in the appalling sight, for two solemn men dressed in white smocks entered the Throne Room from the small room behind known as the Ante-Throne Room. They carried a stretcher.

"Excuse me, Ma'am . . . gentlemen, miss." A short, sturdily built, middle-aged man standing near me spoke cheerily at the same moment, squatting down by Mr. Pettibon's corpse. The man's suit jacket was off. He was pulling latex gloves over his fingers which were as bloodless as the corpse's face. "Some of you may not care to witness what I'm about to do."

But his hand had alit on the sword's hilt before any of us had time to consider a decision. Such an action was un-doubtedly old hat to the scene-of-crime officers—they looked on expressionlessly. As for the rest of us: The Castle Governor, General Sir Paul Hebberton, blanched visibly when he realized what was to happen. I must confess, I couldn't bear it. As the sturdily-built man, evidently the pathologist, grunted with the effort of pulling the sword from its scabbard of solid flesh, I quickly turned my head away and found myself gazing at the Queen. Her Majesty looked on, seemingly imperturbable, allowing herself only one sad slow gentle lowering of her eyelids when the weapon made its exit. The next I looked, the pathologist was sealing the bloody sword, a short model, into a large plastic bag and handing it off to an officer. The stretcher-bearers moved in swiftly.

"Oh, look!" I cried aloud, not really intending to sound so intense. But as the deadweight was being carefully shifted from the floor onto the stretcher I noticed something the earlier drama had caused me to overlook. Mr. Pettibon, not a big man by any means, had been wearing dark blue trousers, loose-fitting on his frame but for one area: just below the left knee the fabric was tightly gathered and tied with what at first glance seemed a thick decorative blue ribbon. "Isn't that—?"

"Looks like a garter," one of the stretcher-bearers grunted indifferently.

"No, it's *the* Garter," the Queen interjected in a cut-glass tone.

It was. As a white sheet fell over the late Mr. Pettibon's body, I could make out part of the famous motto, HONI SOIT QUI MAL Y PENSE, embroidered in gold thread along the length of the ribbon, and the glitter of the gold clasp that secured the buckle. When a new Knight is being invested in the Throne Room, one of the Pages of Honour kneels and places the Garter around the recipient's leg below the knee (around the left arm, in the case of lady Knights). Since the Garter is the most prestigious order of knighthood honour in the land and there are only twenty-seven Knights at one time, there aren't a heap of Garters lying about. You can't buy them in a job lot. You won't even find one at Harrods.

"What on earth was Mr. Pettibon doing wearing the Garter?" I exclaimed.

"Well you might ask," one of the men responded drily.

"And whose could it be?" I persisted.

"Well, I was just saying to these gentlemen—" the Queen began, her voice in my ear sounding a note of dismay, "I was just saying, I have the most unhappy feeling that it may be mine."

2

THE ROUTE WINDING from the Norman Tower in the Upper Ward down past the Round Tower to St. George's Chapel in the Lower Ward was lined with a mighty throng undergoing a light sauté in the noonday sun by the time I lit out to secure my patch. I had, of course, been delayed by the morning's drama which still, as I elbowed my way behind the protective line of Household Cavalry resplendent in their scarlet State uniforms, reverberated obscenely in my mind: Roger Pettibon in the pool of blood, the crimson bloom on his shirt, the sheer bone-chilling yukkiness of the weapon being released from the wound. I had dashed past the stretcher-bearers before they could bring their burden through the doors to the Ante-Throne Room and quickly made my way to the floor above to fetch the rug that, I hoped, would ably hide the stain from Her Majesty's guests.

There are, as you might imagine, a gajillion rugs and

carpets over the acres of flooring in the Royal residences, and I've passed a carpet sweeper or a vacuum over one heck of a lot of them. Familiarity, I guess, breeds . . . well, not contempt so much as a certain obliviousness, at least in the housemaiding business. I couldn't tell you the colour or pattern of the Axminster in, say, Windsor Castle's White Drawing Room, though I've certainly stared at it enough times in my work. I'm not sure I even remember what the rug in my own tiny room at Buckingham Palace looks like, but I did have a decent recollection of a certain rug in a room above the State Apartments because I had spent some little time standing on it that very morning.

Among the temporary residents in the Castle was an artist, Victor Fabiani. Fabiani was occupying a suite of rooms while completing a portrait of the Queen. During the period of the Easter Court I had accidently barged in on him and Her Majesty during a sitting (or a standing, actually) and the Queen had laughed and suggested me as a substitute should her schedule limit the numbers of sittings she could give the artist. I'd thought nothing more about it until that morning.

I was making fresh beds—this was around nine-fifteen—when Fabiani glimpsed me in passing and asked, would I mind posing for a few moments? Well, I did sort of mind—I wanted to get through my work rota as quickly as possible—but the idea of substituting for HM was kind of intriguing (and it was a break from routine) so I parked my equipment and did as he bid. Hang the bed-making. Besides, it meant I got to wear the blue velvet mantle of the Garter—Her Majesty's mantle no less! (Yes, the very one she was wearing when we talked in the Throne Room a few hours later.) Eton College Heraldic and Genealogical Society had commissioned a portrait of the Queen in her Garter robes and Fabiani was at a stage, I guess, where he was worrying over the way the fabric draped. Of course, a few moments stretched into the best part of an hour as Fabiani, a rather intense sort of fellow, carefully composed the folds and drape of the mantle.

Really, posing for a portrait is dead boring. Fabiani, who had been somewhat brusque and inattentive to the Queen's conversation when I had barged in on them at Easter, met my poor attempts at chitchat with little more than grunts before, defeated, I finally dwindled into silence. I couldn't move from the pose, of course, so all I could do was marvel once again at the Queen's ability to stand motionless for long periods without complaint. Because Fabiani was concerned with the costume and not my distinctly *un*famous face, I could, as long as I didn't unfold the folds, move my head about without raising his ire. So I ended up examining things in his temporary studio. Among them, the rug.

Fabiani was absent from the room when I arrived at a sprint just before noon, which was just as well. I didn't fancy having to explain why I was absconding with his rug. And it *would* fit, I thought, eyeballing the rug's dimensions. The blue-and-purple weave was well worn, as so many behind-the-scenes things are in royal residences. But no one would care, certainly not the old rich friends of the Queen who had houses full of battered bits and bobs that you and I would probably think of as tatty. I lifted the rug, gave it a little shake, rolled it up, and dashed back to the Throne Room in double-quick time.

I can't say it's a wholly edifying experience unrolling a rug over a blackening bloodstain, especially with the source of said blood so fresh in the mind, but I managed to do it without losing lunch.

"Any idea when this stabbing took place?" I asked an officer who stood nearby, the only one left in the room. His arms were crossed over his chest, his tie loose about his shirt collar. He regarded me (or perhaps what I was doing) with a frown of disapproval.

"Earlier this morning," he allowed.

Brilliant. I'd figured that out.

"No later than ten o'clock, because that's when the body was found." He addressed *my* frown. "Probably between eight-thirty and nine-thirty. That's only preliminary. There's no rigor mortis set in and the body was still warm to the touch."

I suddenly saw the north face of Windsor Castle as an architectural cutaway, like Queen Mary's famous fabulous dollhouse not a hundred yards away in its own room on the ground floor: Me, a tiny figure, blithely scrubbing lavs on one level, while on the floor just below another tiny figure is stabbing stabbing stabbing someone to death. Ooh, to be so close and yet so insensible.

The astonishment must have shown on my face.

"And just where might you have been during those hours?" the officer asked.

"Interrogating me, are you?"

"I might do, if you give me any more clever answers."

I sighed. "I was upstairs, then. Skivvying. I'm a house-maid."

"I can see that." He gave my uniform a corrosive glance. "Upstairs where? It's a big bloody pile, this Castle."

"Above the State Apartments, mostly. There's some rooms—let's see—between the Cornwall Tower and King George IV Tower. That's above where we are now, here in the Throne Room, but there was a bit of damage from the Great Fire, so they're still not quite in use. And they're small rooms. And then there's some larger rooms between the George IV Tower and the Royal Library. That way," I added, pointing west toward the sumptuous rooms of the State Apartments, above which I had been beavering that morning. "We work on a rota. And that area is part of my responsibility for the week. I have to do other parts of the Upper Ward as well."

"You work by yourself, then."

"In teams of two sometimes. I think one of the daily ladies is to join me tomorrow. But, no, I was by myself this morning."

"You're permanent staff, I take it."

"Buckingham Palace is home. But some of us get sent here to Windsor for the Easter Court and for Royal Ascot. Her Majesty has lots of guests at those times."

My interlocutor, so to speak, tugged at his chin—he had a lean, long, deeply lined face, the face of a heavy smoker—and shook his arm to release his watch from the cuff of his shirt. "We'd best be off," he said sourly.

I made for the door to the Ante-Throne Room; I couldn't help noting the brass handles had been dusted for fingerprints.

"Were there prints on the sword?" I asked.

"Clean, I'm afraid. Where do you think you're going?"

"I'm going to take the stairs off the King's Dining

Room. It's more private. The Queen's guests are probably assembled in the Waterloo Chamber by now, so we wouldn't want to run into them."

"Christ! More stairs. I brought my in-laws here once and I don't remember all these bloody stairs."

"Well, the tourists use the Grand Staircase and they think that's probably all there is. But there's lots of staircases in this area; they're just sort of concealed. Let's see, there's sets either side of the Waterloo Chamber, a couple between here"—We were in the King's Drawing Room by this time—"and the Queen's Drawing Room over there. There's stairs off the Queen's Guard Chamber. And, of course, a couple of staircases up and down the Library. Why, Windsor Castle is absolutely lousy with staircases."

I must admit I was rather enjoying his discomfiture, the sulky bastard. All the access points to the Throne Room would add up to a nightmare for any investigating officer. That on top of it being a murder in a royal home.

"And all these stairs are connected to the rooms over the State Apartments, I suppose," he observed.

"Oh, yes."

He groaned.

"Wait a minute," he commanded as I moved away from him. We were standing by the large French marquetry desk in the bay window of the King's Drawing Room.

"Did you see anything . . . unusual while you were up there this morning?"

"Not really, no."

"Well, who lives up there then?" His eyes went to the cream-and-gold ceiling with its Garter Star-shaped mouldings.

"Mmm, Prince Edward has a suite for the times he's at Windsor. But I think he's away. In Canada, opening some games or something. There's an artist with temporary lodgings. He's painting a portrait of the Queen."

"Was this artist there this morning?"

"Yes."

"Anyone else?"

"No, that's it."

"But you said the Queen has all these guests."

"Yeah, but today's taken up with the Garter Ceremony. The stay-over guests for Ascot Week won't start arriving until this evening. Most of the overflow occupies the towers on the south side, you see, but because the fire cut down on space, some of the overflow overflows to this north side."

He regarded me with something like mild irritation, which I don't think I deserved. "I see," he said evenly. "And what's your name?"

"Jane Bee. And yours?"

"Detective Chief Inspector George Nightingale. Thames Valley CID."

"Oh? Won't the Met be doing this?"

"*I'm* the investigating officer."

"I see," I said, not seeing. Some squabble over whose patch was whose, I supposed. "Well, you've got your work cut out for you, Inspector."

"*Chief* Inspector."

"*Chief* Inspector. A murder at Windsor Castle. Can't be the first, though, in a nine-hundred-year-old castle," I mused.

"It's the first murder at Windsor Castle for me. And on the eve of retirement, too," Nightingale grumped.

"Could be the feather in your cap if you solve it." Or, I thought, the pie in your face if you don't.

Nightingale's expression suggested the latter was more to his thinking.

"Anyway," I continued, anxious to depart, "if I think of anything, you know, relevant, I'll let you know."

"See that you do."

He must be, I decided as I made my way back to my room in Clarence Tower, one of those menopausal males you read about. Too bad—he had such a lyric surname. I wondered if he'd ever sung in Berkeley Square. Or if anyone had ever written an ode to him.

Likely not.

Elbows are fine things. I used mine to superb effect to make my way down to the Lower Ward through the holiday crowd that, on the whole, happened to be in a congenial mood anyway. There was much exchange of smiles as I passed in a litany of excuse-me's through clouds of perfume and after-shave and essence of sun creme toward the spot I favoured: the final bend in the processional pathway across from the barracks where the Scots Guards were stationed, at the point where the Garter procession turns toward the Horseshoe Cloister and the west front of St. George's Chapel. Only as I edged toward the front of the crowd did I begin to get peevish looks.

"Excuse me, I'm a doctor, let me through, please," I crisply commanded an assembly of male paunches as effective an obstruction as the Thames Barrier.

"You're never a doctor, girlie," retorted the most porcine of the gentlemen. His face was a dewy beetroot in the blazing sun.

But I was granted egress through the wall of flesh nonetheless and I soon slipped into a choice spot behind the thin white guard rope, next to a woman in a wheelchair.

"*Are* you a doctor?" she whispered just before the Scots Guard Band struck up its salute to Mozart. She tilted her head to look up at me. Under the wide brim of a straw hat was a rather sweet heart-shaped face, slightly flushed, dark eyes dancing with merriment. She looked faintly familiar. "You seem much, much too young."

"Oh, gosh, no," I laughed.

"Good. Doctors give me the pip. You must be keen to see the Queen, then . . ."

"Er—" Not precisely true, I thought. I've seen the Queen. Close up. Many times.

". . . although occasionally I think I come just to see the Guards—"

"Oh?"

"—topple over in the heat. Cruel of me, I know. But their breastplates make such a great clanking noise when they fall! They look so virile and then they're pools of red and white before you can say ouch, poor things."

A different pool of red and white flashed ominously in my brain. I thought of poor Roger Pettibon and shuddered.

"You're not chilled, are you?" the woman asked, astonished, opening a fan of intricate Oriental design.

"Oh, no. Just a . . . spasm. Something I ate, I guess," I explained lamely. I hoped I wasn't having some sort of delayed reaction to the unpleasantness back in the Throne Room. I didn't want to faint and look a fool. I glanced at the Life Guard nearest us. Sunlight glinted off his steel backplate. The plume of white horsehair high atop his helmet spike, looking from the back like a pencil's wig, seemed to gleam with its own light. God, I thought, in those stuffy uniforms they must be fit to die. Then I wished I hadn't thought that.

I slipped on a pair of sunglasses I'd been holding in my hand and with feigned nonchalance scanned past the rows of Life Guards spaced every ten feet along both sides of the walkway toward the stone walls of the barracks in front of which were three neat rows of Scots Guards. I was looking for somebody. Damn, I thought: With tall bearskin caps practically falling over their eyes and thick gold chinstraps biting into chins, each soldier was virtually indistinguishable from the other. Was he among them? I realized I'd never even asked his rank. Got a first name, though: Jamie.

I wasn't sure quite what was possessing me—well, I *was*, in a way—but I also felt a contrary need to push such things from my mind, so I turned back to the woman next to me. I wished I'd brought a fan, too. I could feel perspiration beading along my hairline. It was odd how quickly the weather had turned.

"Did you come by yourself?" I asked, thinking about the effect of Windsor Castle's slopes and cobbles on a wheelchair.

"Yes. I'm motorized, you see."

"Oh, so you are." I noted the large black contraption at the base of her chair.

"I was to meet a friend, though. But she hasn't arrived and I don't know where she could be. I'm beginning to worry. She's not usually so unpunctual. And I can't go across because of this rope—" She flicked her fan at the security line in front of us "and because of the Guards, of course. I don't fancy being stabbed with one of those swords. My friend just lives over there." She pointed the fan kitty-corner across the bottom of the Lower Ward.

"In Salisbury Tower? Are you a friend of Mrs. Pettibon?" I hoped the surprise and dismay didn't register on my face. Roger Pettibon's wife may well have been in Salisbury Tower but the poor woman was probably in shock, oblivious to the ceremony that was shortly to take place.

"Oh, do you know Joanna?"

"Well, not really," I replied. "You see, I work here and since Mrs. Pettibon's Curator of the Print Room in the Royal Library I've met her once or twice. I remember having a brief conversation with her last year during Ascot Week. And then, of course, there was the memorial service at Easter time for her daughter. I said a few words to her and her husband afterwards. I guess that's where I'd seen you before, at the service at St. Margaret's. Wasn't it just the most tragic thing?

"Wasn't it?!" she echoed. "To lose a child like that! Poor Joanna. I thought she would crack under the grief. But she seems to have pulled through marvellously. You do, of course. You must."

The observation seemed to warrant a moment of contemplative silence. Mrs. Pettibon's daughter by her first marriage—Philippa was her name—had drowned in the Thames downriver at Runnymede on Good Friday evening. A day student at St. Mary's School, Ascot, she was hardly fourteen, a small, dark, rather serious-looking girl, as I recalled from the few times I'd seen her come through the Henry VIII Gate and turn toward the Salisbury Tower in her somber little blazer and skirt. She intrigued me a bit because, though I had a room in a Windsor Castle tower at Easter and Ascot Week, she had a whole house in a tower all year round. At her age, I would have been thrilled to bits to live in such a romantic setting. I could have stood in the high window overlooking the town and let down my hair, Rapunzel-fashion. Late one afternoon in the week before she died, I almost asked her if I might look around her home, but she'd turned toward me at the iron gate to the Salisbury Tower's small forecourt with such an uninviting and somehow troubled expression that I'd changed my mind. The inquest had ruled her drowning an accident, but it also said there had been evidence of drugs in her system.

"What do you do here, if you don't mind my asking?" the woman in the wheelchair said, as if she felt the need to change the subject.

"Oh, I'm just a housemaid," I replied, as glad to get off the subject of death myself.

"Not 'just,' surely." She laughed, cocking her head toward me. "You're a housemaid in a castle. Must be rather fun. Do you ever see the Queen?"

"She comes past on occasion. Some of the other girls jump into nearby rooms or into alcoves if they hear her coming. Or hear the corgis, I mean, because they're Her Majesty's early warning system. But she always says a nice hello. I don't know why some of the others feel so intimidated." I shrugged.

"I expect there's still a great sense of deference in this country however much we pretend there isn't anymore. You're not English, are you? American?"

"Canadian."

"Of course. Commonwealth connection. What brought you here?"

"I took a year off university to tour Europe, ran out of money, and thought I'd take a job. I answered an advert in the paper for domestic work and it turned out to be at Buckingham Palace. Oh!"

I felt suddenly the whip end of a lash of excitement passing down through the crowd. The band with newfound enthusiasm lit into what the program indicated was a Glenn Miller medley, and the people around us began craning their necks to catch the first glimpse of the Garter Procession.

"I guess the show's on the road," I said, looking at my watch. Yup. Two-forty-five. There's not often a missed cue in the royal ceremonial business. But there'd be a few minutes before the Knights wound their way to our vantage point.

"Anyway," I finished my thought, "I've been in service ever since. It's a few years now. What do you do?"

"I'm the volunteer coordinator at the Windsor Cultural Centre. We do various programs in the arts, music, drawing, painting, theatre and such."

"Oh, that's interesting. That wouldn't be how you know the Pettibons, would it?"

"Yes, actually. Joanna volunteers with a painting class one evening a week. I met her years ago. And Roger does a drawing class with children on Saturday mornings. Or at least did."

Did? Did she know after all that Roger Pettibon was dead? I looked into the face looking up at me. Candid. Impossible.

"Since Pippa's death, I think he's found it difficult to be around children," she explained. "Joanna keeps up her end, though. She says she finds it therapeutic."

"I'm Jane Bee, by the way," I interjected. "I should have introduced myself earlier."

"I'm Lydia Street. Very nice to meet you, Jane. That's a lovely skirt, by the way. I'd meant to say that to you when you first arrived."

"Thank you."

"Good to see people dress up a bit. I can understand if you haven't got the money, but really," she continued, dropping her voice, "you'd think this was Blackpool, the clothes some people have chosen. My generation's fault, I suppose. Blue jeans with everything. Now we're paying the price." She added wistfully: "There seem so few occasions where one might dress up that it's a shame not to if you have the chance."

"Mmm," I murmured noncommittally, feeling less than pure in motive and less than fresh in the wilting sunshine.

"The Guard have been good, haven't they?" Lydia continued.

"What do you mean?"

"None have gone crash bang boom. This may be a first for such a hot day. Oh! And here's Sir Paul—"

The Governor of the Castle, looking much sprightlier than he had earlier in the day, turned the corner, breezing smartly past in his scarlet uniform and plumed hat to the beat of the Scots Guard Band. There was a smattering of applause around me, and the mechanical cricket-chirrups of camera shutters. Despite the heat, the sardine conditions, and the long wait, a feeling of good cheer washed over the crowd. The Garter procession is an odd thing in a way: It's quite grand with the costumes and all, but at the same time it's cosy—no horses, no coaches. You can practically reach out and touch the participants. Although of course you wouldn't dare. As Lydia noted, those are swords in the hands of the Household Cavalry.

The Military Knights of Windsor Castle came next in their cocked hats, terribly fierce and proud as they stepped along. But they're old sweeties, really, thirteen senior retired Army officers (as determined by tradition) who live in a row of lodgings built against the inner wall of the castle across from St. George's Chapel. Following the Military Knights were the Officers of Arms in their splendid tabards embroidered with the Royal Arms in rich shades of blue, red, and gold. Their titles are medieval mind-ticklers: Portcullis Pursuivant, Rouge Dragon Pursuivant, Norfolk Herald Extraordinary, and so on and such.

"They always remind me of the playing cards in *Alice in Wonderland* painting the white roses red before the Queen of Hearts catches them out," I remarked to Lydia.

She laughed. "Yes, you're right, you know. I suppose it's the squarish shape of their tunics. Substitute hearts and spades for the heraldic lions and they could do a turn as the arches in the Queen's game of croquet."

"First we'd have to find flamingos for the mallets and hedgehogs for the croquet balls."

"Perhaps the Duke of Cheshire would do for a hedgehog. Oops, I must keep my voice down. It's a wonder they don't hear us."

But they do, I'm reliably told. Davey Pye, who sometimes does carriage duty when members of the Royal Family travel through London by open landau on State occasions, claims he can hear perfectly well what people lined along the street are saying. "What a dreadful hat" and "My, doesn't he look grumpy" are the two most common. Davey figures if *he* can hear, then *they*—that is, they sitting in the coaches, smiles affixed, hands turning imaginary lightbulbs—can hear.

The Duke of Cheshire, as one of the two freshly-minted members of the Order of the Garter, had the honour of leading the other Knights two-by-two down to St. George's Chapel and was but six feet away when Lydia spoke. And she did have a point. His Grace was, it was true, a rather short and rotund individual, hardly the stereotypical profile of a member of the aristocracy (which usually runs to the tall and the thin) and would, I had to agree, probably make a fine hedgehog. At least in a pantomime.

At the sound of his title, his head turned and he gave Lydia and me a penetrating gaze from under his Tudor bonnet. But he turned as quickly back to his companion, the philanthropist industrialist person, who towered over him like a maypole and who was walking carefully with the aid of a stick.

I'm told when Edward III founded the Order of the Garter in 1348 he was harkening to the knights of the Round Table, Camelot's chivalric order of young vigorous men. And maybe the Knights of the Order of the Garter in Plantagenet times or Tudor times were at the peak of their physical prowess, but today members of the Order tend to be, well, not to be unkind, a bit geriatric. They all look terribly resplendent in their blue velvet mantles with the Star of the Order embroidered on the left breast, heavy gold collars draped from their shoulders, and plumed hats, but a few of them are quite doddery. The most infirm elect to travel in a car which follows the procession.

"Are we there yet?" one elderly peer inquired plaintively in a carrying voice, looking around him confusedly as he passed us.

"Mph!" whispered a male voice behind me. "Bit gaga, that one. Looks like he's missing something."

"Which one?"

"I don't know. I'm not sure who he is. Oh, there's Lady Thatcher."

"And there's the Duke of Wellington."

"No, love, *that's* the Duke of Wellington."

"Are you sure?"

Their debate was smothered by growing cheers, acknowledged by the Knights, their hands somewhat encumbered by their mantles, with faint smiles or awkward little bows from the neck. Some of them, I think, are uncomfortable being on display, even if they are dukes and viscounts and barons; a retiring lot, on the whole. Only a few I recognized, mostly former prime ministers I'd seen in newspaper pictures.

"I tell you, there was a fwightful pong in the Fwone

Room, didn't you think?" one of the Knights said argumentatively to his companion as they passed by us.

"Your nose must be rather more sensitive than mine, Arthur," the other answered drily, then turned his head to respond to applause from the other side.

"What could that have meant, I wonder?" Lydia muttered.

"Haven't a clue," I lied.

The cheers and clapping grew steadily louder as the Royal Family came into sight. First, in earnest conversation, Princess Anne paired with the Queen's cousin, the Duke of Kent. Then, by himself, Prince Charles, smiling and waving, the crowd smiling and waving back. The applause abated slightly for the six officers of the Order, of whom I could recognize only the Dean of Windsor, the Queen's chaplain who you see wandering about the place, and Black Rod, the Order's disciplinarian, who was carrying, of course, a black rod.

But then the cheering claimed a greater fervour. Cameras took to a fierce paroxysm of clicking as the Queen stepped into view, seeming untouched by the heat, her smile as radiant as one of her own tiaras. With her was the Duke of Edinburgh, whose smile could never be described as radiant, but who nonetheless favoured the assembled with a benign expression.

My attention, however, was drawn to the two Pages of Honour carrying the train of the Queen's mantle. You could read the concentration on the face of the further boy as he held his end and kept pace with Her Majesty so he would neither bump into her nor jerk her backwards. But the second, Hugo, seemed to have lost all colour from his face. He slowed suddenly and appeared to wobble. You could tell the Queen was sensing the tension grow along the length of her train, for she turned her head and mild surprise registered in her eyes. The throng, locked onto the figure of the Queen, however, thought she was noticing them and they cheered all the louder.

But I could see what was about to happen. Hugo dropped the train, his hands flopped weakly to his sides, and he tottered like a carnival doll. Then he toppled onto his back with an ugly thud, almost at my feet. The crowd caught a collective breath, then groaned sympathetically. An officer with a chest full of medals walking directly behind Hugo narrowly averted stepping on the fallen boy's head. The other Page, in a swift movement, grabbed the fallen end of the train while the Queen, aware that something was wrong, looked back with dismay and concern as a nurse from the St. John's Ambulance seemed to materialize from thin air at Hugo's side.

But Her Majesty couldn't stop. The show, of course, had to go on and the procession's finale, a detachment of the Yeomen of the Guard, oblivious to the little drama just around the bend, was pressing relentlessly forward.

"Poor boy," Lydia murmured beside me.

"Hey! I thought you was a doctor, girlie," came a sarky voice behind as I stooped down to see if I could be of any assistance. But the nurse was already nimbly loosening the lace jabot at Hugo's neck and unbuttoning his scarlet coat. A policeman had stepped forward to direct the Yeomen around the scene of the accident while two men in St. John's Ambulance gear slipped in carrying a stretcher.

Hugo's fall had had the effect of driving the small sword Pages of Honour wear as part of their uniform into his coat so it looked, absurdly, as though a tent pole were concealed within. When the two men lifted Hugo onto the litter, the side of the knee-length coat fell away and I noted something that at first made little sense.

There was no sword. There was only a scabbard.

Odd, I thought.

And then I thought a darker thought.

3

IT IS A truth universally acknowledged—or at least universally acknowledged among those inquiring into murder—that suspicion quickly flies to the luckless soul who happens to find the corpse. Worse, if the murder weapon happens to belong to said luckless soul, then said luckless soul truly is luckless.

"Poor boy," Lydia Street had said of Hugo FitzJames.

Poor boy indeed, I thought, but for reasons other than Hugo's abrupt withdrawal from the Garter procession. The crowd would assume the boy had collapsed from the heat, and perhaps the brutal sun was sufficient trigger. But I suspected the shock, of which Her Majesty had warned earlier, was the real cause, kicking in at a most awkward moment. But was it shock at coming upon a dead body? Certainly that would be trauma enough for a boy only fourteen or fifteen years of age. Or was something almost unthinkably worse involved?

The sword sticking from Roger Pettibon's back had to have been Hugo's. I was certain of it. The page simply wouldn't have got away with insufficient and inappropriate dress. Members of the Royal Family are absolute sticklers for detail in uniforms; the Queen can spot a misplaced military decoration at ten paces, and without her spectacles. She had *chosen* to let Hugo fulfil his duties as Page of Honour improperly attired.

I guessed the Queen had noted the detailing on the hilt of the sword in the dead man, knew what kind of sword it was and to whom it likely belonged, but, with characteristic concern for the smooth running of Garter ceremonies and for Hugo's well-being, had kept the knowledge to herself until an opportune moment arose later in the day, after the Garter service. Certainly, nothing in Chief Inspector Nightingale's gloomy manner suggested that the policeman had found his solution in Lord Lambourn and could tie a neat bow around the murder in the Throne Room.

Was HM worried Hugo might be responsible? *Could* a boy of his age commit an act so heinous? The grim truth, I realized as I watched Hugo being borne away on the stretcher, was that the idea of a young teenager—or younger!—as a murderer was no longer beyond imagining, not these days. But Hugo FitzJames, grandson of the Duke of Cheshire, an Eton scholar? Ought I to perish the thought?

I knew very little about him, really. The Queen has four Pages of Honour, all of them sons of her friends, all between twelve and fifteen years old. Their duties are hardly arduous. Carrying the Queen's train on ceremonial occasions is the extent of it. Train-carrying isn't done just because it makes a pretty picture, although it does. The trains are heavy, particularly the eighteen-foot-long crimson velvet number worn for the State Opening of Parliament. If there weren't four sets of gloved hands carrying the thing by its ermine trim, the Queen would barely be able to drag herself forward. I'd half glanced at Hugo while watching the State Opening on telly back last November, but this was the first time I'd seen him live and in colour, as this was his first Garter gig. Of course, he's never been anything to me—or to most people, I expect—but a supernumerary on the great stage of British pageantry. Now, I wondered, was he about to upstage the formidable lead actors?

I mentally reviewed what I did know: Before Eton, Hugo had attended Ludgrove, the same prep school near Wokingham, about twelve miles southwest of Windsor, at which Prince William and Prince Harry had boarded. When he wasn't at Eton he lived with his grandfather at Umbridge Trigoze, the Duke of Cheshire's estate in Gloucestershire. And . . . That was all I could remember. There was something odd about his parents, I was sure. But what? Davey would know.

Of course, Hugo, however highborn, was, at base, a teenage boy. Strange creatures, teenage boys. I seem to recall finding them enormously fanciable at one period in my life, some time after my horse phase and before reaching my majority, I think it was. Who knew what went on in their hormone-hijacked little minds? In their early teens, particularly, boys seemed subject to odd passions, little secrets, and stupid cruelties which, now I think of it, were pretty much the fundamentals of life for girls the same age. Perhaps we were worse. It's difficult to recall. My mind then seems to me to have been a fog.

Anyway, might Hugo have harboured some peculiar resentment toward Roger Pettibon and expressed it suddenly, and fatally, in the Throne Room? Certainly stabbing somebody had the air of a sudden fit of passion of some nature. Yet, whatever might have captured young Hugo FitzJames's mind, it was hard to imagine Roger Pettibon having any place in it as an intended victim. What possible animosity could Hugo have held toward a Royal Library Staff member? I doubted they even knew each other.

"Well!" Lydia exclaimed, pulling the brake on my train of thought. "That's not happened before—a fainting Page. I do hope there's nothing wrong."

I didn't respond. The last of the Yeomen had disappeared through the passageway that leads to the Horseshoe Cloister, the aptly named complex of half-timber medieval-looking cottages opposite the West Door of St. George's Chapel, and a fanfare had sounded to mark the Queen's arrival, met with yet another burst of cheering from the crowd.

"Are you staying for the drive back?" I asked Lydia. After the short service in the Quire of St. George's, the Queen and Prince Philip return to the Upper Ward in an open carriage. The Knights return by car. It *is* uphill.

"I think I'll stay," Lydia replied. "I've got my fan. I shan't perish. Perhaps Joanna will make an appearance." Worriedly, she looked across to Salisbury Tower. "Wherever could she be?"

I smiled weakly. "Perhaps she was somewhere else in the Castle precincts, got trapped in the crowd, and couldn't get through."

"Not as cheeky as you! Doctor, indeed!" Lydia laughed, her face lifted from the shadow of her hat brim as she looked up at me.

"She'll show up. Anyway, I think I'll elbow my way back. It was very nice to have met you."

"And to have met you. You must come and visit me. We're always looking for volunteers. Or you could take a course."

"I'm only here for a few weeks each year."

"I'm sure we could find something for you to do. What are you good at?"

I thought about it. "Turning beds?"

"Nonsense. I'm sure you have many other talents."

Putting on a nice outfit, I thought with a sigh as I made a final scan of the Scots Guard and turned back into the throng, had been a wasted effort. What had come over me? What difference did a bloody dress make, for heaven's sake? Did I think he was suddenly going to break ranks (presuming he was among the ranks), overcome with my dazzling beauty, dash over, and . . .

It didn't warrant thinking about. Annoyed with myself, feeling sticky, crumpled, and uncomfortable from the heat, I trudged up the hill, past the Middle Ward shop, amob with souvenir-mad tourists, toward the Upper Ward and the castle keep that I call home. Like Cinderella back from the ball, it was to be off with my frock and back into my tattered gray gown to sift the ashes, sweep the floor with my meagre broom, and hold the mice at bay. Well, okay, I exaggerate: My morning's posing for Victor Fabiani had put a spanner in my schedule and I had a few tasks left to complete in the skivvying department.

For some reason, however, Lydia Street's innocently asked question gnawed at me. It had hit a nerve: Well, what *was* I good at? Turning beds wasn't much to recommend me. Was I wasting my time? Had I tarried too long in Her Majesty's service? My parents sure thought so, and said so often enough by letter and phone. My father, a Royal Canadian Mounted Police officer in Prince Edward Island, had even come to visit me one Christmas at Sandringham and tried to petition the Queen—I tell no lie—to send me back to Canada, to university, to stuffy career, to everything *he* thought I ought to do. Fortunately, HM suggested to my father that he let me follow my own lead. I was dead chuffed.

Now I wondered if my father was right all along and the Queen had just been being diplomatic. Maybe I *was* wasting my time. Maybe I should never scrub another loo, hand in my resignation to Mrs. Boozley, clear my savings from the Clydesdale Bank, and take the next flight home from Heathrow. The airport's only twenty minutes east of Windsor, very convenient.

I don't often fall into a funk like this. I'm quite enjoying my life. Really, I am. It's a lark living in England, staying in various stately royal homes, travelling with other members of the Household and Staff from one part of the kingdom to the other as the Queen makes her annual progress. I've lots of mates among the below-stairs crowd, and there's no end of things to do. The pay's not great, but the room and board's free and, best of all, I've a ringside seat at the world's longest-running serial drama: The Trials, Tribulations, and Triumphs of the Windsors.

It's the heat. I blamed the newfound heat. I wasn't wanting for something, as my gran back in PEI would say. I just needed a cool shower and perhaps—this was the ticket!—the chance to set my mind on something else. How fortunate that the morning's drama provided the very thing!

Why, I wondered not ten minutes later as water cascaded (well, sprinkled; English showers being rather feeble) over my shower-capped head, would anyone take such a dislike to Roger Pettibon as to want to dispatch him suddenly, and with violence, from this comedy we call life?

Pettibon seemed like the most ordinary of men, really; pleasant, polite, soft-spoken. The first and only time I'd had a conversation of any length with him was at Easter—this was Easter over a year ago—when Court was at Windsor. Not fancying the grub on offer in Servants' Hall one Saturday noontime, Heather and I had gone down through a cold spring drizzle to The Royal Oak on the Datchet Road, almost at the foot of the great chalk mound upon which Windsor Castle was originally built. A coach party of o.a.p.'s, arriving at the same time as Heather and I, had so swarmed the pub's several rooms there were few places left, but we did manage to dart past a clutch of less agile wrinklies and snatch a choice table at a window overlooking Riverside Station where the trains arrive from London Waterloo. Mean of us, I know, but we felt we needed a reward after another hard week on our feet hoovering and such, and *standing* at the bar was not an attractive prospect.

Mr. Pettibon arrived shortly after our food arrived. Given the available seating, he was soon a guest at our table, though the *Daily Telegraph* rolled protectively under his arm suggested a solo meal had been his original intent. Propinquity plus a vague awareness of each having seen the other before soon led to introductions and the usual ice-breaking inquiries. What Heather and I do for a living isn't much of a conversation sustainer (unless we tell people we skivvy in a *royal palace*, thus opening the interrogatory sluice gates) so we were, before long, onto what Mr. Pettibon—*do please call me Roger*—did at the Castle.

Roger was on staff in the Royal Library, in the Print Room as it happened, where he was an assistant curator responsible for the loan of prints and drawings to various exhibitions. On the surface this would seem sort of bureaucratically drab, but for the fact that the prints and drawings he was helping manage were the works of such people as Leonardo da Vinci, Michelangelo, and Raphael.

"It's a huge collection, isn't it?" I commented conversationally, tucking into a moussaka which had arrived with a glass of white wine.

"Staggering, really, when you think about it," Pettibon agreed. "About half a million prints in all. Some thirty thousand Old Master drawings and watercolours. Six hundred works by Leonardo alone, the largest single collection in the world."

"Gosh, how do you keep track of everything? A print could go missing and you'd never notice."

"Oh, we're computerising, of course. Joining the modern age. The entire Royal Collection, everything—the paintings, the drawings, the furniture, photos, Fabergé eggs—from all of Her Majesty's residences is going on a computerised inventory. It's been an amazing opportunity, really. We've found things we didn't even know we had."

He smiled complacently, his lips disappearing momentarily under a bushy gray-speckled mustache. I thought him then to be somewhere in his mid-to-late forties. The hairline beginning halfway atop his skull and the graying hair combed neatly to a tiny flip touching his collar (an arty eccentricity in an otherwise conventional appearance) affirmed me in my guess. He had a round, gentle, almost childlike face. Only his eyes, bright and black as a spaniel's, hinted of adult worry or tiredness or sadness.

"If you're involved with loaning the Queen's things, do you get a chance to travel at all?" Heather interjected at that point.

Heather's keen on the *idea* of travel. She left her home in Edinburgh, determined to do so, and got as far as London. She now pesters me to recount adventures of my Grand Tour, taken a few years back before my present gig OHMS; she reads the travel sections in the colour supplements with dreamy expressions, and hops it back to Edinburgh whenever she gets the chance, usually when her mother, a hypochondriac (in my view), takes a turn.

"Occasionally." Pettibon addressed Heather's question as he carefully unwrapped a knife and fork from its napkin casing. "Thank you." He smiled up at the harried server who was hovering over him with his steak and kidney pie, scowling.

"Occasionally," he said again as the plate was dumped unceremoniously in front of him and a few peas bounced to the floor. "Most often the prints and drawings travel within

the UK. I'm working toward an exhibit of Leonardo drawings for The Queen's Gallery next year. Some Holbeins are
travelling to Leeds shortly."

"Oh," Heather said disappointedly.

"I was in America last year, though," Pettibon added,
stabbing the crust of his pie and releasing a lava of gravy.
"Some Canaletto etchings were travelling to Chicago. Let
me see, I've been to Japan with drawings by Flemish masters—Rubens and Van Dyck and others—to Italy, to Thailand, Poland . . . to Australia on two occasions with—"

"Ooh, Australia," Heather cooed. "I've always wanted
to go to Australia. Do you watch *Neighbours* at all?"

"Er . . . ?"

I groaned. "It's an Australian soap opera."

"Oh? No. I think my daughter may watch it, though.
Or one of them. I do seem to hear a lot of Australian accents
pouring from the television when I get home some days."

His daughter. Or stepdaughter, to be more precise.
Pippa. The ceremonial aftermath of her death was the last
time I'd spoken to Roger Pettibon, and then it was only a
few words of condolence. The only other time, I recalled as
I turned off the shower tap and groped for a towel, had been
a mere exchange of hellos at Ascot last year. Do-please-call-
me-Roger had been in the usual Moss Bros. morning dress,
standing in the Royal Enclosure with his wife, Joanna, and a
tall young man with neatly clipped red hair below his top
hat, who I was not to see again for nearly a year, and only
then because he tried to pick me up at a Windsor disco.
That day, the day at Ascot racecourse, Ladies' Day it was,
had been wonderfully sunny yet not hot—not as bleedin'
hot as this afternoon had turned out to be—and the mood of
the crowd seemed exceptionally jolly. The Pettibons and
companion, however, all wore the fraught expressions of
people suppressing one of humanity's uglier emotions and I
could feel a swell of tension as I passed. Mr. Pettibon looked
almost relieved to answer my cheery hello, though I wasn't
sure he even recalled who I was.

What kind of a relationship did the Pettibons have, I
wondered as I towelled myself off. And what about the
young man with the ginger hair? I knew now, from the disco
encounter, he was one of the Scots Guard stationed at Wind-

sor. And I knew, too, he was Joanna Pettibon's brother. (I told him I'd seen him at Ascot with her and her husband.) But I didn't have his name. I'm sure he told me at the time, but discos blare so. At any rate, after what happened at another Windsor watering hole Saturday night, I'm not sure I cared to know.

A couple of hours later, after completing my housemaiding tasks for the day, I hopped down to Servants' Hall for a refreshing cuppa and a continued brain-tease. A splendid rib-vaulted room on the ground floor below St. George's Hall, Servants' Hall had suffered some damage wrought by the gallons upon gallons of water poured over the State Rooms to combat the Great Fire of '92, but renovation had lightened and brightened its gothic grandeur, and the late afternoon sun pouring across the Quadrangle through the mullioned windows over and around dust motes in the air seemed to bring a dazzle to the room. It was like taking tea in a radiant church.

Few were about. I poured my tea at the self-serve and aimed for a seat near the far west wall when I noted behind one of the central row of columns a pair of black buckled shoes resting on a table. Rounding the column I found a figure in black trousers, a stiff white shirt, and a bow tie leaning back against a chair, eyes closed as if in sleep. A scarlet tailcoat (for semi-State occasions such as Royal Ascot week) rested on the back of an adjoining chair. This person also had his index finger swimming in a cup of tea.

"Davey," I addressed the figure, "you'd think someone with your manners and training—Thanet and all—could do better than to stir his tea in that fashion."

"I am not stirring my tea, Jane dear," Davey drawled lazily, his eyelids firmly closed, "I am soothing my poor finger. One of the corgis bit it and the warmth of the tea is ever so nice."

"Shouldn't you see a doctor?" I said, pulling up a chair.

"Whatever for? It's not the first time one of the blighters has taken a fancy to some part of my person."

"How do you know those dogs won't give you a disease or something? Tetanus, rabies . . . whatever."

"You know perfectly well these islands have been rabies-free for centuries. Quarantine laws."

"Maybe a rabid fox finally made its way through the Chunnel from France."

"And raced up the M20 in search of Mother's little loves? I think not. But thank you for your concern," he added, continuing to stir gently. "I'm sure I'll live to carry on another day."

Once upon a time, David Pye was but one of thirteen footmen in the Master of the Household's department. He served at table, fetched things to and fro throughout the royal residences, attended to guests' needs, did occasional carriage duty, and thoroughly indulged his fondness for drink and gossip. Then, one day, Her Majesty noted that her beloved corgis seemed to take a shine to him. I firmly believe that Davey secreted a lamb chop somewhere in his livery to seduce them, for the way to HM's heart is through her canine chums. And Davey, who is terribly devoted to Mother, as he persistently calls the Queen, thought promotion to one of the Queen's *personal* footmen would be just the thing to put himself more firmly within Her Majesty's orbit. Damned if it didn't work. Unfortunately Davey found that, in addition to an augmented workload (he still had to fulfil a number of the above tasks), greater attendance upon the Queen's person really meant greater attendance upon the Queen's dogs, who want walking at least twice a day. We've titled him Corgi Minder Extraordinary. Of course, once the corgis realized Davey wasn't a walking lamb chop, they turned snappish on him. Bit fingers are a frequent consequence.

I glanced out the window toward the statue of Charles II on horseback baking in the sun at the foot of the Round Tower. There was something I wanted to ask Davey, but I didn't want to necessarily tip him off about the murder.

"Davey," I began. "Do you know . . . ?"

He yawned extravagantly and noisily, opening his eyes for the first time.

"Gosh, I'm absolutely knackered. Must be this sudden wretched heat. I was walking the dogs in the Home Park and felt quite faint for a moment there."

"Maybe if you *drank* your tea rather than used it as a finger bath, you'd feel revived."

"There's a thought." He blinked tears of yawning from his eyes, withdrew his finger from the teacup, flicked away a few adhering drops of tea, and stuck the finger in his mouth.

"Still hurt?"

"Yes," he whimpered theatrically.

"You're as bad as Heather's mother."

"Tch! I'm having you on, Jane dear. Now you were about to ask me something: 'Do you know . . . ?' Do I know who? Or is it 'whom'?"

"Hugo FitzJames, the Queen's Page of Honour."

Davey studied the tip of his index finger. "Do I know him? Not really. We don't seem to travel in quite the same social circles, Jane. And, of course, he is half my age."

"I mean, Davey, do you know anything *about* him? Is there something . . . odd about his parents?"

"Quite odd, if you consider death to be odd."

"Oh?"

"No, no, I shouldn't say that. No one is quite sure if Hugo's father, the Marquess of Graven, is dead or not. At least, no one's had any luck finding him if he is alive. The Marchioness is dead, though. Quite dead. I think she was some sort of model in the early seventies. I guess they didn't have supermodels in those ancient times. Merely models." He frowned. "Arboreal nickname, I think she had. Tree? Twig? No, that's not right. That was Twiggy. Branch? Root? Stem? Bud? Or was it floral . . . ?"

"What did she die of?"

"Oh, she had a dreadful drugs problem. Overdosed." Davey took a slurp of his tea. "Such a shame. I'm told she was quite stunning in her day."

"Poor Hugo!"

"Yes, well, as it happened, the old Duke had stepped in sometime before her death. Went to court to get custody of Hugo. Put up quite a battle, I understand. But he won. Rupert—that's the Marquess, and . . . Poppy—yes, that was her name! How could I forget the irony? Any road, they were just too *too*, don't you know. There wasn't an opening or a launch or a lunch without the FitzJameses. But they went quite off the deep end. Drink, drugs, decadence, the whole bit. Don't you recall this? It was all over the press when the Duke of Cheshire was trying to get custody, great bloody headlines . . . oh, of course, silly me, this was before you joined our happy band at Buck House." He scowled. "Don't your newspapers over there cover the more depraved members of our aristocracy? It's enormously entertaining!"

"No. Canadian papers are more interested in constitutional affairs."

"You don't say?" Davey peered at me over the rim of his teacup as if he thought I was the ambassador of the most impossibly dull country on earth. "You make me warm to the Finns, you do."

Ignoring this jibe, I continued: "And what about Hugo's father?"

"I believe the expression is: 'Wanted for help in our inquiries.' By the police. Suspicion of foul play and such. If I remember correctly, there was some question if his wife's overdose was self-inflicted or administered by someone else, notably Lord Graven. You see, there was much bruising on Poppy's beauteous body and face, and her body was in some sort of harness thingy. It came out that they liked to explore new and exciting forms of interpersonal communication."

"Into kinky sex, you mean."

"Spot on, m'love."

"So Lord Graven may have fled the country."

"Or killed himself from remorse. Nobody's ever been found, however, and there was a whisper that his cousin, Canon Leathley, one of the clerics here at St. George's Chapel, helped Graven slip out of the country." Davey fingered the rim of his cup. "There's still the occasional sightings report. There were an awful lot of those at first. You know, the usual: the Antipodes, India, some jungle somewhere, golfing with Hitler in La Paz or motoring through Mexico with an entourage of space aliens. Mad! For myself, I think Graven's probably enjoying sundowners with Lord Lucan in Botswana even as we speak."

"What a good thing the Duke of Cheshire got Hugo away from all this."

"Mmm."

"Nice of the Queen to give him a gong—the Duke of C that is—I mean considering all this embarrassing stuff that's happened to his family."

"I think it's Mother's view that parents aren't to bear the burden of their children's failings forever. If she did she'd have been poleaxed years back. Besides, she and old Freddie are both horse-mad. He was her racing manager for a time. That's half the reason why he got the Garter. The other half is he's a delicious old gossip and always serves Mother the latest treats. Telephone, telegraph, and tell Cheshire, they say."

"I suppose," I said abstractedly, taking a slow sip of my tea.

"What?" Davey was regarding me with amusement. "What's so funny?"

"Do all these questions of yours have something to do with Roger Pettibon's rather unexpected demise?"

I caught my breath. "How do you know about that!?"

"Really, Jane," Davey drawled theatrically. "The tom-tom's have been beating through the Upper Ward since luncheon. Wherever have you been?"

"Watching the Garter procession, then finishing up a bit of work here. But—"

"I was too tired to watch the Garter procession this year, I'm afraid," Davey interrupted with a sigh. "I had to serve at table. And then help some of the Knights into their robes and regalia, rather a struggle in a few cases. Really, some of them are quite dotty. Lord Dingleberry kept rabbitting on about some odour in the Throne Room."

"That's because Mr. Pettibon was killed in the Throne Room. There was no time to air the place."

"I did manage to figure that out, Jane." Davey yawned. "Beg pardon. But do tell, why this interest in the Duke and his grandson?"

"Because not only did Hugo find the body, it was his sword sticking out of Mr. Pettibon's back!"

"How odd."

"You knew?"

"No."

"You don't seem too astonished."

Davey smiled at me with a kind of malicious glee. "I

expect you're thinking: What's bred in the bone comes out in the flesh, that sort of thing, aren't you, Jane? Because Hugo's parents were a gruesome twosome, inevitably he, too, would go off the deep end in a hideous rampage of—"

"I was thinking no such thing! But Hugo's sword *is* the murder weapon, I'm sure. I can't help but wonder."

"Yes, I'm sure. I know something of your Bee brain. It's buzzing, isn't it? You're intrigued. You're thinking: Who might have killed nice Mr. Pettibon? Might it really be that angelic schoolboy, Hugo FitzJames? Or perhaps his roly-poly grandpapa? What about *Mrs.* Pettibon? Who knows what evil lurks in the heart of that dear lady. Or—"

"Oh, stop it!" I laughed. "Look what you've made me do!" I had spilled tea on my uniform.

"Well, few know how to remove a spot as well as you, I expect." He rose from his chair and reached for his tailcoat. "You should enjoy yourself during Royal Ascot, Jane. Relax a bit. Take a walk in the Great Park. Flirt with the Guard. Windsor should be your playground." He gestured expansively and hit his hand against the column. "Ow! My poor savaged finger!"

"You're right, of course. None of this is my business anyway."

"Yes, everything is well in hand," he continued, grimacing, waving his smarting hand. "Your invaluable talents won't be required this time."

"Huh?"

"It's all over, Jane, dear." Davey shoved his arms into the sleeves of his tailcoat. "The riddle's been solved. The murder's been cracked. There's been an arrest."

"There has?"

"And you don't know who it is, do you? This is delicious!" He fiddled with a gold button and grinned wickedly at me. "I do so like having something over you."

"Who is it, then? Who? Who, Davey?"

"Would you care to guess?"

"I'll do you one worse than those corgis, if you don't stop teasing me. Now *who* have they arrested for Roger Pettibon's murder?"

Still grinning like a madman, Davey began a little

mime, dabbing at his open palm with one hand, then raising his arm in a gesture that reminded me of . . .

"Not—!"

"Yes, my dear, him." Davey bowed to my acumen. "Artist and portrait painter, Victor Fabiani, poor chap."

LUNCH AT ONE o'clock.

Sitting at two.

Such is a typical weekday afternoon for the Queen if she's not had to preside over a formal luncheon, say, or do one of her Queen things outside the Palace like open a box factory or visit a new seniors' residence. There's always some worthy organization, some charitable enterprise, some establishment or institution seeking a portrait of Her Majesty, and Her Majesty more often than not complies with the request. So midafternoon HM's likely to be found—should you happen to be looking for her—in the Yellow Room on the north side of Buckingham Palace overlooking the Mall, sitting or standing as still as can be, bedecked in one or other of the robes of the many orders of which she is grand pooh-bah, or in a gown, or even a workaday frock, while some anxious (probably) painter tries to affix the regal image to a piece of canvas.

Portraits aren't often done at Windsor Castle, I'm told. Windsor is a weekend retreat for the Royal Family. Buck House is the office, and sitting for a portrait is more work than pleasure (as I can personally attest), so sittings are usually done in London. However, because this latest portrait had been commissioned by the Eton College Heraldic and Genealogical Society, and because Victor Fabiani had been quite agreeable to staying at the Castle while engaged in his work, the sittings had been scheduled for the Easter Court when, in effect, the "office" moves from Buck House to Windsor.

None of this would have trickled into my consciousness, normally, but for one occurrence: I inadvertently barged in on them—the Queen, Fabiani, and Jonathan Bremner, one of HM's assistant Private Secretaries—one afternoon the week after Easter, just as the artist was beginning to sketch Her Majesty. Mrs. Boozley had quite clearly put some of the State Apartments on the north side of the Upper Ward on my schedule for a light dusting, which seemed a little strange as the Private Apartments on the south side (where living people actually reside) were normally the objects of dust-seeking missions. Mrs. B. hadn't quite got the hang of her new computer at that point, so sometimes our schedules lacked a certain logic. But who was I to point out anomalies?

Anyway, I had been running my trusty furniture brushes over the gewgaws and bric-a-brac in the King's Closet and the King's Bedchamber and my trusty carpet sweeper over the Axminsters as per schedule in a cheerful mood (the State Rooms are grand and it's wonderful to have them all to yourself), when I burst through to the King's Drawing Room singing a chorus of "Some Day My Prints Will Come" (sparked by a local photo shop's delay in developing my roll of film) expecting, of course, no one to be there.

Only to hear a high voice completing the rest of the chorus as I came to a dead halt.

"Sorry, Your Majesty," I said, *quite* surprised, tugging my stupid schedule from the pocket of my uniform and curtsying all at the same time. "I didn't know anyone would be here."

"Well, never mind," the Queen said brightly as I scrutinized my schedule yet again. She was standing in her Garter regalia on a temporary dais at an angle to the great bay window through which a gray light washed from the drizzly skies over the Thames and Eton College beyond. White sheeting covered much of the floor. "You might just as well go about your business, Jane. I'm sure Mr. Fabiani won't mind, will you, Mr. Fabiani?"

"Mmmm," was the artist's strangled reply. "No, Ma'am," he said in a deep virile drumroll of a voice, removing some sort of drawing instrument from his mouth, ignoring me while he stared with intensity at the Queen's face, in three-quarter profile. The light from the north window silvered her hair, softening the lines of age around her eyes and mouth.

It was the first time I'd seen Victor Fabiani. He was a big man, thickset, in a rather shabby pair of old trousers and a sweatshirt. Masses of thick dark hair shot through with gray tumbled past his collar in unkempt fashion. His shoes, a pair of trainers, were paint-spotted to a degree that suggested they'd lasted through several portrait commissions. I'm sorry to report that if I'd passed him on Peascod Street, Windsor's main shopping thoroughfare, I would have thought him derelict. He certainly looked nowhere near my imaginings of a society painter; if he had been given any dress suggestions prior to meeting Her Majesty, he must have ignored them. But, I later learned, Fabiani had been highly recommended, having painted the portraits of a number of titled and wealthy folk. The last of which was of the Duke of Cheshire, to hang in the great hall among his ancestors at Umbridge Trigoze.

"Mr. Fabiani was just telling us a little about his family, Jane," the Queen continued. "Relatives in Canada, I think you were saying. Jane's a Canadian."

Fabiani flicked me a disinterested glance from in front of his easel. He had thick straight rectangular eyebrows and full heavy-lidded eyes. There was a suggestion of annoyance in the latter. "I have some cousins in Winnipeg," he said neutrally. "I've never met them. I believe one's a journalist."

"My mother's a journalist." I turned to my attention to the French lacquer and gilt bronze cabinet next to the fireplace. "In Prince Edward Island. Quite a ways away. I think my father was once posted to a small town near Winnipeg, though. But that's before I was born."

"Canada's such an extraordinarily large country," the Queen continued as if the fact still amazed her. "The countryside around Winnipeg, the prairie, is so flat and it goes on for miles and miles. Days, really, if one travels by train. Quite astonishing."

And the conversation continued on for quite some time in this vein, either I or Mr. Bremner contributing a comment or query where appropriate. Her Majesty, as I recall, was quite animated that afternoon. A drink at lunch, perhaps, or just happy to be away from her interminable Boxes. It occurred to me then that the Queen actually likes posing for portraits. It's an opportunity for her to have normal aimless chitty-chatty conversations with people outside her family, instead of the usual perfunctory exchanges her job usually obliges her to have.

Mr. Fabiani, on the other hand, was a brooding sort of presence, his moodiness slowly growing and filling the room like a balloon filling with air. At least that's how it seemed to me as I went about my business. The Queen, Mr. Fabiani, and Mr. Bremner discussed the tragedy of the Pettibons' loss—for Pippa's drowning had occurred only a few days before, and HM was interested in the arrangements being made for the memorial service. Fabiani contributed the irony that he had only just *found* a daughter; or, rather, that a daughter, of whose existence he had been unaware, had recently found *him*, but what I recall most vividly that April afternoon, what I was reminded of talking with Davey in Servants' Hall, was Fabiani's growing impatience, an anger even, a kind of atmosphere, the sort my father could create in our house when he was in a particularly grumpy mood. I felt, and wondered why the others couldn't feel, the charged atmosphere that precedes a thunderstorm. But maybe they couldn't see, as I could see from my vantage point near an ebony writing table at the centre of the room, Mr. Fabiani

running his hands through his hair and flinging a ⸜
charcoal to the soft sheets on the ground. Finally,
stepped aside from his easel and shouted in a voice that
carried like cannon fire:

"*Your Majesty, would you please stop fidgeting!*"

Mr. Bremner stiffened, aghast. I felt a thrill of horror
pass through me. But the Queen serenely returned her
hands to sweeping back the Garter mantle, to the pose presumably, and raised her head, allowing herself only a tiny
grimace in reaction to the artist's blast.

"Thank you!" Fabiani snapped and stepped back to
examine the few strokes he had made on the canvas.

I looked at the Queen. Without moving her head, she
raised an eyebrow in the direction of Mr. Bremner and myself, and rolled her eyes. I couldn't help but snicker. The
tension, you know. HM repressed a smile. Fabiani turned
and glared at me.

"If you tire of me, Mr. Fabiani," Her Majesty said in
finely chiselled tones, "you might consider using Jane in my
stead. We're the same height."

Though hardly the same size, I thought. But, oh well.
Fabiani made no apology.

He had, I saw in that moment, quite a temper. But a bad
temper does not a murderer make. Necessarily. So when
Davey gave me the news that the police had arrested Victor
Fabiani for the murder of Roger Pettibon, my reaction was
immediate and unequivocal:

"I can't believe it!"

"Now why would you say that?"

"Because I can't. Fabiani couldn't have killed Roger
Pettibon. Could he? Oh, surely not!"

"Then why would he go to all the trouble to say he
did? Seems an odd thing to do," Davey muttered, brushing
at the sleeve of his tailcoat.

"I haven't a clue. Where do you think you're going?"

"I thought I might—"

"Sit down, mister," I snapped, feeling a little hard-
boiled. "I want to hear more. It's practically the quiet hour,
anyway. You haven't got any urgent duties."

d at his watch. "Well, I sort of thought I
to, um . . ."

or heaven's sake?"

ensong at St. George's Chapel," he replied
quie...ts at five-fifteen."

"You...idding. A church service? You haven't a pious bone in your body, except where members of the Royal Family are concerned. Well, some members."

"I like the bells and smells," he pouted.

I stared at him. He looked faintly embarrassed. "Then hear 'em and sniff 'em later. You can go to evensong any day of the week."

Davey appeared to weigh this argument. "Oh, all right!" he exclaimed sulkily, plunking himself back down in the chair.

"Now, then, what's going on? Why did the police arrest Fabiani? On what evidence?"

"None, as far as I know."

"That's nonsense."

Davey licked at his sore finger. "Perhaps I haven't explained things quite correctly. Fabiani is in police custody. He's being detained . . ."

"I don't understand."

"He confessed, you see."

"He *what*!"

"Confessed. Has floor wax invaded your ears, my dear?"

"I cannot believe this!"

"You keep saying that. *Why* can't you believe it? Fabiani has been living here at Windsor for months now. Perhaps he got to know and hate Roger Pettibon, although, come to think it, Pettibon seems rather too dull to take strong feeling against. Anyway, the two of them are around the same age, I'd wager. Maybe they knew each other in the past? Went to the same school. Had the same woman. Or—oh!—they're almost in the same business, aren't they—art, drawings, paintings, and suchlike. So . . ." He shrugged and looked again at his watch. "Perhaps some business thingy. See! Not so unbelievable. Now, perhaps, I'll just leave you after all—"

"Davey, I'm not talking about motive. I'm talking

about opportunity. Pettibon's body was found soon enough after death to make a reasonably decent estimate about the *time* of his death. Inspector Nightingale told me Pettibon died this morning probably sometime between eight-thirty and nine-thirty."

"So?"

"I was with Victor Fabiani for part of that time!"

"Really? How delicious! I say, this *is* worth staying for. I had no idea you two were an item, Jane. I had a sense you had your eye on one of the Guard."

"I'll bean you with this teacup."

"Ooh. Sex and violence. *And* tea! You do know the way to an Englishman's heart. Speaking of which, my cup's empty. And, as I seem to be lingering here in Servants' Hall, perhaps . . . ?"

When I returned with two cups of fresh tea and a couple of biscuits from the self-serve, Davey had removed his tailcoat again and was folding it across a chair.

"What I meant, Davey, as you know perfectly well," I carried on, pushing his cup in front of him, "was that I was with Mr. Fabiani in his room this morning while he was painting the Queen's portrait. I wasn't *under* Mr. Fabiani."

"You do disappoint."

"I was tidying in some of the rooms up there and he asked me . . . well, commandeered me, really, to pose for him in the Garter mantle. Something to do with the way the fabric draped. He has a cloth dummy—looks like a dressmakers' model—but it wasn't good enough. Anyway, I was wearing the thing from about, oh, nine-fifteen to ten o'clock, which happens to intersect very nicely with the time when—allegedly—he stabbed Roger Pettibon to death."

"Which simply means, Jane dear, that Victor did the deed earlier, while you were elsewhere, up to your armpits in bed linen."

"It's possible, I suppose." But I agreed reluctantly.

"Probable, really. Fabbo had forty-five minutes before he shanghaied you into posing."

"But, Davey, don't you think a person who'd just murdered a man might be the tiniest bit *agitated* afterwards?

Could you return to your room after shoving a sword into someone and carry on doing fine work with a paintbrush? You'd have to have extraordinary control. I don't think Fabiani has that kind of sangfroid. Do you know, he actually yelled at the Queen when she first started posing for this portrait?"

"I heard. Well, you told me. Shocking lèse-majesté. Still, I've listened to Father give her a piece of his mind over the breakfast table when he's in one of his funny moods."

"What does she do?"

"Ignores him. Goes back to her crossword. But, Jane, it strikes me that people who are quick to anger might just as easily be quick to cool. Mightn't Fabiani be one of those changeable creatures?"

"You are determined to convict."

"I am not! I just can't think why anyone would confess to a murder one didn't commit. Wouldn't be good for one's health, in the long run, I shouldn't think." He bit into a biscuit. "So he had to have done it sometime before you came to his attention this morning," he mumbled through crumbs. "Simple!"

"The Victor Fabiani I was with was totally preoccupied—*with his work*. He was composed. He was intense—he fills the room with his intensity—but he was composed. Completely focused on the portrait. He couldn't be that changeable! I just can't believe I was in a room for part of an hour with a man who'd just murdered someone."

"Did the two of you talk?"

"He made a sarcastic remark about the Queen recommending me for the posing job. But we didn't talk much. Fabiani doesn't like to be distracted."

Davey sighed. "Well, then, is there any chance the time of death could be wrong? That he did it *after* you were with him? You left . . . when did you say?"

"At about ten o'clock. I did a little tidying in Prince Edward's suite."

"Oh."

"What? You look surprised."

"Well, I was up there just a little after that time. I was sent to fetch Mother's Garter regalia. Her dressers—can you believe it?—realized at the last minute Fabiani had everything."

"And was Victor there? In his room?"

Davey nodded. "He was a trifle shirty about my taking the mantle and such. I don't think the man even realized today was Garter day." He sipped his tea thoughtfully. "Perhaps you're right. Fabiani is a rather preoccupied sort of artist chappie. Wonderful portrait, though, don't you think? He's done the hands so well. Hands are a beast to do. Mother will be pleased when it's finished . . . *if* it's finished, that is."

But my mind had flown elsewhere: to a blue band buckled round Roger Pettibon's leg and to Her Majesty's expression of dismay in the Throne Room.

"Did you know," I said, "that Pettibon was *wearing* the Garter when he was found dead?"

Davey gasped. "You don't say! Below the left knee? The cheek of the man! Wherever would he have got one of those?"

"My question. Or where would the murderer have got one, if it was the murderer who strapped the Garter on his leg? I can't remember seeing a Garter in Fabiani's room when I was up there, and I know a glimpse of the Garter shows in the portrait. The Queen was wearing her Garter around her left arm when I happened to walk in on them during one of the early sittings at Easter . . ."

"And here I thought you were doubting Fabiani's guilt."

"Lots of people—even Mr. Pettibon—could have nicked the Garter from Fabiani's room earlier, couldn't they? And how about this: The Queen worried aloud in the Throne Room this morning that the Garter clamped to Mr. Pettibon might be hers!"

"Oh, I shouldn't think so. Mother's Garter? No, no. Im-bloody-possible."

"Why?"

"You do have wax in your ears, Jane. I *just* said—didn't I?—that I'd gone to Fabiani's to fetch Mother's Garter glad rags? Well, there *was* a Garter in his room."

"Then why, you pompous footperson, was Her Majesty not wearing her Garter when she was wearing everything else unto the floppy hat? And why did she say she thought the Garter that Pettibon was wearing was hers?"

"Ah!"

"Ah, indeed."

Davey grimaced and cleared his throat. "Because . . ." he began with a guilty expression. "Because I dropped the Garter on the way to Mother's rooms. I was sent back to find it—that's what I was doing, or trying to do, when I was told to find you and pack you off to the Throne Room. I do so hate being ordered about that way. You don't know which task to perform first."

"And you found the Garter?"

"Yes. I'd dropped it near the White Drawing Room."

"Well, I guess that lets the Queen off the hook."

"Jane! How shocking! You'd imagine for a moment . . . !"

"Why not? The Queen's human. Anyone might be capable of murder if they're desperate enough. *Even* the Fount of Justice herself."

"Well, I grant you Mother does on rare occasion display a little Hanoverian spleen, but *really*!"

I sighed: "Then I wonder whose Garter it was, wrapped around Pettibon's leg?"

"Indeed. You can't buy that sort of thing in the ladies' lingerie department at Caleys Department Store."

5

THAT EVENING I went down to the Star Tavern on Peascod Street on me own tod, so to speak. Heather didn't fancy
coming along, particularly after what had happened the last
time we'd been there, two days before, Saturday evening,
following our hat-shopping spree at Caleys. And none of the
other girls could be persuaded either, particularly since the
latest edition of the *Windsor & Eton Observer* happened to
splash Saturday's event on its front page.

I don't know what they were afraid of. Headlines always make things sound worse than they really are. But,
then, none of my Buck House mates have had a newspaper
editor for a mother to school them in one of the central
contradictions of journalism—civic responsibility vs. profit.
There's nothing like a juicy headline to draw the punters,
and for otherwise sleepy Windsor,

Blood runs down walls as rival squaddies fight it out

PUB RUINED BY BRAWLING SOLDIERS

is about as juicy as it gets. But the outcome couldn't be that bad, surely, I thought as I made my way round the bend in Peascod Street and in through the door of the pub.

And it wasn't. Or at least it didn't appear to be. Granted, when I cast my eye about the room there did seem to be fewer bits of furniture, particularly near the back, past the central bar, towards the Garden & Games Room where the snooker tables are located. But the walls looked the same. No rivulets of coagulated blood stained the paper black. The fruit machines were twinkling away as per usual. "Everybody Wants to Rule the World" was the Muzak of the moment. The landlord was wiping one end of the bar. Two barmaids were giggling at the other end. A few knots of people at various tables were in quiet conversation. Everything looked pretty normal to me. Normal as rising unemployment. Hardly ruined.

As it had been early Saturday evening when Heather and I struggled in with our hatboxes. The two of us had decided this year we would splash out a bit for headgear. The wearing of hats is de rigueur at Royal Ascot, and that includes female members of Staff who attend the annual rite. Heather and I had made do in the past with modest straw affairs but we thought this year we, too, would join the Hat Brigade. Not in an ostentatious way, mind. We couldn't afford Philip Treacy designer creations. And neither of us felt like calling attention to ourselves the way some women did—starlets and the like—by wearing over-the-top millinery shaped like man-eating mutant daisies or replicas of the New York skyline. At Caleys, though feeling enormously silly in front of the mirrors with various bits of felt and feather plunked on our noodles (for who wears hats these days other than female members of the Royal Family?) each of us managed to find something suitable from the leavings of Windsor townswomen who had tornadoed through earlier on the same zealous quest.

I don't know why Heather and I settled on the Star

Tavern for dinner and a drink. It's not exactly on the way back to the Castle from Caleys, which is close by, on the High Street. I suppose we'd just turned the corner and wandered down the cobbles of Peascod Street, past the thinning tourist hordes (who bugger off smartly after six o'clock), lackadaisically window-shopping and finally realizing we were a mite peckish right about the moment we'd got as far as the Star. The pub's not as posh as The Royal Oak but it's all right, the nosh is decent. Heather and I picked a corner table, just inside the door, in front of one of the windows looking onto Peascod Street where it intersects with Oxford Road, and ordered a meal, the daily special, a chicken curry.

It was an ordinary sort of day, really. I can hardly remember what Heather and I talked about as we sat there, eating, drinking gins, occasionally glancing at people as they trickled into the pub, their faces glowing with the kind of anticipation unique to Saturday nights. We considered heading back to Clarence Tower to dump our things and then striking out elsewhere in the town for some aimless thrills, but we found ourselves instead growing inordinately fond of our little nook, feeling as contented as cats curled in a sunny window box. Oh, it was the drink, I suppose. But it was the sun, too. The day had brought mostly patchy rain, but the sun had broken through when we came out of Caleys, and now it was pouring down narrow Oxford Road so the street blazed like a golden funnel, flaming the red brick of the shop fronts, streaming through our window, and falling into our laps, soft and warm as unspooled wool.

I turned my head at one point, not toward the bar where the activity naturally drew one's attention, but toward the window—*drawn* to do so, I felt later—where I suddenly saw . . .

Oh, I could come over all Mills & Boon if I wanted to. I've read those sorts of books from time to time, guiltily. I could say, as such books might, that the face I saw gazed into my very soul with deep-set dark brown eyes; a beguiling smile played along a delicate mouth, golden locks in an aureole of sunlight tossed recklessly over a clear high brow, a romantically dark shade brushed cheeks, upper lip, and virile chin. As this staggering spectacle met my eyes, I felt my whole life soar to a crescendo in a searing blinding moment of truth. In a flight of ecstasy, I suddenly knew—oh, lyric love!—the meaning of life, the purpose of art, the beauty of music, and the weather forecast for Hertford, Hereford, and Hampshire every day until the year 2016.

Yes, I could say all that.

But that would be silly.

And yet, and still, in that moment, I felt . . . well, I felt *something*, for heaven's sake. Something I hadn't felt before. At least not to that degree.

But then, too soon, alas, the spell was broken. This paragon took a step forward and fell over the sandwich board the publican had placed on the pavement to advertise the daily specials. There was a muffled clatter of wood and chalkboard hitting cement. I burst into laughter. I couldn't help myself. A couple of passersby edged around the fallen figure, regarding him with tight-lipped disapproval, but he was quickly on his feet, dusting the front of his shirt and straightening the sandwich board. He smiled at me sheepishly through the window.

Madness seized me. I signalled for him to come and join us.

The barmaid had a bruise on her cheek, I noticed when I ordered a half of lager two days later.

"Is that from Saturday night?" I asked, touching the same spot on my cheek. I knew she had been on duty through the fracas. She had served Heather and me our meals.

The woman, whose heavy red-gold hair sat on her head like a maladjusted wig, rolled her eyes as she pulled the pint. "My face had a sudden meeting with the side of a chair. I'm all right, though. More the shock, really." She pushed the glass of lager toward me.

"Ta."

She took my two pound coins and gave me change from the till. "Still don't know what they were on about. We don't usually get aggro from squaddies. Well, nothing like that, any rate."

"The paper makes it sound like a shoot-out at the

O.K. Corral." I pointed to an *Observer* someone had left on the bar.

She made a dismissive noise. "There was a bit of cleaning-up to do yesterday. I was recovering from my wounds, though, so I couldn't help." She smiled conspiratorially, sat on a low stool, and heaved her ample bosom onto the bar. "But it wasn't as grim as that rag says. Well, you were there that night. I served you and your friend a couple of gins."

"You've got a good memory."

"Keeps me in this game."

"Do you remember the guy we were sitting with?"

"Mmm. The single malt? Nice-looking bloke." She flicked me a sly glance. "Fancy him, do you?"

"Well . . ." I murmured, while somewhere inside a "yes!" was bursting to get out. "I just wondered if he was okay, you know. He sort of hustled us out when the fighting really got going. He was with the Guard, he said, so I wondered if he got hurt or whatever . . ."

The woman scrunched her face in thought. "I couldn't rightly say. I was knocked out in the first round, so to speak. Bert!" She shouted down the bar to the landlord who was in low conversation with an older man wearing a tartan tie. "Bert, do you remember a young, oh, sort of sandy-haired bloke, slim, smart-looking, involved in Saturday's ding-dong?"

The landlord turned to her with an exasperated look on his face. "Jesus, Molly, they all look like kids to me. Can't tell 'em apart."

"More like officer material, I think," she persisted at him. "Had a bit of class." She turned back to me. "Did he tell you his rank, luv?"

I shook my head.

"Still haven't a clue," Bert responded and resumed his conversation with the customer.

"Sorry, luv," Molly told me. "Try calling Wexham Park Hospital in Slough. A few got taken there by ambulance."

"Have you seen him in here before?"

"No. *I* haven't, any rate. I'd remember him though, no danger. I may be forty-six, but I'm not dead. Yes, luv?" she said, sliding her bosom from the bar surface and moving around the bar to attend to another customer, leaving me alone to brood.

His first name was, as I mentioned earlier, Jamie. Why didn't I know his last name? Why, indeed. We just seemed to play it informally. "Hi," I said nonchalantly after he'd gone to the bar and come to our table with a Scotch in hand, "Are you hurt? You took a nasty spill."

"Well worth it if I was able to make you laugh." His voice held just a touch of irony.

"I'm sorry," I said, dismayed. "I didn't mean to. Really. It's just that—"

"No, don't apologize." His blue eyes twinkled. "I don't get many opportunities to do a comic turn in my line of work."

"What do you do?"

"I'm with the First Battalion Scots Guards. And what do you do?" he asked before Heather or I had a chance to comment.

"We're . . . flight attendants," I said suddenly and then immediately regretted it, the least because Heather kicked me rather hard under the table.

You idiot! I admonished myself. *What are you playing at?* But "housemaid" had suddenly seemed so . . . so *ordinary*, so unimpressive, so likely to lose someone's attention, particularly if that someone also works in Her Majesty's service and knows the pecking order. And I felt compelled beyond reason not to lose this guy's attention. But of all the occupations to choose! The one with the silly party-girl reputation.

Predictably—and to my chagrin—his eyebrows went up a notch. He said with interest, "Flight attendants? Really?"

"With Air Canada. We're here on a layover. Isn't that right, Heather?"

"Oh, aye," she replied brightly, warming to her sidekick assignment. "On a layover."

"You're Canadian, then," he addressed me. "I thought

you might be American. You're not, though," he said to Heather.

"Heather was with British Airways, but thought she might like a change," I explained.

"Fancied a change," Heather echoed reassuringly.

"My family's from Scotland, too," he said.

"Normally we have our layovers in London," I gabbled on, making it up as I went along, "but we thought we'd stay in Windsor for a change. It's so close to Heathrow after all."

"Close to Heathrow." Heather nodded. I kicked *her* to indicate she should *stop parroting me*. Heather grimaced. ". . . And we thought we might like to tour the Castle and all," she added through her teeth.

"And shop, I can see." He was eyeing our hatboxes. "Caleys. You've bought hats?"

"For Ascot," I replied.

"Really? But surely layovers are only a day or two."

"Well, layover plus some vacation time," I allowed, digging a deeper hole. "We're here for the week or so, so we could attend Ascot."

"You must have booked your hotel early. It's hell finding accommodation in Windsor during Royal Ascot otherwise. Where are you staying?"

"At the, um . . . oh, what's it called, Heather? It's slipped my mind."

"Oh, aye, our hotel. The, um, the Rocking Horse Hotel, I think it is."

"I don't know that one."

"It's new."

"Oh? Well, we've been stationed in Northern Ireland for a time, so I guess I wouldn't know about new construction here."

"Well, it's old, actually. They took an old . . . building and renovated it."

He let this pass. I was beginning to think we were hopelessly unconvincing, but his expression gave no sign of questioning our sincerity.

"Will you be in the Royal Enclosure?" he asked, sipping his Scotch.

Heather nodded enthusiastically.

"You do have your vouchers, of course."

Heather's face fell. My heart sank. Heather and I would be in the Royal Enclosure all right: We had Staff tickets permitting entry. But *he* didn't know that. We were essentially presenting ourselves as a couple of tourists, rather dumb ones at that.

"You have to write to the Ascot Office in St. James's Palace and you really need to do so in January or February." He addressed me: "And you'd probably have to apply to the Canadian High Commissioner in London. Do I take it neither of you did so?"

"Um . . ." we chorused.

"What a shame," he said sympathetically. "Anyway, I'm sure you'll enjoy the spectacle from the Grandstand."

We smiled at him wanly. He looked out the window to the sunny street, his face in repose like a—oh, never mind, I'm too embarrassed to even record it. I sighed inwardly. Our apparent ineptitude (or something) seemed to have led us to a conversational cul-de-sac. I looked past him toward the central bar and the phalanx of people hiding the taps from view. The place had filled nicely in the interim and there was a steady drone of conversation.

"There's the Garter Procession Monday . . ." our guest began, looking at me with a strange and disconcerting intensity.

"We do have tickets for that," I lied.

"We do?" Heather piped up.

"Don't you remember?" I kicked her again.

"Ow, aye! Garter Procession. I can't wait."

"This is silly. We should introduce ourselves," I interjected lest Heather stick her foot in her mouth and give the game away. "I'm Jane Bee. And this is Heather MacCrimmon."

"I'm very pleased to meet you," he said, looking at me. Into me. I could feel a Mills & Boon reprise coming on. The violins were cranking up. "I'm Jamie—"

But his words (and the violins) were lost in a sudden explosion from the back of the Star, from somewhere near the snooker tables. It was more of a roar, really: Enraged male voices beat the air, followed at once by a sickening series of sounds as bone met flesh and wooden furniture splintered and crashed to the floor. The steady hum of conversation ceased abruptly like a generator switched off while bystanders nearest sidestepped quickly, opening to view the unchoreographed spectacle of flying fists and falling bodies. The face of one of the combatants stood out, caught for a second under a spotlight like photographer's prey in the flash of a camera, distorted by concentrated fury, his red hair familiar. Everything happened so fast it was hard to take in.

Jamie's head had turned at the noise. "Some of our men," he said grimly, rising. He looked back at us. "You'd better leave."

Heather didn't need a second invitation. She reached down to gather her hatbox. "But . . ." I said. *His last name. I wanted his last name.*

"This could get out of hand. I wouldn't want you hurt."

That diverted me. "We can take care of ourselves, thank you," I bristled.

"No, you can't," Jamie shouted impatiently over the rising din. "Not in this situation."

"C'mon, Jane. Let's leave." Heather handed me my hatbox as a shattering of glass rent the air. I watched Jamie shoulder his way through the ring of spectators while Heather tugged at my sleeve. "I can't stand this," she cried, dragging me through the doors into Peascod Street where a few others of the weak-of-stomach variety had already gathered. "My brothers were always fighting, always coming home done over. I'm not watching it. I'm not. I don't know why men have to do this."

"Pompous ass," I said, staring at the door, half wondering, half worried whether he had gone forward to join the fray or try to stop it, either of which could result in injury.

"What?"

"I mean him. Jamie. Whatever his last name is."

"A bottle could have come flying our way, Jane. He was being thoughtful. You don't know. You've only got sisters."

"He was being chauvinist."

"Well, I'm not arguing with you. Oh, look . . ." A panda car, its blue light flashing, had rolled up the cobbles. "Let's go. Before we get nicked."

"For what? We were just having a quiet drink, for heaven's sake."

But Heather had turned up Peascod Street. Far off, the persistent klaxon of an ambulance grew. Reluctantly, hatbox in tow, I followed my comrade housemaid. In the distance, beyond the top of the street, the Round Tower of Windsor Castle shimmered like a mirage.

6

MOLLY TAPPED THE bar near me with a red-lacquered fingernail. I glanced up from my lager, feeling foggily that the last few minutes had taken me a million miles away.

"Here's someone who might help you," she whispered, stony-faced, squinting toward the door to the Star.

I looked over my shoulder and noted with a slight shock a crown of red hair and a face below more than matching Molly's for bruising. It was Joanna Pettibon's brother. The slight rock to his gait as he approached the bar suggested he'd already hoisted a few elsewhere.

"Look," he said thickly, coming up beside me, addressing Molly, "I'm sorry about the trouble Saturday. If there's anything . . . you know, that I can do." He shrugged as a scowling Bert stepped forward. "Help pay for any damage?" He glanced around. Green eyes fell on me and lingered a second.

"Look, lad," Bert interjected before his barmaid could open her mouth, "I've talked with Major Strathmore at the Barracks and he says you lot are banned from coming in here."

"I'm not with the Guard."

"Yeah? Well, by rights I ought to bar you anyway. I don't need any aggro."

"I'm not with anyone. There won't be trouble. It was a one-off. I only wanted you to know I was sorry. And wondered if I could perhaps make some sort of amends."

Bert considered him, frowning. "I've discussed compensation with the major," he said curtly. "But . . ." He paused. He seemed to thaw a little. "Thanks for the offer anyway."

Bert received an ingratiating smile for his pains, and the request: "Do you think I can have a drink, then?"

The landlord's response was to scowl more deeply as if he realized he'd been smarmed. "Oh, Christ, give him a drink, Molly," Bert sighed finally, moving off, muttering.

Molly's well-plucked eyebrows ascended her forehead inquiringly.

"A large whiskey, please. And whatever this lady's having," came a faintly slurred response.

I'd been looking at him with interest—no, not *that* kind of interest. I'd assessed him, in that unfathomable way one has, back at Stripes disco at Easter, as not my type. Too pleased with himself. What I found interesting was his current demeanour. His sister had just lost her husband a few hours ago—murdered, yet! the poor woman had to be devastated!—and here he was in a pub down Peascod Street near to well-oiled. I recalled, too, that the time he'd tried to pick me up at Stripes had not been more than a week after his niece Pippa's funeral. It didn't appear observing the niceties was his strong suit.

"This *lady* will have a half, Molly," I said, responding to the invitation. "I thought you *were* with the Guard," I added as Molly poured the drinks.

"I was with the Guard," he replied obliquely, pulling a money clip from his pocket. He assessed me brazenly as he peeled a ten-pound note off a thick wad. "We've met before, I'm sure."

"Stripes. At Easter."

"Ah. I remember now." His expression changed to mild amusement. "Fancied my chances, did I? I'm guessing from your tone."

"As we say where I come from—you struck out."

A cocky grin creased a battered cheek. "Have one yourself," he urged Molly as she proffered the change. He turned back to me. "Perhaps I should try for a home run this time. Is that the right expression? Home run?"

"Right expression," I agreed evenly. Wrong attitude. *Very* wrong attitude. Nonetheless he intrigued me, for reasons stated above. And more: Here was the widow Pettibon's brother! Perhaps he'd learned something that could snuff the tiny doubt that flamed in me every time I thought of Victor Fabiani picking up a paintbrush moments after killing another human being. My original reason for being in the Star Tavern flew from my head. Suddenly there were other fish to fry. With a side of mushy peas.

"I'm Iain Scott, in case you've forgotten." He settled on the next stool; half his drink disappeared down his throat in a single gulp.

"Jane Bee. And I don't think I ever knew. You're Joanna Pettibon's brother, aren't you?"

He wiped drops along his mouth with his finger. I noted the knuckle rash from Saturday's fight. "How did you know?"

"You told me at Easter. I'd seen you last June at Ascot with your sister and brother-in-law, looking about as festive as a rainy bank holiday."

"Ah. Well, we'd been having a disagreement, if I remember correctly. My brother-in-law's a bit of a—" Iain's upper lip curled. "—Never mind."

I sipped at my lager, a little perplexed. Then it struck me with force: Was it possible Iain didn't know Roger had died, was indeed murdered?

"How do you know my sister?" he asked. "Or did you tell me this before?"

"Probably. Anyway, I work at the Castle."

"Really? Haven't seen you about."

"I've only got into Windsor late last week. I'm a . . . I'm in service at the Castle." God, I was doing it again—

tarting up my résumé. I added quickly: "Does this mean you're living at the Castle?"

"I've been staying with Joanna and Roger for a bit."

"Since leaving the Guard?"

"Since leaving the Guard."

"What? Were you court-martialled or something?"

"Of course not!" Iain replied belligerently. "It was a short-service commission. Three years. It ended. I'm taking a little time off while I consider my . . . career options." He contemplated his half-empty glass.

"Sorry."

"S'alright." He turned on his stool and regarded me candidly from under heavy lids. "Tell me, Jane, what precisely *do* you do at the Castle?"

"Jane?"

I didn't realize I had been staring at him until the prompting registered along one of my more alert brain cells. "Where on earth," I began, my amazement growing, "have you been all day?"

He shrugged. "I don't quite understand."

"Well . . . I mean . . ." His face, with its smattering of freckles across the nose, was one of such utter booze-dulled complacency, such self-absorbed nonchalance, I felt like adding to his injuries. "I don't want to intrude or anything . . . I mean, I hope I'm not the first to tell you this, but: Did you not know your brother-in-law was found *dead* this morning?"

"Yes, I know." The rest of the whisky disappeared down his throat.

"You *do*?"

"Yes."

"Murdered!?" The word extruded from between my locked teeth.

"Uh-huh."

"Well! You're awfully damn cool about it."

He shrugged again. "I'm sorry. I didn't very much care for the fellow and I'm not going stand around pretending I do now. God knows why my sister ever married him in the first place."

"Jeez, you might show a *little* concern."

"*Well, Roger didn't show any bloody concern for me!*"

The outburst was swift and unexpected, loud enough to send a few heads in the uncrowded pub swivelling in our direction. Bert slammed down the glass he was polishing at the end of the bar. "Look, mate," he said tersely, jabbing a finger at the sulking ex-Guardsman. "I said I didn't want any bother."

"It's my fault," I piped up hastily. "I . . . provoked him."

"Sorry, landlord," Iain muttered insincerely, pushing his empty glass forward. "I'd like another large whisky if you don't mind."

"It's okay. He's with me," I apologized.

Bert deliberated, then silently refilled the glass. "And mind you don't provoke him again," he warned me, moving off, muttering something that sounded distinctly unflattering. I'm sure I heard "bloody" and "women" in the same sentence.

"C'mon." I shifted off my stool. "There's an empty spot in the corner over there."

Iain followed obediently and settled himself heavily into one of the chairs ringing a table near a fruit machine. He quickly drained half his glass, then smiled at me with a kind of libidinous interest the booze unwittingly twisted into a half-smirk. My own, but differing, interest was piqued.

"Why, if you don't mind my asking—I wouldn't want to be provocative—did you say Roger never showed any concern for you?"

"It's nothing." Iain turned his attention to the golden liquid in his glass. "It doesn't matter now."

"But I'm curious."

"Why?"

"Because, well, because when someone's been murdered you wonder *why* they were murdered. I met Roger once. He seemed nice enough to me. But there might have been something about him that drove Victor Fabiani to murder. Not that I mean to blame the victim exactly—"

"Wha . . . ?" Iain looked up. His eyes focused unsteadily on me. "What are you talking about?"

"Victor Fabiani. This afternoon—I'm told—he confessed to murdering your brother-in-law . . ."

There was a slack-jawed aspect to Iain's face that wasn't difficult to read.

"You mean you didn't know?"

"Who the hell is Victor Fabi . . . onion . . . ee?" He strangled the vowels.

"Fabiani. He's a fine artist, a portrait painter. He's been staying at the Castle the last few months working on a portrait of the Queen. You've never heard of him?"

Iain shook his head slowly. "Christ! I don't believe it!" He drained his whisky in a sudden movement, then dropped the glass on the table. "I need another one of these."

"No, you don't."

"I bloody well do, too." He shifted himself awkwardly in his chair, trying to pull the money-clip from his trousers pocket and trying to rise at the same time.

"Look, let me get it," I sighed. Better than him falling flat on his face.

He grunted assent, sat back, and peeled a fiver from the clip. "Brilliant day on the horses," he grinned lop-sidedly. "Go on, then. Have yourself another."

"No, thanks. I haven't finished the last drink yet."

When I returned with his whisky he was staring glassily at the twinkling lights on the fruit machine, his face wreathed in a sort of idiotic smile.

"How is your sister coping?" I asked, resuming my seat.

"Eh?"

"Your sister. Joanna. How is she?"

"Oh, you know . . . women." He shrugged.

Was he so indifferent? Or were tears and worse (the meaning, I assumed, behind his careless misogyny) the reason he was in a pub and not playing a supportive, perhaps even *comforting*, role back at Salisbury Tower?

Useless male!

"Well," I continued, the unhappiness of Joanna's situation suddenly washing over me, "it must be absolute hell for her to lose her husband. Especially after losing her daughter a few months ago."

Iain's expression hardened the moment the words dropped from my mouth; the dullness vanished from his eyes. "That was cruel," he said sharply, enunciating his words with complete clarity for the first time. I withered under his gaze.

"Oh, gosh, I'm sorry. I meant to be sympathetic."

"No. I meant what happened to Pippa. The sheer bloody insane cruelty of it!" He spat out the words and grabbed his drink, his face black with anger. We drank in silence for a few moments, Iain apparently lost in thought.

"Sorry," he mumbled grudgingly, finishing the last of the whisky, newly aware of my presence. "It's just when I think about what—"

"No problem." Not fancying another outburst, I cut him off. I'd noted Bert glaring at us earlier. "Shouldn't you maybe be with Joanna? I'm sure she could use family around her at a time like this."

"Hillary's coming up from Oxford if she can get her husband and kids sorted out. Another sister," he added by way of explanation. "Got three." He raised four fingers. The tide of clarity was quickly ebbing.

"Still . . ." I added meaningfully.

"I had some business to attend to. Unavoidable. Fancy another of these." It was a statement, not an invitation. He shook his empty glass.

"I think you've had enough."

"Rubbish."

"No. C'mon. You're practically legless already. The landlord'll never serve you anyway."

"You fetch it. Like last time."

"No."

"Then where's . . . Molly." He swerved around in his seat, managed to catch her eye, and raised his glass. The barmaid flicked a glance at me. I shrugged helplessly. Shaking her head, Molly reached for a fresh glass.

"I would have thought the police might have at least had the courtesy to tell your sister they've got her husband's likely killer," I commented while we waited. "If even to give her a little peace of mind."

"Perhaps they have." Iain ran a hand through his coppery hair. "I haven't been home."

"Wait. I'm confused—"

Molly's substantial shadow travelled over our table.

"This is the last one, sunshine." She plunked the whisky down and marched off.

Iain grunted. He raised the glass and squinted at me over its rim. "What's the problem? What were you—?"

"I said I was confused. How did you know Roger was dead if you haven't been home? I doubt the news has spread much beyond the Castle."

"No, no. I mean, I haven't been home this afternoon. But I was home this morning when the police came to talk to Joanna. I'd only just arrived myself—" He took a healthy swig of his drink.

"Don't tell me they kept you over the weekend at the hospital? You don't look that bad." I examined the sharp cut along his chin and the welt on his left cheek.

"What're you talking about?" The glass rattled as it hit the table.

"That." I pointed to his cheek where the bruise was beginning to fade to a sickly yellow colour. "The fight Saturday night. I was here, at least for the first part of it. You seemed to be in the thick of it."

He rubbed his jaw, then made a dismissive gesture. "It wasn't much of anything. I gave better than I got." He made a jabbing motion in the air with his left fist, then added sulkily: "But someone laid me out. So I ended up in hospital in Slough. They checked me over, then released me." He tried manfully to focus on my face. "I called a friend in London and she picked me up. The night was still young, you know."

What woman would sacrifice her Saturday night so she could drive through London traffic to pick up some guy at a hospital on short notice, I wondered? Either a devotee or a doormat.

"Anyway . . ." Iain's voice became more slurred, ". . . what the hell was I saying? Oh, yeah. Anyway, they never mentioned this Fabi . . . this artist—"

"They? Who?"

"The police. They never said a thing to Joanna about him this morning when I was there."

"That's because the police didn't know. Fabiani turned himself in this afternoon. I said that earlier."

"Oh? Right. Sorry."

"And you don't know Victor Fabiani?"

"Never heard of the bugger."

"So you don't know why he'd have it in for your brother-in-law."

"Haven't a clue." Iain pulled a face. "Not sorry he did it, though. Roger was a sod. A real bastard. Manip . . ." He belched quietly. ". . . Manipulative. Devious bugger. Did I say cheap? Cheap as a . . . as a . . . whatever—the tight bastard. He wouldn't . . ." Iain swayed slightly, picked up the whisky, and finished off the glass. His eyes struggled to focus. He stabbed his finger in my face. "You know what Roger was? He was evil. That's what he was. That's the word. Evil. Fucking *evil*."

"That's a bit over the top, surely."

"You don't know the half of it, darlin'. Say, you wouldn't care to continue this conver . . . this talk over a meal."

"No, thanks."

"S'alright. I'm not hungry, anyway, really." He lifted his empty glass. "So, here's to Victor Ffff . . . ah, whatever the hell his name is. Here's to you, Victor. Cheers!"

Needless to say, my half-pint did not leave the table-top. I just remembered why I'd come to the Star Tavern that evening in the first place. "Speaking of names—"

But, unfortunately, there was no joy there. Iain Scott slumped in his seat. He had passed out.

7

ON TUESDAY ROYAL Ascot week begins in earnest, which means house parties and houseguests and for those of us in the housemaiding business, more beds to change, more loos to clean, more rooms to hoover and so forth. What's holiday for some is toil for others. Housemaids' karma. Fortunately, for the occasion, a detachment of reliable local daily ladies joins our ranks, so what would otherwise be an exhausting week really isn't so perspiration-making after all. Besides, at this point in my brilliant career, I could just about fulfil the duties in my daily rota in my sleep. It was, in fact, in a somewhat somnambulant state that I was pushing a carpet sweeper down the Grand Corridor bright and early Tuesday morning, thinking about this, that, and the other—either Jamie Sans-Surname and assorted feelings in that direction; the question of Victor Fabiani's confession to murder; what item in my meagre wardrobe I was going to wear to Ladies'

Day at Ascot; or whether cats eat bats or bats eat cats. The nice thing about this job is that the actual work occupies about six percent of your brain. The other ninety-four percent you can employ usefully on other phenomena.

The Grand Corridor is indeed rather grand. It runs around the inner perimeter of the south and east wings of the principal floor of the Upper Ward, with fireplaces and sundry doorways on the wall side leading to the main rooms of the Private Apartments, vintage portraits of the long-dead and unremembered (at least by me) all over the walls and, at regular intervals, marble busts of more forgotten nobs on malachite pedestals minding the passage like grim sentinels. In the mornings, the Grand Corridor is a bit gloomy. Tall mullioned windows face west and north onto the Quadrangle and catch no sunlight. With the routine that both members of the Royal Family and guests breakfast in their rooms, there is also very little traffic. I feel at such moments, when tidying the Corridor is my lot, as if I'm pushing my carpet sweeper through a vast and empty art gallery.

Except for the breakfast dash. You'll be sweeping along drowsily when suddenly there'll be a little pattering of feet in the distance. Before you know it, various members of Staff are trotting along in a great hurry, silver trays in hand, darting through doors all around the hall, delivering breakfast before the food gets cold, a challenging task given the Windsor kitchens are probably half a mile off. Five minutes later, it's all over, and you're back to solitude.

"This is the *second* time I've brought a soft-boiled egg to that man," Davey groaned with exasperation as he scurried by me, naming a certain neophyte guest to the annual house party.

"It'll be hard as a knot by the time you get it to him," I opined, jerked out of my reverie.

"Well, *precisely*, my dear!" he called over his shoulder. "I've tried explaining. Do you think he understands this? And he practically runs the Bank of England!"

He vanished behind a door.

The piqued phantom of Davey Pye sent my mind back to our conversation the previous afternoon in Servants' Hall. As we talked I had begun to wonder what I ought to do. I was *still* wondering what I ought to do. My evening diversion at the Star Tavern had no more lent perspective to the problem of Fabiani's astonishing confession to murder than it had brought resolution to my riddle of name-that-soldier.

"I wonder if I should go to the police," I had said then to Davey as he slurped his third cup of tea, fetched by me, noisily.

He grimaced over the rim of his cup.

"I take it that's a 'no.' "

"Jane, dear," he said patiently, returning cup to saucer, "they'll bust you for messing about with their investigation, for being an . . . obstruction or whatever they call it. Do you really want to spoil your Ascot Week?"

"And what about the course of justice, Mr. Pye?"

"Ooh, 'course of justice,' is it now? I do beg your pardon. I'll just fetch your blindfold, your sword, and your set of scales. We do have police and a court system in this country, you know, darling."

"That's not the point."

"Then what, pray tell, *is* the point?"

"The point is this: The investigators should at least consider every bit of evidence before they go about prosecuting. I was *with* Fabiani for at least part of the time he's supposed to have stabbed Roger Pettibon. Not to mention that he didn't act much like a man who'd just killed someone."

"Mmm," Davey demurred. "They won't wear it, you know—a little thing like you sowing doubt where no doubt ought to be sown—"

No, I suppose they won't, I thought, DCI Nightingale coming quickly to mind. He seemed a man in want of a quiet life and there's nothing like a quick confession to a serious crime to supply it.

"—and our artist friend mightn't welcome it either," Davey continued. "If Fabiani's gone out of his way to confess to a murder, then he must have a jolly good reason to do so. For instance: He did it! Otherwise he'd have to be completely bonkers and nobody's ever noticed."

"You're looking at your watch, aren't you? Evensong over?"

"Er . . . yes, I suppose it is."

I regarded Davey with curiosity. "Why, may I ask—" I began.

"I've seen Roger Pettibon there quite often, you might be interested to know," he cut in quickly. "At evensong. At Sunday services, too."

"So . . . ?"

"I never used to see him. And he's often in the company of Canon Leathley, too. The Canon's a nephew of the Duke of Cheshire, don't you know."

"You're trying to distract me."

"I am not, darling. I'm merely trying to keep your persistent curiosity in channels pertinent to the murder enquiries you seem to love so much. Pettibon has been consistently in Church since Easter. Don't you think that's terribly terribly interesting and meaningful?"

"No, I think it's dead boring. Pettibon's stepdaughter died tragically at Easter. He probably turned to the Church in his grief. Not unusual. As for Canon Leathley . . . It's also not uncommon to turn to a clergyman in times of great stress. Part of the therapeutic package, I guess. My question is: Why have *you* turned to the Church?"

"I find the choreography and the millinery enchanting."

"I thought it was the bells and smells."

"That, too." A flush of red had crept above Davey's collar and was slowly making inroads into his podgy cheeks.

"Hmmm," I began teasingly, "I seem to recall some comment about Windsor being the most roman*tique* castle that is in the world. Pepys, wasn't it?"

Davey gave me a long sorrowful look. He whimpered: "Oh, it's hopeless."

"What is?"

"He's one of you lot."

"You mean he's really a woman?"

"Don't be silly."

"Then who is he?"

"One of the choristers. One of the *adult* choristers, a lay clerk," he amended to what must have been an expression of creeping horror on my face. The choir of St. George's Chapel consists of sixteen boys and twelve men, but for some reason I always think of it as a boys' choir. "He's gorgeous. I can't help myself."

"How long has this been going on?"

"Since last winter. Pathetic, isn't it?"

"You are a drip. Stop going if nothing's going to come of it."

"I'm a fool for a pretty face."

You and me both, mate, I thought.

"Besides, this madness only happens at those weekends I'm on duty and Mother's at Windsor," Davey continued. "And this Easter. And now Ascot, of course. Oh, dear." After a moment's frowning contemplation, he added cheerily, "I'm sure it's only a temporary departure from my usual serenity."

"I'm sure." Indeed it was rather unusual to see Davey damp in spirit. Nevertheless he eyed me as if my words of concurrence were a sarcastic swipe.

"So," I continued hastily, not quite keen on further exploration of this topic, being a bit arid in the romance department myself. "Canon Leathley is the Duke of Cheshire's nephew."

"Mmm, yes." Davey straightened in his chair. An opportunity to display his knowledge of the noble families of England always perks him up. "His Grace's sister's son. Mary, I think her name was, one of those exhaustingly good good good people, if you know what I mean. Or so I've been told. Against her family's wishes Mary married this impoverished parson-person, the Reverend Somebody-or-other Leathley, equally afflicted with blinding goodness. They went off together to Borneo or Papua New Guinea or somewhere equally devoid of flush loos and good claret, bearing the white man's burden. This is after the war, in the fifties, I think. Hard to imagine people doing that, even then. Missionary zeal seems so nineteenth-century. But I expect people are still making an nuisance of themselves doing it today. Anyway, at least they had the sense to leave young St. John, our Canon Leathley, at home in England. He was brought up in the Duke's household. He and Rupert, the Duke's son, were virtually raised as brothers."

"So the Leathleys sort of set up permanent shop in

Borneo or wherever. You'd think they'd have at least sent for their son at some point."

"Never had the opportunity, I'm afraid."

"Why?"

"The Leathleys' mission to the darker-skinned people of the world was brief, I'm told. They became somebody's dinner in rather short order."

"You mean . . . ?"

"Yes, I'm sure the natives quite resented two busybodies insisting they abandon their charming world-view to worship some first-century Israelite who died in an unpleasant fashion. Can you imagine, Jane, living in a sweet little village here in England and suddenly have some eager fellow in a sarong and his grass-skirted jolly hockey-sticks wife bother you into worshipping the Great Oogyboogy or whatever these people revere? I'm not sure I'd have them *for* dinner, but I wouldn't have them *to* dinner!"

"Perhaps they were just a mite peckish and the pig harvest had been poor that year," I suggested.

Davey snickered. "Well, there *is* no accounting for taste."

"Samuel Pepys?"

"Noel Coward, I think."

"Interesting that their son went into the church. You'd think his parents' experience would have scared him off."

"Loyal to their memory, perhaps. Or bred in the bone, as I mentioned earlier. At least the Canon's had the wits not to go off to Bongobongo Land and offer himself up as an entrée in Christ's name, amen. Still, he seems to me a bit, oh, *evangelical* for C of E. I think he may actually believe in God! He's spotted me, you know. Ever since I've started making my little appearances at services, he's been pressing pamphlets on me, and inviting me to tea for improving chats, no doubt. I can hardly tell him my *real* reason for personally pushing Church of England attendance above the national two percent average."

"Perhaps he fancies you rotten."

Davey waved away the notion with a flick of his hand. "A gorgon wife and two lumpish teenage daughters, don't be silly."

"So," I mused. "Leathley is a nephew of the Duke of

Cheshire, who was installed as a member of the Garter this very morning. He's a cousin of the Marquess of Graven and he may have abetted Graven's disappearing act after his wife's death. And Leathley's also a cousin of sorts to Hugo, little Lord Lambourn—"

". . . first cousin once removed, I think, is proper."

"—whose very sword, I'm damn sure, was lodged in Pettibon's back. Sort of sets the mind to spinning. Perhaps I shouldn't have dismissed your remark about Pettibon having confabs with Leathley so lightly."

Davey groaned. "I wish I'd kept my mouth shut now. You can't seriously entertain the notion that the FitzJames family would have anything to do with this?"

"What exempts noble families from scrutiny?"

"You *are* determined to be democratic, aren't you," Davey commented dryly. "Nevertheless, I say you're wasting your time. Fabiani confessed to it. Fabiani did it."

"I say there's a reasonable doubt he didn't. And . . ." for it had just occurred to me, "just how does everyone know Fabiani confessed anyway?"

"Oh, that old gossip, Nigel," Davey explained, referring to one of the other footmen, Nigel Stokoe. "He was at the police station on Alma Road. I'm afraid Nigel was caught—*ahem*—misbehaving in a public place with one of the Household Cavalry. No charges laid. I think he'd been obliged to appear for a dressing-down. Anyway, Nigel was there when Fabiani made his entrance and blabbed all."

"Blabbed all? Including *why* he was claiming to have done this damn silly thing?"

Davey shook his head. "However, of course, we Staff have been threatened with a spell in the dungeons if we talk about this spot of unpleasantness outside these four walls or four hundred walls or however many walls this castle has. I'm sure, dear, you'll get your lecture soon from Mrs. Boozley. Good-bloody-luck keeping this one from press and public, I say. Poor Mother. And this being her favourite week in the year . . ."

If the police really are sure Fabiani is their killer, then they'll make their own announcement, and soon, I thought

as I continued pushing my carpet sweeper down the Grand
Corridor. As for the Queen, well, in my experience, she
wasn't averse to solving a puzzle, whether jigsaw, crossword,
or murder.

"And I'll bet Her Majesty would be dead pleased if
Fabiani turned out not to be the killer. She'll want that
portrait finished," I'd said to Davey last thing.

"Well, if by some slim chance you're right, darling,"
he mused, "then we may all have to face the fact a murderer
is loose in Windsor Castle. Mother *won't* be pleased about
that!"

True, I thought, as I passed a window facing onto the
Quadrangle. An odd sound coming from the other end of the
Grand Corridor pulled me from my musings. The Grand
Corridor, all five hundred feet of it, runs at almost a ninety-
degree angle and I thought peering from a window along the
east side might indicate the source of the noise on the south
side, but no joy there. The Corridor had gone all quiet in the
wake of the breakfast rush but for this sound which in a way
was not unlike that of the carpet sweeper, a sort of *swoosh*,
only continuous and growing louder, faster and more ominous by the second. Feeling oddly alarmed, I set aside my
sweeper and moved forward to investigate. The Grand Corridor has a deflection where the east and south wings meet, a
sort of diagonal cut. On one side is a great Gothic doorway to
the Sovereign's Entrance and Her Majesty's suite of rooms
in the Queen's Tower. On the other side, jutting into the
Quadrangle, is what I'm told was once the gloomy old Oak
Dining Room from Queen Victoria's day, now a modern
drawing room. I turned at the first angle of the Corridor, the
noise now a kind of dull roar.

There was a blur, a figure careened toward me at great
speed, and then the next thing I knew, ooph, I was flying
through the air, my head landing, ouch, on the edge of my
carpet sweeper. Birds do not tweet in these instances, as
they do in cartoons, I have learned from this painful experience, but I could see stars in irregular orbit around the pan-
elled ceiling and tiny suns exploding. The wind was quite
knocked out of me. I lay there dazed.

"Harry!" The voice of more than forty Christmas broadcasts was sharp, "I believe you've been told you mustn't . . . you mustn't—"

"Rollerblade, Your Majesty," I wheezed from the floor.

"—*rollerblade* down the Corridor."

"Sorry, Gran."

The words were formally contrite but through my interstellar fog my ears detected a tone of glee. Imp!

"Are you hurt, Jane?"

"Oh, I'm just fine, Ma'am."

"And you, Harry?"

"I'm okay, Gran."

I must say, the floor's an odd angle from which to view the Sovereign. Her head seemed so far away, up among the stars I thought dreamily. A sun exploded near a newspaper she had folded in her hands. Ah, the *Daily Telegraph*. She's doing the crossword, of course. How . . . how . . . *Her*. I could feel hot meaty breath pouring onto my face and something wet and rough running along my face. *Yuck*, I had the presence of mind to think, *what is that?*

A corgi!

What else?

The stars and planets vanished. I struggled to my elbows. Two liquid brown eyes regarded me balefully. Teeth and tongue were not far away.

"Harry, help her up if you would, please."

Tottering on his Rollerblades, Prince Harry bent over and grasped me by my underarms, his blades nearly shooting out from under him. We struggled awkwardly but—really!—I was fine, and I managed to get to my feet without falling into a heap with His Royal Highness, who was more hindrance than help.

"And, Harry . . . ?" The Queen prompted, making a gesture with her free hand.

"I'm sorry," he said, taking the cue, turning to me.

"Oh, think nothing of it, sir," I responded airily.

"I hope you aren't hurt," he continued, brushing back his hair, favouring me with a cheeky grin.

The Queen regarded me thoughtfully. Pale morning light, diffused from a skylight above, glinted off her spectacles. "You do look a bit off-colour, Jane." She indicated a pair of varnished doors with a crenellated frame opposite. "I think perhaps you should come with me."

Her Majesty ushered me through into the Oak Drawing Room, herself remaining in the frame of the open door. "Harry, do please take those things off." I heard one of the chairs against the Corridor wall creak as a body fell into it. The Queen lingered a moment, ensuring, I suppose, her grandson really did unlace his Rollerblades. "Very good," I heard her say finally. "Now off you go, Harry."

"I suppose one should have signs posted: 'No Roller-blading in the Corridor,'" Her Majesty sighed, shutting the door after one of the corgis, swaddling us once more in silence. "He had Hugo—Lord Lambourn—tearing down the Corridor yesterday on those things." She smiled at me. "Now, are you quite sure you're feeling well enough? It looked to me as if your head might have hit that sweeper of yours."

I pressed my fingers to the back of my skull as Her Majesty fiddled with a switch in the door frame. A crystal chandelier dripping from the centre of the ceiling like a stalactite blazed diamond-bright, illuminating the showpiece of the room, a statue of the Queen's favourite racehorse, Aureole. "There, that's better," she said.

"Really, Ma'am, it's nothing. His Highness just knocked the wind out of me, that's all."

"Because if you've had concussion you must see the doctor, you know."

"I think my hair saved me." I patted my housemaid's knot.

Her Majesty examined me more closely a moment. She seemed satisfied.

"Well, come and sit down for a moment, then." The Queen gestured to a cream-coloured chesterfield near one of the corners of the semioctagonal room.

Past white-and-gold draperies, I glimpsed deep shadows of the crenellated Castle battlements reaching over the lush grass of the Quadrangle. I felt oddly disconcerted, and it wasn't the aftermath of my tumble. It had entered my mind then to raise my qualms about the unpleasantness in the Garter Throne Room. If something is wrong, I've

learned, it's far better to tell HM, however unwelcome the
news might be, than have her find out later and be cross
And unwelcome I thought the news might indeed be, given
not only the potential to tarnish Royal Ascot week, but to
cast a cold light upon both HM's friends and the community
nestled within the castle's ancient walls.

"You were of great service yesterday in quite dreadful
circumstances, Jane," Her Majesty began solemnly, sitting
down, placing her newspaper on her lap. "Happily, my
guests were spared knowing what had preceded them in the
Throne Room." A tiny smile played about the corners of her
mouth. "I think perhaps I shall even make the extra rug a
custom of the Garter Investiture."

"Thank you, Ma'am," I answered, sitting in turn, not
really knowing how to respond. The Queen rarely thanks
people for doing what, after all, is their duty. But I suppose
lending a hand at the scene of a crime was somewhat above
and beyond the call of said D.

"As I'm sure you know, there's been a resolution," the
Queen continued briskly, petting the corgi that had settled
beside her. "Most surprising, really. And rather discouraging
to learn that one's portrait is being painted by a murderer
. . . well, *alleged* murderer."

I clung to the word "alleged" like a former royal princess to her divorce settlement. "Ma'am . . ." I began nervously.

A regal eyebrow rose over spectacle frames.

"Ma'am, I think there's something a bit odd about all
this business with Mr. Fabiani."

There. I said it. And I didn't sink through the floor and
into the dungeons below.

Her Majesty gave me one of her cool assessing looks.
"Really," she responded neutrally. "Are you quite sure,
Jane?"

"Ma'am, I talked with Chief Inspector Nightingale after I put the rug in place and he told me the time of death
was estimated sometime between eight-thirty and nine-
thirty yesterday morning."

"Yes . . . ?"

"Well, the time of death didn't mean anything to me
at all, until I heard Mr. Fabiani had claimed to have stabbed

Mr. Pettibon. You see, Ma'am, I was with Mr. Fabiani . . . well, at least part of that time.

"Posing," I hurried on to say as HM's eyebrows made a further ascent. "I was working in the rooms near his suite and he sort of insisted that I put on Your Majesty's Garter mantle and pose for him while he painted. This was about nine-fifteen."

"I see." She added gently, "But if the Chief Inspector's right, then Mr. Fabiani had a good forty-five minutes when he wasn't in your sight."

"Yes, Ma'am, that's true, but . . ."

I rushed on to assert what I had argued with Davey: that Fabiani had shown none of the distress you might expect of one who had so recently slaughtered another human being. He'd been utterly concentrated on his work. Davey, too, I reported, agreed Fabiani had seemed perfectly unruffled when he'd seen him, not long after ten o'clock. "Unless, Ma'am," I concluded reluctantly, "Fabiani's, like, some sort of complete psychopath."

"No, I shouldn't think so," Her Majesty responded. She didn't elaborate. Since I figure after more than seventy years in the people-meeting business Her Majesty is a pretty shrewd judge of character, I was pleased she seemed to be moving to my point of view on the subject of Fabiani's culpability.

"How very peculiar," Her Majesty added pensively, reaching down absently to stroke the corgi's golden head.

"Ma'am," I braved, "you don't happen to know why Mr. Fabiani confessed?"

The dog's face lit with pure pleasure as her mistress's fingers caressed between her furry ears.

"Yes, I do," the Queen replied at last. "I was briefed last evening. Mr. Pettibon, it seems, was a blackmailer." She shot me a penetrating gaze. "Or at least this is Mr. Fabiani's claim."

"Wow. So Mr. Pettibon was blackmailing Mr. Fabiani. Over what, though?"

"Forged drawings."

A largish question mark must have settled along my features for Her Majesty explained: "Apparently, when he was younger, when he was, I suppose, struggling to make a living as an artist, Mr. Fabiani forged the work of some very well-known artists. Some of that work seems to have found its way into the Royal Collection. Mr. Pettibon, who you probably know was the assistant curator for exhibitions in the Print Room, detected—somehow—these fake drawings, connected them with Mr. Fabiani, and then set about blackmailing him.''

I mulled this over for a moment. What I knew about the world of art came mostly from catching Sister Wendy on telly in the Staff lounge, and occasional forays into the National Gallery and the Tate on my days off. Questions began to bloom in my brain like penicillin in a petrie dish, the most obvious being nonart-related:

"What did Mr. Pettibon want, Ma'am? Money?''

"I'm afraid so. As I understand it, he had been threatening Mr. Fabiani with exposure—which would certainly ruin his reputation—if certain sums weren't forthcoming. Mr. Fabiani consistently refused to pay. Yesterday morning, Mr. Pettibon went to Mr. Fabiani's rooms—''

"His *rooms*?''

"Yes,'' Her Majesty replied calmly. "His rooms. They argued. Again, as I understand it, Mr. Fabiani pursued Mr. Pettibon down the stairs, through the State Apartments, and into the Throne Room where he happened to come across the short sword that young Hugo had left behind.''

"And . . . ?''

"Mmm. Mr. Fabiani claims he was so overwhelmed with rage he barely knew what he was doing. Acted on impulse, I suppose one could say. Mr. Fabiani is, you'll allow, Jane, somewhat short-tempered,'' Her Majesty added drily, giving me a knowing glance.

Yes, I had to admit he did seem to be. And I could all too easily imagine Fabiani erupting into anger. The artist just seemed the type. I could even see in my mind's eye, in comic fashion, the hapless, reedy, Milquetoasty Roger Pettibon fleeing through the Castle before Victor Fabiani, no match for the larger, heavier, impassioned artist who had finally been pushed to breaking point. It all *seemed* plausible.

And yet, I thought.

"And yet,'' I said out loud to the Sovereign, "Mr. Fabiani displayed no great emotion while I was with him that morning. He wasn't winded. Or sweating. Or shaking. And Davey—David Pye—can attest to the same when he went to pick up Your Majesty's Garter things later. He was cool as a cucumber, totally absorbed in his work.

"And," I continued, growing more confident, "if there had been some sort of blazing row I'm sure I would have heard it. Not only was I posing for Mr. Fabiani from nine-fifteen on, I was in the vicinity for nearly an hour before-hand!"

The Queen absently ran her fingers along the strands of pearls at her neck. She looked beyond me, toward the window, seemingly lost in thought.

"Jane, are you quite sure you would have heard something if the two men had been arguing while you were doing your work?"

"Pretty sure, Ma'am. I know the walls are thick, but I had all the doors open in the suites I was working on to give them a proper airing."

"Well," Her Majesty considered after another moment's thought. "I grant you—this is most peculiar. One would be very unhappy to see Mr. Fabiani punished for something he didn't do, if he didn't do it, of course." A certain enthusiasm crept into her voice. "You've presented an interesting dilemma, Jane."

"Oh, thank you, Ma'am." I felt a slight blush of pleasure creep up my neck. "Of course, Ma'am, if Mr. Fabiani is innocent, the question is—"

"Why would he make a confession?" Her Majesty finished the thought. "Why, indeed."

8

THE QUEEN PICKED up her newspaper and rose from her seat. I thought at first it was her signal for dismissal, but, instead, she beckoned me (and the corgi) to follow her across the room. She switched on a couple of Anglepoise lamps, placed the paper to the side, and removed a large piece of card that lay overtop an oak table. Revealed was a jigsaw puzzle, potentially an enormous one judging by the size and placement of the few completed portions. The puzzle looked utterly daunting, with about two hundred shades of green, and hardly any discernible shapes.

"A landscape, Ma'am?" I groaned within.

"I expect so. I asked them to hide the lid to the box, so I'm not quite sure." She picked up a piece. "I often find this helps me think." She contemplated the puzzle piece's irregular outline a moment, then thought better of her choice.

"I must say, Jane, I do find your description of Mr. Fabiani's calm demeanour yesterday morning when you were with him really very interesting. He'd have to be rather a Jekyll-and-Hyde type—wouldn't he?—to kill one minute and behave quite normally the next. Although I suppose it's possible." She tilted her head, chose another segment, and tapped it against her chin thoughtfully. "Oh, surely not. Perhaps the truth lies somewhere else in his background."

"Does Your Majesty know much about him?"

"Let me see, what *does* one know of Mr. Fabiani that might be useful?" the Queen mused. "Born in Devonshire, grew up near Newton Abbot, I believe. His father came to this country from Italy after the war and married an Englishwoman. I think he had a brother here at the time, who subsequently went to Canada. Oh, yes, we talked about that during the first sitting. You were there, Jane."

Her hand darted out and she snapped the puzzle piece in place. She continued: "He took his one-year Foundation at the Exeter Polytechnic. Studied at the Slade in London. Spent some little time in Rome furthering his studies, I believe. At the British School. And perhaps visiting family." The Queen frowned slightly. "I'm not sure this is very helpful. Some biographical details were supplied to me when my approval was sought for Mr. Fabiani to receive the commission, but they're not very telling."

"Did Your Majesty and Mr. Fabiani talk about other things in general?"

The Queen looked off into the middle distance, then picked up another jigsaw piece. "We talked about horses, I seem to recall—"

Gosh, what a surprise. Prince Philip once said that unless something eats grass and farts, his wife isn't interested, which isn't at all true, as I can attest. But it is, in its sarky way, an indication of one of Her Majesty's main passions in the life.

"—he very much liked to sketch horses when he was young—their musculature, I think, he found challenging—and there were stables nearby . . .

"Oh, and we talked of the East End. There's a rather strong artistic community in the East End, I understand, and I'm quite interested in the renewal in that part of London.

The war destroyed so much of it, of course. Mr. Fabiani also mentioned he'd been living in a loft in Clerkenwell but was in the process of selling it."

"I wonder why?"

"He didn't give a reason," she replied, expertly placing another jigsaw piece in its rightful place. "I wonder if this is a jungle landscape of some nature. It's quite vivid. What do you think?"

"I can't make any of it out, ma'am."

"Hmm. Well, it'll come." The Queen paused. "Anyway, as I was about to say, the Duke of Cheshire told me that Mr. Fabiani had recently separated from a woman—that may be the reason for bringing in the estate agents to sell his loft. I expect Mr. Fabiani spoke rather more freely with Freddie . . . with the Duke. I understand Mr. Fabiani is quite a man for the ladies. No wife in the picture, however. Not in the customary sense." She paused again and considered her handiwork. "I had a feeling that Mr. Fabiani was in a bit of a muddle, actually."

"Separating from this woman probably, Ma'am."

HM nodded. "Possibly. Perhaps Windsor has been a haven for him." She pushed into the right spot a puzzle piece of acid green. "And, of course, there was this daughter of his," she continued. "Do you recall, Jane, Mr. Fabiani mentioning his daughter at Easter?"

"Yes, Ma'am," I replied, watching her match another piece, "I remember you were talking about the Pettibons having just lost a daughter and Mr. Fabiani saying something about finding one and how ironic it was and such."

"Well, Mr. Fabiani did elaborate later. I'm afraid he was a bit tense at that first sitting. People so often are. But he was rather more personable at subsequent sittings and we did have some pleasant conversations.

"Apparently, the young woman had sought him out, oh, last winter sometime. He'd had a child when he was a very young man, which the child's mother later gave up for adoption. I believe the relationship between Mr. Fabiani and the woman in question had ended well before the child was born. I'm not sure if Mr. Fabiani even knew he was a father at the time. Anyway, he seemed to be quite delighted that this young woman had entered his life. I think it's part of the reason why he agreed to come to Windsor to paint one's portrait."

The thought flitted through my mind that any portraitist with an eye to his c.v. would probably agree to hump it to the North Pole for the chance of painting the Queen.

"In fact, Jane," she frowned slightly, discarding an unworkable bit with a slight blue tinge, "Mr. Fabiani's daughter works here. She's a restoration expert of some nature. I wonder what she thinks about this business with her father, poor young woman."

"His daughter's one of the people working on the fire-damaged rooms?"

"A plaster-modeler, I believe. One of a team. They've done splendid work on the ceilings in the Crimson and Green Drawings Rooms. Now, let me think: She has a rather poetic Christian name." Her Majesty cast about the room as if the woman's name lay hidden beneath the sideboard. "Ah! Miranda. I'm sure that's correct. As for surname, I don't believe Mr. Fabiani said. Of course, it would be different, as she was adopted."

"She might be worth talking to," I considered.

"Unfortunately only a skeleton crew is working this week; I'm not sure Miranda would be one of them," the Queen explained. "It was decided, in view of Ascot Week and my guests' comfort, to offer a week's leave." The corgi suddenly yawned with great noise and spectacle. "Are you bored, my darling?" The Queen regarded the dog indulgently. "Just a few more moments and we'll have Mr. Pye give you a very nice W-A-L-K-I-E."

The dog barked excitedly.

"Perhaps one should start using French."

"*Une promenade?*" I offered, relying on my high school learning.

The dog barked again.

"Or perhaps German." The Queen picked up a portion of the puzzle almost shaped like Prince Edward Island (only much smaller) and immediately found the right spot. "There! Look, those two parts join with that part."

"Oh, I see. A bit of sky through . . . treetops?"

"I expect so."

"Mr. Fabiani may have been in a muddle about his

life," the Queen resumed after a moment, "but he wasn't muddled about art. Quite passionate on the subject. Not surprising, I suppose. But I'm afraid most of it went over my head. In my family, my sister is the one knowledgable about trends in art. I did quite like the copies of the portraits I was sent, though."

"Ma'am . . . ?"

"I was sent photographs of Mr. Fabiani's previous work when my approval was sought. And I did see the Duke's portrait when I visited Umbridge Trigoze. His paintings had some inspiration, I thought. A bit of life to them. He seemed quite good at getting the details utterly real without being brutally frank. I suppose I thought his work was a bit old-fashioned in a way. Or perhaps it's the new fashion. I've no idea. Anyway, I thought some inner substance came through in the portraits of his I was shown. Rather like the best of the Old Masters, in a way, with their generous view of humanity. Including one. One hopes."

"Oh, I think the portrait—what he's done so far—is quite wonderful," I said and meant it. "He must have picked up a thing or two studying in Italy. Which," I added reluctantly, "seems like an argument for Mr. Fabiani's supposed ability to duplicate Old Masters."

The Queen raised her chin. "I'm afraid there's more. Mr. Fabiani's father worked as an undertaker, you see—"

I didn't actually.

"—we talked a little about the affect of this on his childhood. Being teased and so forth. But the Duke told me more: As a boy, Mr. Fabiani would steal into his father's place of business and make sketches of the deceased—"

"Eeeooo."

"—some of which weren't always . . . whole, if you understand my meaning. Quite disagreeable, really." The Queen's lips formed a thin line as she turned her attention back to the jigsaw.

"Like Renaissance artists, studying anatomy the only way they could at the time, Ma'am," I supplied.

"Quite. So you see, Mr. Fabiani's passion for art is rather considerable. And I expect this . . . early training, if one may call it that, has served him well."

"Your Majesty means in making fakes as well as originals."

"Possibly. Apparently, among the works Mr. Fabiani has counterfeited—allegedly—are Leonardo drawings of the anatomical sort as well as drawings of horses."

Feeling a bit deflated, I commented hopefully: "There must be more to making a convincing forgery, Ma'am, than being able to imitate a famous artist. You'd have to make it *look* old, somehow."

"Yes, I expect so. But one would have to ask an expert about that."

"And even if Mr. Pettibon could recognize a fake," I wondered out loud, "what would lead him to Mr. Fabiani?"

The Queen's fingers sieved through a mound of jigsaw pieces. "Knew each other in the past, perhaps," she replied, selecting one. "They're around the same age, I would guess. Although Mr. Pettibon took a curatorial route, I expect they may have had similar educations, gone to the same schools perhaps."

She tried the puzzle piece in a number of spots but was unsuccessful. "Oh, well." She frowned slightly, then made one of her imperceptible gestures which indicated our interview was drawing to a close. As she replaced the card over the jigsaw, she gestured to the nearby newspaper. "Have you seen today's *Telegraph*?"

"Oh," was all I could say when I opened it. There, above the fold, was a photo of Hugo FitzJames caught in midfall along the Garter procession route, the Queen's mantle stretched like taffy, and the Queen herself, head turned toward the camera, captured with a look of mild perplexity.

"Is Lord Lambourn okay, Ma'am?" I asked, returning the paper to her.

Her Majesty's response was not immediate. "I hope so," was her ambiguous reply.

"And . . ." I almost hated to bring it up, "was the weapon that killed Mr. Pettibon Lord Lambourn's?"

"I'm afraid it was," she said shortly. The Queen refolded the paper to the crossword and we moved down the room to the door, corgi in tow. "Perhaps the wisest thing for you to do, Jane, would be to go to the police and tell them what you've told me," she added firmly.

But I knew what this guidance cost her. If not Victor Fabiani, then who? But the weapon used to kill Roger Pettibon belonged to her Page, Hugo FitzJames, and Hugo FitzJames was the grandson of her friend, the Duke of Cheshire. Hugo couldn't be eliminated.

And then, the image of the Garter Procession before me, something else rose in the old bean like carbonation in a fizzy drink. "The Garter that Mr. Pettibon was wearing: It wasn't Your Majesty's after all, was it?"

HM looked faintly puzzled. "No, I suppose it wasn't, in the end."

"Let's see, Davey found Your Majesty's Garter, which had been in Mr. Fabiani's room; therefore the one around Mr. Pettibon's leg couldn't have belonged to Mr. Fabiani," I said brightly.

"Unless Mr. Fabiani had another one."

Brightness faded to dark.

"I very much doubt it," the Queen added, folding the paper under her arm. "Although . . . hmm, I wonder . . ." She paused at the door. "You see, Jane, when a Garter knight dies I receive his nearest male relative in Audience and he returns the Garter insignia to me. Or to the monarch of the day, as the case would be in the past. So, in theory, there are no insignia in a sense . . ." HM gestured vaguely, ". . . out there."

"In theory, Ma'am," I repeated.

"Yes, well, they're not all in safekeeping, at least here. Winston's—Sir Winston Churchill's—are on loan. You can see them at Chartwell. And I believe the Duke of Wellington has the Badge of the Garter that was worn by Charles I at his execution."

Her Majesty's right hand drifted to her neck. Unconsciously, I'm sure.

"I'm not quite certain how the Badge came into Wellington's possession," she continued. "I know Lord Kitchener's Garter things went down with him when his ship sank during the First World War, and . . ." HM paused, her hand traveling a few inches south to her pearls. She ran her fingers along the strands thoughtfully.

"However—and this is important, Jane—the insignia returned to the Crown does *not* include the Garter itself.

Only the Garter Star and the gold collar, which are both rather valuable. So the Garter remains within a family and, one presumes, is passed down. And, if I remember correctly, there have been a few occasions when Garter insignia have shown up at auction too, which shouldn't be allowed, but there you go . . ."

Her Majesty's face brightened. "I have an idea." She clapped her hands with almost girlish pleasure. "I shall contact the Secretary of the Central Chancery of the Orders of Knighthood.

"Sir Bernard Scrymgeour-Warburton administers the Chancery," HM explained, "and keeps the records, so he may well have some idea where this extra Garter could have come from. We do know it couldn't have been one of the new Garters for yesterday's Investiture. I saw both of them lying on their presentation cushions."

Unseen hands slowly began to open the door. (It's amazing how Staff always know where HM is.) "Well," the Queen said in a hushed voice in a summing-up sort of fashion, "I shall look into this Garter business. I should like to know what the police have made of it!" she added parenthetically.

"And you, Jane . . ." She smiled encouragingly. "Do what you must. Perhaps this daughter of Mr. Fabiani's can shed some light. But do go into town as soon as you can." She nodded to the purposefully blank-faced footman who now stood by the door. "I'm sure you know what I mean."

There are a few hours, after breakfast and before the Family and guests return to their rooms postluncheon to dress for Ascot, when we below-stairs denizens finally get the chance to make beds, scrub loos, and generally bring order out of varying degrees of chaos. With the Corridor swept, I was due to join the daily assigned to me, a local woman named Fleur Aiken, in York Tower to begin attacking the mountain of linen. But there was one task I thought I could accomplish quickly in the meantime. Storing my sweeper in a housemaid's cupboard in one of the gloomy below-ground passages, I made my way upstairs and into the forest of scaffolding that is St. George's Hall. There I understood a few members of the restoration teams to be at work despite the Ascot week furlough.

I strained my ears. St. George's Hall, really a vast tunnellike chamber, seemed as deserted as a schoolroom at recess. Tools and sawhorses and lumber lay forsaken where they had been dropped. Only from the far western recesses near the top of the soaring ceiling could I detect a sound, a rhythm, a sort of curious scuffing noise that hinted of human activity. At least, I thought as I navigated the pathway of wooden planks over the ribbing that would eventually be a new oak floor, St. George's Hall and the adjacent State Rooms are relieved of the horrible musty reek suffered during my first stay at Windsor. So much water had been poured through to quench the great fire, it'd taken these rooms years to dry properly. Now the Hall smelled like my father's workshed as sunshine, streaming through the tall cathedral windows, warmed the new wood, penetrating the piles of wood shavings and sawdust, pinching my memory so that I felt a pang of homesickness.

"Hello!" I called.

No response.

"Hello!" I called again, louder, cupping my hands over my mouth for a megaphone effect. The scuffing noise continued unabated. Tiny particles of wood dust, turning and dancing in the shaft of sunlight, assaulted my nose. I sneezed.

I squinted up through the maze of scaffolding to the temporary floor under the ceiling. The climb looked daunting—St. George's Hall soared to three or four stories—and I'm not a huge fan of heights, but under the adage that it's best to conquer your fears (and aware that time was a'wasting and Fleur Aiken would be p.o.'d if I were late), I started up the succession of ladders and walkways, breath coming a little quicker with each step, until finally, with relief, I poked my head through an opening and climbed into Gothic rafters that seemed in close-up so monstrously huge my first expression was:

"Wow."

A man wearing a forest-green construction helmet and a matching green T-shirt turned from blueprints he was holding in his hand and glanced at me.

"Where's your hard hat? You must have a hard hat if you're going to be on site."

"Sorry," I replied, still distracted by the tracery of new oak blazing a warm gold in the light of arc lamps. Another man, younger, identically attired in green, was pushing a large metal blade against a mammoth rib of new oak with smooth regular strokes, sending ribbons of wood curling over the side. His face glistened with perspiration.

"I'll just be a sec." I brushed some sawdust from my hands where I'd gripped the floor. The space under the ceiling was quite warm. "I'm looking for a woman."

"Join the queue," grumbled the chiseler, not pausing in his rhythmic strokes to look up.

Ignoring him, I addressed the older man: "A Miranda somebody. She's a plaster-modeler. Probably worked on some of the moldings around here." I noted the pointed arches at the top of the Gothic windows, still black from the fire. "Or at least in the Drawings Rooms."

"Gerry, didn't you try it on with some bird from Turner Associates? A Miranda, wasn't it? Black hair—"

"Yeah," Gerry growled between puffs from exertion.

"Is Turner Associates the firm she works for?"

Gerry nodded. "In Slough. They were subcontracted for some of the plaster restoration work."

"You a friend of hers?" The younger man paused in his work to address me, running the back of his hand across his brow.

"Sort of," I lied. "I was just wondering if she'd been at work this week."

"You know, I thought I caught a glimpse of Miranda yesterday in one of the below-stairs corridors when we were coming in," the older man mused. "Might be wrong, though. I doubt she was scheduled to work."

"What time was this?"

"Nine or so."

"Funny you being a friend and not knowing her last name." Gerry regarded me sceptically.

"I forgot it. We'd just met."

"Walter, then. Miranda Walter. Surprised she's got any friends." Gerry leaned into his blade and resumed chiseling. "Cold bitch, that one."

The older man glanced at his colleague and then at me. He shrugged apologetically. "Anyway, you'll have to ask someone else if she's been around. Phone Turner's. They'd know her schedule."

"Thanks. I guess you wouldn't happen to know where she lives? In Slough?"

"Gerry . . . ?"

"She lives *here*," Gerry replied testily. "In Windsor. St. Margaret Place, if you're so keen to know."

"Hard hat next time." The older man tapped on his headgear as I turned to pop back down the rabbit hole. "This Miranda sure got to you, mate," was the last thing I heard.

Well, I thought, trotting along vaulted stone passages to York Tower, at least I've got a full name and an address. An address that echoed of something, as it happened. I knew St. Margaret Place was not far from Peascod Street, west of St. Leonard's Road. I'd seen it on a map but I'd never traversed it. It was a bit off the main drag.

When I climbed the York Tower stairs and entered the Prince of Wales's suite on the principal floor, Fleur was already in full froth.

" 'Bout time!" she announced in merry imperious fashion, glancing up from a tabletop she was energetically dusting in the sitting room. "Blimey, what's he readin' now?" she added before I could respond, picking up a book lying open facedown on the table. "*Visud* . . . I can't read it."

"*Visuddhimagga.*" I pronounced the title as phonetically as I could, taking the book from Fleur's hands. It was thick, with a purple leather cover, the title embossed in gold. "By Bhadant . . . I give up. By Somebody Buddhaghosa. Buddhist text, I guess. Look, here's the translation: *Path of Purification.*" I flipped through the pages, keeping one finger where His Royal Highness had left the book open. There were no pictures or conversations. And what, one might ask, is the use of a book without pictures or conversations? "Looks like a total snore."

"Buddhist! And him one day going to be Head of the Church of England! His poor mum!" Fleur shook her head.

"Here. Put it the way you found it. You know what he's like if you move his stuff, particularly his books and papers."

"I know, I know." Fleur's quick eyes darted about the sitting room in search of dust and disorder. The place sparkled. "This'll do. If we don't get through this lot they'll be charging back to change for Ascot. C'mon."

Cleaning gear in hand, she led the way through a curved passage that led to the bathroom and bedroom. In her wake wafted the ghost of chips past. After mornings skivvying at the Castle and afternoons skivvying for private clients, Fleur worked evenings at a fish-and-chips shop in St. Leonard's Road. Try as she might, the aroma of frying fat never quite deserted her. I wasn't sure if she knew she made your stomach growl, but it seemed heartless to tell her. She worked so hard, such long hours, and still and all was somehow managing to raise two children without benefit of a husband (or reasonable facsimile). One of her kids, her daughter Cath, was twelve years old, and Fleur had only a few years on me. I admired her pluck, not half because she remained so determinedly cheerful. She was a devil of a worker, too; her tireless capacity for speed and thoroughness was probably why Mrs. Boozley overlooked the ring in her nose and her short blond hair, almost cruelly butchered, streaked lime or raspberry, as the fancy took her.

"At least His Nibs is a tidy sleeper," she observed, pulling the counterpane back over the six-foot-wide mattress and brushing her hand over the bottom sheet to smooth out creases. "C'mon, Jane, pull your finger out. We've not got all day."

I had moved to the window, diverted not so much by the view of Windsor Great Park in green splendour and the Long Walk lost to a mirage, as by the guard posted right below at King George IV Gate. "More like officer material," Molly, the woman in the Star Tavern, had opined of Jamie Sans-Surname. I knew well enough: Officers weren't sentries. And all I could see anyway was the top of a bearskin hat, glossy black hairs glistening in the midmorning sun, and the shoulders of a scarlet tunic. Poor bugger, I thought as

Fleur dragged me back to the work at hand. Must be scorching in that getup.

"What's all this talk about a murder then?" Fleur demanded after a moment, as we both plumped pillows. "I hear tell someone got it proper in the Throne Room. Some bloke from the Library. I think Cath had him for Saturday morning art classes at the Arts Centre. Pettibon." She snorted. "Last name's worse than my first."

Fleur's mother, according to Fleur, had been captivated by some swan-necked bit of gossamer in a televised Edwardian soap opera before her pregnancy. Her legacy to her daughter was a lyric name the child grew out of, rather than into. Fleur was as plain a woman as any I knew, and blithely aware of the discrepancy, too.

"How did you find out?" I asked. "About the murder, I mean."

"Not from you lot, that's for sure," she groused good-naturedly as together we pulled the counterpane over the bed and tucked it around the pillows. "I heard it in the chippie last night. Two coppers from Alma Road getting take-away just before closing. Didn't think I was listening. But I was. They said that artist painting the Queen did it. The one with the rooms north side of here."

She regarded me with astonishment. I shrugged. "Apparently," was my lame response.

Fleur shook her head. "You're not even safe in this pile of bricks." She whisked some petals that had fallen on a cabinet top from a vase of flowers into her hand and then into a bin liner. "I've seen him, you know. Fabiani," she added, lifting the vase and dusting around it.

"What? Here in the Castle where he's doing his painting, you mean?"

"Oh, yeah, seen him here. That's how I know what he looks like. But what I meant was—across the road. That's where I've seen him last few months. Going in and out of this girl's flat."

Something tweeked my brain. "You live on . . . ?"

"St. Margaret Place. I've told you before."

Illumination! That's why St. Margaret Place seemed more than just a street name to me. Fleur had even invited me to her flat at Easter but I hadn't been able to make it for some reason.

"She's an odd sort," Fleur prattled on. "Keeps herself to herself, if you know what I mean. Doesn't seem to have a lot of friends. Not that I've seen going in and out. No men friends. And then suddenly this bloke. Well, isn't she the clever one, I thought. And old enough to be her dad, too. Dirty old sod."

I laughed. "That's because he *is* her dad!"

"Never!" Fleur gasped at me through a mirror she was polishing.

"No lie. Her name's Miranda Walter and Fabiani's her father. Her biological father. Natural father, whatever. She was adopted right at birth. He didn't even know he had a child. Apparently she went looking for him, did a search, and only just located him."

Fleur frowned and attacked the mirror with greater speed. The glass squeaked in protest. It occurred to me that perhaps she was worrying her own children might one day do the same thing—seek their father. Or father(s). Fleur always determinedly avoided mentioning the paternity of her children.

"Maybe that explains it," she said quietly, after a moment.

"Explains what?"

"Cath said he never stayed the night."

I laughed. "I wondered how you kept up on your neighbours' doings, what with all your jobs."

Fleur smiled weakly. "She's a right little snoop, that kid of mine. Knows too much for her age already. And bright! I'm not just saying that because I'm her mum. Now," she added obliquely, "if I can only keep her from making my mistakes." She picked up her box of cleaning gear by the handle and sighed. "Anyway, shift yourself. There's the loo yet to do."

We were scouring the porcelain together, me the sink, Fleur the tub, when it occurred to me she might have an idea of Miranda's movements the day before. Or her inquisitive daughter might have.

"Not clapped eyes on her in days myself, I don't think," she replied when I broached the subject, the tub an echo chamber for her voice. "Last week was maybe the last time I saw her in the street. I'm not sure about Cath. She hasn't mentioned anything." There was a pause. "Poor Miranda. She's only just found her old dad and then off he goes and sticks someone."

I hesitated before a framed Jak cartoon of the Prince of Wales to which a few specks of toothpaste had adhered. Ought I to confide my reservations to Fleur? This wasn't like the death in Buckingham Palace I'd once helped HM investigate. Then it had appeared one of us from the lower orders had been the culprit and so you had to be a bit cautious about who you talked to. This was different. Besides, Fleur was only a daily. She wasn't really a part of the Castle community.

"Well . . ." I said in sufficiently doubtful tones to pique her curiosity.

"Well . . . ? Well, *what*?"

"I have this gnawing feeling that Fabiani might be innocent."

And I told her why.

"Blimey!" She had seated herself on the loo lid and had grabbed a toilet plunger sceptre-fashion, which made her look a little like . . . well, never mind.

"So you think someone else . . . ?"

"I just don't *know*. But there's something a little weird about all this."

Fleur rose from her throne. "I saw *him* Sunday. Fabiani. I was coming home from the chippy about nine or so and he passed me. I'd seen him come out of her flat. Dead angry he looked, too. Oop, they've had a row, I thought. Lovers' quarrel. Guess I was wrong there." She scooped up a number of damp towels piled on a stool near the tub. "But I've not seen her. I wonder if she even knows what's he's done. Confessed and all. It's not hit the papers. Not yet."

"I'm not saying he absolutely didn't do it, Fleur."

"Hmm. Well, anyway, let's press on." She glanced at her watch. "There's the half the bedrooms on this side to do before eleven. And I've got two houses in Clewer to do today. Then there's the chippie this evening . . ."

9

THE NARROW STREETS and lanes of the old town of Windsor cling to the great gray garrison standing over it like a cobweb to a stone wall. Little wonder, I suppose, for Windsor Castle, high on its hill, has been the town's protector, its benefactor, its reason to be for nine centuries. I've stood on the battlements and looked down upon Thames Street curling around Curfew Tower like an arm and tried to imagine the scene in days of yore: the horses, the carriages, the timber-framed buildings, some of them butting against the very flanks of the castle, the public houses and hostelries, the route teeming with tradesmen and soldiers and yeomen. Today, of course, the street teems with camera-toting, fanny-packing tourists changing not their horses but their travellers' cheques while the hot-blooded youth of Windsor gather at Ye Aulde Pizza Hut for ye vegetarian special. But I think something of the essence remains: Life flows on. Only the costumes have changed. The castle remains eternal.

As Her Majesty might say: How very reassuring.

Crossing Thames Street where it joins Peascod Street, I felt somewhat in need of reassuring as I was facing the daunting task of going to the authorities and telling them I thought there was something rotten in the state of Denmark, or at least something a trifle malodorous. But I seemed to draw encouragement somehow from the everyday life around me. Peascod Street, a pedestrian mall, was awash in sunlight. Hand-holding couples strolled over the cobbles; grandmothers sat with prams outside Marks & Spencer; carrier bag-ladened tourists wandered from the shop to shop. Birds were singing. Everything was bright and beautiful.

And then I glimpsed Andrew Macgreevy, reporter for the *Evening Gazette*, member in good standing of the Rat Pack, that swarm of journalists who watch the Windsors like ferrets watch rabbits. He was staring into the window of Methven's Booksellers, which was run riot with heaving piles of Jeffrey Archer's latest novel. A cloud appeared on my horizon. Whenever I've been of assistance to Her Majesty during the occasional spot of unpleasantness that has besmirched one of her stately homes, Macgreevy has shown up to play the villain, serving his own self-interest, of course, and that of the egregious Reuben Crush, proprietor of the *Gazette* and two dozen other media sewers worldwide. I once dreamed Macg. tied me to a railway track. He'd even grown a handlebar mustache.

Fortunately, his back was to me. *Un*fortunately, I'd had to step between a street vendor's display of Pamela Anderson posters and a potted tree, and found myself cruising too close for comfort. Perhaps he saw me reflected in the window glass. I could have pretended not to hear him. After all, there was steady hum from the passing crowds and a busker up aways was making a bit of a racket with an accordion. But I was completely halted in my tracks when he shouted after me:

"Jane!"

In my salad days . . . well, a while back, when I'd first encountered Macgreevy (he'd accosted me in the Underground at Green Park in London), I'd hastily assigned myself a *nom de guerre* to fob off his inquiries about a certain premeditated demise at Buckingham Palace. I'd used the name of Stella Rigby, a minor character in a long-running British television serial, and he'd found this enormously amusing ever since. He never failed to address me as such, har-de-har-har, ha ha ha, and so on. The fact that he'd just used my proper name sort of cleaved the earth in front of me. He must be ill, I thought, turning.

"Where you off to?"

"I'm going to the po—" I bit my tongue.

"The po?"

"Um, the po . . . etry reading at the Culture Centre, down St. Leonard's Road."

Macgreevy frowned, flicking the cigarette he was holding. "Sounds boring."

"And what are you doing here?" I asked hastily before he could inquire further. "It's well past two. Shouldn't you be at Ascot making a nuisance of yourself?"

He looked away. "I'm on holiday, as it happens."

"And you're spending it in Windsor? Within spitting distance of the Royal Family?" I was incredulous.

"Okay, I'll be straight. I've been suspended for a couple of weeks." He looked defiant. It didn't stop me:

"Ha! You're kidding! From the *Gazette*? What possible misdemeanour would get you suspended from the *Gazette*?"

"Watch it, you!" he said defensively. "It's possible. It's *bloody* possible." He dropped his cigarette and crushed it with the toe of his shoe. "Didn't you read my piece about the bishop? The R.C. one? Do you *read* the Gazette at all?"

"Was it *intended* to be read? Okay, sorry. Yes, I glance at the *Gazette* from time to time. This isn't the story about the bishop and the Land's End love nest? Run to ground—"

"Yeah, yeah," he interrupted grimly.

"What's the problem? Carnal clerics are the staff of life for papers like yours. That, and romping royals. Which leads me to ask: Isn't the church a little out of your line?"

"It was a slow couple of weeks at Buck House."

I stepped out the way of a small child whose ice cream looked perilously close to dropping on my shoes. "So why were you suspended?"

"She was his bloody *sister*!"

"Oh." I smiled but aimed it at the mother of the ice-cream-smeared child. "Odd. You've done worse to Fergie. Have you never been suspended before?"

"No, but Crush sits on some ecumenical quango thing. They wanted a pound of flesh as well as an apology. They got both. The pound of flesh is coming out of me."

"Andrew, that still doesn't explain why you're spending your 'holiday' here in Windsor." Oh, hell, I thought as I said it. He knows about the Pettibon murder and he's doing some extracurricular snooping. "I mean," I hurried on, "you could have spent a relaxing time in the French countryside. Or Italy."

Macgreevy shrugged. His eyes had wandered over to the posters of Pamela Anderson and her surgically enhanced breasts.

"Have a meal with me," he said suddenly.

I wasn't sure if I cared for an invitation that came on the heels of an eyeball scan of Ms. Anderson's endowments. There was also no telling what Macgreevy was up to. He was always trying to cultivate a mole in the Palace. I opened my mouth to say no.

"At the Riverview Inn," he added, his expression giving nothing away.

The Riverview Inn, just up the Thames, was one of the best restaurants in Britain. Its nosh was fabled. "Don't be a fool!" my brain cautioned. But my stomach was taking a different view. I hesitated.

"What are you staring at? Is there something on my lip?"

"I was just wondering what you'd look like in a moustache, that's all."

"Are you coming or not?" he snarled, annoyed.

"But it's Ascot Week," I protested, playing for time. "The Riverview's probably been booked for months."

"No problem. I can get a reservation any time."

Gad, I thought. The maître d's probably got some sexual peccadillo and Macgreevy has the photos to prove it. He looked faintly smug, too. He had lit another cigarette in the meantime and his eyes squinted at me through the smoke.

With his oat-coloured hair and his perennial newsroom pallor, Macg. was not the most attractive of men. Not my ideal, anyway.

But hell, a girl's gotta eat.

"I'm not talking about the Royal Family or the Household," I warned.

"Oh, conditions, is it?"

"I'm just telling you now so you won't be disappointed later. And no other funny business."

"All right." He held up his hands in mock surrender. "Just mates. No ulterior motives. Just a nice little dinner."

"Okay, I accept." My stomach cheered though my brain stomped off in disgust. "When, though?"

"Tomorrow. I'll fetch you at eight at the Henry VIII Gate."

"No! I'll meet you. I think that would be better. Where are you staying?"

"At the Castle Hotel. On the High Street."

"How long have you been here? In Windsor?"

"Just arrived this morning."

Good, I thought. Hasn't had time to put his ear to the ground, if that's what he's intent on doing. Or had he?

Oh, what had I done? Ten seconds after leaving Macgreevy, I immediately regretted agreeing to join him for dinner. Was this a date? Davey had teased me remorselessly during a certain murderous fracas at Sandringham, HM's Norfolk residence, insisting that Macgreevy fancied me. Was it possible? I certainly didn't sense any sexual tension. What I sensed, or thought I sensed, was a maneuver in some strategy. What was he doing in Windsor? Was it simply a case of being so wedded to his job he had zero private life? Can't tear himself away from the Windsor watch?

And then, as I turned into Clarence Road, a worse thought entered my addled brain: What if someone from the Royal Household is at the Riverview and recognizes me dining with the enemy? It was Ascot Week. The Riverview was just the sort of watering-hole to which the upper echelons of the large-bottomed gray men of the Palace bureaucracy would gravitate of an evening. Breaking the nondisclosure clause in the Staff Agreement we all sign when we're hired on at the Palace means an instant sacking. I had no intention of disclosing anything, but a member of Staff witnessed supping with one of the more scabrous members of the Fourth Estate would certainly raise an upper-class eyebrow, and in the land of understatement it's always dangerous to trigger eyebrows. Perhaps being out of my monotonous white housemaid's uniform and my hair done up differently I would be unrecognizable. Or perhaps I could borrow a *chador*, one of those enveloping garments Moslem women sometimes wear.

Or I could always renege.

Cowardice!

Because St. Margaret Place is on the way to the police station on Alma Road, and because the farther I got from the Castle, the less sure I felt about my mission, I thought a quick visit to Miranda Walter, as Her Majesty had suggested, might not be completely out of order. Perhaps, as Victor Fabiani's daughter, Miranda was party to later developments: Her father had recanted, the confession was a neurotic episode, my doubts had been confirmed, and carrying on to the police station wasn't worth the bother. Or, on the other hand, despite the confession, a charge had not been brought against Fabiani, pending further evidence. I could then lend Miranda encouragement by telling her I was bravely marching on to the cop shop to champion her father. Or: Miranda could tell me the jig was up, Fabiani was indeed the culprit, and I could at least offer my sympathies. Anything might be a help.

Fleur lives at 10 St. Margaret Place, on the top floor. Unsure of Miranda Walter's number, Fleur's description indicated one of two terraced houses across the road, each divided (as indicated by a set of brass nameplates and an entry phone) into three flats. A Dunphy's "To Let" sign jutting from the second-story brickwork of one of the homes gave me pause. The nameplate I saw once I'd mounted the steps to number eleven had a telling gap next to the top flat, the weathered backing of the wood where the nameplate had been suggesting the flat had been on Dunphy's books for some time. The other names listed were Durling and Gowerlock. No joy there.

Oddly enough, the brass plate next door at number nine was the same: names were listed for each of the lower two flats—Ford and Page—but none for the top flat. If anything, the vacant space for the top plate was even more weathered, as if the flat had been empty since the reign of George VI. I turned from the door. The neighbourhood was unpeopled but for a tall, slightly bent man loping up the pavement. I surveyed Fleur's house across the road. I was sure I was judging the angle of Fleur's view correctly. Turning back to number eleven, I began to ring the doorbells in succession. But though I could hear muffled buzzing within, no one responded. Well, surprise: It *was* midafternoon on a workday.

"Looking for someone?" The high reedy voice came nearly at my ear. I flinched.

"Sorry to startle you."

It was the man I'd noted earlier. He was holding a bulging, beaten Gladstone bag awkwardly over one skinny shoulder, the weight of it obliging him to stoop so his head nearly touched the door as he fumbled with his keys. He had twisted his head around his upraised elbow and was regarding me candidly with pale watery blue eyes. Despite the heat, he wore a woolly beret, of hunter green, and beads of sweat had formed a necklace under the brim. He made me long to scratch.

"I'm looking for Miranda," I replied casually. "I *think* I've got the right place."

"Have you come from America?"

"No," I replied with some exasperation. What a silly question. "Has Miranda been expecting a visitor from America?"

"I'm not sure." The man appeared to consider this as if the question had some gravity. His face was very lined, though I guessed he couldn't be more than fifty years old.

"I'm Canadian," I allowed.

"Ah," he said cryptically, lowering his bag. "Canada."

His staring was beginning to unnerve me. I glanced

down. I noted the hem of his trousers flapping well above the top of his trainers.

"Miranda *does* live here?"

"Oh, yes. She lives here. Top flat. Would you care to join me for tea?"

"Actually, I have another appointment this afternoon," I said hastily. "I just thought I'd drop in on Miranda for a moment on my way."

"How very nice. I don't believe she gets many visitors, although her boyfriend came looking for her yesterday afternoon. I've tried to interest her in my books, but . . . oh, well." He pushed his key into the lock. "Are you sure you wouldn't like some tea? I'd be happy to show you some of my literature."

"Gosh, very kind of you but, you know, time presses. You haven't *seen* Miranda lately, have you?"

"Oh, yes. I saw her yesterday. If I showed you my books, I'm sure you'd find them most interesting. They're all about the secret teachings—"

"Really, no, I couldn't. I only had a few moments and I was hoping to see Miranda."

"Oh," he said, surprised, "Didn't I say? She's gone away. I saw her stowing some cases in the boot of her car. Taking a holiday, I expect. Or perhaps a retreat. There's a community in the West Country somewhere."

"Community?"

"I'm not sure what it's called exactly. More of a coven. I believe Miss Walter's a witch."

"A what!?"

"A witch."

"Oh, I thought you said . . . oh, never mind."

"I don't know why she's not interested in my literature. I'm *very* sympathetic. I'm a pagan myself." He pushed the door open. "You're quite sure you wouldn't like to come in, now? I don't want to press," he added hopefully, heaving his bag over the threshold.

"Wait! What time did she go?"

"Miss Walter?" The bag hit the hall floor with an audible thud. "Oh, now, let me think. Late morning, I believe. Yes, that's right. I was on the phone to—"

"And you think she was travelling to this 'community'?"

He looked anxious suddenly. "Oh, heavens, I don't really know. I was just making an assumption. Miss Walter prefers to keep to herself. I happened to see her from my window, that's all. See," he gestured toward the ground-floor flat, "this is where I live. I'm Geoffrey Gowerlock."

"So you really have no idea where . . . ? Or how long?"

"Sorry."

I eyed the door to number eleven. I was aware of a little tingle of excitement travelling through my spine and into my limbs. "You say she left late morning? About what time?"

"Oh, elevenish, I should think."

And that older guy working in St. George's Hall had mentioned something about seeing Miranda at the Castle earlier that very morning.

Was this meaningful?

"There's no nameplate here like the others," I observed, wondering if Miranda had taken the marker along with her luggage, signalling a trip more permanent than a vacation.

The man leaned back and craned his neck to see past me. "How odd. I've never noticed before."

I started down the steps.

"If I see Miss Walter, I could maybe tell her you called, Miss . . . ?"

"Rigby," I replied over my shoulder.

"Eleanor?"

Something so wondering in the tone of his voice caused me to stop and turn. "No. Stella. Why?"

"Oh." Disappointment shadowed the lines of his face. He said sadly, "I thought maybe you'd been sent."

Sent?

"Eleanor Rigby," he said. "The Beatles. They're part of the secret teachings. I could show you . . . ?" He reached down to his bag and began to fiddle with the catch.

But before he raised his head, I was halfway up the road.

• • •

"May I," I asked of the desk sergeant not ten minutes later at the front desk at the Thames Valley cop shop, "see Chief Inspector Nightingale?"

"He's very busy this afternoon, I'm afraid," I was told with a touch of rebuke. I'd been sized me up in an instant and, I expect, found wanting. "Is there something I can help you with, perhaps?"

"No, it's the chief inspector I need to see."

"I'm afraid it may be some time before you'd be able to speak to him," the sergeant continued even more officiously. "If you'd care to wait over there, I can take your name."

Ah, the runaround.

"Would you tell him it's about the Pettibon murder," I said more perseveringly, running around the runaround. "It's sort of urgent."

"Sort of?"

"*Is,* then."

His mouth narrowed to a thin line. "Your name?" He pulled a pen from his uniform pocket.

"Jane Bee."

"As in . . . ?"

"Yes, the stinging insect."

He flicked me a cold glance. "Would you sit over there and wait. Thank you."

Still, I had to cool my heels for the best part of half an hour, the not-so-clever tactic all bureaucracies use to indicate who holds the upper hand. It shouldn't have mattered. I was used to police stations. Nay, I'd frequented them. Not through chronic naughtiness on my part, though, but simply because I'd often enough waited for my father at RCMP headquarters in Charlottetown while he finished his shift. Police waiting rooms pulse with nameless anxiety, though, and by the time I was fetched and led upstairs through a maze of white corridors to the chief inspector's office, even police-station-weaned I was feeling less than optimistic.

Nightingale greeted me politely enough, rising from a black leather chair that, relieved of his weight, snapped metallically. He showed me a nearby seat, then pushed aside an

untidy stack of papers along with a heaped ashtray and settled heavily on the edge of his desk.

"Yesterday you suggested I come and see you," I said
for openers, unhappily aware he had chosen his higher perch
straight out of the Intimidation 101 handbook. "I mean, if I
thought of anything else related to Roger Pettibon's death."

He said nothing.

"I know Victor Fabiani has confessed. It's all over the
Castle. Everybody knows . . ."

Nightingale's fingers drummed along the underside of
the desk. He frowned slightly, deepening the lines around
his mouth.

". . . but, um . . ." I smiled weakly. "I wonder—"

"Come, come, let's be having you, Miss Bee. I'm a
busy man. I've a roomful of reporters downstairs chomping
at the bit for confirmation about this homicide."

"Okay, then. Do you think it might be possible Mr.
Fabiani's not guilty?"

"Well, anything's possible, I suppose." Nightingale
crossed his arms over his chest and said with ill-disguised
sarcasm: "Am I to take it you've come all this way to entertain me with possibilities? Such things are not unheard of in
my line of work, you understand."

I could feel a little fume building somewhere inside
me. "But isn't there a possibility—?"

"Miss Bee, guilt is determined in the courts. We're
police officers. Mr. Fabiani has confessed to a crime. He
hasn't been charged. But we are detaining him for the time
being. We take no homicide lightly, but you can imagine the
gravity that attends a murder in the vicinity of Her Majesty
the Queen."

"Yes, I know—"

"Then what is it you've come to say?"

"I thought you might like to know that I was with Mr.
Fabiani in his rooms over the State Apartments for at least
part of the time when he was supposed to be in the Throne
Room stabbing Mr. Pettibon."

"I see." Nightingale tugged at his moustache. "And
what period of time would that be?"

"From about nine-fifteen to around ten o'clock. You
see, I was skivvying in some of the other suites on the north

side, above the State Apartments, yesterday morning. At about quarter after nine, Mr. Fabiani asked me if I wouldn't mind posing for him—"

Nightingale's eyebrows shot up a notch.

"—in the Garter robes. To help him with his portrait of the Queen. We're the same height, the Queen and I. Anyway, you said Mr. Pettibon had probably died sometime during the hour after eight-thirty—"

"That was yesterday, Miss Bee. The postmortem indicates a time of death at the earlier end of that spectrum, likely no later than nine o'clock."

"Time of death can only ever be approximate, of course."

He regarded me stonily.

"My father's a cop. He also says any time there's a murder, there's usually someone who comes forward with a bogus confession."

"And did your dad also tell you we can spot the nutters a mile off? Victor Fabiani is not one of them. We're taking his confession extremely seriously."

"But the other thing, Chief Inspector," I pressed on, "is that Mr. Fabiani in no way conducted himself around me like a man who'd stabbed someone to death only moments before." I furnished further details of the artist's demeanour as he obliged me to pose in the Garter robes for his portrait. I finished by telling the chief inspector I'd overheard no argument between Pettibon and Fabiani in the latter's rooms, and I was sure I would have if Pettibon had truly come upstairs to confront the artist for refusing to pay blackmail.

Nightingale said nothing for a moment. Then he issued one of Her Majesty's beloved words, noted for its ambiguity: "Interesting."

"Isn't it." Mine was not a question.

"It's hardly evidence, Miss Bee."

"Well, it's *something*!"

"My dear young woman, I've met more psychopaths than you've had hot dinners. There *are* people who can kill without a trace of remorse and go to the pictures the same evening."

"I don't think psychopaths go in for confessing their crimes."

Nightingale's fingers drummed along the desk once again. "Well, I'll grant you that one," he commented sourly.

"So you think it's true Mr. Fabiani faked Old Master drawings and that Pettibon was blackmailing him?"

His eyes narrowed. "And how did you know that?"

"Gossip grapevine." I shrugged.

The chief inspector looked annoyed. He said shortly, "We've consulted with his wife, who I'm sure you know is the curator of those very drawings, and we are dealing with other experts. We also have a preliminary match for blood-stains found on Fabiani's clothes. Now . . ." he pushed himself off the desk, "there are other matters requiring my attention. So if you would be so kind—"

"What about the Garter!" I exclaimed, trying to maintain a toehold. "What explanation did Fabiani give you about that?"

"Miss Bee, I can't continue discussing the details of this investigation with you. It's early days. Your views will be given every consideration, I can assure you." He smiled patronizingly. "Good of you to come."

Reluctantly, I rose from my chair.

"Can I see Mr. Fabiani?"

"Are you his counsel?"

"No."

"Family?"

"No."

"Friend?"

"Well . . ."

Nightingale moved around his desk and reached for his phone. "You're not his lover, are you? Is that what this is all about?"

"No, I am not his lover!"

"Because he does seem to have gone through a fair number of women in his time."

"He's ancient!" I spluttered.

"Depends on your perspective. I'm sorry, Miss Bee. I'm afraid I can't allow you to talk with Mr. Fabiani. Sergeant?" Nightingale spoke sharply into the phone. "My visitor was just leaving. Would you be so kind as to escort her from the building?''

The way back to Windsor Castle took me past the Windsor Cultural Centre, a great ugly redbrick pile that resembles a Victorian train station. I glanced up the few steps to the entrance, half-wondering how Lydia Street, the woman I'd met at the Garter procession the day before, accessed the building in her wheelchair, and half-wondering if I ought to talk with her. She was, she'd said, a friend of Joanna Pettibon's. Surely she was—had been—a friend of Roger's as well. However discouraging my interview with the chief inspector had been, I'd still come away feeling that my own sensibilities about the murder were not completely cockamamie. So my question to myself was: If Victor Fabiani wasn't responsible, who was?

The pavement seemed to shimmer with heat, and the prospect of a cool interior made my decision for me. As I entered the Centre, it occurred to me Lydia might not even know about Roger Pettibon's death. The news had spread within the Castle's barricaded walls, a seed had travelled to the police station, but what of the town in between?

There was a slightly fusty smell in the foyer. I wondered if the walls of Day-Glo lime, orange, and yellow had been chosen as a distraction from the depressing odour. No one seemed to be about the place. There was an exhibit of children's art on the walls and a countertop full of brochures for various activities and entertainments. Only the muffled crash of a piano and the sound of shuffling feet somewhere above (a dance class?) suggested a bit of life. Then I heard a distinctive click and whir and suddenly Lydia appeared through an archway from a passage beyond, holding a sheaf of letters. She smiled at me vaguely, then a light of recognition sparkled in her eyes.

"Oh, hello, Jane," she said in greeting. "Have you come to volunteer, after all?"

"I'd like to," I replied with the excuses of the half-hearted, "but I'm only here for Easter and Ascot, as I probably mentioned yesterday, so . . ." I shrugged. "Actually, I was just passing and I thought I'd pop in. I was wondering if you caught up with Joanna Pettibon yesterday?"

"No, oddly enough. Well, there was such a crowd in the Lower Ward after the procession it was almost impossible to get over to Salisbury Tower, so I found myself more or less swept through the gate and out into the street." Lydia regarded me with mild curiosity. "I tried phoning later but only got her answerphone. And I haven't had a chance today to—Why? What is it? Is something the matter?"

"Lydia, could I talk with you privately?"

Her welcoming expression turned grave. "Of course, yes. We'll go to my office."

In silence, we went down a corridor, up a gentle ramp to a large outer office, passing a young woman with frizzy blond hair on the telephone who smiled at me, and then into a smaller inner office, as tidy as Chief Inspector Nightingale's had been chaotic. Neatly, with precision born of practice, Lydia quickly maneuvered her chair behind a round table with several chairs and a telephone and invited me to sit opposite.

"First—would you care for tea?"

"Only if you're having some."

Her eyes searched mine. "I think I'd rather hear what you have to say. Oh, dear. There is something the matter, isn't there?"

There seemed no best way to tell her other than to blurt it out:

"Roger Pettibon's dead."

Lydia gasped. "Dead?"

"I'm sorry to have to tell you."

One hand fluttered to her forehead. "Oh, my lord! Poor Joanna! Oh, and she only just lost Pippa, too. How *awful*! I can hardly take it in." She seemed to look through me. I might have been glass.

"There's worse, I'm afraid."

She flinched, as if seeking to ward off the worst.

"He was murdered."

A groan sounded somewhere from the back of her throat. "But when? Where?" she murmured after a moment's stunned silence.

"Yesterday morning. In the Garter Throne Room, as it happens. He was found stabbed."

"Stabbed," she whispered. "Roger. Murdered. But . . . who? Do they know? Have the police . . . ?"

"Have you heard of a portrait painter named Victor Fabiani? He's been staying at the Castle working on a portrait of the Queen."

Lydia frowned. "I think I may have seen a piece about him in the local paper. Do you mean he's . . . ?"

"Yes. He confessed to the police yesterday afternoon."

Bewilderment settled on Lydia's face. She opened her mouth to speak and then, changing her mind, reached for her phone and pressed a button. "Wendy, would you bring tea, please. Two cups. Thank you." She set the phone down. "I think I may need it," she said to me. I smiled sympathetically and asked:

"Did Mrs. Pettibon—Joanna—ever talk about Victor Fabiani with you? Or did Roger?"

Lydia shook her head. "No. Never. I really haven't had that many conversations with Roger, except during those times he volunteered here. And the times I've seen Joanna socially . . . No, she's never mentioned this portrait painter. But why on earth . . . ?"

I sighed. "Well, apparently, Roger had been blackmailing Victor Fabiani."

"What?"

"Apparently," I said again, emphasizing the word, "there are some forged Old Master drawings in the Royal Collection. Fabiani faked them. Roger knew about it—apparently—and was threatening to expose him. I suppose it was an ideal opportunity from a blackmailer's point of view: the scandal of an art faker painting Her Majesty's portrait. Anyway, Fabiani was finally—I guess—driven to the edge."

Lydia shook her head in disbelief. "And was this for money? . . . Oh, thank you, Wendy."

The door had opened. The woman who'd smiled earlier entered and placed a tray on the table.

"And, Wendy, would you see that I'm not disturbed for the next little while?"

Wendy flicked me a curious glance. "Sure," she said,

shrugging. "But Wilton will be wanting those changes soon."

"He'll have to wait."

"Okay." Wendy shrugged again.

"You have a lot of responsibility," I commented neutrally as Wendy departed.

"We're trying to keep all our programs alive. And with governments cutting funds we're dependent ever more on volunteers and private fund-raising." She raised her eyebrows. "Would you like a cup? Milk?"

"Please. And to answer your earlier question—yes, Roger was apparently blackmailing Victor for money." Lydia poured milk into the bottom of two souvenir mugs. Each had a drawing of Windsor Castle on the side. I proceeded in what I hoped was a gentle fashion: "Had the Pettibons seemed, oh, flush lately? Or have they been wanting for money?"

"Well, they both earn rather decent salaries, but . . . Can you reach?" She pushed the mug of tea across the table toward me.

"Thanks, yes," I said. "But . . . ?"

"They did come into some money. Or Roger did. An old unmarried aunt, or great-aunt, left him a certain sum, I don't know how much—fairly decent, though. Or at least that's the story. Good heavens, I guess it *was* a story. Could it be?"

"When did Roger get this inheritance?"

"Oh, last summer, I think. Yes, that's right. That's when they bought that BMW. But I can't think of any other particular extravagance since. And I wouldn't regard them as desperately wanting for money, particularly. But you never know, do you? People will do mad things for money."

She sipped her tea thoughtfully. "Joanna's brother, on the other hand, I think, has made some demands on them in the wake of Roger's inheritance . . . but, of course, you'd hardly blackmail someone on behalf of your brother-in-law." She shook her head again. "I must say, I'm having trouble taking this all in, Jane. I do hope Joanna has some family around her, one of her sisters—"

"I've met her brother a time or two."

"Iain?"

"I happened to witness a brawl at the Star Tavern on Saturday between some squaddies from the Guard and the Household Cavalry. Iain was in the thick of it."

"Sounds like Iain. But I was sure he was a junior officer, a subaltern."

"Not any longer. His commission ended."

"I didn't know that. I'll bet he wasn't invited to stay on."

"You don't like him." I couldn't help note the editorial tone in her voice.

"Well, I don't really *know* him. I've met him but once or twice, but it was enough to convince me he's a rather spoiled young man. He's much younger than Joanna and her sisters. Came as a surprise, you understand. And, because he was the only boy, very much doted on. Best schools, and such. Eton. But he manages to get himself into trouble. I would say he has a gambling addiction, from what I've been able to gather from Joanna, reading between the lines."

"Really," I interjected between sips of tea, intrigued.

"Oh, there've been incidents with bookies and unsavoury characters and moneys owed and so forth. Joanna is unrealistically inclined to view it as boyish scrapes and high spirits, but I don't know . . . . And he drinks and he has a dreadful temper, too. So I'm not surprised he was in a pub brawl." Lydia shook her head. "I can't think he's going to be much of a comfort to poor Joanna." She looked off into the corner of the room. "Blackmail," she intoned. "Roger Pettibon blackmailing someone. It's so astonishing—"

"Well, *allegedly* blackmailing someone."

Lydia looked at me as if truly seeing me for the first time. "Allegedly? 'Apparently' you kept saying before. The police aren't satisfied . . . ?"

"I'm not sure, really. They might be. But . . ."

And I shared my doubts with her.

10

THE DOOR OPENED. "Can you take a call?" Wendy said hesitantly to Lydia, grimacing apologetically.

"Who is it?"

"The chairman."

"Oh, I see." She sighed. "Would you excuse me, Jane? Just for a moment. He's the sort who wants his hand held."

Lydia picked up the phone, punched a red light throbbing impatiently on the set, and began a monologue consisting largely of "yes," "no," and "don't worry." I tuned out, my mind wandering instead to Iain Scott, a young man with an inclination to violence and a need for money. His sister, as Lydia described her, was a soft touch. Had Roger been? I doubted it. Would any man feel like advancing money to an irresponsible brother-in-law? Mightn't he even forbid his wife to do the same? But with Roger out of the picture . . .

The idea rolled around my head like a pea in a barrel.

But where was the opportunity? Iain had gone from Wexham Park Hospital, Slough, Saturday night, to London where he'd stayed the rest of the weekend—by his account—with some woman or other until he returned to his sister's home in Windsor Castle late Monday morning. At nine o'clock that same morning (the latest time of Roger's death, according to Nightingale) Iain would most likely have still been in London. The train from Waterloo Station to Windsor takes only fifty minutes; less time by car. Of course, this *was* Iain's account. However, I thought, there was a way to check.

"There's no need to worry overmuch about this, Ken," Lydia said heatedly enough to break my reverie. "No. Yes. Look, *I'll* talk to the Shillingtons. Now may I call you back on this? Yes, I do have somebody with me. Yes, of course. Thank you. Good-bye."

Her hand gripped the phone receiver over the cradle for a moment longer than seemed necessary. Finally, giving me a wan smile, she gently replaced the receiver.

"I do apologize."

"Trouble?"

"Oh, nothing we can't handle," she replied thoughtfully, biting on her lower lip. "Anyway, would you care for more tea?" She reached for the creamer. "You were saying you had some doubts that this artist was responsible for Roger's death."

I continued my tale. "And," I concluded, taking one of many sips of tea, "if the new money Roger got last year was through blackmail and not through inheritance, that means he'd been blackmailing Victor for some time—at least a year—and not merely since Victor arrived in Windsor at Easter. And that means, he's known—I mean, he *did* know—Victor for some longer time. Is that possible?"

"How old is this artist?"

"Mid-to-late forties, I think."

"So is—was—Roger. They both have art backgrounds, although Roger went into the curatorial side. But he taught drawing to the kids here."

"But why, then, would Fabiani arrange to stay at Windsor Castle when it would put him nearer his blackmailer, his tormenter?"

"To kill him, perhaps?" Lydia laughed out loud. "I'm sorry. I shouldn't have said that. I suppose it's the shock. But, really, Jane, it does sound plausible . . ."

"But do artists have that kind of money? To pay off blackmailers?" I argued, feeling somewhat crushed.

"Well, I shouldn't be surprised that some portrait painters do rather well. This Mr. Fabiani was commissioned to do a portrait of the Queen, which must be some indication of his reputation and the fees he's able to charge. Didn't the newspaper article say he'd recently painted the Duke of Cheshire?"

It was my turn to laugh. "You're determined to make this difficult for me, aren't you?"

Lydia smiled. "I know the police do make mistakes, Jane, but I'm inclined on the whole to trust their judgment." She paused. Then the smile collapsed. "But if they are mistaken—" She looked at me and a certain grim intelligence passed between us.

"I wish I hadn't told you about the inheritance and Iain's problems and such, Jane," she said with dismay.

"Murders so often run in families."

Lydia accepted this with a deep frown. "But Iain wouldn't inherit," she insisted.

"But you indicated Joanna indulges her brother. Roger's money would come to her."

"Joanna may indulge Iain, but she's not a fool. Besides, Jane, if you were planning to kill a relative for his money surely you'd need to be more subtle if you wanted to get away with it. Use an undetectable poison. Or artfully arrange an accident. You know, the sorts of things you read in mystery novels."

I had to admit Roger Pettibon's murder did seem to lack a certain finesse. Unless the very artlessness of it was part of some awfully clever scheme. There was, of course, the Garter around Roger's knee. *That* certainly smacked of a ritual or planned aspect. Still, I was beginning to feel a certain sense of futility.

"Did Roger Pettibon strike you as having been the sort of person who would *be* a blackmailer?" I asked, trying a different tack.

"Do blackmailers share certain characteristics?" Lydia countered.

I shrugged. "I suppose the situation creates the blackmailer. What was Roger like, then?"

Lydia's face shuttered abruptly, inexplicably. "I'm not sure I can really help you there," she said slowly, leaning back in her chair. "I know Joanna far better than I do Roger, and even that's largely through my work here—" She gestured toward the outer office—"and through occasional lunches with Joanna. We're not childhood friends or old neighbours or anything like that. And, on the whole, we do travel in different circles."

"Well, how long have—had—they been married, for example," I asked, feeling somehow she was devaluing her friendship with the widow Pettibon.

Lydia sighed. "Not long, really. A little over two years. Although they knew each other longer, of course."

"Were you at the wedding?"

"No, it was quite small. Family only. You see, it was a second marriage for them both, so . . ."

"Oh, Roger was married before?"

"To a woman in London. Well, that's where he worked before coming to Windsor. He was at the Courtauld, I think. Anyway, the marriage ended in divorce some long time ago, I'm sure Joanna told me. And of course you know about Joanna's first husband . . ."

"Not really."

"Oh? Well, Spencer—Spencer Clair. He was a lovely man, really. He was shopping at Waitrose late one afternoon—it was only a few weeks before the Great Fire, I remember—and he simply collapsed. An aneurism. He was dead before the ambulance arrived. He wasn't yet forty years old. This is why I feel so dreadful for Joanna. They say trouble comes in threes, but this is much too much—losing three people you love in a row. It's hardly fair."

Silence seemed the only way to observe this lament. There's truth in banality, I suppose. It *was* hardly fair. *Life* wasn't fair. But perhaps life is a struggle against the unfairness of the world. How I do grow in wisdom! In my view it was hardly fair for the wrong man to go to prison for something he didn't commit, if he didn't commit it, that is.

"Any idea why they married?"

"Joanna and Spencer?"

"No, Joanna and Roger."

"Goodness, why does anybody marry? I haven't a clue, really. Joanna was a widow with a young child. Roger was, well, *there*, I suppose."

"Doesn't sound like a big endorsement."

Lydia looked at me sharply. "Roger was pleasant and polite, a little formal perhaps. He seemed a nice man. A gentle man. I suppose."

She hesitated, then explained: "You see, Spencer had been curator of the Print Room and Joanna had been deputy curator. She took Spencer's place after his death and I suppose that caused a certain shuffling of positions. Anyway, Roger joined the Print Room staff about a year later. As I say, Joanna was still a relatively young woman with a child to raise and Roger was, well, a presentable sort of male and he was within her orbit. So I suppose I do understand their marriage on one level—a comfortable arrangement between two people in middle age. At least, that would be my interpretation. I certainly can't recall Joanna waxing passionate on the subject of Roger. Of course, she wasn't a teenager. But I suppose I was a little surprised when they decided to wed."

"Why?"

"He simply wasn't Spencer. I know that's unfair, but Spencer was so vital, so outgoing, so charming—and Joanna seemed so very much in love with him—that Roger in comparison appeared a poor second. A sort of compromise." A guilty look flitted across her face. "I feel as though I'm speaking ill of the dead."

"Not really. I don't think evaluating someone is necessarily speaking ill of them."

"Mmm." She studied my face a moment. "Did you ever meet him? Roger?"

"Once," I replied. "A year ago Easter. At The Royal Oak." And I described the encounter Heather and I had had.

"And?" Lydia said.

"What did I think of him?" I shrugged. "He seemed nice enough. A bit gray. Sort of civil servant-y, if you know what I mean. But—" I suddenly thought of Iain Scott's drunken rant about his brother-in-law.

"But what?"

"Well, Roger wasn't universally appreciated. In the pub last evening, Iain called him a sod. Described Roger as manipulative . . . devious, I think. And a tightwad. Oh, and *evil*."

"Really?"

"But by that point Iain was practically blotto."

Lydia shook her head. "Bitter over some money issue, I would guess. Odd, though. I can't say I would credit Roger with any such strong characteristics. Perhaps a trifle controlling, but only a trifle, the way men are sometimes." She frowned. "On the whole," she continued, seeming to choose her words carefully, "I think I would ultimately describe Roger as . . . opaque."

"Opaque? As in, sort of, 'hazy?'"

"Yes, in a way. I know it seems contradictory to define someone as having a lack of definition. But Roger has always seemed to me to be missing something. Some dimension. Some *edge*. He does seem nice enough, to me at any rate. He has a nice face. Had . . ." She trailed off. "Of course, people are rather like icebergs, aren't they? Ninety percent is below the surface. I wonder . . ."

"Wonder?"

"Oh, nothing, really." A smile snapped back on her face. "I suppose I'm still trying to wrap my head around this . . . terrible tragedy."

I sighed inwardly. None of this was much to go on.

"Did Joanna's daughter get along with her stepfather?"

"Oh, I think there was a period of adjustment," Lydia replied shortly. "There always is. But I think Pippa grew to accept the situation."

"But then this drowning? There were drugs involved, the paper said. Ecstasy? Something like that."

"Apparently. But I don't know much more than you would. Since Pippa's death and the funeral, I've only talked to Joanna briefly, more in passing, when's she been here. I didn't even know Iain was no longer with the Guard. Monday was to have been our day to catch up. Roger decided to drop his volunteer activity so I've seen nothing of him, and of course," she added wryly, gesturing to the wheelchair, "I don't get about quite as easily as some."

"Sorry."

"Don't be. You cope."

"I wonder how Mrs. Pettibon's coped."

"In work, to a large degree. Although I'm sure Joanna's been very depressed. She's sounded awfully low over the phone. I was rather hoping we'd be able to have a good talk yesterday but, well . . . now this."

"There was a bit of talk that Pippa's death might've been suicide," I interjected, aware I was perhaps pushing things.

Lydia jerked up in her chair, dismay registered in her face. "I've not heard that. Are you sure?"

"Yes, the rumour was going around the castle at Easter. No one could figure why a girl her age—what was she? Fourteen?—was hanging around Runnymede on a Good Friday. She was nowhere near a club or the usual places these drugs are sold. Besides, she was too young to get into clubs and such."

"I'm shocked. I can't believe it. Pippa never struck me as a particularly troubled girl. She was a rather serious and studious kid but, oh, dear . . . ." She stared at the telephone as if it held answers, then returned her attention to me, brow furrowed. "But the paper said the inquest ruled accidental drowning. There was no mention of suicide."

"I know." I shrugged. "It's just a rumour. I don't know how these things get around. If there were any truth to it, I'm sure the ruling would have been different."

Lydia worried a fingernail. "Yes, I suppose," she said reluctantly. "I must admit I was surprised about the drugs, though. But children today seem to get involved in these dangerous practices at younger and younger ages . . ." She glanced again at the phone and then at her watch. "I hope you don't mind if I cut this short, Jane. There are some calls I really should make. It's been very interesting—"

That word!

"—talking with you."

"I'm sorry to be the bearer of bad news," I said, rising,

somewhat reluctant to go. I'd only scratched the surface. "Although it'll all be in the papers tomorrow, of course."

"Oh," Lydia commented unhappily, wheeling herself around the table to join me at the door, adding: "Did you happen to see the papers today with the picture of the fainting Page?"

"Oh, yes. Poor kid. I'm sure his mates will be unmerciful."

"I hadn't realized *that* was Hugo FitzJames. Joanna mentioned him once or twice as being a friend of Pippa's. I think she was a little worried that perhaps the two of them were a little closer than they ought to be at that age, getting up to things at weekends and such."

"Really?"

"Yes," Lydia replied, startled at my vehemence. "I mean, I realize he's a duke's grandson—"

"No, I didn't mean that. It's just that . . . well, the murder weapon—it was a short sword—was Hugo's. It's part of the Page of Honour's livery."

"Good heavens! But how . . . ?"

"The story is Hugo left the sword behind in the Garter Throne Room earlier in the morning. He and Wills or Harry were horsing around, or something. Later Fabiani snatched at it and used it to stab Roger. Apparently."

"Apparently," Lydia echoed. There was no irony in her voice. Only a thoughtful look on her face.

"Anyway, thank you, Lydia." I opened the door and turned to her. "Maybe we can talk again another time."

"Yes, of course," she said. But they were automatic words of good-bye. Her mind seemed to be elsewhere. The door closed behind me.

I was halfway out of the Cultural Centre when I realized there was one more thing I wanted to ask her. A long shot, really.

"Excuse me, Lydia," I said, putting my head through the door. I'd caught her with the phone at her ear about to dial a number. "Do you know if Roger Pettibon happened to have a Garter?"

She gaped at me, then laughed weakly. "Are you asking me if Roger fancied wearing women's clothes?"

"No, no. Sorry. I mean, did he have a capital 'G' gar-ter, as in Knight of the Garter."

"No," she said slowly. "Don't you have to *be* a Knight to have a Garter?"

"More of an old Garter, I think. From a dead Knight."

"I . . . I really have no idea."

"Oh, well. Doesn't matter. Sorry to disturb you."

I closed the door quickly, somewhat red-faced. The woman probably wondered if I was a loony.

The bells in the Curfew Tower struck quarter to five o'clock just as I walked up the cobbled causeway to King Henry VIII Gate at the southwest corner of the Lower Ward. It's occurred to me there was probably a drawbridge at this spot in days of yore—the archway is flanked by two broad octago-nal towers that seem to glower at you on gray rainy days—and the gate *is* the principal entrance to the Castle for any-one who has a reason to be in the Castle (principal *exit* for tourists). Those who drive to work at the Castle and have permits park up the hill and usually enter at King Henry III Tower, but if you were walking to work at the Castle, as I reasoned Miranda Walter would do, she would most likely enter at the Henry VIII Gate as I was doing now. So would Iain Scott, returning from London. But would anyone re-member either of them, what with all the daily to-ing and fro-ing? Maybe. Tourists were largely absent until the Castle opened at eleven o'clock and—of course!—Garter Day the Castle was closed to all but those who had tickets to view the Garter Procession.

"You weren't," I hopefully asked one of a pair of hel-meted PC's minding the gateway as I flashed my Staff pass, "by any chance on duty yesterday morning, were you?"

"I was, yes," he replied over my head, signaling a car to pass through the gate.

"You wouldn't happen to remember seeing a woman named Miranda Walter? She's working on the restorations in the Upper Ward. Young, dark-haired?" Having never met her, I'd little more to go on than Fleur's description. I re-called the attitude of the workman in St. George's Hall. "Fairly attractive?"

134 ❖   C. C. Benison

His eyes monitoring clumps of dazed and confused tourists, he replied, "Plaster modeler?"

"That's the one!"

"I'm afraid the Castle is now closed, madam," he recited crisply to a woman whose fleshy arms and face were mottled with heat rash.

"Oh," she whimpered, her face falling. "The damned thing's closed, Laverne!" she shouted down the causeway to another ample and perspiring woman of indeterminate age. "When's it open?"

"The Castle precincts are open eleven A.M. tomorrow. But the State Apartments are closed this week while Her Majesty is in residence."

"I'm gonna kill that travel agent when I get back to Biloxi!" the woman fumed, stomping away.

"Yes, she was through here yesterday," the bobby continued to me, not missing a beat. "Before nine o'clock, I would say."

"How much before?"

"Twenty to the hour? She's quite regular."

"And did you happen to see her leave?" This was exciting.

He shook his head. Sunlight danced off the silver shield on his hat. "I'm afraid we're more concerned with people trying to get *into* the Castle. And yesterday morning, people began to arrive for the Garter procession."

"Then, how about a young guy, red hair, a bit banged-up-looking in the face?"

The PC glanced at me curiously. "I've been asked that already today."

"Oh? By whom?"

"Those investigating yesterday's homicide. Well, I'll tell you what I told them: A young man by that description came through at about eleven yesterday morning."

"And he wasn't in or out of the Castle any time before that."

"No. My shift began at eight and I was here the entire morning, no break, God love me. Yes, madam . . . ?"

"Y'all couldn't let us take just a little peek now, could you?"

Mrs. Heat Rash had waddled back.

"I'm very sorry. You may, if you wish, attend evensong at St. George's Chapel, madam. I can let you pass through then. It starts in about fifteen minutes."

"Evensong? What the heck's that?"

"A church service."

Her fat face scrunched with doubt. "Hey, Laverne! Wanna do a church service?"

Laverne shook her head like a fly-tormented water buffalo. "Can we sit down?" she called plaintively.

"Of *course* we can sit down, Laverne. It's a *church* service, for God's sake." Under her breath she added to us, "We *can* sit down, can't we?"

"Of course."

"I'll take them," I told the PC.

"I thought a l'il trip to England might cheer Laverne up, but I don't know. She lost her husband a few months back," my new companion confided as we waited for poor Laverne to puff her way up the causeway. "What part of the States you from, honey?"

The economically annexed part, I nearly said. "Canada," I replied instead with a polite Canadian sort of smile.

"Oh, that's nice," she said vaguely. "I'm Wanda. This is Laverne. Laverne, this little girl is going to take us to this chapel. St. George's, is it?"

I nodded. Laverne smiled bravely, struggling to catch her breath. There were great damp patches under the arms of her muumuu. We passed under the archway.

"Look how thick this wall is, Laverne. What did you say your name was, honey?"

"Jane."

"Do y'all work here? I saw you with some pass card. Laverne, look at that soldier with that hat. Just like the ones at Buckingham Palace."

"I'm a housemaid."

"No kiddin'? Ever see the Queen?"

"Once or twice."

"No kiddin'? What's she really like?"

"A fire-breathing dragon."

"No kiddin'? She looks like a sweet l'il ol' thing on TV. Too bad about those kids of hers. I like Diane, though."

"Diana."

"Laverne, will you look at that getup. Isn't that cute!" Wanda pointed to a figure hurrying toward the chapel. "Maybe I can get a picture."

It was Davey in his semi-State footman's livery, scarlet tailcoat, and black trousers. Wanda was fumbling with a camera slung around her neck. "What's he supposed to be, honey?"

"A footman."

"No kiddin'? What's a footman do?" She took a practice aim with her camera.

"They take care of the Royal Family's feet. Sort of like a chiropodist."

"No kiddin'. Boy, I could sure use one of those right now. Poor Laverne, her feet are going to drop off, aren't they, honey?"

"Sure are," sighed the long-suffering Laverne. "Do you think there's a chance . . . ?" She looked despairingly to me. We had reached the south porch of St. George's Chapel.

"They're only allowed to touch royal feet, I'm afraid."

"Hello, Jane. Hel*lo*, ladies," Davey smarmed in his best meet-the-tourist fashion, coming upon us.

"I was gonna take your picture, if that's all right." Wanda beamed at him.

"It would be my very great pleasure. Shall I pose here?" Davey framed himself under the pointed arch of the south porch, in the sunshine a blaze of red against the dark void. Just as the camera clicked, he vogued like Madonna doing Marilyn Monroe.

"That's great!" Wanda exclaimed, oblivious. Laverne gaped at him. "So, does the Queen have nice feet?" Wanda continued conversationally, tucking her camera into its cover.

Davey gave me a flying glance. "Madam, Her Majesty has the most charming feet anyone could imagine, even into her eighth decade. Dainty and soft. Beautiful nails. And, confidentially, I can tell you Her Majesty has never had an ingrown toenail in her life. Of course, we footmen give excellent service."

"No kiddin'! Laverne, wait'll we tell everyone at home we met the Queen's Footman!"

"And now here's the door opened. I think you may go in, ladies. So lovely to have met you."

We held back as the two women passed through the door ahead of us.

"I wish you'd done the 'six-toes' version, Davey. It really gets them going."

"Jane, darling, why must you provoke the tourists so?"

"I just can't help myself. Something's triggered when they ask what part of the States I'm from, I guess."

"Are you coming to evensong?"

"I think I will. Can you introduce me to Canon Leathley?"

"Still snooping about, are you, my love? Fabiani was the one wot done Roger in, I say. But who am I to dampen your little enthusiasms—"

Bollocks, I thought unholily, as we entered the delicious cool of the nave: Someone else might have done it. Hugo FitzJames, friend of the late Pippa Clair, had the means. I couldn't forget it was his sword that slayed Roger Pettibon. Iain Scott had a motive—money, love of which is the root of all evil (or so they say; I could use a pay raise myself). And what about Miranda Walter, the alleged murderer's daughter? Opportunity there, I'd say. She's at the Castle—on her day off, no less—around the time of the murder and then, a few hours later, she and a set of luggage are on their way out of town. Certainly an *interesting* conjunction of events. So there! Someone else might have done it!

"Did you say something?" Davey queried, ushering me through the Quire doorway in the middle bay of the stone screen dividing Quire from nave.

"Was I talking out loud?"

"You were muttering about someone named Dunnit. No, no, sit over there," he whispered, gesturing to the stalls on the south side of the central aisle. "That fat woman has a *disease*, I'm sure."

"It's only heat rash, Davey."

"Never mind. The view's better from this side anyway."

"View of what, I wonder? Or perhaps I should say 'whom?' "

We climbed to the third tier of carved stalls and settled into wooden seats. Evensong attracted very few people, it seemed. In the soft glow of the stall lamps I recognized a couple of members of the Castle community in the stalls opposite. They wore sober dress and lacked souvenir-stuffed carrier bags. The remaining few were tourists, one man in a T-shirt with Yankees emblazoned on it, nursing a video-camera, and a few Japanese women in neat attire, rustling plastic and paper in a vain attempt to stuff recently acquired loot under the narrow benches. Across from Davey and me, Laverne and Wanda gawped at the spectacle in their midst.

Of course, the Quire of St. George's Chapel is fairly gawpable. Frozen music, some sage once said of architecture, and St. George's Quire, with its extraordinary delicacy and beauty, is an entire symphony of vaulted stone, burnished wood, and luminous stained glass. It quite ripped me away from hot summer, mysterious death, the twentieth century. The air itself was radiant, as though we were dwelling somehow inside a precious jewel.

"Your mouth is hanging open." Davey elbowed me as he reached for the hymnbook.

I had once wandered aimlessly through St. George's with a herd of tourists, but this peace bought a chance to better examine the site where the Knights of the Garter had assembled yesterday for their Installation. Indeed, the Quire is everywhere a reminder of the Order. High above our heads were the helmets, crests, and banners of each Knight Companion, the latter eruptions of primary color, red, yellow, and blue, emblazoned with heraldic devices that, if you could decipher them, would identify the particular Knight. (I couldn't.) At the back of each stall are enamelled golden plates displaying the arms of past Knights. So many have the centuries provided, that the wall opposite seemed to shimmer. I turned to look at the stall plates behind my head. The inscriptions were in French, the language of the Court, I guessed, when the Order of the Garter was founded in the fourteenth century. On many of the plates, too, was the Garter motto, French again: *"Honi soit qui mal y pense."*

The motto was everywhere at Windsor Castle, from plaster moldings in the ceiling to the pattern in the rugs, from the decoration on the china to the embroidery on the linen. I generally paid it about as much mind as I paid adverts on television. Now, in the Quire of St. George's—at Garter Central (so to speak)—in the wake of Roger Pettibon's murder, the motto suddenly took on a greater urgency. I'd attached a possible significance to the mere fact of Pettibon's wearing a Garter, a piece of regalia that oughtn't, in the usual run of things, to belong to someone such as he, being no Knight. Now I wondered if the words themselves held significance. From my Canadian French-immersion education I thought I could get the last bit, "qui mal y pense"—something like "who thinks badly of it" or "thinks there's evil there." But "honi"? I knew there was the verb, *honnir*. Despite its resemblance to the English word "honour," it actually meant pretty much the opposite. But . . .

"Davey, what does *honi soit qui mal y pense* actually mean? In English?"

" 'Shame on him who thinks this evil.' "

"Oh, I see. Of course." I repeated the motto in my head, *en anglais*. Was Roger's wearing the Garter in death meant as some sort of message? Or was it just somebody playing silly beggars?

"The use of a woman's garter's got something to do with one of the Plantagenet kings, doesn't it?"

"Edward III. Shh. They're coming in. I'll tell you later."

There was an expectant hush and in through the Quire doorway entered the verger, gravely bearing his verge in front of him. We all stood as the clergy filed in, followed, in two lines, by about a dozen boys in white surplices over red cassocks, each with faces serious and full of grace. I could see Laverne and Wanda smiling, as I was doing. You couldn't help it, they looked so sweet and—yes—angelic. Following them, similarly dressed, were half as many young men. The lines parted, and in orderly fashion they moved into the stalls to take their places.

"Which one is he?" I whispered to Davey, referring to the object of his romantic yearnings.

"Second row, third along."

A slim man, remarkably blond, the hair tousled, looked with attention toward the choirmaster, his fine features alert in the glow of the lamp. A bit too pretty, I thought, but just to tease my fellow communicant I whispered:

"Ooh, he is a snack. I think I'll go after him myself."

"I thought you had Jamie of the Guard on your mind."

"Then I'll keep him in reserve."

"O Lord, open thou our lips," one of the clergymen intoned. There followed a second of the purest silence and then the mouths of angels opened. Their first note was so resonant, so beautiful, my heart dropped straight to my stomach. Suddenly, the Quire was filled with a golden liquid sound soaring to the fan vaulting. I was transfixed. But from across the aisle a different noise soon drew my attention away. Laverne had burst into tears.

11

"IT SEEMS," DAVEY began in the kind of whispered voice church surroundings seem to encourage, "Edward III was doing some sort of medieval version of the macarena with the Countess of Salisbury at a postjousting tournament ball at Calais, and the Countess's garter slithered down one fetching little leg onto the floor."

"Yeah?" I said. We were standing in the south Quire aisle of St. George's Chapel under a portrait of Edward III impaling the crowns of Scotland and France on his sword. Edward thought he had a right to said crowns. Hence the Hundred Years War.

"Well!" Davey continued. "Didn't everyone find this enormously amusing. Gales of derisive laughter from assorted courtiers and such. But the gracious monarch, with a kind of boudoir gallantry, snatched up the garter, tied it around his own leg, and told them all to get knotted, in a chivalric sort of way, mind: Shame on him who thinks this evil. *Honi soit qui mal y pense.* And then he said something about how he would turn the Countess's garter into the most honourable ever worn by making it the emblem of the new Order he had founded. A sweet tale, methinks. What think you?"

"I'm thinking of laundry."

"You are truly the most dedicated of housemaids."

"You know what I mean, Davey."

We both glanced again at the portrait, underlit with a spot bulb in the shadowy alcove. It had been painted three hundred years after Edward III's long reign in the fourteenth century, so it had few claims to accuracy. I could sniff—dedicated housemaid that I am (well, sometimes)—a cleansing in the depiction of the king, as I did in the story of the Countess of Salisbury's garter.

"The thing is—there seemed to be rather a lot of countesses of Salisbury at the time," Davey added. "The countess of the tale is said to be Joan. She was the second Countess of Salisbury for a period, but the silly cow had another husband at the same time, so her marriage to the Earl of Salisbury finally got the chop. Anyway, it's doubted Joan was ever at that ball in Calais.

"Then there was a Catherine, who was the wife of the first Earl of Salisbury, but she seems an unlikely candidate for some reason I can't remember. And then there was a woman named Alice. She wasn't a countess of Salisbury but was closely enough knitted to the Salisbury line—Montagu, I think, was the family name—that she was mistakenly called countess."

"You want dusting yourself, you know." I interrupted. "Where do you *get* all this old stuff?"

"There is a point, Jane dear, if you will only pay attention, a rendering of the tale I believe you will find . . . piquant."

"I like a point."

"Good. Now . . ." once again Davey lowered his voice conspiratorially. "It seems King Edward found Alice, Lady Montagu, imminently shaggable. Fancied her something awful, don't you know. But the feeling wasn't reciprocated. Alice was married, a modest little thing, I think. But the king, of course also married, went out of his way to ensure she was, you know, at hand. If there's any truth to the Garter story at all, it's most likely this Alice Montagu was the 'countess' with slippage in the undergarment department."

"Yes. And . . . ?" I interjected impatiently.

"Well, the story is Edward finally had his way with Alice. She wouldn't give him to him, however much he begged, so he raped her, in effect."

"What do you mean, 'in effect'?" I demanded, incensed on the woman's behalf even if she was six centuries dead. "Either he raped her or he didn't!"

"Shhh. Did, then. Bound her, gagged her, and was such a beast, she was left all battered and bleeding."

I scowled up at the portrait. "So much for the age of chivalry."

"Worse." Davey sighed. "Her husband went rather off her, turned into a bit of a bad egg all around, and finally beat the poor woman to death."

"Punish the victim! Isn't that just bloody typical! He should have gone after the king."

"Jane, dear, if Montagu had 'gone after' the king, as you so charmingly phrase it, he would have found his head separated from his shoulders in short order."

"Hmph," I hmphed. "So the Order of the Garter and all the notions of chivalry wrapped around it may end up, in a perverse sort of way, honouring a woman victimized not only by her—ha!—*noble* husband but by the Order's founder, a monarch who couldn't keep his trousers zipped."

We had wandered up the south Quire aisle, lingering in the wake of evensong, anticipating Canon Leathley, who had found himself almost borne aloft by Laverne and Wanda and their outpourings of enthusiasm for the (admittedly) beautiful service. So engrossed had we become in things Edward III in the meantime that we failed to hear the Canon slip between us and the sunlight filtering through the south windows.

"Have you been libelling the Order's founder, Mr. Pye?" The voice, a resonant cultivated baritone, was amused.

I started. My head swivelled. The light dazzled my

eyes so the face floating before me seemed a black moon eclipsing bright sun.

"I'm afraid Jane has an interest in deeds most foul, Canon," I heard Davey say slyly.

"Do you now?"

The vertigo passed, the pixels resolved. The Canon was scanning my face with interest through a pair of gold-framed spectacles. His own face was rather hawkish, the jaw long, the nose Roman, the gray eyes deep-set. But the mouth was ample, almost too generous, and a smile lurked in its corners.

"You must be Jane, then," he prompted.

"Where *are* my manners!" Davey interposed. "Jane, this is the Reverend Canon St. John Leathley. Canon, Jane Bee, who is one of Moth—who *acts* as one of Her Majesty's housemaids when she isn't . . . ouch!"

"Sorry, Canon, my leg's developed a nasty tic." I smiled in what I hoped was a dazzlingly distracting manner. "Davey was just giving me an alternative version of the lady with the loose garter."

"I see." Leathley glanced at the portrait of Edward III. "The one concerning Alice, Lady Montagu? A version better appreciated by scholars, I should think."

"Actually, I think ordinary people would find it really interesting."

"Presuming any of it's true," he demurred, leading us away from the portrait toward the nave. "The story of the dropped garter at the ball is the stuff of romance, I believe. As I understand it, ladies of the fourteenth century didn't wear garters of that type. And given its design, the way it buckles around a Knight's leg, the Garter better resembles a sword belt. It's more likely a symbol of brotherhood."

"Why not say so?"

"What!" Davey exclaimed. "And let daylight in upon magic?"

Leathley laughed. "Educated views on the Order's founding are available to anyone who cares to seek them out, Miss Bee. We do find most people prefer the fable."

"But do you think the story of Edward raping Alice Montagu is true?"

"The politics of the day lie behind the establishment

of the Order of the Garter, not the story of the ball. So the king's relationship with Alice Montagu, whatever its nature, has nothing to do with the Garter."

"It has something to do with the Order's claims to honour and chivalry and morality and all that stuff," I argued.

"Such severity in one so young!"

"Rape is a crime."

"There is forgiveness of sins." Leathley tucked his hands under his surplice, tilting his head. "Edward ruled for fifty years. He is one of England's great kings. He was, I daresay, a complex man and I'm sure he was capable of being as contradictory as any of us may be. I like to think he felt remorse."

"And it was ever so long ago," Davey chimed in, sighing.

The sun streamed through the stained glass of the west window, casting pools of colour over the pews and smooth stone floor, warming sombre gray masonry to creamy gold. Earlier, I'd found the nave's coolness delightful; now, despite the chapel's early evening glow, despite the appearance of warmth, I'd begun to feel chilled in my thin top. I shivered slightly as Canon Leathley turned his attention to Davey.

"Have you had time to read the literature I gave you the other day?"

"I'm afraid I haven't, Canon," Davey replied with a show of sincerity. "The week is so frightfully busy with the Garter ceremony and Royal Ascot and such . . ."

"I quite understand. Certainly Garter Day consumes *our* energies."

"Do you attend the Investiture in the Throne Room?" I asked. "You, meaning the canons from this chapel?"

"No, by tradition, the prelate in attendance is the Bishop of Winchester. Windsor was once part of his diocese."

"Oh."

"You seem disappointed."

"Jane has an interest in Roger Pettibon's death." Davey smirked. "She's wondering who was *lurking* about the Upper Ward yesterday morning. Aren't you, Jane?"

"Davey!"

"I was in the Upper Ward yesterday morning, briefly," Leathley said without hesitation, stopping by the white marble tomb of King George V and Queen Mary. "My cousin's son—"

"Hugo FitzJames?"

The Canon nodded. "He'd spent the weekend with my wife and me and I took him up to prepare for his duties as Her Majesty's Page of Honour. Hugo found Roger's body. Poor boy, he had a dreadful shock. Delayed reaction. He was ill during the Garter procession."

"I think Jane's wondering if you saw anything in the Upper Ward," Davey interjected, giving me a mad grin from behind the Canon's back.

"I'm not sure I understand."

"Anything suspicious. You see, Jane thinks—"

"Do you mind, Davey! *I'll* tell it."

And I did, as I had done for Lydia Street. "I don't know why Mr. Fabiani has confessed," I concluded, "but I just can't believe he did it."

"I see. Well, I'm not sure I can help you, Miss Bee. I can't think I noticed anything out of the ordinary yesterday morning. I delivered Hugo to the Private Apartments, you see. On the south side."

"And how did you return?"

It was innocently asked, but the Canon hesitated. "The way I came, of course," he replied finally, smoothly. His spectacle lenses had turned to gold disks in the west window sunshine. Behind them, his eyes were inscrutable.

Might Leathley have travelled the maze of the Upper Ward and exited somewhere in the vicinity of the State Apartments and the Royal Library on the north side? I stepped slightly away from where Their Majesties' effigies lay in repose for all eternity, the better to see the whites of the Canon's eyes.

"So I guess you didn't happen to see Roger Pettibon yesterday morning?"

Leathley scrutinized my face. A smile played at the corners of his mouth. "The last time I saw Mr. Pettibon was at Eucharist Sunday morning."

"How was he?"

"We didn't speak."

"But you have been talking with him over the last few months, though."

The nascent smile turned suddenly severe. "Mr. Pettibon has—had, rather—been in considerable distress following the death of his stepdaughter at Easter. I'd been counselling him. Now, if you'll excuse me, I must attend to other duties." He turned abruptly and began moving up the north aisle, his robes fluttering after him.

"I'm only asking because I'm trying to find a motive for his death," I said apologetically, hurrying after him, leaving Davey behind sticking his tongue out at me in reproach.

"There is nothing I can tell you, Miss Bee. I would be breaking the seal of the confessional if I did."

"So he did confess something!"

"He participated in the sacrament of confession, yes. I think, perhaps, you may be taking the word 'confess' in a manner more evocative of the police and the courts."

Though rebuked, I asked nonetheless: "Would you go to the police if the things Mr. Pettibon told you were serious enough?"

"If anyone told me something in confession I thought warranted police attention, I would encourage that person to seek police help on his own."

"And if he didn't?"

Leathley turned to face me. The gloom of the north Quire aisle enveloped us, the scent of recently extinguished candles heavy in the air. "I'm sure you're quite sincere in your intentions," he began with a kind of obligatory gentleness, "but I do think this business with Mr. Pettibon is best left to the authorities."

"But they're not interested in what I have to say!" I felt all mulish and stubborn. Also annoyed because the Canon hadn't answered my question. I temporized: "What if you were told something *outside* the seal of confession?"

"Miss Bee, please, I find these questions rhetorical."

"What if a family member told you something extremely serious? Family members wouldn't come to you for confession. What if . . ." I was plucking at straws to get some response from him. Something Lydia Street had said propelled me: "What if your cousin, Lord Lambourn, had told you something serious about Pippa Clair, for instance . . . ?"

Leathley's brow furrowed. "I don't know what you mean."

"They were friends, Hugo and Pippa."

"Yes, I'd some idea they were." He glanced down into a softly lit adjacent chapel where George VI is buried. "Who told you this?"

"A friend of Joanna Pettibon's."

"Hugo has said very little to me about Pippa."

"Did Mr. Pettibon ever talk to you about Pippa?"

Leathley didn't reply.

An engraved plaque on George VI's tomb caught my eye. *"I said to the man who stood at the gate of the year,"* the verse began, *"give me a light that I may tread safely into the unknown . . ."*

I wish somebody would give *me* a light into the unknown, I thought irritably as Leathley's voice jerked me back to the present.

"You might find this story about Edward III interesting, Miss Bee. You, too, Mr. Pye," the Canon added.

"There was a murder in the town of Great Yarmouth in one of the years of Edward's reign—after the Order of the Garter was founded, I believe, sometime in the 1350's. The murder went unpunished by the authorities and the king was not pleased, so he imposed a penance on the town. Indeed, one of the earliest letters we have in the aerary here at St. George's is from the bailiffs of Yarmouth on the very subject of this penance, from the fifteenth century. The penance, you see, was made in the form of a grant to the Dean and Canons of St. George's each year. And this yearly grant went on until, oh, sometime in the eighteenth century. Now, would either of you happen to know what the grant consisted of?"

"Do tell, Canon," Davey replied brightly.

"Well, as you know, Great Yarmouth is on the Norfolk coast and its wealth came from the North Sea. So the town was ordered to provide St. George's each year with fish, a 'last' of fish, which is a quantity of thirteen thousand, two hundred."

He paused as if for effect. "The fish were all," he continued, gray eyes glittering, "red herrings."

He smiled tightly. "Now, you really must excuse me. There are things I must attend to. I do hope, though, we will see you both at future services."

Davey pulled a face after the Canon had swirled off down the aisle. "That seemed a bit fraught, don't you think? Whatever did he mean?"

"I think priests like to talk in parables."

"About Edward III's able judgment, I suppose."

"Or something," I added more ominously as I beelined for the south exit.

Stepping outside the chapel into the summer light felt like walking into a blaze. It was after six o'clock, the quiet hour in the royal day, and the Lower Ward seemed very nearly desolate, baking in sunshine. One scarlet-tunic'd guard stood rigid at his black sentry box by the barracks and, across the way, a Military Knight fussed at some plantings along his stone porch.

"Surely that's not . . . ?" Davey muttered as we rounded the St. George's Chapel bookshop, its shutters closed. He was peering up the road toward the Round Tower.

"Bugger," I said.

It was. The hair, the face, the loping stride. Andrew Macgreevy was stepping toward us, carrier bag in hand. My strained conversation with Canon Leathley and its implications flew from my head. Please, Andrew, my mind begged, please please please don't say anything about The Dinner.

"Hello, Andrew, you silly old sod. I thought I could see knuckles scraping the cobbles." Davey greeted him cheerily, adding, "Weren't you with the rest of the Rat Pack at Ascot this afternoon?"

Andrew's eyes slid over to my direction. "I'm on holiday," he replied evenly.

Davey reacted the way I had earlier in the afternoon. With great lashings of incredulity.

"Can't I be a tourist like everyone else in this bloody town?" Andrew retorted. He lifted his carrier bag as if to prove it. A bird's-eye view of Windsor Castle in dark green was emblazoned on the sides.

"Prezzies for your . . . nieces?" Davey giggled.

Andrew scowled. Cold-shouldering Davey, he asked me, "How was the poetry reading?"

"Oh, fine," I replied weakly. "Very nice."

Davey rounded on me. "A poetry reading? Really? You?" -

"They were having a very interesting reading at the Windsor Cultural Centre this afternoon. I just thought I might enjoy something a little above the yobbo culture of the footmen's lounge, Davey, if that's all right with you—"

"Well!"

"—Don't you have some corgis to feed?"

"Fed 'em before evensong, of course." Puzzlement reigned over Davey's chubby features.

"So it's poetry readings for you." Andrew regarded me suspiciously, his glance skipping to Davey. "And church for you."

"And tourism for you," I appended.

Andrew looked away. We all did, each aware that the whole truth and nothing but the truth wasn't much in evidence.

"Jane came to evensong with me," Davey interjected hopefully, as if this shone a light in the murk.

Andrew's eyes returned to me, narrowed. "Poetry readings *and* church. Attend often? Been a naughty girl, have you?"

"I've only been this once." I shrugged uneasily. "Just to see."

"The Reverend Canon St. John Leathley in attendance?"

"I say, Andrew, you do have the Royal Household down pat!" Davey effervesced.

The reporter bowed his head in acknowledgement. "I'd best be off," he said curtly. Relief shot through my nervous system.

"Will we see you at Ascot?" Davey inquired. "Your charming intrusiveness will be missed."

"Look, mate. I'm on my holidays. Okay?" Macgreevy smiled at me. "And I'll see *you*—" A pause that stretched forth like taffy at a taffy-pull. The horror, the horror must have shown in my eyes. The smile turned into a cruel grin.

"—later."

"I still say he fancies you, Jane. Are you well? You look faint."

"It's the heat."

"And what was all that about a poetry reading?" We trudged up the cobbles toward the Middle Ward.

"I wasn't at any poetry reading. I ran into Macgreevy in Peascod Street. I was on my way to the police to tell them about—well, you know—and nearly spilled the beans. *Poetry* was my recovery."

"I don't believe for a minute this nonsense about his taking his hols here at Windsor. Especially as Mother happens to be taking hers here at the same time."

"Look at this," I said, moving to the sign outside the Middle Ward gift shop. "Closed at four forty-five. It's six-thirty now. There!" As I said it, the bells in the Curfew Tower sounded in the distance. "They usually have most of the tourists shooed out of here by five-thirty. So what's Macgreevy been doing for the last hour, I wonder? What's he doing in the Castle at all?"

Davey studied a display of souvenir china in the shop window.

"No good, I would say, Jane m'dear. No good at all."

QUEEN'S PAINTER HELD
IN WINDSOR MURDER

"Makes him sound like some bloke doing up her sitting room," Fleur remarked next morning between swipes at a tabletop with a dust cloth when I read out the headline in *The Independent*. Somebody had left a copy near the self-serve in Servants' Hall, and I'd snatched it during a flying visit for a midmorning bun en route to joining Fleur for the usual round of skivvying (having missed my alarm and breakfast).

"'Portrait painter' or 'portraitist' probably wouldn't fit the space," I murmured, knowing from my mother, the journalist, the problems with headline writing. I began to scan the story. Being *The Independent*, the story was below the fold and the prose quite sedate.

"I popped into Forbuoys before coming here to get a packet of gum," Fleur chattered on, mentioning the news-agents on St. Leonard's Road. "So I looked at a few of the tabs. Big headlines. Horrible pictures. Oh, and the *Gazette* had a picture of the picture inside."

I looked over the top of the paper.

"You know, the portrait what's-'is-name has been painting? It's not done yet but the Queen looks all right in it, not like that one someone painted back when, that made her fingers look like sausages and—"

Macgreevy! It had to be! He probably bribed someone to gain access.

"—showed her nails all broken and bitten. What're you glaring at me for?"

"Sorry, Fleur, I was just thinking about something." Mostly increasing regret at having agreed to dine with the devil.

"Here. Take these things and let's get onto the loo."

"Just a sec."

I read on. For me, there wasn't much new. "Glad to know he's forty-eight years old," I said. "Victor *Winston* Fabiani?"

"Funny, that were me stepdad's middle name, too. Must've been the war that did it."

" '. . . separated from his companion of five years, Irina Kvaternik," I read on. " 'Victor has a simply dreadful temper,' she's quoted as saying. 'I finally couldn't take it anymore.' *He's* the one that left, though," I noted. "Irina says she doesn't know anything about his forging drawings or paintings. That's encouraging. Oh, and it says the forged works in the Royal Collection remain as yet unidentified! Ha! Even more encouraging."

"Jane!"

"Wait, wait! Hmm, not much on Roger. Roger *Gervase* Pettibon. I guess the name's supposed to have more tone . . . . Damn, they *are* the same age . . . both went to the Slade School in the sixties . . . small circle . . . years of ferment, blah blah blah, later studied conservation at the Camberwell School of Art and Design . . . let's see, married previously, victim's wife . . . see Pettibon, page twelve."

I rattled the pages.

"Jane . . . !"

"No mention of Fabiani's daughter, I see."

". . . put that bleedin' newspaper down. Here, stick it in this bin liner."

"I wonder if Miranda's seen this?" I asked rhetorically, obeying orders.

"It were on telly last night. And I heard it on radio this morning. How could she miss it?"

"She's gone, you know. I went to her flat yesterday. Some nutty neighbour of hers told me she'd left Monday morning *in* her car *with* luggage."

Fleur regarded me sceptically. "Mr. Gowerlock? With the green beret he never takes off? You don't want to believe him. Soft in the head, he is. Thinks the Queen's boss of some secret society that controls the world. Like . . . like druids or something, I don't know." She shook her head so her nose ring wriggled. "Barmy. Cath knows what he's on about. I wish she'd keep away from him, though. Gives me the willies." She gave a theatrical shiver.

"Well, he's odd, to be sure. But I don't think he'd make up her going off in her car. By the way, you don't happen to know what she drives, do you?"

"One of them 2CV's. You can't miss it. She'd done it up it up all red and a cream sort of colour, red on the doors, like, and the cream bits framing it all around, if you see what I mean."

"Sort of. Bet you don't know the licence number."

Fleur just rolled her eyes.

"Question is," I sighed, "will she be back?"

"She should be, if he's her real dad, if she cares about him. Even if she did it, y'know, the way you're thinking—"

"I didn't say I'm sure, Fleur. It's just a . . . a hypothesis."

"Whatever. She shouldn't let her old dad hang for it."

"But if she doesn't come back to Windsor . . . ?"

"Then 'guilty,' I suppose."

"Well, not necessarily," I temporized. The previous day had suggested some other tantalizing possibilities that I'd become loath to dismiss.

"Suddenly," a familiar male voice disturbed our confab, "I have a most *peculiar* yearning for fish-and-chips."

I turned. It was Davey, and he was sniffing the air like a poodle in a perfume shop. "Hello," he said to Fleur.

"Have you two met? Davey Pye, Fleur Aiken. Davey's one of Her Majesty's *personal* footmen." *Minds the Corgis*, I mouthed to her.

"Charmed," Davey purred. "And I do more than mind dogs. I can read lips, for instance, Miss Bee. I say, Fleur, absolutely amazing nail varnish. Wherever did you get it?"

"Do you like it?" Fleur giggled uncharacteristically, wriggling her fingers. Each stubby nail was coloured a ghoulish shade of green. "It's called Puke. Got it at Boots."

"Brilliant. I must get some."

"Are you here for fashion tips, Davey?" I asked pointedly.

"Eh? Oh. No. I've a message for you, Jane. You know, I think this is the second time this week I've had to run you to ground somewhere in this magnificent swell of granite. *Quite* enervating!"

"You don't mean . . . !" I was alarmed. Not a *second* untimely you-know-what.

"Don't be silly. Of course not. Come with me into the other room. You must excuse us, Fleur." He gripped my arm and tugged me away with him.

"You know," he said in a low voice as we exited, "I'm sure that chip shop smell is coming from *her*."

"Shush. It is. But don't say anything. I'm not sure she knows. She works evenings in a shop down St. Leonard's Road. She's got a hard life. Two kids. No responsible male helpmate-type person. Now," I said impatiently. "What is it?"

Davey smiled and began to whisper sweet somethings in my ear.

"She does?" I responded, startled. "You're kidding. When? But what about . . . ? Taken care of? But my clothes—!"

"But me no buts, Jane dear," Davey added airily, stepping away to take in my unfetching white housemaid's uniform with a jaundiced eye. "Mother's wish is your command."

Half an hour later I stood in the Queen's Sitting-room, dressed in a reasonably sombre cinnamon-coloured wrap dress and wearing chunky heels. Ascot Week was proving to be a strain on my meagre wardrobe. I'd brought one posh frock for Ascot itself and a couple of spares in case some other entertainment presented itself. But the remainder, besides my uniforms, was jeans and shorts and tops, the sort of clobber I expected to wear for a casual week in sunny (or rainy) Berkshire.

Leaving Fleur to cope, with the promise someone was taking my place, I'd raced back to Clarence Tower, still wondering exactly why I was wanted, splashed a bit of water about my person, fiddled with my hair, dressed, rushed to the Queen's Tower, and was ushered into the Presence by Davey. He was suppressing his amusement by being his most ostentatiously footman-y self.

"Miss Jane Bee, Your Majesty," he announced with a grand gesture as he opened the door, adding in a whisper as I passed before him, "*So* sorry we couldn't have a flourish of trumpets for you."

"Do stop teasing, David."

"My apologies, Ma'am."

I curtsied. The Queen assessed my choice of apparel with the quick discernment she accords a line of soldiers on parade. She herself was wearing a turquoise-and-lilac silk dress.

"That will do very well," she said without preliminaries. "Now, I'm going to pay a condolence call on Mrs. Pettibon this morning, Jane. And I thought it might be a good idea if you came along."

"Of course, Your Majesty," I responded, faintly gobsmacked.

"David?" The Queen gestured toward a side table on which lay a cone of cut flowers.

Davey fetched the flowers, his movements followed by a couple of ankle-famished corgis, and handed them to me. Their fragrance tickled my nose and I sneezed.

"Bless you," Davey said. The Queen settled a white handbag into the crook of her left arm and smiled.

"Well, then," she said crisply to me, heading for the door, "come along, Watson."

•   •   •

Of course, the Queen doesn't just drop in on people unannounced. You might imagine the shock as folks pulled curlers or something from their hair, realizing that the lounge hadn't been dusted in a fortnight and the dog had eaten the last biscuit. Joanna Pettibon had been alerted. There was a policeman posted at the gate to Salisbury Tower and he snapped to attention when we arrived. Similarly, the poker-backed Guard in the adjacent sentry box saluted smartly when we hoved into view, the Queen, yours truly, and HM's current minder, her Private Protection Officer, Derek Landerer, who followed discreetly in our wake.

Of course, too, not many in the kingdom receive a personal condolence call from the monarch. But the Queen regards Windsor Castle as her home, and the people dwelling within as her concern. So this was more a neighbourly visit from one member of the village Women's Institute to another. Certainly none of the two or three people we met winding our way down to an almost deserted Lower Ward appeared startled to see Her Majesty among them in the middle of the morning. And I suspected that while most people would find a condolence call from the Queen anxiety poured on grief, the villagers within the Castle were used to her presence. As curator of the Print Room, Joanna Pettibon had probably met and talked with the Queen many times.

As we walked through bright sunshine, I gave HM a précis of the previous day's events. To Iain Scott and his money troubles, she offered little comment. But news of Miranda Walter's movements Monday morning brought a more animated response.

"That fits rather decently with my thinking," she remarked.

"Ma'am?"

"Well, if your conjecture is right, Jane; if Mr. Fabiani is indeed innocent of this crime, then he would have to have a very strong reason for claiming responsibility for it. Don't you think?" The Queen rivetted me with her china blue eyes.

"Er . . . oh! You mean—"

"Mmm. The best reason I can think of for confessing to a crime you *didn't* commit is to protect someone who *did*."

"It's a dire thing to do, Ma'am."

"And the sort of thing one would only do for a member of one's family, I'm sure. Or perhaps a very dear friend."

Yes, I thought to myself with a zip of excitement, HM's premise had a tidy logic. But for one vital aspect.

"Why, though, Ma'am? What reason would Miranda Walter have to stab Mr. Pettibon?"

"Well, that *is* the rub, isn't it? Good morning, Major Simms," she called to the aged Military Knight outside number 5 Lower Ward, who stood to attention and bobbed his graying head. "Lovely garden."

"Good morning, Your Majesty. Thank you."

I smiled at Major Simms. One of thirteen retired officers dwelling in lodgings built into the walls of the Castle, he was forever outside tending his blooms when he wasn't engaged in the official duties of the Military Knights—attending St. George's Chapel every Sunday on behalf of the Knights of the Garter and attending all the ceremonies of the Order. Which reminded me:

"I understand," I began with some reluctance, not wishing to impugn the Queen's friend's grandson, "that Lord Lambourn was a close friend of Mrs. Pettibon's daughter, Philippa, though I'm not sure if that's important."

"Really," Her Majesty remarked neutrally. I noted her lips pursing thoughtfully. She said little else. Her Majesty can be quite self-contained at times.

The forecourt of Salisbury Tower, facing as it does northeast, had gathered into shadow by ten-thirty in the morning. Outside the door, flowers and herbs in terracotta pots drooped as if wanting for sunlight, though I suspected, noting dark splashes on the paved surface, that water, only recently applied, had been the true need. The spindly ivy demanded a pruning. It had crept over the doorframe and was threatening the windows of the ground floor and upper stories, its dull purple fruit a black stain against the sober gray stone. As we passed the Pettibon BMW, and the policeman opened the black iron gate for us, my eye was arrested by a flash of white in the first-story glass, a ghost face, I thought, that vanished in a thrice. A moment later, just as we reached the stoop, leaving Landerer to wait in the forecourt, the heavy oak door opened on protesting hinges, and an unsmiling Joanna Pettibon appeared, clad in a sombre navy dress, a small pink cloth-covered book in hand, her face immediately shrouded as she bent her head and dropped into a deep curtsy.

"Your Majesty," she said in a slightly out-of-breath voice, rising, tottering a little as she did so.

I caught my breath when she rose. Joanna Pettibon's lingering doll-like beauty was shattered. Hollows hung under pale cheeks; the recesses of her eyes were bruised as if recently punched; her eyes were red-rimmed. Lipstick, I noted, had been unevenly applied as though in haste; her chin-length chestnut hair, though combed, hung limply.

The Queen smiled tentatively. "Mrs. Pettibon, I'm so very, very sorry for your loss."

"Thank you, Ma'am," she said hollowly, adding unnecessarily, "please come in."

She stepped aside, and as I passed her in the Queen's wake I couldn't help but detect just the slightest Scotch haze intermingled with the scent of perfume. My heart sank a little.

"This is Jane Bee." Her Majesty introduced me without benefit of further explanation after we'd entered the cheerier parlour.

"I'm very sorry for your loss, too, Mrs. Pettibon," I echoed the Queen, handing her the bouquet of flowers. The widow received them wordlessly, glancing at me as she did so, but with no apparent curiosity or recognition.

"I hope these will bring you some cheer," the Queen added as Joanna placed the book she'd been gripping onto a nearby secretary desk, then unwrapped the flowers and dropped them into a blue-and-white porcelain vase on a three-legged table before the window. Her Majesty glanced at me. I could sense she, no more than I, was not wholly at ease. Despite the room's visible charm, there remained somehow a cheerless atmosphere no flowers could ameliorate. Perhaps it was a certain damp coolness despite nearly two days of constant heat. Or perhaps it was because our hostess was more visibly desolate than I might have imagined, her feelings lending the room its atmosphere. I thought: This is going to be a bit grim. I wasn't even sure of my own protocol in this unusual coffee-morning.

"Very kind. Thank you, Ma'am," Joanna belatedly responded to the Queen's respects. "Will you both please take a seat?" She indicated a rather thronelike chintz-covered wing chair for the Queen, angled away from the fireplace on the north wall, and for me a squashy cream-coloured two-seat settee strewn with colourful petit-point pillows.

"What a lovely room," the Queen said conversationally, smoothing her dress as she sat, placing her handbag on the floor. As she did so, a ginger-coloured cat slunk out from under the fringe of the chair between Her Majesty's ankles which, truth be told, are thickening a little.

"Oh, hello, puss," said the Queen, reaching down to pet the animal, who received Her Majesty's attentions with an ecstatic expression, digging its claws into the Oriental carpet and stretching full length while the royal hand stroked its long fur.

"My daughter's cat, Maggie."

Maggie settled on her haunches and stared at Her Majesty. Her Majesty endured the impudence for a moment, then blinked. She looked from Joanna to me, eyebrows peeking over the frame of her glasses. We'd both remained silent, myself charmed by the cat's catlike insolence.

"Proof, Ma'am, that a cat may look on a queen," I said without thinking.

The Queen laughed. A smile even crept to the corners of Joanna's mouth. She bent down to scoop up the cat. "I think I'd better remove this rude thing."

"No, don't do that," the Queen protested. "I quite like cats."

Prefers dogs and horses ten to one, I thought, knowing HM was just being polite.

"This one sheds terribly," Joanna explained, hugging the cat to her like a baby, stroking its orange fur. "And she's wont to jump on your lap. She's a relentless little beast. Quite demanding of attention since Pippa—" The words stopped. Maggie sagged in her arms.

"I'll just get the coffee, Ma'am."

• • •

HM was right. The room was lovely. In the silence that enveloped us after Joanna had departed with Maggie, we both scrutinized the interior. The walls were a soft daffodil yellow, the colour repeated in the patterns of the upholstery, in the needlepoint rug, and along the zigzag fringes of the drapery. Softly lit by porcelain lamps, it was a cosy room in the indelible English country style, yet smart—the clutter kept to a judicious minimum. You could tell someone had put considerable thought into the room's effect, for it seemed almost contrived to be an all-encompassing shaft of sunlight in a space that saw little sunshine. A happy room in a happy home. At least once upon a time.

On a table to the left of the fireplace, lit by a painted ironware candelabra, stood a cluster of photographs in silver frames. Prominent among them was a picture of Joanna's daughter, Pippa, a studio portrait, likely taken at school, of her in her school uniform. She resembled her mother as much in her dark pretty looks as in the gravity of her expression. A child with secrets, I thought. Another recognizable photo featured a red-haired young man in a Scots Guard uniform, holding his busby in the crook of his arm, smiling with great self-assurance into the camera: Joanna's brother, Iain Scott. There were others to the front: Joanna and two women of like age and resemblance, two sisters perhaps; an older couple, Joanna's parents, judging from the woman's red hair and the shape of the man's eyes and forehead that so favoured the children in neighbouring photos; and a photo of a youngish man with a wave of soft blond hair over his forehead, a long face, and sensitive features, that seemed somehow an anomalous note. Might it be Spencer Clair, Pippa's father? The subjects of the remaining photos cluttered toward the back fell out of view.

To the right of the fireplace was the secretary desk, the top cabinet displaying a collection of blue-and-white Chinese porcelain, the desk itself open to reveal small drawers and open pigeonholes filled with tidily bound correspondence. The only contemporary note, besides the pink book, which resembled more a pocket diary, was a black telephone and matching answerphone. The latter's little red light blinked insistently. On the walls, more pictures, watercolours in the main, landscapes like the Prince of

Wales's holiday daubs, but some pen-and-ink drawings, too. One group in particular caught my eye: Over the fireplace, several framed sketches in different styles of a child and a cat, a mother and a child, and a young woman with a cat.

It was easy, all in all, to forget you were inside a very nearly round castle tower that had likely once housed soldiers and used straw for floor covering.

A tap on the door pulled me from my thoughts. I rose and opened it.

"I'm sorry," Joanna apologized. In her hands a tray laden with china tinkled delicately. "I forgot I'd closed the door so firmly. The cat . . ."

But Maggie followed her into the sitting room with an air of entitlement, tail raised high. "Um . . ." I began helplessly as I watched the feline jump onto the arm of the couch, then thought better of saying anything. Joanna's back was turned as she placed the tray on a table next to the chair she'd assigned herself near the secretary desk.

"I was admiring the artwork on your walls, Mrs. Pettibon," the Queen said. "Are some of the pieces your own?"

"Yes, a few, Ma'am. I try to paint whenever I have a moment. Some are prints. The rest are photographic reproductions. You may recognize one or two from the Royal Collection. They're among my favourites . . . . Black or white, Ma'am?"

"White, please. One sugar."

"Miss Bee?"

"Black, thanks."

Joanna's hand trembled ever so slightly as she poured coffee from a white china pot into delicate demitasse cups. It was with an effort of control that she managed not to spill. Resuming my seat, I turned my head to avoid embarrassing her. The Queen's attention remained on the pictures.

"I've been rather curious about this unfortunate business of forgeries," Her Majesty continued. "I hope you don't mind my mentioning it."

"Not at all, Ma'am. I'm grateful for the distraction."

The Queen examined Mrs. Pettibon's strained face as the latter bent to offer the coffee cup. "Have you someone to help you at this difficult time?" she asked gently, taking the cup, concern written on her features.

"One of my sisters lives at Oxford. Hillary's driving up sometime today." Joanna handed me my cup with slow careful movement. She had managed to fix her lipstick during her kitchen interlude, but her hands, small and delicately tapered, I noted for the first time, were quite raw and red. "Oh, Maggie!" she chided the cat. "How did you get in here again?" She continued, "And there's my brother, Iain. He was with the Guard until quite recently. He's been staying with us while he . . . considers his future. My parents, I'm afraid, are visiting my other sister in Australia."

Joanna proffered a plate of chocolate wafer biscuits and fruit scones around with cake plates and small linen napkins. As I unfolded a napkin across my thigh, Maggie sprang onto it with a dainty movement.

"Let me take her." Joanna hovered.

"No, I don't mind at all." The cat draped herself across my thigh. Her eyes followed the movement of the biscuit in my hand as I took a bite.

"If you're sure . . ."

The preliminaries over, Joanna sat and returned her attention to the artwork. In reply to Her Majesty's earlier query, she said gravely, twisting her hands together: "I don't know quite what to tell you, Ma'am, about Victor Fabiani's forged drawings in the Royal Collection. I had no idea Roger even knew Victor before he came to Windsor to paint Your Majesty. I . . ." She faltered. "I'm shocked and embarrassed about this blackmail business. I truly am. I can't explain it." She paused and looked down at her hands. The constant kneading, it seemed, was making them red.

The Queen asked: "Is it possible there really *are* forged Old Master drawings in the collection?"

Joanna tried controlling her fluttering hands by clasping them over her lap. "Oh, yes, Ma'am, I'm afraid it is possible," she replied finally, reluctantly. "Old Master drawings are very difficult to authenticate. There are tests that can prove something to be a forgery, but nothing that can prove a work to be genuine beyond any doubt. There are more than thirty thousand Old Master drawings and watercolours in the Royal Collection, a vast number, and unless one of them is challenged on grounds of authenticity, say during periods when we're cataloging them, then we're apt to regard them as the genuine article."

"Mr. Fabiani must know which ones he's responsible for, I should think," the Queen observed.

"The police have been to see me about this. Mr. Fabiani doesn't seem to remember how many artworks he may have forged—he apparently executed them twenty-five years ago or more—but he did name a few that are cataloged in the Print Room now, and a few Leonardos, one or two of which are currently on exhibit at the Queen's Gallery, a study of a horse, I believe."

The Queen's Gallery lies just behind the Palace on Buckingham Palace Road in London. It holds a succession of public exhibitions every year.

"The police asked me to examine some of the works in question yesterday morning and give them an opinion," Joanna continued. Her attention was caught suddenly by the light blinking on her telephone. "I . . . Oh!"

"You've switched the bell off," I observed, sipping my coffee. "Reporters?"

"We're ex-directory, but still they've managed to find the number somehow." She stared at the phone anxiously. "But then I worry it might be a family member or a friend."

The light on the phone stopped and the answering machine clicked into operation. "*Mrs. Pettibon, I'd like to talk with*—" a wheedling male voice began, but Joanna's hand darted to the volume control before we could hear another word. "The *Gazette*," she told us. "That's the fifth time this morning for them."

I was relieved the voice was not recognizably Macgreevy's. The Queen, who knows a thing or two about journalistic harassment, shook her head in dismay. "At least you're living within the Castle walls," she remarked.

"I'm worried the reporters will be camping in the Lower Ward," Joanna said fretfully.

"I think not." A smile of satisfaction crossed the Queen's face. "The Castle will be closed for the remainder of the week. On one's orders. It's a crime scene. I'm not having any nonsense."

Brilliant, Ma'am, I wanted to say. The Japanese tourists can take their trade to Hampton Court Palace.

"Oh, I am grateful, Ma'am." There was a measure of relief in Joanna's voice. "Thank you."

The Queen raised her coffee cup in acknowledgement. "What opinion did you give the police about the da Vinci drawings?" she prompted.

Joanna shifted uneasily, worrying a button on her blouse. Choosing her words carefully, she murmured: "I . . . I thought that they were quite probably . . . not originals."

"Really," HM said evenly.

"A preliminary opinion, Ma'am. And strictly my own. On examining them carefully, I thought they lacked Leonardo's vital nervous touch." She gestured to one of the drawings over the mantle, a pen and wash of a mother supporting a naked child, evidently a Leonardo reproduction. "You see how sensitive and spontaneous his style is? Leonardo never developed a convention of drawing the way Michelangelo and Raphael did, so he's not easy to imitate, though Victor Fabiani is very, very good."

Her voice on a familiar subject became less anxious. When HM nodded, she continued: "The Leonardos named by Mr. Fabiani that I examined closely yesterday in the Print Room, excellent as they are, appeared to me to have the slightly lifeless quality, the sort of dreary line, that sometimes marks the work of even the best copyist. I may be wrong in my conclusions, however."

"Your view has satisfied the police." It was a statement from the Queen, not a question.

"I've recommended a forensic paper expert to them, Ma'am. And suggested other notable authorities on Old Master drawings."

"I see."

"Gosh," I interrupted, after finishing another biscuit. "To be so accomplished so young. Mr. Fabiani, I mean. To be able to copy great artists like Leonardo da Vinci and have the work go undetected."

Joanna flicked me an apprehensive glance. "Mr. Fabiani's not only an excellent painter," she said, pursing her lips, repressing a frown, "he's a superb draughtsman. I've seen his work at various exhibitions, including an unusual one that featured the artists' preliminary sketches. And I've seen his early sketches for Your Majesty's portrait.''

"You did have opportunities to talk with Mr. Fabiani, then,'' the Queen said, looking wistfully at the biscuits, her hand hovering over her plate.

"Yes, he would come into the Library from time to time, I suppose when he wanted a break. He was extremely interested in the Old Master drawings. If you'll remember, Ma'am, I'd helped the Librarian arrange a display of some of the drawings, including Leonardos, for the dine-and-sleeps at Easter. Mr. Fabiani spent some time studying those. And then he showed me his sketches of Your Majesty. His work is very fluid, very vigorous. Drawing's almost a dead language today, but Mr. Fabiani's evidently fluent in it. Largely self-taught in that regard, I believe. So, yes, I would say it was possible to be so capable at so young an age. It *must* be possible, otherwise . . .''

She didn't finish the thought. But I could. If it wasn't possible that a young Victor Fabiani had capably forged the work of Old Masters, then the case for his murdering Roger Pettibon rather fell apart. At least on the grounds of blackmail over forged artworks.

"I'm a bit confused,'' I said, as the cat relinquished my leg and hopped off the couch, her eyes alert to a piece of scone in the Queen's hand. "Are these works that Mr. Fabiani forged 'new' Leonardos—new in inverted commas—some work thought lost that sort of 'reappeared' in recent times and then were bought for the Royal Collection? Or are Fabiani's forgeries very good copies of genuine works that have been in the Collection all along?''

"The latter,'' Joanna answered while the Queen awarded the cat the sort of freezing stare she gives trespassing journalists on the Balmoral estate. "The Leonardos came into the Royal Collection in the seventeenth century during the reign of Charles II, a complete set of about six hundred, and there've been few additions, although I believe one did disappear earlier in the century. There are, in fact, copies of Leonardos in the Collection. But they were made by his pupils and they've been authenticated as copies.''

"But how would Fabiani's fakes have found their way to Windsor?"

Irritation flashed briefly in Joanna's hazel eyes. "Well, a number of ways, I suppose," she replied impatiently. "When the drawings have been removed from Windsor for exhibitions elsewhere, most likely. The first full exhibition of Leonardo drawings was at the Queen's Gallery in 1969, and there've been Leonardos in subsequent thematic exhibits since. There was also extensive conservation work done on the drawings in the early seventies. They'd been poorly mounted on board earlier in the century. So if Mr. Fabiani made these copies early in his career, as he says he did—in the late sixties and early seventies—there would have been opportunity at that time to make a switch."

"This suggests collusion on the part of someone on Staff, doesn't it?" The Queen frowned over the edge of her cup.

Joanna pulled her lip inward with her teeth and looked down at her hands. I noticed she had not touched her coffee.

"There would have to have been others involved," she replied to HM's question with evident reluctance. "Copying Old Masters is one way—a quite legitimate way—students learn to draw. Someone, perhaps, noted Mr. Fabiani had a particular facility in drawing and decided to exploit his talent." She looked off into the middle distance. "Someone knowledgable in period papers, correct inks, where to find them, how to make them, age them . . ." She trailed off. ". . . Yes," she sighed worriedly, "I suppose someone on Staff could have been involved. Over the years there have been many curators and conservators employed in the Royal Collection Trust. Most would certainly have the knowledge . . ."

"I suppose there will have to be an investigation," the Queen commented.

"Oh!" Joanna exclaimed, adding almost as a lament, "yes, Ma'am, I expect there will." A new cloud of doubt and worry seemed to settle along her already drawn face.

"One would like the original drawings back in the collection."

Joanna looked pained. "Original Leonardo drawings that were supposed to be in the Royal Collection would be very difficult to sell, Ma'am, even on a black market. Most likely the substitution of copies for originals would have been done to order, on behalf of some wealthy connoisseur."

The Queen frowned. "I wonder if Mr. Fabiani has revealed who he was working for?"

"Not that I know, Ma'am."

None of this explains Roger's involvement, I thought to myself as I watched Maggie rub herself against Joanna's legs. How did Roger know there were forged Old Master drawings in the Royal Collection? (*If* there were forged drawings. For despite Joanna's accounting, I remained, at gut level, unconvinced.) When did he know? Had he kept to himself for a quarter-century the knowledge of Victor's misdeeds, waiting for an ideal moment to show his hand? Or might he have been involved in this supposed fraud himself? It struck me that Roger Pettibon, with curatorial and conservation training and extensive connections in the art world, was just the sort of person with the experience and opportunity to fiddle about illicitly with valuable works of art himself.

"Might the fakes have entered the Collection at a later date? Even quite recently?" I asked.

"Well, I suppose they might have," Joanna replied, kicking gently against the insistent cat. "The drawings have certainly travelled more frequently and farther afield in the last twenty years, after they were placed on special mounts to protect them from atmospheric changes and so forth, allowing them to be handled easily and safely. There would be opportunity then. The exhibition of Leonardo drawings currently at The Queen's Gallery travelled last fall to Australia and New Zealand, for instance."

"Mr. Pettibon travelled with them," I stated baldly, taking my chances.

"Yes," Joanna responded, startled, pushing at the cat which had begun to paw the air around her knees. "Roger did. But how did you know?"

"He happened to sit at my table at a pub a year or so ago and was telling me about it."

Joanna's pale face paled further, and her features sharpened. "Are you suggesting *Roger* substituted the copies?" Her voice grew thin with astonishment.

"Gosh, no," I lied. I could feel the Queen's warning eyes on me. "I just wondered if that's when Mr. Pettibon noticed some of the works were the fakes Mr. Fabiani had made all those years ago. I mean, I guess I'm wondering exactly when did the blackmail start? When did your husband seem to suddenly have this extra money?"

"I . . . I don't know," Joanna said vaguely, her eyes dragged to the telephone, which had begun to flash again. "Roger was in Australia a year ago May, and again in the fall when the pictures travelled, and stopped over briefly in Malaysia. I suppose he could have substituted . . ." She paused, watching the answerphone blink. "It was shortly after that that his aunt died, or his great-aunt. Or at least that's what he said," she added doubtfully.

"You see, Ma'am," she continued, turning her attention to the Queen, "Last spring we were quite suddenly in receipt of a rather decent sum of money. Or at least Roger was. He told me an old aunt of his had died in Cumbria some months earlier and that he was her sole beneficiary. He'd never mentioned this aunt to me before. I'd no idea she existed. But I had no reason to question it . . ."

"Was this aunt or great-aunt a Pettibon?" I asked. It flashed through my mind that there was some way of checking wills. I was sure my father had mentioned, alluding to some police work he'd been involved in back in PEI, that wills were public records. And wasn't there some place in London where they were all kept? If I could go there and investigate, then at least I might have a better way of determining if this blackmail business had any foundation.

"Yes, I think she was a Pettibon," Joanna answered. "At least that's what Roger said, although . . . Cumbria?" Her brow furrowed and her hands began again their manic movement. "Roger's family was rather sparse. He was an only child. The few cousins he had, who came to our wedding, were from Surrey." She groaned faintly. "Perhaps he was blackmailing Victor then . . ."

"The papers say they went to the same art schools in London, that they knew each other," I pointed out. "Perhaps—"

"Mrs. Pettibon," the Queen interrupted, "did your

husband also talk with Mr. Fabiani those times he came into the Library?"

Joanna looked down at her hands. "Yes," she replied.

"It was clear that they knew each other, then."

"I didn't think about it at the time, Ma'am, but, yes, I suppose they did. I can't recall making introductions . . . and, thinking on it, there was a certain tension between the two of them. I sensed it the few times I found them together, although I never thought to ask Roger about it later."

"Well, it's a very sad business," Her Majesty said sympathetically, then drained her coffee cup. "Perhaps if your husband had not been in the Throne Room that morning . . ." The Queen paused in thought. "Whatever, I wonder, *was* Mr. Pettibon doing in the Throne Room Monday morning? It's rather odd for him to be there, on the whole."

"I've no idea, Ma'am," Joanna replied bleakly. "I wasn't even aware Roger was in the Library at all. The Library staff had the day off in honour of the Garter ceremonies. I'd gone in early to do a bit of paperwork in my office. As I told the police later, I saw or heard no one—Oh, Miss Bee!"

"It's fine, Mrs. Pettibon. The coffee hit the napkin, thank goodness." Joanna's declaration of being in the Upper Ward during the time her husband was murdered had surprised me just as I was lifting my cup.

"As I was saying," she continued, "I was back here at Salisbury Tower by ten. I was to meet a friend later for the Procession and needed to get ready. I was still in the bath when the police came with the . . ." she dropped her eyes ". . . with the terrible news . . ."

"Oh, dear."

". . . so, Ma'am, I don't know what Roger was doing. Perhaps he had arranged a meeting with Mr. Fabiani. The police haven't told me. Or perhaps there was something in the State Apartments he wanted to study. The copy in the Ante-Throne Room of the painting, 'George III at a Review,' which the Canadian government loaned us after the original burned in the fire, I know had been on his mind. There was some thought of it being incorporated into a travelling exhibition." Her voice grew strained. "With no tourists in the State Apartments Garter Monday, it was probably the best time to attend to it . . . oh, I don't know . . . ."

Her nervous hands stilled. There was an ominous silence. She stared in space, stricken. "It seems . . ." Joanna began in a tortured voice, all the repressed emotion rising quickly to the surface and filling the room, "it seems my husband was leading a secret life."

One hand, balled into a fist, covered her mouth. Tears swam into her eyes and drizzled over her cheeks. "I'm sorry, ma'am," Joanna whispered, gripping her napkin with the other hand and dabbing her puffy eyes. The cat, staring, stretched up along her leg, drawn by her mistress's cries.

"Don't be," the Queen said soothingly, regarding Joanna with sorrow. "It's perfectly all right. You've had a dreadful time of it."

Joanna jerked in her seat suddenly with an agonized cry, startling us all. The cat fell to the floor in a ginger heap, revealing a thin red line beading along Joanna's calf. Her stocking was slashed.

"Oh, Mrs. Pettibon!" I exclaimed, rushing to her, crouching and folding a clean part of my coffee-spotted napkin to her leg. "A soak in salt water or ammonia solution will get rid of this blood," I muttered as I dabbed with the linen, housemaidery coming to the fore in a crisis.

"I know that!" Joanna wailed impatiently, putting her own hand to the napkin and rubbing against the pain. "Oh, my leg! That silly cat! She's never done that before!"

"I expect she's been affected, too, Mrs. Pettibon," I heard the Queen say behind me. "Animals can be extremely sensitive to atmospheres."

It was shortly after that, after some further words of condolence, that we departed, HM and I. We hadn't quite got out the gate when a large Ford Scorpio came through the Henry VIII Gate and pulled up beside the Pettibon BMW with an abrupt halt. As the driver, a larger, heavier version of Joanna, stepped from the car, a couple of rubber balls came bouncing out after her onto the stones of the Lower Ward.

"Oh, my goodness!" the woman exclaimed, her astonished eyes darting from the Queen to the miscreant toys. She bent to retrieve them but they bounded vexatiously out of reach.

"Your Majesty," the woman fluttered, curtsying awkwardly.

"You must be Joanna's sister from Oxford," the Queen said as Inspector Landerer waited patiently with one of the balls he'd smartly caught in midbounce. I'd caught the other as it had dribbled into the forecourt.

"Yes, I'm Hillary Elliott. Oh, thank you so much," she addressed Landerer with a harried smile. "They're the dog's. I think I've been sitting against them the whole way down from Oxford. Er . . ."

"I'll put them back in the car, then, shall I?" Landerer asked, taking the second ball from me.

"Oh, yes, please. Do. Thank you."

"We've been visiting with your sister, Mrs. Elliott," the Queen continued as Landerer opened the backseat door and a black Labrador bounded out.

"Oh, goodness. It's all so awful." One hand went helplessly to her cheek. "I've only just been able to get away. The children . . . I mean . . . Oh, the dog! Come here, Sally. How is she . . . Ma'am?"

"I'm sure she'll be better for seeing you," the Queen replied assuringly as Sally strained from her mistress's grip to sniff Her Majesty's hand. Hillary Elliott regarded the door to Salisbury Tower worriedly as the Queen stroked the dog's head.

"Now we mustn't detain you," HM said after a moment, moving away. "Good-bye, then."

"Well," said Her Majesty as we began tracing our way to the Upper Ward, "what do you make of all that?"

"Ma'am," I replied, "There's only one thing I know for sure: the cat's not going to be too pleased when she sees Sally. As for the rest: Well, I suppose I'd have to say I'm sort of disappointed."

13

WELL, I WAS.

Not just disappointed. But quite crushed, really. I suppose I'd hoped Joanna Pettibon would immediately pooh-pooh this forged Old Master drawings claim of Fabiani's and come to the aid of the party (mostly me) in search of her husband's real killer. But she had put her considerable expertise as the curator of the Print Room behind the notion that the drawings named by Fabiani stood a good chance of being forgeries, and I, of piffling art education, was in a poor position to say nay, nyet and nix. Perhaps, I thought, in the glimmer-of-hope department, in her weakened state Mrs. Pettibon had yielded to police blandishments. A fast solution to her husband's murder was in her interest, too: After all, it would help bring needed closure to someone who'd suffered two family deaths within three months. It's a wonder, I pondered as the Queen, her minder, and I rounded the Round Tower, Joanna wasn't prostrate with grief.

HM walked along in a contemplative silence, frowning a little, her chin dug into her neck in a Queen Victoria-ish sort of way. Perhaps, I considered, she's thinking of the two-thirty race at Ascot. Perhaps she was adjudging my performance in the Pettibon parlour. Perhaps . . .

"Did you notice, Jane," the Queen said, "that Mrs. Pettibon had no photograph of her husband among those pictures on her table? Most odd, I think."

"Perhaps it'd got shuffled toward the back, Ma'am. The table was pretty cluttered."

"No," HM countered firmly. "I made a point of looking when we rose to leave."

"Or perhaps it's too painful to have in view, given how recently Mr. Pettibon died . . ."

"Mmm, possibly. But her daughter also died recently, and her photograph is quite prominently in front."

And, I thought to myself, Joanna was among those flitting about the Upper Ward Monday morning, joining a growing list which now included Hugo FitzJames, Canon Leathley, Miranda Walter, and—I mention this with reluctance—the confessed killer himself, Victor Fabiani. Had Joanna allowed some malice toward her husband to fester, only to lose every restraint Monday morning in the Garter Throne Room? The bosom of the family is hardly the unlikeliest place to nurse a murderer. But Joanna had been quite candid about working in the Royal Library Monday morning. It didn't, I think, behoove a murderer to admit propinquity.

"Well, I shall leave you here, Jane," Her Majesty said, after we'd found our way back into the Grand Corridor. "I must prepare for the afternoon events."

"Ma'am, may I ask you a question?"

"Of course."

I felt rather squirmy asking this. I could feel my face begin to flush. "Was I all right as a sort of . . . lady-in-waiting?"

The Queen smiled. "I'm sure you'd learn in time," she replied somewhat ambiguously. "Most things in life are a matter of training."

Oh, I thought. Truly a one-off. But, then, what was I thinking?

"Anyway," HM continued, "I think your qualities better suit you to other tasks—"

Housemaiding?

"—so, yes . . ." she tapped her chin reflectingly, ". . . hmmm, yes, you know, I think you ought to carry on. You needn't frown, Jane. I meant with your *extracurricular* activities . . . . Oh, hello, my darlings."

The door to the apartments in the Queen's Tower opened and a pair of corgis scampered through and gathered about her ankles, pink tongues hanging like tiny hams in a butcher's window. "So much nicer than cats, I think." She looked from one to the other indulgently. "Are you walking them now, David?"

"Yes, Your Majesty. Diamond and Kelpie have been particularly snappish this morning so I thought some exercise might do them good."

The Queen glanced at Davey's plump figure pressed as it was into its uniform. "Yes, some exercise *would* be a good idea," she commented, adding, "Are you on carriage duty this week?"

"Tomorrow, Ma'am."

"Ah. Jane? Do you have your tickets?"

"I've chosen tomorrow as well, Ma'am."

"Oh, good. Well, come along then, Derek," she said to her minder, heading for the great oak door as Davey and I nodded and bobbed in curtsy as gender dictated. She turned. "Oh, and David—it's getting awfully warm out there this morning. Do be careful. Don't overheat them."

"Yes, Ma'am."

"Diamond tore my best trousers this morning," Davey grumbled, as he bent to attach leads to their collars. "I don't know what's gotten into the little buggers. They were scrapping something dreadful at breakfast."

"I think this heat's starting to get on people's nerves. Hard to believe it looked like rain when we woke up on Monday. Perhaps you shouldn't take them outside."

"I shall exercise them outdoors 'till they have heat-stroke! Be still!" he hissed to the recalcitrant Kelpie.

"And then you can present Her Majesty with a couple of dead dogs. Should prove interesting."

"My apologies." Davey rose and fluttered his hand about his face like a fan. "Perhaps *I'm* getting heatstroke." He eyeballed my unhousemaidlike apparel. "I must say, that is a charming frock! I neglected to compliment you earlier. Harvey Nicks, is it?"

"Oxfam. Kensington High Street."

"Then don't tell anyone."

"I won't."

"And how was poor Mrs. Pettibon?" We headed around the bend in the Corridor. "Not one of the merry wives of Windsor, I expect."

"Davey, that's not very kind. Besides, she's a widow."

"Merry widow, then."

"Stop it. Mrs. Pettibon's . . . under considerable strain. Not surprising, I suppose."

"You sound a trifle skeptical."

"My nature, probably. Or my nurture." My mother and her occasional journalistic critiques of our lives in these times popped into my head. "Davey, do you know where you go in London to look up a will?" We stopped by the door to Clarence Tower.

"I don't know," he hastened to add. "I've never been asked that one. Can't tell you how many times I've been stopped on Buckingham Palace Road—usually by some tourist, but not always—only to be asked, 'Where can I find Buckingham Palace?' 'Right in front of your nose, you ninny,' I want to say, but I'm ever so polite, of course. But no one's ever asked me where they can look up a will."

"Great. And here I thought you knew everything about London, Davey Pye."

"I prefer to confine my erudition to Belgravia and Mayfair. And choice portions of the capital's more select neighborhoods."

"Never mind. I know who'll know."

•   •   •

I caught the 1:11 train to London. I was skiving big time, I know. But I decided to extend my brief secondment through to the afternoon and figured Mrs. Boozley probably wouldn't notice. The Castle's so huge you could send out a search party and then you'd have to send out a second search party to find the first. I figured only Fleur or Heather would notice my absence and I could deal with them.

I'd phoned my great-aunt Grace who lives in Long Marsham, a town northwest of London about as far as Windsor is due west.

"Somerset House," she'd replied immediately when I'd posed my question. "Why do you want to know about wills, Jane?"

Being as I was in the Staff lounge where the ears are jumping and the gossip is high, I said I really couldn't say.

"How intriguing," Grace remarked in her usual understated tones. "My church meeting has been cancelled for the afternoon and I'm at a loose end. I was half thinking of coming up to London to do some shopping, but this sounds more interesting. May I join you?"

And why not? Grace, my grandfather's sister (a Bee like me) was good company, liberal in her views (for an old person, I thought with my young person's prejudice), and very discreet. She'd been a sounding board for a previous (mis)adventure at Buckingham Palace and had never breathed a word. I particularly loved visiting her cozy cottage weekends in winter when cavernous Buck House was chilled and we were advised to put on a sweater if we didn't like it. Grace turned up her central heating just for me!

We arranged to meet at two-thirty just outside the arched entryway to Somerset House in view of St. Mary-le-Strand Church.

I half-dozed as the train clattered through the countryside and straggling suburbs to London Waterloo from Windsor's Riverside Station, waking sharply at various stops along the way, then sinking back into a kind of torpor in my sunny window. Jerked awake at Richmond, a little better than half-way into the fifty-minute journey, I glimpsed a stout late-middle-aged woman on the platform. She wore a fussy flower-print dress and frowned and tugged at a pair of gloves so bleached white they seemed to glow in otherworldly fashion.

"O why do you walk through the fields in gloves/Missing so much and so much?/O fat white woman whom nobody loves" drifted through my mind, a peculiarly memorable smidgen of poetry. A footman had recited it last year at Ascot, when one of the lesser-liked imperious gloved wives of one of the more supercilious of the gray men who run the bureaucracy that is the monarchy waddled into the refreshment marquee and hoovered up the strawberries and cream. Gloves, I thought sleepily, as the train pulled away again. Ought I to wear gloves at Ascot? Did I wear gloves last year? Do I *have* gloves? Alice had gloves. White kid gloves. The White Rabbit dropped them on his worried way to see the Duchess and Alice picked them up. I was quite sure. Did she give them to the Duchess, the Duchess, the Duchess? The Duchess had a large cat that grinned from ear to ear. A Cheshire cat. But the Duchess of Cheshire was dead, how sad. The Duke was a widower. He had a wicked son. And a nice grandson. Who wore white gloves that blazed in the sunshine as they gripped the Queen's mantle . . .

I awoke with a start as the train lurched into Waterloo Station. Gloves. Hugo FitzJames wore gloves. Or had gloves as part of his kit as Page of Honour. There'd been no fingerprints on the sword. The weapon was clean, Chief Inspector Nightingale had told me the morning of the murder. Either wiped or never handled with bare hands in the first place, which was a possibility given the—ha!—white-glove treatment of things in royal palaces.

Of course, I considered, heading through the fusty heat along the passage leading to Waterloo Bridge, you might wipe a murder weapon with a handkerchief (if you had one) or perhaps with a shirttail, but would you be so cool and meticulously self-possessed if you'd killed impulsively, rashly, in the heat of some moment of passion, which I was sure had driven Pettibon's murderer? I thought not. And Fabiani was the impulsive type. If he'd been careless enough in failing to destroy a smock with blood on it, would he have been at the same time careful enough to wipe a murder weapon clean of fingerprints?

The sword had been left behind in the Throne Room Monday morning. No one except Hugo had known it was there. If Hugo didn't fatally stab Roger Pettibon, if he wasn't the murderer (still dreadful to think of a fourteen-year-old murderer), then surely the real murderer had come across the sword by chance that morning and used it in haste, on impulse.

And, yet, no fingerprints.

Hugo wore gloves, I thought again, welcoming the lovely cooling breeze on my face as I crossed the Thames over Waterloo Bridge, distracted for a moment by the sight of the Palace of Westminster floating like a Gothic barge under the hazy blue sky. Would Miranda Walter wear gloves in her restoration work in the fire-damaged rooms of the Castle? Quite possibly, given the plaster dust, the smoke stains, the cracked and sharp edges, the caustic materials. And what about Joanna Pettibon? Once, for a project in high school, I'd visited the PEI Archives in Charlottetown. To handle the precious old documents and drawings, I'd been required to wear a pair of cotton gloves supplied by the curators. I had little doubt the Print Room made the same demands on its staff.

And Victor Fabiani? No portraitist painted with gloves on. And it was June. You didn't need gloves for the weather. The frosty Canon Leathley flitted through my mind, too. Do clerics wear gloves? Vestments, yes. Gloves, no.

What *did* become of the White Rabbit's kid gloves anyway?

Somerset House is tucked well off the Strand. It's an imposing-looking compound, with four grim gray mansions grouped around a huge courtyard, but there were always so many cars in said courtyard, I'd presumed it was some sort of upmarket carpark until I learned it was really an upscale eighteenth-century office building instead. Grace met me outside, on the Strand, and, like Davey, made approving noises about my dress, which time had given me no opportunity to change.

"Quite like the old days when we used to dress to come up to London," my aunt remarked a touch wistfully. "We wore hats then. And gloves."

It was my opening to fill her in on events of the last few days. I did so as she led the way through the car-choked courtyard to the south entrance where the principal registry of the family division was located. As she had the first time I'd had an adventure in murder at Buckingham Palace, Grace listened sympathetically.

"I'd read about the murder in the *Guardian* this morning," she commented. "I half wondered if you might have got yourself drawn into it somehow, since trouble tends to seek you out for some reason. But is a will, or lack of a will, sufficient evidence to bolster your point of view?"

"Well, no," I admitted. "I guess I'm just trying to chip away the best I can at Nightingale's notions. All the police have got, as far as I can see, is a confession, an artist's smock with bloodstains, and a sort of qualified confirmation that a few of the Leonardos in the Royal Collection are, to use the nice word, copies. I can't make judgments about the blood and the art, but I'm sure the confession is bogus!"

"But if the legacy from a relative in Cumbria is a fiction," Grace reasoned, "then this Roger Pettibon's sudden wealth may quite possibly have been gained through blackmail, just as your artist friend claims."

"I suppose," I allowed, not keen to concede this. "But he might have switched the Leonardo copies for the genuine drawings all by himself, and made a killing. Or he might have won . . . the National Lottery or—"

"But why would he lie to his wife about it?"

"—or maybe he won it on a horse!"

"Would his wife mind if he won money on a horse?" No, I thought. Unless.

"Unless," I said out loud to Grace, "the money has something to do with Iain Scott, Roger's brother-in-law, who I'm told is a sort of gambling addict. Perhaps Roger won great gobs of money on a tip from his brother-in-law and knew Joanna wouldn't approve."

"Or perhaps he did inherit money after all."

I smiled at Grace. "I've got my fingers crossed."

• • •

The wills registry at Somerset House had the appearance of a popular library, so many people did there seem to be at the pulpitlike bookcases, each containing rank after rank of volumes bound in the same sepulchral purple.

"I've been here once before, to look up my grandfather's will. Your great-great-grandfather," Grace commented in a low voice as we both scanned the room. The place seemed to demand silence.

"I wonder if people do this as a form of recreation," I said, noting the casual dress of all but a few in suits who might have been solicitors. "Did my great-great-grandfather leave heaps of money and a palatial home somewhere in Gloucestershire, say?"

"If he had, Jane, I think both your life and mine would be quite different now, don't you think?"

"I suppose," I said dreamily as we walked, looking at the dates on the spines of the books. "Then I would be employing housemaids, instead of being employed as a housemaid."

"Your great-great-grandfather left a tidy sum for those days. I can't quite remember the amount. However, his sons got greater shares than his daughters."

"What!"

"Shh. The presumption was, in those days, the daughters would be in the care of their husbands."

"Death to patriarchy!"

"I might point out we're the descendants of the sons."

"Yea, patriarchy!"

"How odd." Grace halted near a window overlooking the forecourt. "The books seem to run out in the early 'nineties. This Pettibon relative died last year, isn't that right?"

"Look, Grace—microfiche." I pointed to a nearby machine. "I can do it."

"I'm not completely antediluvian, you know."

But I was already flipping through the much-thumbed red binder of microfiche cards for P names of the recent past.

"Found it! Card thirty-one."

Grace switched on the light and I slipped the transparent fiche under the magnifier and began scanning.

"It should be there," I wailed after a moment, pointing at a spot on the screen. "Right after Petter, James Paul and before Pettman, Ada May."

"And you're sure the death was last year? Probating the will wouldn't take too long . . . . I wonder . . ."

"What?"

"Pettibon is a bit of an odd name, you'll allow. Makes me wonder if the family was originally Huguenot French way back when, or it could go back as far as Norman French, I suppose. Might the spelling of the name have changed?"

"In this century?"

"Worth a try. Hand me card thirty." I stepped aside and let her fiddle with the machine. "Here," she said after a moment. "Right after *Petit, Noel Herbert: Petitbon, Edith Mary*. See? The fourth and fifth letters have been switched around as if to make the name more English-looking. Goodness, Edith Mary was born in the last century. And, look, the address is Cumbria: Cherry Cottage, Great Broughton. Shall we try it?"

After filling out a form, paying a small fee, and waiting about ten minutes, we had the last will and testament of Edith Mary Petitbon in hand.

"Not a long document." I noted three typewritten pages as we sat down at one of the oak tables.

"Let's see. Her solicitor was her trustee. Three beneficiaries to be paid immediately. Look: She's given thirty thousand pounds to a school, forty thousand to her parish church, and—here . . ." Grace pointed at a line near the bottom of the first page.

"Aha!"

"You are vindicated, Jane! One hundred forty thousand pounds to Roger Gervase Pettibon—new spelling, but right person, I assume."

"Well, that's a nice little sum. That would explain the flush of money in the Pettibon coffers of late. Why blackmail someone when you've just been given a load of loot?"

"He could have been *very* greedy, Jane."

"Hmph." I demurred. "What does the rest say?"

"Hmm." Grace turned to the second page. "Residuary estate. What's left from the sale of property and payment of taxes, funeral expenses and so forth. Oh, look, the school, the church and Roger Pettibon benefit again, in the same proportion, so he would get, let me see—"

"Two thirds."

"Yes, two thirds of any subsequent money generated. So he'd be even richer."

"What's this bit?" I looked at the bottom of the page.

"Certain items on safe deposit, it seems to say. In care of the trustees. Also to go to Roger. Family mementoes, I expect. Small items that had been handed down. Perhaps jewellery—"

"Funny, you'd think Joanna Pettibon would have remembered jewellery. But she seemed barely aware of the dimensions of this nice little windfall. Perhaps Roger kept it from her. She said he was secretive."

"Or perhaps it wasn't jewellery . . . ."

A Garter? The thought elbowed its way into my head. Might the Petitbons/Pettibons count some Garter Knight in their ancestry? I supposed all the descendants of all the Garter Knights over the centuries might amount to quite a few people. Was dull old ordinary Roger Pettibon among them? Perhaps only the fellow from the Central Chancery of the Orders of Knighthood knew for sure.

Grace readily accepted my invitation to accompany me to the Queen's Gallery. I wanted to look at the Leonardo exhibit, particularly at the drawing claimed as one of Fabiani's fakes. I also thought I might successfully catch a ride back to Windsor from the Palace, since there was much to-ing and fro-ing between London and Windsor when Her Majesty was staying at the Castle longer than her usual weekends.

"What's the nearest Tube stop, I wonder? Embankment?"

"Oh, let's have a taxi, Jane. My treat."

Given that we couldn't talk about You-Know-What in front of the cabbie, conversation swung, inevitably, from the riddles of murder to more prosaic family matters: My eldest sister, Jennifer, had passed her residency and had set up a shared practice as a pediatrician in Halifax; Julie, the sister married to Mr. PotatoHead on PotatoHead Acres back on the Island, was pregnant with her second child; and my parents, though still separated, seemed to be—go figure—"dating."

"And," I added, sighing, looking out the cab window as we crawled past Charing Cross Station, "most of them, one way or another, bug me about what I do, and when I'm going to smarten up and stop this nonsense, come home, and knuckle down to something or other. Jennifer's a doctor, and I'm a housemaid. Julie has babies, and I'm a housemaid. Dad keeps upping the ante as far as going back to university is concerned. I think he'd just about pony up for Oxford if there was any chance I could get in. Even my mother, who's always been really supportive, now drops these 'maybe your father is right' bits into the conversation when she phones. Jennifer doesn't say much, but she's been so busy she hardly writes," I added rather fiercely.

"It's my fault—" Grace raised her voice to be heard above the rattle of a power drill. If the traffic on the Strand was bad, the road work in progress was worse.

"Oh, Grace, don't be silly."

"—if I hadn't encouraged you to respond to that mysterious 'situations vacant' notice in the paper, you'd likely be well on your way to finishing your education."

"But I *like* what I'm doing. I'm enjoying myself enormously. Really, everybody is being so . . . so *middle-class!* There's nothing wrong with being a housemaid."

"But where does it lead, Jane?"

"I don't know." Housekeeper? I shuddered, thinking of Mrs. Harbottle, deputy Housekeeper at Buck House, our immediate boss, a woman who makes you warm to Margaret Thatcher. "Anyway, Auntie, if it hadn't been for you, how else would I be having these, you know . . ." I glanced at the back of the cabbie's head and said under my breath, "*adventures?* And how else would I have met—"

"Met . . . ?"

"Oh! I meant . . ." Too late. "Well, I've sort of met someone . . . interesting. I think. Well, I don't know, really. I've hardly talked with him—"

Grace remained silent, glancing out her window as we inched past Trafalgar Square, but I could *feel* her smiling.

"—and he sort of ordered me about, which I don't care for," I amended darkly, rattling on.

"Ordered you about?"

"He's with the Scots Guard." So I told her about the dust-up at the Star Tavern Saturday evening.

"The young man sounds like he has good common sense," Grace responded. "You might well have been hurt, Jane. And, think, if you'd been sent to hospital or hadn't been able to work Monday, you wouldn't have been in a position to question Mr. Fabi—pardon me, *the artist's* confession, now would you?" Her eyebrows, curiously black though her hair was steel gray, rose fractionally.

"It was meant to be, you mean?"

"I wouldn't go quite that far. I'm not sure how detailed the divine plan is."

The taxi chugged through Admiralty Arch and we picked up speed down the Mall, Buckingham Palace in sight. I glanced at Grace in profile. She was old, really; nearly as old as the Queen. And she was a spinster (awful word! I mean *unmarried*), having fallen in that old-fashioned way, as the youngest daughter of a large family, to caring for her own aged parents, my great-grandparents. Between her and me stretched a span of two generations and yet, at times, I found her much easier to talk with than my own mother. The grandmother syndrome, I suppose.

"You know . . ." I began tentatively, feeling my face flush around the edges, "when I saw him, Jamie that is, in the window at the pub, I had this sort of . . . oh, Barbara Cartland moment."

Grace laughed. "It *was* meant to be, you mean."

"Perhaps it was the drink. Or a trick of the light."

"Perhaps not."

"How do you know for sure?"

"You don't, of course. You can only let nature take its course. Dull advice, I know, but there you are. I'm a dull old thing."

"Oh, hardly."

"Are you seeing him again?"

"I don't know." I sighed. "I like to think he had a Barbara Cartland moment, too, though I don't think men would describe it that way. They're from Mars and we're from Venus, after all. And then—oh, what an idiot I am!—I went and told him I was a flight attendant for Air Canada staying over the week at Windsor."

"But you were only a moment ago arguing for the honour of being a housemaid."

"I was, wasn't I? I don't know what came over me. He seemed so handsome and smart and nice and in the Guard and all, that being a skivvy suddenly seemed so plain and ordinary. I felt like Cinderella before she got wind she had a fairy godmother. God, I'm as bad as they are—men—saying they're race car drivers or something when they're chatting you up, you knowing all along they're only lorry drivers."

"Call him and explain. Oh, you didn't catch his last name, did you?"

"I suppose I could hang around outside the gates at Victoria Barracks."

"I think there's a name for those kinds of women, Jane. Driver, this will do." Grace snapped open her handbag as the cab made an abrupt U-turn in Buckingham Palace Road and came to a halt outside the entrance to the Queen's Gallery.

I scrambled out and waited on the crowded pavement while Grace paid with a five-pound note. As my aunt stepped from the cab, the driver leaned from his window toward me, wagging his finger.

" 'Oh, what a tangled web we weave,' miss," he intoned, " 'when first we practice to deceive.' "

And then he quickly pitched his cab back into the snarling traffic on Buckingham Palace Road and sped away.

I recall my mother saying once, when she was moaning over submissions to an evening class she taught in journalism, that taxi drivers appearing in feature stories to dispense wisdom was one of the worst clichés of feature writing. Well, I thought, stepping through the doors of the Gallery, I'd finally met the cliché. And I wasn't sure I appreciated the wisdom. I wouldn't have put him in *my* story, if I were writing one.

"This is good of you," I said to Grace as she shelled out once again, for the tickets. She waved the tribute away

and we headed through the Gallery shop down a passageway
to the exhibition space.

The room, a two-story volume of sea blue baize, was
delightfully cool and twilit so it felt like a church, really. (No
complete surprise. The Gallery was built from the ruins of
the Palace's private chapel, gutted by a German bomb during World War II.) Our voices dropped automatically to a
reverent hush. I had only been in the Queen's Gallery once
before: during the London stop on the Grand Tour that had
brought me to Europe in the first place, I'd breezed through,
in vacuous tourist mode, to take in an exhibit of . . . I can't
even remember what I'd seen. Now I felt for the first time
in my life a more vital connection to works of art, which was
oddly satisfying, even if the connection did come about
through a murder.

The Gallery was not terribly crowded, for a day at the
beginning of the tourist season.

"Do you know which one it is?" Grace asked, moving
toward the first da Vinci drawing, a study of a woman's
hands, charcoal on a pale buff-coloured paper.

"I've a description," I replied, rubbernecking as best I
could around the people. "It's a study of a horse. But I don't
know where it might be."

"These are lovely, aren't they?"

Long and elegant, the hands were drawn with great
sensitivity and extraordinary anatomical precision. Not
merely were they some idea of womanly hands. They were *a*
woman's hands, unique. Davey's comment about the difficulty of getting hands right in a painting and how superbly
Fabiani had managed to depict the Queen's hands flitted
through my mind and sparked a moment's doubt. Perhaps
old Fabbo was capable of faking a masterwork. Not this one,
not *this* woman's hands, but *a* woman's hands. Or a face. Or
feet.

We moved from drawing to drawing, the early ones
studies of faces and limbs, following a pair of Japanese girls
in pressed blue jeans and Hard Rock Café T-shirts. They
gazed at each drawing with reverence, whispering together
until they reached some pen-and-ink studies of human
skulls. These seemed to excite them considerably. The

rapid speech and, particularly, certain gesticulations made me wonder if they weren't medical students.

"I'd forgotten Leonardo da Vinci wrote backwards," Grace commented. Several lines of handwriting below the skull, though (probably) in fifteenth-century Italian or in Latin, did indeed appear to be running right to left. "You'd have to hold it in front of a mirror," she added.

"*That* would be difficult to copy, I'll bet. Oh, look." My eye was drawn to an irregularity in the marshalling of framed drawings a little further down along a temporary wall. I led Grace around the Japanese girls. "There must be one missing. There has to be."

Not only was there an awkward gap, an ever-so-slightly faded rectangle of wall-covering and tiny holes where screws had been indicated the former presence of a drawing. So, too, did an even smaller faded rectangle, presumably where a title card had been affixed. "And look—the ones on either side are studies of horses. So surely the one that was here was of a horse, too. They must have taken it away. Just a sec."

I darted over to a pinched-looking man dressed in a kind of blue livery with red collar and cuffs that made him look like the doormen at Claridge's.

"Excuse me. Was the missing drawing over there a study of a horse, or a study of part of a horse?"

"Missing?"

"Yes, the missing drawing. See that blank space over there, beside where those two women in the T-shirts are standing?"

"There isn't a drawing missing."

"Of course there is. Anyone can see."

"It isn't *missing*. It's been *removed*."

"Removed, then. Was it of a horse?"

"Yes," the gallery minder replied tartly as if he were giving away a state secret. "It was removed before opening this morning."

"The fake! Or the alleged fake, anyway."

"Shh. We're trying to keep it quiet. How did you know?"

"Wasn't it in the papers?"

He studied my face. I belatedly realized the specific

forgeries—specific *alleged* forgeries—had not been mentioned in the press.

"Okay, I'm in service at Windsor Castle," I explained to the skeptical little man. "There's been, you know, rumours about which ones were the fakes. I was just curious."

He appeared to thaw a little. "This murder! Well, the drawing's been removed for examination," he allowed in a whisper. "We're telling people the frame was damaged by cleaners."

Right, blame the domestic staff, why don't you.

"Did it look . . . *different* at all to you?"

He shook his head. "I don't know a thing about art," he replied as if it were a badge of honour to be so ignorant. "I only work here."

"Gone, I'm afraid," I sighed to Grace. The Japanese women had moved on. A May-September couple moved into their place, he draping a heavy hairy arm over her thin shoulders like a bear possessing a doe. "To some expert for evaluation, I guess. Mrs. Pettibon said she'd suggested some people to the police."

"I don't think we'd have known the difference anyway, Jane."

". . . Frightfully sensitive, so spontaneous, don't you think?" the man was articulating with ringing confident vowels as he came up beside us. The young woman's reply was inaudible. "His draughtsmanship has such enormous charm . . . and, oh, there's a drawing missing here, I'm sure. We shall have to ask for our money back, shan't we, darling?" He laughed assuredly and drew her tighter. The hair on his head was thick and black, but the bald spot at the crown was deep enough to hold a golf ball.

"It's been removed," I addressed his back, taking some perverse pleasure in interrupting their love-fug. "They say it might be a fake."

He turned a big, deeply tanned face toward me. The woman, pale and delicate, gazed at me with vacant eyes.

"You don't say! How extraordinary!" he boomed. "Say, how do *you* know? Oh, it doesn't have something to do with this murder at Windsor I read about in *The Times*, does it?"

"Yes, actually, it does. That's what the guide over there says."

"I have heard of Victor Fabiani, of course. I know *of* him," the man continued airily. (It went without saying, apparently). "And *certainly* I've seen his work. He's quite good, but I wouldn't have thought him capable of forging copies of Leonardo's work."

"Why not?"

"Well," he waved his free arm in the air like a lecturing professor, "I mean, it's . . . Leonardo never developed the sort of formality of drawing that could be easily copied, not the way Raphael or Michelangelo did. There's no little trick to it that one can pick up easily. Not to mention the knowledge of period papers and recipes for inks—"

"Still, it could be possible," I argued for the prosecution.

"Well, anything's possible, I suppose," he replied witheringly. "But I wouldn't have said Fabiani forging Old Masters was even probable. People who counterfeit art, I've found, are usually motivated by envy or jealousy or have some quarrel with society. Or they love intrigue. Forgers may actually be great artists—almost, but not quite. There's always something missing." He gave me a sour smile. "From what I know of Fabiani, he doesn't quite fit the profile. Still—"

"Are you an artist yourself?" my aunt inquired.

"No." His smile broadened, compacting the tan lines around his eyes. "You could just say I'm a collector." He didn't elaborate.

"The papers say Fabiani made these copies when he was young, when he needed money," I interjected.

"He would have to have been *extraordinarily* talented. Look," he added with impatience, drawing our attention to a drawing of a figure on horseback. "There's another thing. You look, too, Ginny, darling," he addressed his lady friend. "You'll learn something. Do you see the diagonal lines of shading, around the neck and over the horse's back and sides?"

"Yes," I replied, somewhat annoyed at his preemptory tone.

Like, *so?*

"Which way are they going?" he continued.

Silence. And then, wanly, in the form of a question from the pixie woman: "From left to right? Sort of up in the left corner down to the right?"

"Very good, darling. And what do you think it means?"

I stared stupidly at the drawing.

"Oh, I see," Grace said in a slightly startled voice. "You'd have to be left-handed."

"Exactly. Leonardo da Vinci was *left-handed*. He shaded from left to right. Now a copyist, I suppose, could learn to imitate that, but it would be very awkward if you were right-handed. I'm not sure the result would be very convincing. As for Fabiani, my guess—"

But I'd stopped listening. I saw Victor Fabiani as he was that day at Easter in the King's Drawing Room with Her Majesty. And again Monday, as I posed for him in the Garter robes. I saw him as clearly as if he were before me right now in the Queen's Gallery. He was standing, his easel turned at an angle, in his left hand, his palette.

And in his right hand, his brush. Like most people, he was right-handed.

How simple!

14

FOR STARTERS—LOBSTER in a white port sauce.

Price—£34.

For *starters*!

Did I dare? I hadn't had a bite of lobster since leaving Prince Edward Island, and I hadn't had a bite of *anything* since breakfast.

I snuck a peek over the top of the menu. Andrew Macgreevy was immersed in his. His high forehead and crown of oat-coloured hair hovered above the blue card. My eyes quickly darted among the tables nearest our own at the Riverview Inn's dining room. I recognized no one. So far, so good.

Or should I go for the foie gras served with a buttery brioche, the cheapest—excuse me, most *affordable*—appetizer? I glanced at the heart-stopping prices. Was Macgreevy on expense account, or was this coming out of his own pocket? (He was on suspension, after all.) Should I offer to go dutch? (I could hardly afford it.) But *he* invited *me*. (Why?)

All I knew is, I could eat a horse (à la beaujolais).

But was I going to be dessert? (Perish the thought.)

"Gosh," I said lightly, hoping for a sign, "I'm spoiled for a choice here."

"Have whatever you like."

Big help.

In fact, I was feeling in a somewhat partyish mood. The case against Victor Fabiani, as far as I was concerned, was melting like ice cream in a summer rain. Roger Pettibon's tidy little financial windfall seemed to have a legitimate source after all. And Fabiani's capacity to have fabricated Old Master drawings was very much in question, as far as I was concerned.

Yes, the lobster! Why not? And perhaps some bubbly?

A waiter shimmered forth, his physique and colouring reminiscent of white asparagus.

"I believe I'll start with the lobster," I announced. From across the table, I sensed a flinch.

"Make that two." Macgreevy's tone suggested I'd presented a challenge. "And a bottle of the Bollinger '85."

The waiter glided off.

"Celebrating something?"

"Celebrating dinner with you, Jane."

Stuff the smarm, I thought, toying with the silverware, casting about in my mind for some neutral conversation. I'd reached Windsor with enough time to race up to my room and grab a pair of sunglasses. I'd borrowed a scarf from Heather. She was cheesed off at me for skiving the whole afternoon.

"Are you impersonating Jackie O, or are you simply unhappy to be seen with me?" was Macgreevy's comment when I presented myself at the Castle Hotel a little later. I hadn't an answer. The short ride to Bray in his Jaguar XJS had passed in relative silence, but for the usual BritChat about the weather. (They worry if it doesn't change at least twice a day, and it hadn't changed at all since Monday). Oh, and chat about the merits of his car, of course. The substitute penis.

"Enjoying your holiday?"

"S'all right, I guess."

"Good thing you toured the Castle yesterday, Andrew. It's been closed off, you know." Hell, I thought, I'm sliding straight into topics I'd vowed to stay clear of.

"I'm not responsible for that photo of the Queen's portrait in today's *Gazette*." Macgreevy looked at me hard while he reached into his suit pocket and pulled out a familiar packet.

"Did I say you were? And you know you can't smoke in here."

"Well, that's what you're thinking." He cursed the smoking laws under his breath.

"Well, Andrew, it is sort of interesting you were in the Castle precincts yesterday. The photo of that painting is up-to-the-minute. So it had to have been taken at some point since Monday."

"How would you know it's 'up-to-the-minute'?"

"Because I was airing some of the rooms on the north side of the Upper Ward on Monday and happened to get a glimpse of the portrait."

"I find it interesting you were on the north side of the Upper Ward Monday." His tone mocked me. "The Throne Room's on the north side. So I learned yesterday."

"I can hardly believe you've never toured the State Rooms at Windsor Castle after your years in the Rat Pack."

He shrugged. "There's never been a reason to."

"Aha! So you *were* there for a reason."

"The reason being my personal pleasure, Stella. I'm a tourist and Windsor Castle is a tourist site."

"Why don't I believe you? Oh!"

A wine steward materialized at our table, startling me.

"By the way, there was no poetry reading at the Windsor Cultural Centre yesterday afternoon. Yes, fine," Macgreevy addressed the steward holding the bottle for his examination. "I hadn't anything better to do, so I decided to catch you up. But you weren't there, and no reading was scheduled.

"But," he sighed, "I suppose if there had been a poetry reading, then I wouldn't have had time to enjoy the Castle. That would have been too bad."

You shit, checking up on me.

"I wouldn't have thought you one for poetry, Andrew." I watched the golden bubbly liquid fill our champagne flutes.

"I like all forms of literature."

"That must explain why you work for the *Gazette*."

"Shall we have a toast?" He smiled and raised his glass. "To . . . To mysteries solved."

I withheld my glass. "What do you mean? And why— mysteries? What mysteries?"

"It's only a toast, for Christ's sake. Mysteries. Life's a mystery. You're a mystery. I'm a mystery. All waiting for resolution."

"All right, then." I'd promised myself I wouldn't be provoked. "To mysteries solved."

But not by you, buster.

The crystal flutes clinked. My eyes happened to glance past Macgreevy's self-satisfied expression to another diner who, in rising from his seat, looked my way. He regarded me blankly, then recognition flooded his roast-beef-fed face.

"What's the matter? Bolly not good enough for you?"

"Hell, it's Jonathan Bremner."

"The Queen's assistant Private Secretary?" Macgreevy's head whipped around.

"Oh, don't do that!" I hissed. "Oh, God, he's seen you."

Bremner's eyebrows ascended his brow tellingly. He turned abruptly and ushered his wife, or lady of equal distinction, from the room.

"He doesn't necessarily know who I am," Macgreevy said evenly, sipping at his champagne.

"Are you kidding? They've got pictures of you guys plastered on dart boards in their offices. Bremner probably thinks I'm the one who took the picture of Her Majesty's portrait and sold it to your bloody rag," I wailed.

"I'm surprised such an exalted member of the Royal Household knows one housemaid from another." Mischief danced in Macgreevy's eyes.

"I should never have agreed to this dinner—"

"If a man and a maid—a housemaid, even—can't have

a meal together then I don't know what this country's coming to."

"Eat your lobster!"

The waiter had appeared to deposit two pale green plates of lobster slices artfully arranged in a pond of creamy sauce. Then he vanished into the ether.

"And I wish the staff here would stop materializing and dematerializing," I ranted with unfocused annoyance, stabbing at a lobster slice. "It gives me the creeps."

"They're good at being unobtrusive, aren't they? Why do you think the Riverview has all these Michelin stars? Your lot could learn a thing or two from these boys, I'd say."

"Oh, shut—oh! ooooh! This is *won*derful." The lobster melted in my mouth and slid down to where the hungry lions awaited. I greedily scarfed down the rest in double-quick time.

"Doesn't Her Majesty feed you?"

"Uh-huh. Gruel. Twice a day. Pass that bread."

He watched with a mixture of amusement and distaste as I swiped at the superb sauce with a *morçeau* of baguette. "I'm not wasting this wonderful stuff," I argued between gulps. "Just because you English think it's rude to sop. The French do it!"

"Not a convincing argument in this country."

"I haven't eaten since this morning."

"Been busy?"

"Very. Ascot week. Terrible." I drained my glass of champagne. I was flooded by a sense of well-being from the food and drink. My worry over Jonathan Bremner drowned like so many rats in a flash flood. More of this sort of nosh, I thought, and even Andrew could have his wicked way with me. "Does your wife know you take other women out to dinner?"

"I don't have a wife."

"Then what's the gold band on the third finger of your left hand?"

"I *had* a wife, years back, before I got on at the *Gazette*. She exploded. One of those human combustion stories. I tried selling it to the *National Enquirer* in Florida at the time, but . . ." He shrugged.

"So you wear the ring for sentimental reasons."

He glanced at the gold band. "You'd be surprised the women attracted to a bloke wearing one of these." He grinned lopsidedly.

"You're disgusting."

"Why don't you decide what dish you're going to inhale next."

I had already decided. The roast duck poached in jasmine tea and roasted in honey. But I glanced at the menu anyway while Macgreevy studied his. I realized I knew next to nothing about him, hadn't wanted to know, not since he first made a nuisance of himself during my early days at Buck House. However, his wearing a wedding ring in the face of a departed (detonated) wife suggested he wasn't completely the hard case I thought he was. Or was the drink lowering my guard?

"Perhaps next time," I said to the waiter, who'd made me flinch yet again, "you might clear your throat to herald your arrival."

"As you wish."

I ordered. Andrew ordered. Out the window, past the terrace, an ancient weeping willow dipped its fronds into the Thames. A paddling of ducks glided across the sun-dappled waters. The view was, not to put too fine a point on it, utterly enchanting.

"So, Andrew," I began, turning reluctantly from the pastoral scene, groping about for a bit of conversation, he being uncharacteristically noninquisitive, "how *did* you get into the wonderful world of journalism?"

"Got a job at a paper in Leicester after going to university there. Worked my way to London. Bob's your uncle. How did your mother get into journalism?"

"I don't remember talking to you about my mother."

"Oh? Wonder how I knew that then?"

"What I wonder is if there's any difference between journalism and spying."

"Don't get your nose out of joint. I probably picked it up when there was that murder at Sandringham and your father was in the picture. Remember? Both you and your father were mixed up in that somehow."

"I'm not discussing any of it. I'm just a housemaid."

"And I'm the editor of *The Sunday Times.*"

In fact, my father and I had become involved in the resolution of a murder one winter at Sandringham, the Queen's private estate in Norfolk, and by some fierce stone-walling to the likes of Andrew Macgreevy managed to keep our names out of the papers. "You know what my father does, and it seems you know what my mother does. What about your parents, Andrew?"

"My father was a London taxi driver."

"Does he like to spout wisdom to passengers?"

"I said 'was.' He's dead."

"Oh, I'm sorry."

"Years ago now. Motor accident. Ironic, I suppose. As for my mother, I don't know where she is."

"What . . .?"

"Walked out on my dad. He brought me up. He sacrificed a lot."

"No brothers or sisters?"

He shook his head.

"Stepbrothers? Stepsisters? Your father didn't remarry or whatever?"

"No. I said he made a lot of sacrifices."

"And you've never tried to find your mother?"

"I could if I wanted to. I know a few tricks in this business. I'm persistent. But she abandoned me and my father, so . . ." He shrugged and looked into his champagne flute. "Am I breaking your heart yet, love?"

"You are a bloody hard case, aren't you, Macgreevy?"

"Have some more champers."

There was the noise of throat-clearing, and a bony hand lifted the bottle and topped up our glasses.

"You know, Andrew, when I saw you on Peascod Street yesterday I figured you'd got wind of the murder at the Castle and practically flew here from Wapping. So far, we've gone through one car ride, had appetizers and drinks, and you haven't once tried it on. I mean, as far as trying to extract information. Not that I have any, of course."

"Disappointed?"

"It's not like you."

He held up his hands. "Look, Jane, it's not my story. I don't care. I'm on suspension."

"And you choose to spend this forced time off in Windsor."

"I heard they do some brilliant poetry readings here. Besides, this murder at the Castle has been resolved. Well, hasn't it?" I must have appeared doubtful, for he asked again, more forcefully: "It has, hasn't it?"

"Of course it has. It's been in the papers."

"Poetry readings . . ." Andrew muttered, one eyebrow flexed. "*Po*etry readings . . ."

"Would you excuse me? I have to . . . I should powder my nose before our entrées arrive."

This was not a ploy to forestall the usually nosy reporter. I had seen across the crowded room the figure of Jamie Sans-surname rise from a table, and I rose too, instinctively. Sweet violins, sunshine, roses, oh! Let the heavens shine upon me! He pulled at a chair the other side of a pillar and from it arose a young woman, willowy blond perfect-complexioned, who smiled at him radiantly as they turned in the direction of the restaurant corridor. They looked perfect together. Oh, blackness and despair! From elation I fell in a thrice, absolutely pig-sick with jealousy. But I was a body in motion, on leave for the loo, and shortly, my brave face affixed, I converged with the golden couple near the bar.

"Jane!"

There was such surprise and delight in his voice that my heart leapt.

"Oh, hello," I responded, fiercely feigning nonchalance.

"I've been looking for you everywhere."

"Oh?" Flustered, in a sort of be-still-my-beating-heart way, I glanced at his companion to register the effect of this dating no-no.

"Jamie, I'm going to have a word with the Newlanders," she said in a pleasant, cultivated TV-presenter sort of voice, moving away with barely a notice of me toward the front lounge.

"Mmm, fine." His tone to her was disinterested. "I looked for the Rocking Horse Hotel," he continued to me, "but I couldn't find it. It must be very new. Even BT hadn't a number."

"Oh, I know, silly, isn't it?" I laughed weakly. "The wallpaper's barely dry."

"I wanted to see if you were all right, and to apologize for having ordered you about like that, and—" He faltered.

"Well, I wondered if *you* were all right," I hastened to interject. "The paper made the fight sound like Cup Final."

"It wasn't as bad as all that."

" 'Pub ruined' the paper said. I was worried . . . I mean, I didn't . . . I didn't actually catch your last name on Saturday—"

"Allan."

Jamie Allan. Jamie Allan. Jamie Allan. Oh, what a *nice* name!

"—but one of the barmaids told me some people were taken to hospital."

"Two or three. Only one of our boys, though. Officially, you understand, no Scots Guard was at the Star Tavern Saturday night." Jamie winked. "It's always been off-limits."

"Oh-oh. Were you punished?"

"No. The rule applies to the lower ranks, I'm afraid. I'm an officer, a subaltern. The lads involved in Saturday's fight got a bit of square-bashing and extra guard duty for their pains. Listen, can I call you?" he added more urgently, glancing across the lounge to where his date was conversing with an elderly couple. "Do you have a number for this Rocking Horse place you're staying at?"

"Um, no. Well, we moved, you see, Heather and I," I blurted, further tangling the web I'd woven, but unsure how to extricate myself with time and other people pressing us both. That he was making a date while on a date bothered me not at all. Oh, where was my head?

"We switched hotels. Heather has some allergies, and all the chemicals from the new wallpaper and carpeting and so forth were getting her down."

"What a shame. Is Heather here with you?" He looked over my head toward the dining room.

"No. She's off somewhere else tonight. That's one of the pilots, just a friend," I explained of Macgreevy, waving my hand dismissively. "He's on a short layover. Flies back to Toronto tomorrow."

God, I thought, I'm weaving so much web it could be my funeral shroud.

"I see." Jamie regarded me expectantly.

"Oh, and yes, my number. It would be nice to see you again." I smiled up at him; my heart sank at what I was about to do. "I'm staying . . ." I began hopelessly, recklessly, "I'm staying at the Castle."

"You were very lucky to find rooms Ascot Week. I'll call you there then. This weekend? Saturday? If you're free, of course."

"Of course." I knew he'd misinterpret. He thought I meant the Castle Hotel on the High Street, the same one at which Macgreevy had parked his person. "I'm here till Monday . . . or longer. It depends . . . oh, look, I should tell you—"

"Wonderful! Look, I must dash." But he seemed reluctant to leave. I didn't want him to leave. He looked so chuffed and I felt so happy that my willingness to fess up instantly evaporated. I had a question, other business, something that had been bothering me, something I thought he might be able to answer.

"You wanted to tell me something . . . ?"

"I just wondered . . . about . . . In the Star Tavern. The guy with the scar, the red hair—"

"You know him? Iain Scott?"

"No. Well, yes, met him once. On another layover." God help me. "Did he go to hospital after the fight?"

Jamie frowned. "Yes. Scott was in one of the ambulances."

"He wasn't admitted, was he? I mean, the hospital didn't keep him overnight?"

"One of my men was kept over for observation, but the others, including Scott—though he's not with the Guard any more—were discharged late Saturday . . . well, early Sunday morning, actually, by the time they were all examined and patched up. There was quite a queue in emergency at Wexham Park that night."

"You wouldn't happen to know how Iain left the hospital, by any chance? Picked up by someone in a car?"

"I think so, yes."

"Did you see who picked him up?"

"Not really. A woman, I think. It was rather dark by that time, though . . . But why . . . ?"

"It's nothing," I said hastily. "I know you have to go." The elderly couple and the blonde had parted company. I wasn't anxious to meet her. "If you have trouble getting me . . ."—as I knew he would—". . . then perhaps I'll call you at Victoria Barracks."

"I say, you have learned a few more things about Windsor than the average tourist. But I don't live at the barracks. I have a flat . . . Oh, look, I must be off. I'll call you." He looked endearingly flustered. "Must go."

And I watched him go. The blonde tucked her arm around his.

"You must have a lot of nose to powder," Andrew grumbled when I'd resumed my place. "Your duck's ice cold."

"I ran into someone I know."

"I saw him. Who is he?"

"Not a member of Staff, if that's what you're wondering. Mmm, this is brilliant duck!"

It could have been oatmeal cooked in a sheep's stomach and still I'd have found it tasty. Food suddenly seemed a trivial matter. I would dine on anticipation. Ah, the violins. They were cranking up once again. The sunshine was streaming through the windows. The roses . . .

Stop it, for heaven's sake!

"Stop what?"

"What?"

"You told me to stop something."

"Sorry, Andrew, I didn't realize I was talking out loud."

A cloud scuttled over in the shape of a blond woman. It began to rain. I flicked a glance at Andrew; he was chewing his lamb pensively.

"What did the priest do when you showed up?"

"What priest?" His tone was sharp.

"The bishop, I mean. It was a bishop, wasn't it?" I gabbled. "The one you surprised in your randy vicar story, the Land's End love nest whatsit. The reason why you're on unpaid leave."

"Oh, that. I didn't talk to him, actually. Well, we had the evidence, didn't we? Bits of torn letters from the rubbish, overheard telephone calls, a photo of the two of them kissing—didn't look like a brotherly peck to me. No sister was mentioned in any of the usual biographical sources. He'd been behaving strangely for months, too. Secretive. So sources said. And then he just disappeared. I was able to track him down to Cornwall."

"Sounds like you were set up."

Macgreevy shrugged. "Maybe. The bishop's a real right-wing bastard. Family values and all that crap. He's ambitious, wants to be a cardinal, and he's got enemies. But my sources swear they thought he had this fancy woman, too." He sighed. "Anyway, the existence of this sister—half-sister, really—turned out to be this deep dark secret of the bishop's family. Bunch of bloody pious frauds is what they are. The bishop's mother was shagging some other bloke while she was married to the bishop's father—this is just before the war—and there was this little slip. The bishop's father found out it wasn't his, he refused to accept paternity, but they couldn't divorce—being Roman Catholic and local nobs—so the missus went to Cornwall for a 'rest cure' for her 'nerves.' The kiddie was put up for adoption. Amazing they were able to keep it secret all these years."

"Then how . . . ?"

"Deathbed confession. The woman's adoptive mother spilled the works. Had some papers to prove it."

"That's pretty dramatic. Not such a bad story."

"Na. Compared to a near-bloody-prince of the church having a bit of fluff tucked away? She was over fifty, but she was a stunner. At least through a telephoto lens, she was. Damn. It was a *great* story."

"But it wasn't *true*, Andrew."

He made a scornful noise between bites.

Of course, I ruminated, looking again at the Thames as the lowering sun bronzed the water, all the evidence could point irrefutably in one direction and yet, for the want of one tiny but oh-so-significant bit of information, be completely and utterly wrong. The challenge, I thought, was to be thorough, to assemble every last piece of information; only then could you even come near to finding a satisfying conclusion. Despite my earlier elation, I realized I was pretty much stalled in seeking Roger Pettibon's killer. All I was really sure of now was that Fabiani *didn't* do it. Whoopee for me.

"How do you find a missing person anyway?" I asked, all innocence, Miranda Walter popping into my head.

His fork hovered between plate and lips. He regarded me warily. "Why do you want to know that?"

"Just curious."

His eyes narrowed. The fork returned to the plate. "You know something."

"About what? What are you on about?" Had I given something away? Did he know about Miranda? Was his lack of interest in the Pettibon murder feigned after all?

"Nothing." His tone changed abruptly. "It's nothing." He smiled. "How do you find a missing person? Well, it depends of course on who the person is, and what information you have to start out with."

"And with the allegedly randy bishop?"

"There was a bit of letterhead from a hotel, a source in his parish—"

"I see."

There were some advantages to Macgreevy's craft: greater mobility, cultivated sources, and, of course, his willingness to insinuate himself, his tenacity, his thick skin. It struck me with awful force: Macgreevy could find Miranda Walter far more quickly than I could, far more willingly (maybe) than an unbelieving police force would. He could be useful.

But at what cost?

The Riverview Inn, for England, has a rare feature: It's air-conditioned. Still, I felt a dew beading at my hairline, a flush growing along my arms and up my neck. Should I do this? Was I about to make a horrible mistake?

"Jane, I think you'll find that food tastier than your fingernails," Macgreevy interrupted my thoughts.

I removed the finger I'd been worrying from my mouth. "Andrew . . ." I began tentatively, "Andrew, have you ever betrayed a source?"

"That's a damned rude question!"

"Well, have you? Have you ever said you wouldn't

reveal the source of some information and then gone ahead and done it anyway, for one reason or another?"

Macgreevy regarded me stonily. "No," he said defensively, downing his fork and folding his arms over his chest. "I bloody well have *not.*"

It was something, I guess, that his eyes remained on mine the whole time and didn't slide off in another direction. Or was body language really just a load of old cobblers, and Macgreevy an adept at the art of fabricating sincerity?

Oh, God, what to do? Was that sulphur I smelled in the air, or had some waiter just fetched in an egg dish?

"What is this, Jane, a quiz about journalistic ethics?" What *would* he look like with a villain's mustache?

"I think there's something I can do for you, Andrew."

"Oh, yeah?"

"But there's something you'd have to do for me."

"Oh, yeah?" he repeated, even more skeptically.

"Look, Andrew, you're not in Windsor for your health. You're up to something. And if it's what I think it is—despite your earlier denials—then I think I can help you. But you'd have to make me a solemn promise."

"A little *quid pro quo*, is it? Well, I can't say I'm not intrigued at this little turn of affairs. Something *you* can do for *me*? I'm not sure about making promises, though."

"You'd have to."

"Scout's honour?"

"Scout's honour."

"I was never a scout. Bunch of little Nazis as far as I'm concerned."

"I thought you worked for a right-wing newspaper."

"It's a pose, love. Pulls in the punters."

"The Bible, then. You'd have to swear on the Bible."

"I'm an agnostic. If that."

"Fine, then, Andrew. I'm not telling you anything. You can get stuffed."

Macgreevy didn't rejoinder. We ate in silence.

"All right, then," he finally said in a pissed-off tone. "What is it?"

"Oh, waiter!" I raised my hand but a fraction. There was an ahem, and the waiter beamed down à la Star Trek. "Waiter, I'd like a Bible."

He blinked rapidly. Probably trying to recall the item from the menu. "I don't think—"

"You've got a number of guest bedrooms here, don't you? Well, I'll bet the Gideons have been around."

The waiter turned helplessly to Macgreevy.

"Get the lady a Bible," Macgreevy growled.

The service at the Riverview truly is superb. Moments later Macgreevy's paw was pressing the purple cover of a Revised Standard Edition. "This is ridiculous," he muttered.

"Promise me . . . Andrew, pay attention! Promise me you will not name me as a source or in any way involve my name in anything you report or write based on what I'm about to tell you. Nor will you embarrass Her Majesty the Queen, her heirs and successors, or members of the Royal Household, including—"

"Steady on! You're trying to do me out of work. What's the Queen got to do with any of this?"

"Nothing, actually," I lied glibly. "Sorry, I got carried away with the oath thing. I just don't want you to involve me. Okay?"

Macgreevy pulled a face. "Yeah . . . all right," he said grudgingly.

"Swear!"

"For Christ's sake. All right, I swear I will not name you and so on and so on." He lifted his hand gingerly from the book. "This had better be good."

"Well, it's not bad." I paused and took a bite of the salad the waiter had brought with the Bible. "Victor Fabiani, you may be interested to know, did not murder Roger Pettibon."

"Oh, yeah?" Macgreevy allowed. "Says who?"

"Says me. During part of the time Fabiani was supposed to have killed Pettibon, I was with him. Fabiani, that is."

Macgreevy leered at me across the table. "I've heard about sex romps at the Palace. Bloody hell, I've *written* about sex romps at the Palace!"

"Oh, get your mind out of the gutter. I was *posing* for Fabiani."

Macgreevy made a salacious noise. "Sounds a bit of all right."

I sighed. "I was posing in the Garter robes. I was working in the bedrooms on the north side of the Upper Ward where Fabiani's temporary studio happens to be, and he pressed me into service. Sort of hauled me in. He's hard to say no to. Something to do with getting the folds of the robe right in his painting, and anyway I'm the same height as Her Majesty, so he thought I'd do."

"You haven't got Her Majesty's heavy bosom, though."

"Eyes up, Macgreevy. So, anyway, I was with Fabiani a good bit of the time. There was little opportunity for him to go downstairs into the Throne Room, plunge a sword into someone, then face me a few minutes later like nothing had happened. *And,* if he did forge Old Master drawings, he'd have to be an ambidextrous genius to fake the Leonardos convincingly. His confession's baloney."

Andrew pushed a piece of lettuce around his plate with his fork. "The police seem to have taken a different view."

"Bird in the hand . . ." I shrugged.

"Then who . . . ?"

"Well, the Queen . . . I mean, *I* think Fabiani must have confessed to protect someone."

"Who?"

"Cherchez la femme, Andrew."

"You want me to find some *woman?"*

"You're good at it. You've just said. Look." I dropped my voice and leaned over the plate. "Fabiani has a daughter, a woman about my age, who he didn't know existed until fairly recently. He had some affair when he was really young and the baby went up for adoption. I guess he never even knew the woman was pregnant. Anyway, his daughter's come into his life and I understand he's quite devoted to her. Not only that, but this woman—her name's Miranda Walter—works at the Castle. Artistic, sort of—like her father. She's a plaster restorer, working on the fire damage in the State Rooms."

"And this woman's going to let her father take the rap?"

"That's what I've been trying to tell you: Miranda's disappeared. She has a flat in Windsor, and she left in her car late Monday morning with luggage. *And* she was seen at the Castle earlier that morning, around the time of the murder."

"What are you having for pudding?"

"Oh, um . . ." I glanced hastily at the menu. "Pistachio *crème brûlée*," I told the hovering waiter.

"I'll have this *île flottante* thing," Macgreevy added, flattening the French with a steamroller accent. "And coffee. And would you care for a brandy, Jane?"

"No, thanks."

"And, please, take this thing away." He regarded the Bible with distate. "Why," he continued casually, when the waiter had vanished, "are you doing this?"

"I'm a gift horse. Look, if you find Miranda Walter, you get a scoop. Your editors will love you—you'll be back in their good graces."

"And what do you get out of it?"

"Truth, justice, and, you know, all that good stuff." Disbelief registered on Macgreevy's lips. "Okay, the real truth is, I'm super browned-off that nobody's interested in my theory."

(Well, almost nobody.)

"I don't want a man to go to jail for something he didn't do, especially when I can prevent it. And . . . well, the Queen would probably like her portrait finished, too. I mean, for all I know."

The waiter—ahem—and the sweet materialized.

"What makes you think I'm interested in this at all?" Macgreevy contemplated the confection on his plate nonchalantly. "I'm on suspension, remember?"

"And spending it in Windsor. Oh, Andrew, spare me. You're interested all right. I can see it in your beady little eyes."

Macgreevy scowled. His beady little eyes narrowed. "You could be dead wrong about this Miranda Walter."

"Don't you think a parent would do something drastic for a child?"

"Then what would be *her* motive for stabbing this Pettibon character?"

"Find her, and we'll all find out."

Macgreevy fell silent. He appeared to be weighing something in his mind, what I didn't know. I actually thought he'd leap on my information like a drowning man on a life raft.

"Okay," he said finally, lifting his spoon. "I'm at a bit of a loose end anyway. I'll see what I can do. What can you tell me?"

"Well, not much, really. Miranda Walter lives at St. Margaret Place. She works for an architectural restoration firm called Turner's in Slough. Let's see . . . she drives one of those 2CV's, cream and red."

"I suppose you don't have a license number? Well, I've useful contacts at the vehicle licensing centre in Swansea. Anything else?"

"She might have fled the country, you know."

"Airline passenger lists, credit card purchases, passport control—all is within my grasp," he said smugly.

"You are truly Satan's spawn."

"A man's gotta do . . . etcetera, etcetera."

"One of Miranda's neighbours suggested something about a retreat in the West Country. Said Miranda was a witch."

"A what?"

"A witch. With a double-u. I'm not quite sure what the neighbour was getting at. He was a bit of a nut. But since I don't believe in witches, my guess would be that Miranda might have an association with some sort of feminist community. Goddess worshippers perhaps?"

"Sounds barmy." Macgreevy shrugged. "And I suppose you want me to keep you informed of my progress—"

"Yup, and otherwise keep me out of it."

"I don't know why you're so set on anonymity. ROYAL HOUSEMAID FINGERS KILLER! sounds good to me."

"Sshhh!" I glanced at the nearby tables. "Jobs don't grow on trees in this world, Andrew. I'd like to keep mine for the time being, thank you very much. Bad enough Bremner saw me dining with you."

"I'm not religious, you know. Bible's a fairy story far as I'm concerned."

"You swore!" I could smell sulphur again. "Is there no

honour among you information thieves? Couldn't you try behaving like a gentleman?"

"Piss on that. I'll tell you what: I'll do your bidding, I'll keep your secret, and I'll do it—" He smiled across the table at me supersmarmingly, "—for you, my love."

I shuddered.

15

AND WHAT IS so rare as a day in June?

Lots of things, really, if you think about it. But a day in June at Royal Ascot is pretty extraordinary. Imagine—oh, go on, try!—a sort of enormous but *evah*-so-jolly mob scene, sixty thousand swells aswarm over lush green new-mown lawn, all peacocked up in silk and muslin and taffeta (if you're a woman) and the *de rigueur* gray morning suits and toppers (if you're a man) like expectant guests at the world's largest outdoor society wedding, with blazing flower displays and merry brass bands and flowing champagne and scrumptious strawberries and cream and horses thundering down turf and hats, endless hats, fabulous frothy confections shielding delicate English complexions from the sun of flaming June. Oh, 'tis an intoxicating sight.

I was a little intoxicated myself as I led the way, macheteing through the crowds along the railings near the summer paddock with my dependably sharp elbows for a chance of seeing the Royal Procession drive past in open horse-drawn carriages. A bunch of us plebs had come the seven miles from Windsor in a hired minibus and had a car boot picnic in the parking lot before crossing over to the racecourse proper. Drink and the midday sun conspired to make my brain come over all fizzy, but then I was feeling somewhat effervescent in any case. My quickie London jaunt with Aunt Grace the day before had advanced me along the paths of righteousness, for Victor Fabiani's sake, amen. The promise—melt! melt!—of a further rendezvous with the dishy dashing Jamie Allan was in the offing (the, ahem, dissembling about my residency and occupation problem I dismissed, for after all, tomorrow, as Miss Scarlett would say, *is* another day).

"Jane! Look at *that* hat!" Heather's urgent whisper, fell in my ear.

"Where?"

"Over there. By all those cameras."

A balcony at the side of the Members' enclosure groaned with the weight of what seemed a thousand telescope lenses and the snapping dogs training them at us, a frightening sight, really: the cameras looked like clusters of small weapons and the camera jockeys all too eager for combat. Below, women keenest to appear next day in the newspapers paraded about like a bunch of Soho tarts, pretending to be utterly oblivious to the clicking and whirring and catcalls of "This way, darlin'." The woman who had caught Heather's eye had perched on the side of her head a jinormous fabrication shaped like a frying pan, handle and resting spatula jutting into the air, cooking on the inside bacon, egg, fried bread, tomato, and mushrooms—the full English breakfast. You had to laugh.

Only I didn't. The cameras reminded me suddenly of, ugh, journalists. And the English breakfast recalled dinner with Macgreevy. This was the raincloud besmirching my sunny horizon, the fly dive-bombing my delicious soup (other than the question of who that woman was with Jamie). I'd tossed a bit in bed last night before falling asleep, and it wasn't because of all the nosh sloshing around in my stomach. Was I a complete puddinghead for putting any trust in the tabloid terrier? Or was I just a puddinghead without the chocolate sauce? Macgreevy made it seem like *he* was doing *me* a favour, the silly sod. And I wasn't happy about his proffered reason: *'For you, my love.'* Yech! The dinner at the Riverside cost a bomb and, of course, when he drove me back to the Castle (I insisted he park well up the Datchet Road past the gate) somehow his left arm found its way past my headrest and then made a sharp right downward.

"This isn't feels on wheels, Macgreevy," I reminded him.

"Can't blame a bloke for trying, especially after a slap-up meal like that. Don't I warrant a kiss? What are you fussing with your handbag for? What is that thing?"

"It's a personal alarm. Care to pull the pin?"

"The sound of the next plane into Heathrow will drown that little thing."

"Wanna bet?"

He failed to take up the challenge. Graced me with an alligator smile instead. Macgreevy made a screeching U-turn in the middle of the road and sped back to the Castle (the hotel) while I walked to the Castle (the medieval fortress and royal palace) wondering, speaking of betting, if I had played my cards right.

Sometime before two o'clock each afternoon of Ascot week, the Queen, members of the Royal Family, and a few extremely important guests speed away from the Sovereign's Entrance at Windsor Castle south into leafy Windsor Great Park in an assortment of hired Rollers or Daimlers. At a certain point in the Park, before a cheerful holiday crowd, HM, TRH's, and the VIP's do the changeover: they exit the cars and mount open carriages for the processional ride down the rest of the Park, west toward Ascot, through the Golden Gates and into the racecourse. They are scheduled to glide into view at Ascot at precisely two o'clock, and at precisely two o'clock they did, for from the stands we could hear this sudden rustling as if a wind has risen in the plane trees. It was the sound of thousands of subjects greeting their Sovereign.

"Ooh, here they come!" Heather gushed, as the champagne atmosphere around us bubbled even more.

"Mmm," I responded vaguely, for I knew it would take another five minutes before we'd glimpse them. On the other side of the railings I'd espied Chief Inspector George Nightingale, eminently mistakable in gray morning suit but quite *un*mistakable for the lined face under the gray top hat. Finery hired from Moss Bros., or did he really own his own rig? Was this the Ascot version of plainclothes duty? Or was he just one of the punters? The woman next to him, as tall as he, wearing a wide-brimmed bonnet swathed in white feathers, was impatiently fussing with the drooping red carnation in the left buttonhole of his jacket. Mrs. Chief Inspector, I presumed. One of the larger hens in the barnyard.

Nightingale didn't see me. My own wide-brimmed number ably shaded my face, but I intended to keep my eye on him. I had a few things I wished to say to the inspector, and thanked the lords of fluke for the circumstances. He couldn't very well kick me out of Ascot racecourse. I had my Staff voucher for the Royal Enclosure. I had a right to be here.

The crowd pressed forward in anticipation, too soon. From the direction of the cheering, one could tell the procession was still a-trot along the racetrack itself.

"Did I tell you you look brilliant in that outfit?" I commented to Heather. She wore a high-waisted white ankle-length dress with pink polka-dots, the wide ribbon around her straw hat of the same material.

"You said back at the Castle," Heather replied impatiently, craning her head. "When I asked you where you'd been last night."

"Are you going to put any money on anything, do you think?" I segued artlessly.

"I'm not going to the betting shop, if that's what you mean."

"Oh, Heather, don't be so wet."

"You do it, then."

"But there's somebody I want to talk to."

"Then get one of the boys to go. Placing bets is *their* job. I'm not going to be the only girl in the queue."

"Look." I took a five-pound note from my purse. "You

give this to one of those guys and tell him to put it on Beatitude to win." I'd seen the name on my race card and savored the entendre. Lousy odds, but I felt lucky.

Wordlessly, Heather took the fiver from me. The Royal party had made the turn behind the racing buildings and was heading into the summer paddock in our direction, two pairs of beautiful gray horses clearly visible pulling the first carriage. Through the haze of heat I could glimpse Davey with another footman perched high atop a seat behind the Queen and the Duke of Edinburgh, their scarlet tailcoats blazing in the sunshine. And lower, another beacon, a white gloved hand raised, palm outward, Her Majesty's, saluting her subjects. As the carriage drew ever closer, the applause grew louder, a few of the more decorous ladies in front bobbed, and the face on a million ten-pound notes emerged, formed and sharpened, the animated smile under the broad brim of the blue-bordered white hat familiar and reassuring as she turned her head gently from side to side, as she had done countless times in her long life, as she must, God knows, sometimes do in her sleep. Her Majesty's glance turned our way as her carriage passed and I fancied her smile fell a little but then it was all over so quickly—the other coaches in the splendid cavalcade breezed by, with the Queen Mother and Princess Anne in one, with Prince Charles and Prince Michael of Kent in another, with more royals and demiroyals in the others. The crush of people had begun to get a little unnerving, my champagne buzz had dulled a notch, and so it was a certain relief I felt when the crowds began to disperse. Heather, timid cow, went in search of some male Staff member who would do the gentlemanly thing and enter the—ooh!—spooky forbidding masculine preserve of the betting shop. And I kept my eye on the chief inspector, who was studying his racing card while his wife gave another woman an air kiss (the only type possible with massive millinery) and fell into conversation.

Opportunity knocked.

"Good afternoon, Chief Inspector," I said brightly, sidling up to him.

He frowned over his racing card. "Good afternoon, Miss Bee," he responded evenly. "I wouldn't have expected to see you here."

"Well, Staff get tickets and can choose a day. Ladies' Day is the most fun, so . . ." I shrugged. "Are you here on business or pleasure?"

"Mrs. Nightingale finds the event congenial."

"Does that mean you don't?"

"It has its moments."

"I see." I didn't see. "Chief Inspector," I continued, emboldened still from the champers, feeling a bit saucy, "did you know that Leonardo da Vinci was left-handed, and that his drawings indicate as much?"

"I do."

I started. "You do?"

"I seem to be getting an education in the finer arts these days."

"Really? So then you must see that it would be very hard for Victor Fabiani, as a *right*-handed person, to—"

The inspector cut me off. "Miss Bee, I'm not discussing any of this inquiry with you. I thought I made that quite clear in my office on Tuesday. And it is, besides, my day off."

"If I were a police detective I'd be interested in what anybody had to say!"

"Anything *relevant,* Miss Bee. You've already given me your views on Mr. Fabiani's movements, or—in your view—lack thereof. I'm not sure if your being a housemaid qualifies you as an expert in fine art."

"George?" Mrs. Nightingale turned from her companion and gave her husband, whose voice had begun to rise, a sharp glance.

"I'm having a conversation, Maureen!" he snapped at her. Maureen shot him a venomous look and turned back.

"Well, then," I persisted, feeling a little heated for reasons other than climatic, "there's something else I know that I'll bet you don't know, Chief Inspector. Something I was going to tell you on Tuesday before you had me dismissed from your office."

Nightingale tapped his race card impatiently against his trouser leg.

"Victor Fabiani has a daughter. She *lives* in Windsor. She *works* at the Castle. And she was *in* the Upper Ward Monday morning. Miranda Walter's her name. She was born out of wedlock and put up for adoption. Fabiani didn't even know she existed until recently. Did *you* know Fabiani had a daughter, Chief Inspector?"

He glared at me. I could see his jaw muscles working marvelously.

"No."

A flush had begun to gather above Nightingale's collar. Of course, the temperature was climbing; it was not weather for suit coat *and* waistcoat *and* strangulating tie, but I suspected the first two syllables of temperature were rising, too—in his case, perhaps both our cases.

"Because she wouldn't have shown up in any of your background checks, that's why," I continued. "And Fabiani wouldn't mention her. He's probably trying to protect her. That's what the Quee—er, I mean, that's my guess, anyway."

"And how do you know about this alleged daughter?"

"Gosh, I'm sure I must have mentioned posing for Mr. Fabiani during the critical time of Roger Pettibon's death. Didn't I?"

Nightingale's flush ascended his fleshy face like mercury in a thermometer.

Regretting my sarcasm, I hurried on: "Anyway, as he painted, we talked. Fabiani told me. I guess because I reminded him of Miranda. Same age, same colouring."

Not quite true. Talk of daughters was during the sitting at the Easter Court. A mere detail.

Nightingale was silent. Then he responded with a bark: "Who else knows this?"

"Well, I do, for one." (I didn't dare mention Mac-greevy.) "Then there's Her Maj—her neighbours, I mean. One of them, anyway. Some people at the Castle, probably. I don't really know who knows. Miranda, I understand, likes to keep to herself."

Nightingale pretended to examine his racing card. "Interesting, I suppose. I'm not sure this information's terribly pertinent."

"What! You're dismissing this, too?"

"I'm dismissing nothing, Miss Bee. But I will not have my business directed by some chit of a girl. If *I* think there's some reason to talk to this young woman, I will do so."

"Well, good luck, Chief Inspector," I responded, gathering my dress with one hand. It was full-length, A-line, navy with a discreet pattern of pink flowers, fairly fetching, I've been told, but also perfect for a bit of drama. I turned, walked a step, and called over my shoulder, irritated, wanting to provoke, the perfect opportunity for a flounce. "And I mean good luck. You see: Miranda Walter has disappeared."

"Who are you, love?" Someone from the photographer's balcony shouted at me as my silver sandals quickly carried me away from the chief inspector and into camera range.

"Nobody!"

Unblinking eyes sought other prey.

Beatitude came in dead last in the two-thirty Ribblesdale Stakes. I heard it announced. Farewell, five quid. The French fancy horseflesh, in the gustatory sense, I'm told. And I'm sure there's a glue factory somewhere in the west Midlands.

Peevish words and thoughts. But then Nightingale had left me feeling peevish. I quite like horses, otherwise. I went through the horse thing when I was about thirteen. Adored them. Then I discovered boys. Adored them. Then I discovered boys were more troublesome than horses.

Oh, the pigheadedness of the man!

Or was it simple defensiveness? Nightingale knew his case against old Fabbo was lame as . . . as a horse that came in dead last in the Ribblesdale Stakes. He had to.

Get me a drink, somebody. Somebody?

What a crush of people! A smashing, positively dashing spectacle, to be sure. But easy to lose someone therein. Where Heather disappeared to, I did not know, and eventually I gave up trying to find her. Besides, there were too many distracting American film stars and British pop stars loitering about among the less easily identifiable moneyed and titled. Clearly, everyone who should be here was here. Even some of those who shouldn't have been here were here. The vetting process doesn't completely eliminate assorted spivs, Eurotrash, and other riffraff. Or so some snobs have told me.

By the beginning of the second race, however, I'd found myself swept along, past the turnstiles, past the bowler-hatted stewards who scanned my Royal Enclosure badge, and onto the lawn of the Royal Enclosure itself. I thought about edging my way through the madding and slightly maddening crowd to the railings to watch the horses churn up the turf at close range, but felt my pointy elbows had already seen enough service for one week. I had no bet on a horse, anyway. I was no student of the sport, not like HM, for instance, who's been horse-mad since her nursery days when she put harnesses on her governess (source: Davey Pye), or others of the country set or wagering persuasion who were, by their shouts and intense scrutiny of their racing cards, taking this day very seriously indeed.

Off to my right, above the finishing post, rose the Royal Box, a bubble of glass swelling over a tiny, beautifully-tended private lawn. Because the day was so warm (indeed the sun, if you were standing in it, was starting to become quite penetrating), the glass curtain of the viewing area was opened to capture the occasional breeze. Clearly visible in the front row of wicker chairs was the dumpling figure of the Queen, talking and gesturing animatedly to an unidentifiable portly older gentleman. The races, I discovered during a previous Ascot week, seem to be the only time Her Majesty forgets for a moment or two in public that she's the Sovereign. Watching her in the throes of delight or disappointment is often more compelling than watching the horses—something other spectators have noted, too, for there were not a few pairs of racing glasses turned from the track toward the Royal Box.

The portly gentleman faded into shadows and the Queen raised her own racing glasses. Judging by angle and sweep, she seemed to be doing her own little surveillance of the throng in advance of the race. The lenses, two glinting black O's, lingered in my direction for a puzzling moment until I realized I was standing one step up from Dame Edna

Everage in a blazing frock and sequined spectacles. The famous scrutinizing the famous, I suppose.

Races are over so quickly. Such a terrific buildup, such anticipation, such electricity surging through the multitude as the announcer trumpets his horse-racey dispatches into the ether and the steeds burst through the starting gate. But in a twinkling, they've all roared past the post, and the delirious undifferentiated roar of the crowd splits in twain, into cheers and groans. I had nothing riding on the Norfolk Stakes, so I found myself in neither cheer nor groan camp, more the couldn't-care-less camp. Dame Edna was in the groan camp, poor love.

So, too, was Iain Scott, who I espied not far off scowling over his race card, his top hat pushed back off his forehead, a woman in a brilliant citrus yellow sleeveless frock tugging at his elbow and giggling like a demented schoolgirl.

"Oh, don't be a grumpy bear, Socky, darling," I heard her burble gaily as I approached. "It's only money."

"Hi, Iain," I said. "Remember me?"

He looked at me blankly. Then memory stirred a wariness in his eyes. "Yes, of course," he replied impatiently as the woman continued pulling at him. "How are you? Amanda, *stop it!*"

Amanda rolled her eyes dramatically. She was slim, with a perfect complexion and straight blond hair streaming to her shoulders from under a wide-brimmed hat. "He's such a *pooh* when his horse loses." Her ample mouth struggled to fashion a pout, but instead she snorted and burst into another gale of laughter. Iain looked to be grinding his teeth. "Amanda, this is Jane . . . ?"

"Bee."

"Jane, this is Amanda Simms. Jane works at the Castle . . . in some capacity or other."

"You're not related to Major Simms, one of the Military Knights, are you, by any chance?" I quickly asked Miranda.

"Mmm. My great-uncle. That's how Socky and I met," she added obscurely, curling her arm through his and shaking him a bit. "Didn't we, darling?" She began again to giggle as if overtaken by some private joke. Or by champagne and hot sun. Or both.

"How are you feeling?" I asked Iain, thinking of his drunken condition Monday evening at the Star Tavern. Though the bruise on his cheek had faded in the days since I'd seen him in the pub in strong light, and the cut on his chin was now not so fresh, they appeared raw, ugly, an unflattering contrast to his Moss Bros. finery.

"Oh, poor Socky-poo," Amanda answered instead, running a finger along his face. "Getting into fights. Protecting my honour."

He flinched, glaring at her. "That's *not* what the fight was about, Amanda." He spoke with exasperation, reddening slightly. "You weren't even there."

"No, I wasn't, was I. Poor me." She made giddy little kissing noises at his ear.

"You must be the one who picked Iain up at the hospital," I ventured, seizing the opportunity to check alibis.

"Eh? Oh?" She snorted again with laughter as if I'd said the funniest thing in the world. "Sorry. Yes, of course. Picked him up and we spent a lovely weekend together in London, didn't we, darling?"

"Amanda, would you stop being so ridiculous."

"Now, don't lecture me, Socky. Or I'll—"

"Stop it, Amanda. You've had far too much to drink."

"Ooh. There goes the pot calling the kettle black." She snorted again.

"Excuse us," Iain said grimly to me, pulling Amanda sharply away.

"Ooph," she cried, giggling, allowing herself to be dragged off into the swarming crowd. "Lovely to have met you, Jane."

What a silly cow, I thought. Wouldn't fancy a weekend with her.

I was wishing I'd thought to ask Jamie Allan the hair colour of the woman who'd fetched Iain at the hospital the night of the fight, and wondering if I ought to take up the search for Heather once again, when I felt a light tap on my shoulder. The tapper in question was Captain Pierson, the Queen's junior equerry, in service dress. I had noted him earlier threading his way around the Royal Enclosure, stopping and chatting now and again. Pierson's job, like that of some other members of the Royal Household, was to engage in a sort of reconnaissance of the Royal Enclosure, see who was hanging about, then report back to the Queen anyone she might know, with a view to inviting them to tea at the next day's race.

"You're Jane Bee," the captain said. It was more statement than question, and absolutely true: I was Jane Bee. "Her Majesty wonders if you would care to join her after the next race."

"Of course," I replied, somewhat startled. What was I going to do? *Refuse* Her Majesty's invitation? "In the Royal Box?" I queried.

"Yes," Pierson replied blandly. "If you go around to the back of the stand and give your name to the steward . . ."

"Thanks, I know where it is."

Tea, I knew from Davey, was routinely served after the fourth race. I was to appear at the Royal Box after the third. Clearly, I wasn't being invited to tea. But, then, what were the chances of that happening? Ha! I watched Pierson's back as he wandered back into the crowd. Then, a few minutes later, I observed the Queen's progress, as she emerged from the Royal Box, race card in one white-gloved hand, and made her way smilingly through crushing crowds of bobbing hats and polite applause to the paddock to inspect the horses, a favourite activity between races. Odd, I thought: the Queen wanting to see me, in the middle of Ladies' Day at Royal Ascot. But, then, she'd spent the morning taking her guests on horseback across Windsor Great Park to Ascot for a private race of their own. So if she'd had any significant gleanings she wanted to impart about you-know-what, there wouldn't have been much time.

About half an hour later, half an hour which I spent in the refreshment marquee enjoying strawberries and cream and watching with some alarm the antics of a certain tired and emotional member of Cabinet before his wife hauled him off to the tea tent, I made my way to the entrance to the

Royal Box, up the sweeping staircase past framed cartoons of ancient Ascot toffs, to the first-floor tearoom.

I was feeling somewhat less than collected. The certain t. and e. member of Cabinet had somehow managed to let fly a very squishy strawberry that landed *sploot!* on the front of my dress. Very annoyed, I'd rushed to the ladies' loo to rub at the stain, and then, pricking my ears to the trumpeted end of the Gold Cup race, raced my own self through the throngs, slicing through air verging on the Turkish bath side of humid. A damp and dishevelled me prepared to present herself to Her Majesty the Queen. Only the Queen wasn't about. To the front of the Royal Box was what looked and sounded like a largish cocktail party in progress with footmen weaving in and around the chattering guests with trays of Pimm's and champagne. At the back I could see Davey in his scarlet livery, standing alone by one of several round tables, fussing with the silver centrepiece.

"Oh, hullo, Jane," he said, looking up. "What brings you here?"

"Guess."

"Ooh, there must be developments, then. Do tell."

I shrugged, glancing at the baskets of flowers, the white-and-gold Minton china tea service, and the gilt chairs, all hauled from Windsor Castle earlier in the week.

"Not much to tell, really. Other than to say Fabiani is looking more innocent by the minute, so there! And what are you doing? I thought it was carriage duty for you."

"I'm doing double duty, is what I'm doing. We're short. Nigel won't get out of bed."

"Ill?"

"No, dear, he's sulking. Ever since he got a wigging for his little indiscretion. Have you been drooling on your dress?"

"It was . . ." I named my strawberry assailant. "He was drunk as a lord and flinging food about."

"Not again! Perhaps the prime minister will kick him upstairs before the next election. Then he can *be* a lord, drink as much as he likes, and no one will give a toss."

"Won't prevent him coming to Ascot, though, will it?"

"Wear a bib in his vicinity next time." Davey unconsciously adjusted his white tie, lowering his voice suddenly to a whisper. "Mother's coming."

I turned as the Queen stepped in unaccompanied and surveyed the room briefly. She was wearing a dress of cobalt blue with a windowpane pattern of stylized white ribbons and bows. A glittering diamond brooch shaped in a bow complemented the outfit, about in the same spot—above the left breast—as my strawberry stain. I curtsied.

"David," Her Majesty said quietly, "would you leave us for a few moments."

Davey bowed from the neck. "Yes, Ma'am."

There was a rather odd expression on the Queen's face: like someone who'd passed through an airlock from one atmosphere to another. From delight in all things horsy to, well, something less delightful.

"Did you enjoy your dinner last evening at the Riverview Inn, Jane?"

Bremner! Oh, that a trapdoor might send me hurtling to the boiling centre of the earth.

"Yes, Your Majesty," I replied unhappily, mustering my courage, "the food was brilliant."

"Yes, it is quite good, isn't it? The chef there once prepared a birthday dinner for me." The Queen's lips thinned. Clearly she hadn't called this meeting to debate the merits of the foie gras. "And the company?" she added. "Did you have a pleasant time?"

"Oh, Ma'am . . ." I felt all feeble and squashy, like a five-year-old caught pinching coins from the Sunday offering. "I'm so sorry . . ."

"I must say, Jane, I was rather disappointed to learn you had been dining with that reporter from the *Gazette*." The Queen removed her white handbag from the crook of her arm and placed it on the chair nearest her. "But I felt sure you must have had a good reason."

"Ma'am, I ran into Mr. Macgreevy by chance on Peascod Street when I was on my way to see the police. His invitation sort of caught me off guard. I said yes in a weak moment—mostly because the food at the Riverview always sounds so wonderful—but only on the condition he not pester me about . . . well, about anything. At least anything to do with life at the Palace." I smiled weakly. "And he didn't. Actually."

"Are you sure? Pestering members of one's staff—and one's family—seems to me to be a condition of Mr. Macgreevy's employment."

"He was sort of subdued, in a way. Not quite his usual self. You see, Ma'am, he's been suspended from the *Gazette*. Punishment for getting the wrong end of the stick on a story about a Roman Catholic bishop and a supposed love nest in Cornwall."

"Yes. That poor man. I saw the article. Most disagreeable. But, Jane, why would Mr. Macgreevy be in Windsor this week? He surely doesn't live here?"

"Well . . ." I could feel myself hovering over the slippery slope. "I'm not really sure, Ma'am. He didn't say. Or wouldn't say. But I don't think it has anything to do with . . . *us,* broadly speaking—the Palace and such."

But as I spoke, the vision of Macgreevy trotting down the Lower Ward late Tuesday afternoon with a Windsor Castle souvenir shop carrier bag snapped in my brain like a playing card turned on a table. Had he really been a tourist? My uncertainty was clearly not satisfying, for the Queen pressed on:

"There was a photograph of one's unfinished portrait in the Gazette yesterday. It seems rather more than a coincidence that Mr. Macgreevy was in Windsor at the same time."

Had there been a camera in that carrier bag? I thought with dismay. Still, there would have had to have been someone on the inside, speaking spyishly, to grant him access.

"I asked him about that, Ma'am," I said instead. "He was adamant he had nothing to do with it."

"And you believe him."

"Yes." It was a sort of rickety yes. More of a "yes?" But Her Majesty appeared reasonably satisfied. A thaw touched her wintry expression.

"Well, then . . ." she murmured, glancing at her handbag. The fourth race was nigh and her racing card was within, probably.

"But, um, Ma'am, there is something else." I took a deep breath. As I've said before, it's far better to tell HM unwelcome news than have her find out later from someone else and be cross. Having the Monarch cheesed off with you is not an edifying experience. "I may have done something foolish."

The Queen's eyes caught mine sharply.

"I sort of made a deal with Mr. Macgreevy."

"You young people are awfully fond of this 'sort of' expression."

"Er, yes, Ma'am." I took note of her renewed frown and barrelled on, my heart in my hand. "I told him Your Majesty's idea about Miranda Walter, being Mr. Fabiani's daughter and that perhaps—"

"What!"

"I mean, I didn't mention Your Majesty, Your Majesty. That is, I mentioned the idea. I didn't give the source. I just sort of—sorry, I mean I more or less presented it as my own idea. You see," I gabbled on recklessly, "I thought Mr. Macgreevy might be able to find her—Miranda, that is—since she seems to have vanished. I know he made a hash of that bishop story, but he was really good at tracking him down. And he's a journalist, and they have their ways and such. And so I thought, since he had time on his hands with this suspension, he might be able to track *her* down. I told him I was sure Mr. Fabiani couldn't be a murderer, and why, and oh, God . . ."

The Queen was silent as I abruptly ran out of petrol.

"I see," was all she said. HM's not the sort of person to explode into anger, although I did once witness a brief episode of major pique in the Throne Room at Buckingham Palace during the resolution to a sad death there. So I wasn't quite sure how she was taking all this. She didn't seem *too* cross, at any rate.

". . . and so," I continued, seizing my courage, "I thought this way there's a chance we might get closer to the truth about Mr. Pettibon's death."

"But, Jane, you said you'd struck a bargain with Mr. Macgreevy. What satisfaction is he to get from doing your bidding?"

"A story, for one, Ma'am. He's got a jump on his colleagues with this new information. And if it proves valuable I'm sure his employer will reconsider his suspension."

"I'm not sure I care to see one of my Staff aiding and abetting that publication."

"I think the end will justify the means, Ma'am." I hope. "Oh! And part of the deal is that he not, under any circumstances, name me as source or involve me in print. I made him swear on a Bible."

Her Majesty's eyebrows rose a notch. "As I recall," she said drily, "Mr. Macgreevy was more than a nuisance to you after the unhappy event at Sandringham the other Christmas. He was certain you were very much part of the resolution. And you were."

"But he couldn't prove it, Ma'am."

The Queen shook her head. "And you're quite sure, are you, that you trust him then not to feature you—and, I daresay, *one*—in his writings?"

Too late now, anyway.

"Yes, Ma'am," I replied, though I thought I could hear somewhere the echo of Marlon Brando, his mouth full of cotton wool, saying: *"Someday, and that day may never come, I'll call upon you to do a service for me. . . ."*

"You see, Ma'am, I think, well . . ." Davey's teasing came to mind. "I think Mr. Macgreevy sort of fancies me."

Sort of.

I'm sure I saw Her Majesty shudder. And it wasn't over the "sort of."

"Tch! You look shattered," Davey said to me. The fourth race had been called and the Queen fetched. Her figure was just visible against the front glass of the Royal Box, racing glasses poised. She had reentered that other, equine, world.

She hadn't been best pleased with my judgment, I knew, but I think she accepted my reasoning. I just hoped—God, how I hoped—the outcome would not prove *horribilis*. However, our tearoom audience did at least end on a cheerier note: HM was greatly interested in the results of Wednesday's London excursion, which I quickly outlined for her. I, for my part, was delighted to learn that the Secretary of the Central Chancery of the Orders of Knighthood, more prosaically known as Sir Bernard Scrymgeour-Warburton, would be joining Her Majesty at the Castle Saturday afternoon "when Ascot's over and my guests have gone," as HM put it.

"He has some ideas about the ownership of the Garter that Mr. Pettibon was wearing," the Queen said.

"Brilliant, Ma'am. Did he sound excited?"

"Mr. Bremner spoke with him, I'm afraid."

"Oh."

"I say, are you well?" Davey examined me more closely. "Your brow wants mopping."

"I'm fine. Just relieved we no longer have absolute monarchy."

"Did you disappoint Mother, then?"

"Let's just say Her Majesty was concerned about something. I think it's okay now, though." I let out a gushy sigh. "What a good thing she hasn't an awful temper."

"Got an iron will, does Mother. Even when Fergie was sucking her financial advisor's toes and Di snuck off to do that Panorama interview, she maintained her regal *sangfroid*. Though I must tell you, my dear, step on one of the corgi's tails and she can become *quite* vehement."

"Speaks an object of Her Majesty's vehemence?"

"Those dogs are scattered like bloody land mines sometimes! Many a tea tray has been overturned."

"Poor you. By the way, the mystery of the extra Garter may be solved."

"The one Roger Pettibon was wearing? Do tell. Does it belong to the FitzJameses?"

"I don't know. Won't find out until Saturday. Why the FitzJameses?"

"Well, the Dukes of Cheshire have Stuart blood—on the wrong side of the blanket, don't you know. Hence the 'fitz' bit. And FitzJameses have served the Crown in various capacities for centuries. Some of them have probably been Knights of the Garter. So I thought the FitzJames family was the most likely source . . . of this wayward Garter, I mean."

"Oh." Fascinating. "So you're suggesting one of the FitzJameses might have tied the Garter around Roger's leg? The Duke? Hugo?"

"Haven't a clue, Jane, dear. You're the one for these little puzzles."

"As a message, perhaps," I mused. *"Honi soit qui mal y pense.* Shame on him who thinks this evil."

Davey shrugged. The sound of the fourth race beginning was a muffled noise in the background.

"Sort of sticks in the mind after a while, doesn't it: *Honi soit qui mal y pense,*" I sang tentatively. The Ascot milieu had awakened a buried tune from childhood piano lessons.

" 'Doo-dah, doo-dah,' " Davey chimed in immediately.

"Honi soit qui mal y pense."

" 'Oh, doo-dah-day.' "

" 'Goin' to run all night,' " we chorused as the sound of the announcer over the thunder of the horses on the turf rose to an excited crescendo. " 'Goin' to run all day. I'll bet my money on the bobtail nag. Somebody bet on the bay.' "

"Olé! Hey!" I whooped as the clamour fell to diminuendo. Heads turned in our direction reprovingly.

"Davey, do you think somebody would kill somebody to settle a gambling debt?"

"I think, Jane, dear, they're going to be galloping in for tea in about two ticks."

16

DOWN THE WINDING staircase of the Royal Box I tripped.
Up the winding staircase past me hurtled Prince William and a tribe of other boys from Eton College, their black tailcoats fluttering behind them, on their way, undoubtedly, to the special tea party the Queen Mother likes to give at Royal Ascot. Among them: Hugo FitzJames, Lord Lambourn. I'd like to talk to you, matey, I thought, clinging to both balustrade and hat lest the boys' jostling pitch me or headgear to the floor below. Hugo glimpsed me through his floppy bangs as he shot past. Recognition flashed for a moment in his dark eyes; his careless smile faded a touch. But he tore up the steps behind the others before I could even open my mouth.
Oh, well, I couldn't very well make him late for tea

with the Queen Mother, even if punctuality is not Her Majesty's long suit.

Another day, perhaps.

Outdoors, after the relative cool of the Royal Box, the air seemed thick and muzzy, like a damp towel swatting your face. I hesitated to move beyond the shade of the Box's porte-cochère and onto the sun-bleached pavement back of the stands, putting my hand instead to one of the porch's deep thick columns. Chill to the touch, the stone felt delicious, lovely, and I leaned my whole bare arm onto it as I observed the gilded in morning suits and pastel frocks across the way crowd the enclosure restaurants for *their* tea. Ought I to venture out on another search for Heather? Back to the refreshment marquee, perhaps? Tea? Glass of Pimm's? Strawberry toss? I fingered the stain on my dress.

More than a nice little drink, I needed a nice little think. A number of notions had presented themselves for consideration in the past twenty-four hours: Among them, the greater likelihood of the extra Garter belonging to the noble FitzJames family than to some average joe. But thinking along these lines required peace and quiet. And p & q is at a premium, don't you know, in a crowd of seventy thousand people.

A low conversation had been in progress the other side of the column while my brain had been semiengaged, and I paid it scant attention until I suddenly heard a clipped accent voice the name *St. John*. Canon Leathley's Christian name, I mused; pronounced *Sinjin*, it's more often a surname, and not that common a one, either.

But then I realized St. John Leathley *was* the person under discussion.

". . . and my nephew has been receiving communications for *years* from Rupert!" The hushed tones couldn't disguise the exasperation.

Rupert. The name of Hugo's father, the Marquess of Graven, who'd fled England nearly a decade ago in the wake of his wife's suspicious death. How curious! Quickly, I removed my hat so the brim wouldn't flag my presence, and stole a quick peek around the edge of the post. Yes, indeed, it was the Duke of Cheshire. Hugo's grandfather was stand-ing, facing in my direction, in the shadow of the next col-umn with another man (both in gray morning suits, of course), his bulldog features partially blocked by the other man's shoulder.

"He was somewhere in South America for a time," the Duke continued in low tones. "Brazil—and then I gather from St. John someone spotted him eventually and so he fled to Thailand, of all places. A year or two ago. I should think the boy will be that much easier to identify among all those slitty-eyed devils, particularly as he's living in some ghastly little village in the hills—Pa Ki, I think St. John said. Odd name. Or was it Pa Ka? And whatever has Rupert been doing for money . . . what?"

The other man's response was inaudible.

"Oh, is it? A drugs haven, dear God. St. John didn't mention that. Rupert has a wretched drugs problem, as you know. I'd always hoped that wherever he went he would have sought help. I couldn't give it to the boy . . . I don't know why we never got on—"

Mumble mumble.

"I don't know what I'm going to do. I've always felt Rupert must come back and face his responsibilities—"

Mumble mumble mumble.

"Yes, but, you see, I never knew where he was. I was sure he was alive, of course. I never believed the suicide rumours for an instant. In fact, I suspected for a long time that St. John helped him escape from England. He and Ru-pert were very close as children, you know, particularly after my poor sister and her husband were killed. And close as young men, too. How differently they turned out—"

Mumble rumble.

"Well, that's just it. I *do* know now, don't I? I don't know Rupert's address precisely, but St. John knows where the boy is, or how to find him. He's always known, appar-ently. Kept it from me. At Rupert's insistence, of course. The police made a nuisance of themselves in the first year or two of Rupert's disappearance. Can't blame them, of course. But I told them Rupert had not spoken to me since that day in court when I took custody of Hugo. He was hardly likely to communicate with me from abroad and . . . yes?"

Rumble mumble.

"But, Dicky, do I inform on my son? There must be some justice for Hugo's mother, of course, but—"

Mumble rumble mumble.

"Well, St. John suddenly thinks it's time. He dropped all this information on me last evening at the Castle. I've been a guest of Her Majesty, you see. I must say, I was more than a little surprised at the extent of my nephew's collusion with Rupert, St. John being a churchman as he is. But I suppose blood is thicker and all that—"

Further mumblings.

"He's changed his mind. I don't know why. St. John says he now feels Rupert must come home. You know, justice for Poppy, as I said. We agreed on that. And some proper rehabilitation, St. John says. I'm not persuaded. Rupert will go to prison, of course. I don't know if he did do that damned stupid thing, but if he isn't responsible for Poppy's death—and I pray he isn't—then he will surely be imprisoned for running off the way he did. He won't get the treatment he needs in jail—"

A longish mumble here.

"Yes, exactly, I was going to say. St. John takes the view that Hugo is mature enough to handle it. I disagree utterly. Hugo's much too young. He's at that stage, you know. Early adolescence. It's just the age when his father started to go off the rails. Rupert was the loveliest little boy and then . . . then his mother, my dear wife, died so suddenly, as you know. And things were never the same for Rupert. The trauma, I suppose. And I'm not having it with Hugo. I'm not. Hugo is my hope. He's done so well. But I worry. He's become a bit secretive of late, unreachable, distant. I can't really put my finger on it, but it reminds me dreadfully of Rupert at that age, after his mother died. Is it just normal teenage mood, I wonder. Or . . . ?"

More mumbling.

"Hugo had a little setback this spring when that girl drowned, a friend of his. And then—well, this wasn't in the papers—but it was Hugo who found the dead body in the Throne Room the other day."

Exclamation of dismay.

"The boy seems to have weathered it, but you never

know what they're feeling or thinking, at that age. So the last thing I want for Hugo now is to have his father back and the past dredged up and the newspapers printing all sorts of rubbish. Most of the other boys at Eton are too young to remember much of the original circumstances, but if there's renewed attention, well, you know what boys can be like at that age. I asked Hugo's housemaster to please make sure that dreadful book about Rupert not be among the boys' things. I even went to the used bookshops on Eton High Street the week before Hugo came to Eton and bought up every copy I could find. Burned them, too, I'm not sorry to say."

Mutter mutter.

"I don't know. What would you do, old man?"

Mutter mutter mutter.

"So nice to be able to talk to someone about this. Been preying on my mind all day. A horse of mine was in the second race and I didn't even—"

Further mutterings.

"Fourth. Quite disappointing. Are you taking tea today with the Queen? Oh, you are? Well, come along then. Where's your wife, by the way—"

And their voices were lost as the door opened and a steward ushered the pair into the Royal Box entrance. Slowly, I settled my hat back on my head and stepped into the sunshine. The heat hardly seemed a bother now.

A few hours later I found myself gazing westward from a window high atop Clarence Tower over the Quadrangle of the Upper Ward, toward the Round Tower and beyond, grateful for a little of the aforementioned and much needed p & q. Royal Ascot is undeniably a must-see, must-do event, but even the most splendiferous of treats can start to pall after a while, like too much ice cream when you're a kid. The sun was on its slow descent over Windsor, the towers and battlements of the castle falling into shadow, the ancient stone flickering into a warm and golden light as if illuminated by some inner source. Except for a single soldier on sentry duty, his boots pounding the stone as he made his regular pacing, no one was about. In the early evening calm, the fortification that William the Conquerer began seemed abandoned.

On the surface, it was odd that it should seem so. The Castle was vast; its population that of a medieval village. But it was also a place of clockwork rhythms: Guards changing, Dean and Canons praying, Staff and other Castle employees shuffling off to predictable duties, Her Majesty herself carrying out her responsibilities in a routine that changed little from one year to the next.

Right now, I knew, the Queen, members of her family, and guests were dressing for dinner. Staff in attendance were arranging the setting and readying themselves. Other Staff, me for one, had just finished their dinner and were giving in to the usual postprandial lethargy. Somewhere off in the Lower Ward, by habit, a lay clerk was taking the evening sun, a Military Knight was watering the plants in his little front garden. For all I knew the ghost of Herne the Hunter, Richard II's huntsman, was looking at his watch, waiting for sunset to start his regular haunting of Windsor Great Park.

Everything was as it should be on a summer's eve in Windsor Castle.

Had it been so on a summer's morn?

I looked to the north of the Round Tower past the corner of King John's tower toward the Norman Gate annex. Here, though hidden from my view, was Engine Court, the principal (though not only) entrance to the Royal Library and to the State Apartments for those who were employed there. Miranda Walter would most likely have come in that way Monday morning. So, too, would Joanna Pettibon. And Roger Pettibon.

To the south of the Round Tower, just barely visible, was St. George's Gate, an entrance to the Private Apartments used by Staff, Castle residents and, occasionally, royals, for day-to-day comings and goings. (HM and I had exited the Private Apartments for the Lower Ward that way when we paid our call on Joanna Pettibon.) This is the way Canon Leathley and Hugo FitzJames penetrated the rooms of the Upper Ward Monday morning.

Garter Day—Monday—was not a typical day for the Castle. Tourist visits were barred; the shops in the Lower,

Middle, and Upper Wards were shut; only those with tickets
were allowed into the Castle to view the Garter Procession.
But the Procession didn't begin until two o'clock; guests to
the Procession were granted egress through King Henry
VIII Gate only after twelve o'clock.

Before nine o'clock Monday morning, it would have
seemed just another typical summer's day during a working
week at the Castle. No one would have remarked at either
of the Pettibons walking through the Lower and Middle
Wards to their jobs in the Royal Library. Or at Canon
Leathley strolling beyond the confines of the St. George's
Chapel with his young cousin who, as the Queen's Page of
Honour, was not an unfamiliar sight. Most of the crew working on the fire-damaged parts of the Castle had leave for
Ascot week, but Miranda Walter showing up nonetheless
would have aroused little interest.

All had a right to be where they were. None were
where they couldn't or shouldn't have been. No one would
have found his or her presence suspect, coming *or* going.
And since the police seemed to have found their culprit with
such ease, no one at either entrance to the Upper Ward, I
suspected, had been anything more than superficially inter-
viewed, and only then in the hours before the Garter Procession, before Victor Fabiani had made his way to Alma Road,
to the police station and his confession.

What a bore. Opportunity galore. Means at hand. But
what, pray tell, was the bleedin' motive? Of any of them?

I left my window view and went to my room on the
east side of Clarence Tower and flopped down on the bed.
The conversation I'd overheard between gossipy telephone-
telegraph-and-tell-Cheshire and the other gentleman had
been tossing around my brain box like an autumn leaf in a
wind. The Rev. Canon, it seemed, could certainly keep a
secret, no mean feat when compared to his uncle who was
prepared to discuss the whereabouts of his long-lost son with
a friend in the middle of Ascot racecourse. But wasn't
Leathley guilty of violating some Christian clerical norm by
withholding information on the whereabouts of a man
sought by police hunting the killer of his wife? A man who
may very well have done the deed himself? (After all, what
did fleeing the country suggest?)

Or was it all under some seal-of-the-confessional type thing?

What would I do, I mused, staring at the ceiling, if—let's say—my sister Julie, wife of potato farmer, killed (or allegedly killed) her husband and ran off somewhere remote, and only I knew her whereabouts? Would I turn her in? Or would I keep quiet?

Tough one. Taking the high road, I thought it would be difficult to deny the demand for an accounting before the law. On a (much) lower road, Julie and I had had more fights as kids than I care to remember, and turning her in would be the topper in the "Did not! Did, too!" match, ha!

Yet, I knew in my heart that I would protect her. If her wish was to hide from the law I would accede and hope that one day she would see sense.

I expected the same sensibilities governed the relationship between St. John Leathley and Rupert FitzJames. Though cousins, St. John and Rupert had grown up in the same household as brothers. They had remained close despite, apparently, wildly different styles of life. Leathley, it seemed, had spent the eight years since Rupert's flight diligently safeguarding the secret of his missing cousin's whereabouts. Suddenly he had changed his mind: Rupert must return to England and face the music. Why? Why *now*?

Under other circumstances, the intrigues of the FitzJames family would be to me little more than the stuff of Servants' Hall gossip. Except that southeast Asia had once again raised its dragon head in conversation. Leathley's parents had been killed somewhere in that area, I recalled Davey saying. Where? Borneo? Malaysia? New Guinea? Davey couldn't remember, or didn't know. And my awareness of that part of the world was nebulous indeed.

Hadn't Roger Pettibon stopped in that part of the world on his way back from curatorial trips to Australia? Was it Malaysia? Hadn't the Queen herself paid a state visit in recent times to Malaysia? Or was it Thailand? One of them was a Commonwealth country, I was sure, and HM's visit had been to a Commonwealth country there. But which one? Joanna had said Roger had been in Malaysia. Really, many people living in the northwest fringes of the planet don't know one part of southeast Asia from the next. I don't. Could Roger have been in Thailand instead?

Rupert FitzJames, Marquess of Graven, was living in Thailand.

Might Roger have run into him? And recognized him? Or was this stretching the bounds of coincidence beyond all recognition?

I imagined Roger Pettibon in conversation at some later date with Canon Leathley, perhaps during one of the counselling sessions after young Pippa's drowning: "Oh, by the way, I saw your cousin, Lord Graven, while I was in Thailand . . . ."

The Canon's reaction? Alarm, surely. But ever so smoothly disguised, I should think. Leathley would disabuse Pettibon of the notion. "I believe my cousin to be dead," he would say sadly. "But I'm quite sure, Canon, that I did see him," Roger would reply, adding uncertainly, "Ought I to go to the police, do you think?"

Or the press! *Quelle* scoop!

Canon Leathley would subtly dissuade. Pettibon would hesitate. A smile, a benediction, and the two men would part. Not an *urgent* problem, really; not on Pettibon's part. He had other, more tragic things to think about. But for Leathley? Roger Pettibon possessed information that would imperil his dear cousin Rupert's safety. Roger was the proverbial ticking time bomb. He had to be stopped! So, one fine Monday morning in June, the good Canon . . .

Oh, but I was letting my imagination run at a gallop.

If Leathley had killed Roger Pettibon to protect his cousin, why, only days later, would he be seeking Lord Cheshire's consent to expose Rupert to the full force of the law and the glare of publicity? This made no sense.

Unless . . . !

Footfalls scraped the steps outside my room.

. . . unless he suddenly needed to get shot of his motive!

"Some of us are going out." Heather's voice sailed across the room, pulling the curtain down over my little playlet. "Are you coming, Jane?"

"Where to?"

"One of the clubs. To celebrate. It's midsummer's eve, did you know?"

"Dead romantic."

Romance.

"Jamie!" I sat bolt upright in my bed. "Oh, God, how could I forget?"

"Forget what? Oh! How did he find you?"

"Not at the Rocking Horse Hotel, you might imagine. Where did you get that one anyway?"

"There really is such a place, Jane. I saw a new sign go up outside a house on St. Leonard's Road. It's just a B and B. Don't look at me like that. What were you doing giving him all that about us being airline hostesses? I don't think we were very convincing, do you? Airline hostesses are all old boots."

"There's a few young ones. When was the last time you were on an airplane?"

Heather fell silent.

"Anyway," I continued, sorry for having got a bit snappish, "I ran into him last evening. He said he tried to reach me at the Rocking Horse Hotel but he couldn't find a number. So I had to tell him we moved because you had allergies—"

"You didn't!"

"I'll sort it out somehow. But remember, if you see him again, you have allergies, okay . . . ?"

"I'll tell him I have pox, too."

". . . and so I told him we were staying here. At the Castle."

Perplexity corrugated Heather's brow. "You mean you *did* tell him the truth?"

"Well . . ."

"Jane?"

"It's sort of a question of interpretation. I mean, it's true, isn't it? We *are* staying at the Castle, aren't we?"

"Yes, but—"

"It's just that there's more than one Castle in Windsor."

"There is? Oh, no! He thinks you meant the hotel on the High Street?"

I gave Heather a sickly grin.

She made a clucking noise. "Oh, what a tangled—"

"Save your breath!" I cut her off. "I get that advice from taxi drivers these days."

"Are you coming with us, or not?"

"Not. I'm going to the Castle—hotel, that is—to see if Jamie left any messages for me. I hope, I hope. And, anyway, Fleur asked me the other day to come by her place. She wants me to meet this genius daughter of hers and tell her what Ladies' Day at Ascot was like. She gets off her other job, the one at the chip shop, at nine. What time is it now?"

"Just after eight."

"That's all right," I said, reaching for my shoes. "Loads of time."

But there wasn't really. First, Heather pulled a slip of paper from her jeans pocket.

"I nearly forgot this. I'm sorry, Jane. Someone handed it to me a while back. I said I'd be seeing you."

My name and a phone number was scrawled on a torn scrap of newspaper. "No name?"

Heather shrugged.

"It's for a mobile phone," I noted.

"Perhaps it's Jamie," she said slyly, leaning against the door frame. "He's tracked you down to your wee lair here at Windsor's one and true Castle."

I looked at the number again with dismay. Had he? He couldn't have. I decided if I had some 'splainin' to do, I'd rather do it where walls didn't have ears. So fifteen minutes later I was at a phone box off Thames Street at the Central Station, the other of the two train stations in town, punching in the numbers, annoyed with myself and excited at the same time.

The phone clicked into life on the second ring.

"Macgreevy!" a voice barked, a swooshing sound in the background.

"Oh, it's only you," I sighed with a mixture of disappointment and relief.

"*Only* me? I think I deserve better than that."

"Andrew! Don't tell me you've already found Miranda!"

"No. But there's no indication she's left the country. Yet, anyway."

"Oh. That's something, I guess. Where are you?"

"On the M25."

"Doing what?"

"Never you mind. Driving. Look, I didn't call to make a traffic report. I've got some information on your Miranda Walter. Fulfilling my part of the bargain, you see. Are you interested or not?"

"Of course, I'm *interested*! I'm more than *interested*! What is it?"

"Miranda was adopted by a couple, Donald and Jean Walter, who lived at Shepperton. When Miranda was . . . just a sec . . ." I heard paper rattling. ". . . when Miranda was nine, Donald died. In an auto accident, as it happened. He had just turned forty. Two years later Jean remarried. Guess who she married?"

The woosh of traffic on the M25 flowed back into the phone in the pause that followed. It was like hearing the ocean in a seashell.

"You don't mean . . . !"

"I do mean. Husband number two was Roger Pettibon. The marriage didn't last long—about four years. But for those years, Pettibon was effectively Miranda's father. Or stepfather, or whatever."

"Wow." It was all I could think to say.

"Doesn't supply a motive, but—"

"At least there's a connection."

"Right. Look, Stell, a tunnel's coming up. I'm ringing off."

"But—"

"Cheers."

The phone went dead. The ocean sound vanished.

Thames Street was quiet but for a few local louts standing on the park benches below the Castle walls, trading insults with a couple of off-duty soldiers leaning out high above from one of the Guardroom windows. I hurried past, my time short, my destination the Castle Hotel up the street, my thoughts on Macgreevy's gleanings.

Choice or chance? Did Roger have a peculiar fondness for widow ladies? Or was the pattern no pattern at all, merely happenstance? I suppose if you're a man past a certain age, the eligible women you're likely to meet come with some sort of baggage. Divorced, in most cases, I should think, if you're in your thirties or forties. But widowed isn't unheard of.

Widows may have widows' pensions, I considered, crossing the intersection at Peascod Street. Was that part of their attraction for Roger? Widows may in fact gain financially, while divorced women more often than not lose. On the other hand, if you marry a young widow you do take on the responsibility of helping raise another man's child without benefit of some spousal support.

But why—I shook the cobwebs from my head, glancing at Caley's window display (hats gone)—was I assuming Roger had some less than wholesome motive for marrying these women anyway? He may have simply fallen in love.

Only his marriages didn't last very long. Roughly four years in each case. Of course, the last marriage had ended rather abruptly. Who knows? Roger and Joanna might have turned into Darby and Joan if someone hadn't taken a notion to stick a sword in the future Darby before he could contemplate a retirement cottage in Devonshire. . . .

"Do you have any messages for Bee?" I asked a moment later at the desk in the Castle Hotel.

"For whom?"

"For Bee."

"I'm sorry. I thought you said 'me.' "

"No. *Bee*. As in the much-loved honey-producing insect."

"Ah." Richard Hawley, Assistant Manager (for that was his name and title as proclaimed by the shiny tag over his suit coat pocket) tapped a few keys on his computer. He frowned. "There doesn't seem . . ." The frown deepened. "Are you Miss Bee?"

"Bee be me."

"Odd. There doesn't seem to be a Bee registered."
He smiled unctuously. "When did you arrive?"

"Oh, I'm not staying here."

"I beg your pardon."

"I'm not staying here. That is, I don't have a room.
I'm not registered."

He blinked, his smile faded. "I see. Well, we don't, as
a rule, take messages for people who are not staying at the
hotel, or who aren't at least expected imminently."

"Yes, I'm sure. But you see, I told someone I was staying at the Castle."

"Why would you do that?"

"Because I am."

"But you're not. You've just said. *And* you're not registered—"

"No, no, I mean I'm staying at the Castle because—"

"Miss, I assure you, this is the *only* Castle in Windsor."

"Have you looked outside your window, lately?"

Jonathan Hawley, Assistant Manager, glared at me.

"I am staying at the Castle—Windsor Castle, the great
huge thing up the hill—because I work there. But, you see,
I sort of told someone I met that I was staying at the Castle
and I realized later that he'd think I meant *this* Castle, not
that Castle." I pointed vaguely in a northeast direction.

J. Hawley glared.

"Sorry about the confusion. Anyway, it would be a
Jamie Allan phoning for Jane Bee. Was there a message?"

"You're missing the point, I think, Miss Bee. Anyone
telephoning for a Bee would have been told that no Bee was
registered. So there would be no message taken."

"Yes, but somebody might remember somebody trying
to leave a message for a Bee." I affixed my best smile. "How
long have you been on duty, Mr. Hawley?"

"Since one o'clock."

"And you're *sure* no one phoned for me."

"I don't answer every call."

"Someone else then."

"Possibly."

"Could you check? Please. It's important."

"One moment." He sighed and disappeared into the
side office. I could hear muffled conversation. A moment

later J. Hawley returned. "It seems," he said with some exasperation, "that there *is* recollection of a telephone call for a person named Bee."

"Oh!" I was both delighted and dismayed. "Did he leave a message?"

Hawley quivered. "No," he said through clenched teeth. "He did not leave a message because he was told no Jane Bee was registered here."

"I see. Well . . ." I could see I had irked the chap in some way. "Would you have a phone book I could look at, do you think?"

A copy of BT's Slough, Windsor, and Maidenhead directory slapped the surface of the counter.

I knew I had to put a stop to this nonsense I'd started. I'd phone Jamie, and explain. He'd said he had a flat in Windsor.

But there was no J. Allan listed for Windsor. No J. Allen, either. Directory inquiries might have a new listing but when I asked Hawley if I could use his phone he said:

"No."

"No?"

"You may not. This telephone is for the use of *hotel guests only*."

Five minutes later, I turned the corner into St. Margaret Place just in time to see Fleur hanging onto the balustrade moving wearily up the steps to her home. Dead tired, she must be, our Fleur "Three-Jobs" Aiken.

But when I drew closer, I realized something else had happened.

"Bloody hell!" she said, when she saw me. "I've gone and buggered me ankle!"

"Oh, no! Here, let me help you." Fleur put her left arm over my shoulder and we went up the last step together. "Did this just happen? You haven't been hobbling around all evening?"

"I came around the church a minute ago and stepped on a piece of loose pavement. Bloody stupid thing to do. I wasn't looking. Ow! Oh! Here's the key."

I managed to open the door. Fleur stepped painfully

over the threshold and we both contemplated the shadowy corridor and two daunting flights of stairs to her top-floor flat.

"Come on, we'll take it slow," I said, pushing the timed light switch to better illuminate our way.

"I don't need this," she wailed, puffing with exertion, as we climbed the steps carefully one by one.

"Maybe you can get compensation. The pavement shouldn't be cracked like that."

"Maybe. But it's not going to do me much good in the short run, is it?" She flinched.

The light snapped off. We were only halfway up.

"Hell!"

"It's okay, Fleur. There's enough light. Barely, anyway. Hang on."

But the light suddenly snapped back on. A small figure appeared at the top of the stairs.

"Mum!"

"It's all right, Cath. I've just gone and twisted me ankle, that's all."

A delicious aroma wafted down the stairwell toward us. "Something smells good," I remarked. But Cath had darted back into the flat. "Couple more," I said to Fleur. "There! We made it."

Fleur winced, then let out an enormous sigh. "Thanks, Jane. You came along at just the right minute. I don't know how I'd ever have got up them stairs."

"I'd have helped you, mum," her daughter said stoutly as we entered the front room of the flat. In her hand was a terry towel and small bowl of ice cubes. She's a quick study, I thought.

"You ought to lie down." One lumpy-looking settee facing the front windows looked large enough for a make-do bed. Fleur regarded it indecisively, balancing on one foot while she continued to hold onto my arm.

"If I get on that thing, I'll never get off."

"Mum, I can bring your tea in here, if you like."

"You want to at least get your leg up," I contributed.

"I think I'll try that chair in the kitchen," Fleur said, pivoting on her good foot toward the back of the flat. She introduced me as we struggled into the kitchen, a bright room taking in all the sun from the west. "And this is my daughter, Cath. My pride and joy."

"Oh, Mother!"

I eased Fleur into a comfy-looking lounge chair while Cath pushed one of the kitchen chairs forward as a support for the injured leg. Cath hovered with her towel and bowl while I fiddled with the laces on Fleur's trainers.

"Ooh, it is swollen," I said, pulling off the sock. The area around the ankle was already bloated and discoloured. "I wonder if you should see a doctor."

"Not if I have to go down them stairs."

"How painful is it?"

Fleur grimaced. "I'll live."

Cath placed ice in the towel and carefully wrapped the cold compress around her mother's foot. She was a small girl, neatly made, her capable hands accomplishing her nursing task as if she had done it a hundred times before. Fleur hardly winced.

"There." Cath pushed a fringe of dark hair from her eyes, regarding her handiwork with solemn satisfaction. With her big dark eyes, pointed chin, and tiny ears, she reminded me of a pixie. But there was a gravity to the child, to the way she held herself, that was interesting to behold.

Fleur released a long sigh. "That feels brilliant. Thanks, luv. You're a wonder. You, too, Jane." She leaned back in the chair and closed her eyes.

"Now don't fall asleep, Mum. Your tea will get cold." Cath's tone was almost maternal. She moved to the cooker, gave something in a pot a brief stir, then reached under the adjacent counter and pulled out a tray. The kitchen table, I noted, had been set formally for one, even unto a tiny vase of flowers that looked like they had been picked from a country lane.

"I've put Jimmy to bed . . . ." Cath continued.

"I'll look in on him later," Fleur muttered in reply.

"And I've fed Mrs. Sheldon's cat and I've done some of the laundry. Miss Bee, will you have some of this with my mother? She didn't say she was having a guest . . . ."

". . . Sorry, luv."

"Oh, that's all right. We'll use a tray for mum so there's a place set here . . ."

"But have you had your tea?" I asked.

"Oh, yes, hours ago."

"Well, it smells wonderful. I'd love to try some. And please call me Jane."

She pulled out the chair from the table and bade me sit, then reached for two plates from a rack over the counter.

"I thought you'd probably bring home things from the chip shop," I said to Fleur.

Her nose wrinkled. She opened her eyes. "Jimmy loves it. And Cath doesn't mind a bit of haddock'n'chips from time to time, do you, luv? But I can't eat it. Some nights I can't bear to look at it. Oh, thanks, Cath. This does look good."

My plate arrived next, with an apology for having served from the pot. "I hope you like it."

In a creamy curried sauce were tiny meatballs and vegetables. Tentatively, I lifted a bit. It melted in my mouth. "This is excellent," I said, failing to disguise the astonishment in my voice. "And you cooked this yourself? How old are you?"

"She turned thirteen in March," Fleur replied with evident pride.

"Gosh, they didn't teach us stuff like this at school when I was your age. I think rice pudding was the most complicated recipe we did."

"Oh, I got this off TV." Cath poured milk into two teacups. "I copied down the recipe. I used mince instead of steak. Steak's too expensive."

"Incredible."

"I told you she was clever."

Imperviously, as if she'd heard praise once too often, Cath silently poured the tea and handed us each a cup. She perched on the edge of a chair and watched us solemnly with her big dark eyes.

"Jane was at Ascot this afternoon, Cath." Fleur spoke between bites.

"Oh! Were you?" Her eyes sparkled and, briefly, she seemed more like the child she was. "Did you see the horses?"

"Yes, well, sort of," I replied, reflecting that I'd hardly

paid any attention at all to the creatures, and wished now I had. For her sake.

"Cath's horse mad."

"I know the feeling."

"Did you once have a horse?"

"No. Wanted one badly enough when I was about your age, Cath. But my parents wouldn't go for it. Well, it was pretty impractical, really. The stables were miles out of town and someone would have had to drive me. And then there was the expense. We used to ride along the beach sometimes—I grew up on Prince Edward Island—it was wonderful, the wind through your hair, just feeling the horse's power—"

"Isn't it brilliant? I'd love to have a horse—"

"Now, Cath," her mother said warningly.

"There's a paper round going at the newsagents on St. Leonard's Road, Mum."

"No."

"Please. It would help us. You're not going to be able to go to work now."

Fleur looked down worriedly at her swollen ankle. "No, Cath. You're too young for a paper round. You'd have to get up so early. I want you sticking to your schoolwork. That's what's important. I'll be on my feet in a few days."

"And then, after, when you're better, I could use the money to pay for a horse myself," Cath continued, as if her mother hadn't spoken. "I've figured it all out. It wouldn't cost us any extra. And there'd still be lots of time for me to mind Jimmy, and do my homework and things around here."

Somehow I believed she could. The child, for all her elfin appearance, exuded a strange sort of self-possession. She was an accomplished thirteen-year-old cook. The flat, including the kitchen, I'd noted, though hardly well-appointed, was neat as a pin—Cath's doing I suspected, as Fleur worked all hours God sent. Her young brother was tucked up safely in bed. And I suspected she'd done all her homework, too. She was a freak of nature. She'd be prime minister one day.

"We'll talk about this later, Cath," Fleur responded to

her daughter's argument in tones a little tired and defeated. "I don't think Jane wants to hear this."

"I'm sorry," Cath apologized to me, rising from her seat. "I didn't mean to be rude."

"Oh, not at all," I said, startled again at her adult demeanour.

"Would either of you care for more tea? Mum?"

"Ta."

"I'll just start on the washing-up," she said as she went from her mother to me with the teapot.

"Oh, leave it, love."

"Mum, somebody has to do it."

Fleur sighed and glanced at me with a kind of resignation as her daughter turned and pushed a short plastic stool in place before the sink.

"Anyway," I continued as Cath stepped on the stool, glanced out the window, and reached for the taps, "there were lots of people you'd probably know at Ascot this afternoon." As I named a few of the television and pop stars I'd recognized, Fleur and her daughter argued their merits, or demerits, who was "in" and who was "out."

"And how about the royals?" Fleur inquired.

"Oh, same old, same old, on the whole," I replied. "Lady Linley's outfit was really smashing, black and cream with a sort of lacy halter top. Princess Margaret's hat looked like a frosted *gâteau*, quite funny in a way. The Queen wore a really nice deep blue dress with a white pattern and a hat with matching blue bows. Suited her."

"Jane's met your friend across the street," Fleur interjected, as Cath stepped off her stool and took her plate and mine.

"Who? Miranda?"

"No, the daft one. Who thinks the Queen's head of some cult or something. Actually, I wish you wouldn't talk to that man, Cath. He gives me the shivers. I hope you don't go into his rooms."

"Oh, Mum, Mr. Gowerlock's harmless."

"But you haven't gone in?"

"No, Mother," Cath intoned as she dipped another plate into the rinse water.

"Tell Jane what he's on about."

"Well, it's something called, let me think—psychoge-ography," Cath explained as she worked away. "Mr. Gowerlock says Britain is run by this secret society called Freemasons, I think it is, and the Queen and Prince Philip are at the top, and all the royal palaces follow Masonic designs, which only Masons can recognize, and that there's these kind of lines, invisible lines like, um, longitude and latitude, only more mystical, I guess, that connect different important places—"

"Daft!" Fleur interjected.

"—so, sometimes when the Queen goes somewhere she's really performing a secret ritual that only Mr. Gowerlock and his friends know about. Mr. Gowerlock says Windsor Castle was built along one of these lines, which connects somehow to Stonehenge, I think . . ."

"I gather he thinks the Beatles are somehow involved." I recalled his confusing me with the fictional Eleanor Rigby.

"Oh, lots of famous people," Cath continued over the sound of running water. "He says there's clues in the words to Beatle songs . . . ."

"Clues to what, I'd like to know," Fleur muttered.

Cath's thin shoulders rose and fell in a shrug. "Oh, and even that John Lennon was shot because he was going to reveal everything."

"I think I agree with your mother. That *is* daft."

"I hope you don't believe any of this, Cath."

"Oh, Mum, of course I don't believe it." She stopped suddenly, both hands in the sink, and cocked her ear toward the door. "Jimmy's calling."

We heard a child's voice plaintively calling "Mum" over and over. Fleur instinctively moved to rise, then fell back with a grimace of pain. "Hell!" she groaned.

"I'll see what he wants if you like," I offered.

"No, I'll go," Cath said. "He'll just be after a glass of water." She reached for a tumbler drying on the rack and filled it.

"Tell Jimmy what's happened," Fleur instructed her daughter. "I'll look in on him later. Make sure he doesn't get up, or you'll never get him back to sleep."

"Don't worry, he won't," the child responded with authority as she passed.

"Time you were off to bed, too," Fleur called after her.

"Why don't I do some of these," I said, rising and moving toward the sink, edging the stool aside with my foot.

"Oh, don't, Jane."

"I don't mind." I squirted some more washing-up liquid into the dull water and turned the tap. Outside the window, the flowers and shrubbery in the cluster of tidy back gardens were melting into the lengthening shadows of the dying day.

"You should come to Ascot next year and bring Cath," I told Fleur, and then wondered if I would still be in service myself.

"They never give tickets to us temps."

"I don't know why not. You work at the Castle as many weeks of the year as I do. More. Next year, take my ticket, and I'll blackmail Heather into giving Cath hers."

"Oh, I don't have a thing I could wear to a posh do like that."

"I got my dress from Oxfam. Dead cheap. You can borrow it if you like." I plunged my hands into the warm water and scrubbed at an eggy-looking encrustation on a plate, thinking the dress would have to be let out.

"Cath would be thrilled," Fleur allowed. "We'll see. It's not for another year. Thanks for the thought, though, Jane. Bloody foot of mine," she muttered. "I wish you'd leave those plates."

"I ran into Chief Inspector Nightingale at Ascot," I by-the-wayed as a diversion, triggered by my use of the word "blackmail."

"You're still set on this artist bloke not doing the murder, then."

"Too right. And I told him so."

My own reasonably good self suddenly stared back at me, a faint reflection in the window. "Oh, no, you mustn't," Cath cried, hurrying toward me.

"I don't mind, really. There's only a couple left."

"No!" She was quite adamant. "It's very kind of you, but you're a guest. Please."

252 ❖ C. C. Benison

I relinquished the brush and picked up a tea towel. "I can at least dry," I said, wiping my wet hands on the cloth.

"Oh, but they'll dry in the rack."

Fleur shook her head, smiling. Defeated, I resumed my seat.

"Jane was just saying, Cath, that she doesn't think this man they've charged with Mr. Pettibon's murder did it."

"Oh."

"I was with him—the painter, Victor Fabiani, that is—very shortly after the time Mr. Pettibon was killed," I explained to her back as she lifted one of the last plates dripping to the rack. "He didn't act like someone who'd just murdered someone. And there's other reasons, too."

"I meant to ask you about him earlier, Cath. He was the one who taught that Saturday morning art class you took at the Cultural Centre in the winter, wasn't he?"

"Uh-huh."

"What was he like? You've never said."

"Mum, you're hardly ever home . . ."

It was not an accusation, more an expression of fact. But Fleur's smile collapsed, as if she had been struck in the face. "I'm sorry, luv. I don't know what else I can do."

"Oh, Mum, I didn't mean that. I just mean that sometimes you're not here when I want to tell you something. And then afterwards, I forget, or it's not important. Anyway, I'm not so sorry Mr. Pettibon's dead."

"Catherine! What's got into you? That's not very nice."

"Well, he wasn't very nice. He was all right as a teacher and all. And he *seemed* nice. But then he went and stuck his hands in my knickers one time after class when I wanted to show him something and so I wasn't so keen on him after that.

"Dirty old man," she added scornfully.

There was a deathly silence on our side of the room. I looked at Fleur with surprise and shock but she had gone ghostly, her limbs stiff, staring at Cath's pale reflection in the window's dark glass.

"So I said to him," Cath continued fiercely, oblivious to our reaction. "I said to him: Mr. Pettibon, if you ever try that again, I'll report you to the police *and* I'll write a letter to the Queen *and* I'll send another letter to all the newspapers. That," she added with satisfaction, pulling the plug, "put him in his place."

The dishwater roared down the drain with a horrible sucking noise. Fleur remained deathly still, her staring eyes glassy as if she were staring inwards. Troubled by her numb response to her daughter's admission, but not wishing to frighten the child, I asked, in as casual and natural a tone as I could muster:

"And do you think Mr. Pettibon did anything like that to any of the other girls in your class?"

Cath was energetically scrubbing the sink. "I think he might have tried it on Elise Shillington because she acted sort of strange one time and then she never came back after that day. This was before he tried it with me, so it was only afterward that I thought he might have tried it with her. Dirty old man," she repeated as if savouring the expression, stepping off the stool and pushing it away from the sink.

"Now I must go to bed," she announced matter-of-factly. "It was very nice to have met you, Jane." She held forth her hand in solemn gesture. I shook it, hardly knowing how to respond to her after what she'd told us.

"G'night, Mum," she addressed her mother, giving her a quick hug, to which Fleur responded mechanically. Drawing away from her mother, she frowned worriedly. "Mum, you don't look very well." Cath glanced at me.

"That's all right. I'll help your mother to bed. You go off now," I told the girl.

And I somehow managed a smile.

17

THE METALLIC CLICK and soft thump of the closing
kitchen door magnified the awful silence that followed. Outside the window, veins of gold and purple shot through the
darkening undersurface of a crosshatch of fine thin clouds
wrought by airplane vapour trails. I watched the subtle shift
of pattern and colour in the sky as the midsummer sun sank
toward the horizon beyond Windsor's tidy confines. My
mind roiled. Roger Pettibon had engaged in inappropriate
touching—extremely inappropriate touching—with Cath
Aiken, with a thirteen-year-old kid, twelve as she was then.
And with another girl at the Cultural Centre, Elise Shillington, and why was *that* name familiar? Roger Pettibon,
who had one stepdaughter, Miranda, now in her midtwen-
ties. How old had Miranda been, I wondered, during her
mother's brief second marriage? And then Roger with another stepdaughter, Pippa, a budding adolescent, dead these

last few months. A sickening sense of horror and helpless-
ness swept through me. What liberties beyond unwelcome
touching had Pettibon taken?

"She handled it well, Fleur," I said at last, turning to
her, my own voice sounding to my ears gratingly cheery.
"She was very brave telling him off."

A wounded cry escaped Fleur's lips. Her eyes, huge in
her strained white face, sought mine. "I've got to go to her,"
she whispered hoarsely, struggling to lift her injured foot
from its resting place.

"No. Don't. Not now, not tonight." I don't know why
I interfered as I did. But I could sense in Fleur a growing
agitation I thought might do Cath more harm than good if
tendered now, in outsized emotion: outrage, anger, and
tears. Cath's maturity was remarkable; perhaps her aplomb
in a situation that would have left me at that age shaken
with fright and confusion was genuine, not suppressed. If so,
she was one of the lucky ones. But there would be time
enough to probe her feelings. Later, in an atmosphere of
calm and consolation, some hour at the weekend, perhaps.
Yes, later would be best. I said as much aloud.

"Cath did the right thing, Fleur. You'll not have to
worry about her. She's got guts."

"Yes . . . yeah, she has, hasn't she," Fleur said hollowly. And then her face crumpled. Tears sprang suddenly
to her eyes and her voice, choked by sobs, turned a keening
pitch. "Not like me."

"Oh, now, don't be silly," I said cajolingly, distressed
by the intensity of her feeling, "you've got tremendous
courage, raising two kids on your own, working all the hours
you do. I couldn't do it . . . ."

". . . not what I mean," she croaked, jamming her fist
to her mouth to control her sobs.

I felt a terrible premonition in my chest at that moment. "Oh, Fleur, not . . ."

She nodded mutely. Impulsively, I reached over to
take her hand. "Oh, you poor kid," was all I could think to
say.

"That's how it started. The groping." She looked up
at me, eyes brimming. "My stepdad, it was."

I groaned. "Oh, God."

"I was Cath's age, too. Younger, maybe."

I felt helpless. "And there was nobody you could turn to."

Fleur shook her head. "There was just me. No sisters, no brothers. Just my mum and she was crazy about him. Wouldn't hear a word said against him. Jack was his name. Jack. I *hated* him." She spat the words.

"Your mother didn't believe you."

"Jack threatened me. Said he'd do me an injury if I ever told." Sagging in the chair, she snuffled noisily. "So I let him do what he wanted. I only told her after . . ."

Her grip on my hand grew tighter. Pulled toward her, I found myself kneeling by her chair, her wretched face before me a pale and tear-stained moon. "I only told her," she repeated, "after . . . after . . ."

"After what, Fleur?" I asked softly, dreading what was to come.

". . . after . . ." Her face twisted as she fought a renewed onslaught of tears. ". . . after I was in the club." She pinched her lips together hard. Her pale, watering eyes searched mine for understanding.

The old expression baffled me a moment. "In the club"? I thought. What club?

And then I knew.

"You mean . . . ?"

She turned her head sharply away.

"Oh, no!" Tears came unbidden to my own eyes. I reached over and cradled her head against mine, the improbable whiff of chip fat assailing my nostrils. Cath was his child. This Jack bastard. This monster of a stepfather. I shivered with revulsion.

Fleur sobbed quietly. "She's never to know, Cath is. *Never*," she said fiercely.

"I won't say anything, Fleur."

"I've never told anybody this before . . . except . . ."

"And your mother didn't believe you . . ."

"She took his side. And I—hid it until it was too late to do anything." She released a shuddering sigh. "He stopped after that. I lived at home another couple of years with the baby—awful years—until I could get out on me own. Met a bloke. He were decent. Didn't last, though. He went to Saudi for work." She pulled away and wiped at her eyes. I scanned the kitchen quickly and lit on the tea towel.

"Here," I said after fetching it. "It's not too damp."

"You look a bit done in yourself." She laughed weakly and blew noisily into the towel.

"It's all right." I dabbed at my eyes with one finger. "You're a marvel, Fleur. I don't know how you've done it."

"Nothing else to do but carry on. Brian helps. He sends some money from Saudi for Jimmy."

"Does Cath wonder about her father?"

"They both think Brian's their dad. Just as well. Brian doesn't mind. They wonder about grandparents more. Brian's are tucked up near Newcastle somewhere and never come down south. I don't know what Brian's really told them about us, anyway. And I've told Cath and Jimmy my mum and dad are dead. And they are, as far as I'm concerned. I'll never forgive my mother, and he's just—" She groped for a word and failed.

"Fleur, you need to talk to Cath about what Roger Pettibon did at the Cultural Centre on the weekend. But, gently. See to what degree it may have affected her."

She nodded. "I'll be home for the next few days anyway." She indicated her foot. "Will you tell Mrs. Boozley?"

"Of course. Can I do anything else?"

"Thanks ever so much, Jane. I'll be okay." A funny little smile lit up her face, still wet with tears. "I've got Cath, after all."

"You do, don't you. She's been a big help, you know. At least I think she has."

Puzzlement blunted Fleur's smile.

"Well," I continued, "I found out earlier this evening that Miranda Walter—you know, across-the-road Miranda—well, I learned tonight that Roger was married for a time to her mother. In other words, Roger was Miranda's stepfather. And, of course, he was Pippa's stepfather, too . . ."

Fleur's mouth fell open in a silent *no*.

"I can't be sure," I said. "But, I mean, his . . . touching Cath and that other girl at the Cultural Centre can't be the first time he's done stuff like that, can it? There's got to be a pattern here. The wonder is," I continued, "that he's gotten away with it all this time."

Fleur shook her head. Sorrowfully, she said: "There's no wonder, Jane. No wonder at all. If they're like I was. Too frightened and scared. Scared to say anything, scared to do anything. Scared to death."

Dark night. Dark thoughts. I walked past the Star Tavern on my way up Peascod Street after I'd helped Fleur to her bedroom and let myself out of 10 St. Margaret Place. I remembered then what I'd forgotten: Jamie Allan. He'd completely flown from my mind. And there was hardly any point in trying to find his telephone number at this hour of the night.

And there was hardly any time next morning. With Fleur out of commission, I was doing double duty. Certain of Her Majesty's guests, for all their trappings, are, I must say, distinctly messy in some of their personal habits. I've a mind, sometimes, to sell the details to *The News of the World* or the *Evening Gazette*. No, *give* the details away, gratis. Even to the likes of Macgreevy. Such prickliness on my part as I skivvied away at my usual tasks was in no small way attributable to my mood of anger and frustration (tidying up after people is, after all, what I'm paid to do) in the wake of Cath Aiken's bombshell. I kept seeing her thin figure turned to the sink, her too-large green T-shirt hanging over a pair of blue tights down to the back of her knees, the dark fringe of her hair grazing the exposed tiny bones at the base of her neck. She'd been a strange mixture of resilience and vulnerability. She might have been me ten years ago, I thought with a frisson of horror. Only—I could thank some deity, I suppose—nobody had ever tried to violate my childhood sense of trust in that unspeakable way.

But with Cath's revelation, I was convinced I had been given a key to unlock the mystery of Roger Pettibon's murder. Or I'd found the unravelling thread in a skein of wool. Or the needle in the haystack. Reader, pick your metaphor. Whatever it was, I felt certain I'd glommed on to something significant, something that tied together the many loose ends. *Felt*, mind you. I've misinformed myself before, and

I've learned from past adventures to be wary of false revelations.

What I desperately needed was some corroborating evidence, some testimony, some confirmation that Roger Pettibon really was more than just some weird old fart who'd taken it into his head to fiddle-dee-dee with a couple of little girls once at a local art class. But Miranda Walter, for one, remained elusive. She must have vanished into some universe where a newspaper never crosses a doorstep or television never fills a lonely hour. Joanna Pettibon? Cath's bulletin about Roger brought a new perspective to his widow. But would she be frank with me? I doubted it. The mothers, as Fleur so poignantly illustrated, were the very ones apt to be drowned in denial. Canon Leathley? The seal of the confession—if child molesting was the sort of thing confessed—was firmly sealed against me.

In the midst of a fold-and-tuck of one of Her Majesty's guest's beds, my mind lit upon Hugo FitzJames, the hapless (or was he?) discoverer of Roger Pettibon's body in the Throne Room, whose very sword had delivered the fatal cut. Hugo had been Philippa Clair's little friend, had he not? A playmate within Castle walls during his visits to his cousins' family circle? Recalling—dimly—my own unfabled early adolescence, I knew there were things you told your friends that you'd never ever tell your parents or another adult. Suppose Pippa had confided in Hugo? Was it possible? I thought I knew just how such a confidence might have been shared. Boys of that age weren't a *complete* mystery.

More of a mystery, at least to me, however, is Eton. After I cross the Thames over Windsor Bridge, I always feel that I'm penetrating some secret world. Eton High Street, long and narrow, has a bright commercial bustle. But once you reach the college precincts, the street splays into lanes and the lanes into passages with tree-shaded walls shielding private gardens and somber quadrangles over which loom buildings of dull red brick and cold gray stone with long windows like melancholy eyes. There never seems to be any identifying signs on anything. Except for the tourists, I'm sure the streets would be empty most of the time. Eton's an island of academic repose, I suppose; and I'm sure many people find the college precincts utterly charming, but I always have the disturbing sense of being watched by unseen eyes. Perhaps it has to do with being female in a preserve of male privilege.

Not, of course, that I've spent a lot of time in Eton. Other than one tourist-mode tour and one or two Sunday walks at the behest of others, I've never found much of a reason to cross the Thames.

Not today, however. After a hasty lunch in Servants' Hall, I darted up to my room in Clarence Tower, shimmied out of my starched white and ever-so-boring housemaid clobber, slapped on a pair of jeans and a top, and quickly made my way out of the Castle, wondering as I did so how I was going to find one Eton scholar out of twelve hundred and not raise an alarm. Or even an eyebrow.

"Next guided tour's at two-thirty," a woman with a sharp nose and soft double chins announced as a clock in the distance sweetly chimed the hour of two. She was seated just outside the arched entrance to Upper School and the School Yard of Eton College, smiling a practiced smile, nimble hands tidying the fan of brochures and publications on what looked like a scarred school desk.

"Oh, I'm not after a tour," I said. "I want to talk to one of the boys."

She looked up, lifted a pair of glasses suspended from a silver chain around her neck, and peered intently at me. "You're not some American journalist trying to ferret out tittle-tattle about Prince William, I trust." She frowned. Her chins grew a chin.

"No, no," I assured her. "I work at the Castle."

"I see." Her eyes ran swiftly over my apparel. "I thought you didn't look much like a journalist. What is it you do at the Castle?"

"I'm on Staff."

"Oh. Well." Suspicion gave way to something more like polite curiosity. "Who is it you wish to speak to?"

"Hugo FitzJames."

"Mmm. I'm not sure I know . . ."

"Lord Lambourn."

"Oh, yes. The boy who fainted at the Garter Procession. The Queen's Page of Honour. I was there, you know.

Saw the poor thing collapse. It's this dreadful heat we're having, you know."

"I was there, too. He practically fell at my feet."

"Of course! You were standing next to that woman in the wheelchair. I remember you now. You were wearing a rather nice dress." This quasi-shared experience seemed to advance me in her estimation. "Well," she continued, "you're probably best off going to the School Office, unless you know which House Lord Lambourn's in."

"I don't, I'm afraid. And, frankly, I'm sort of hoping to catch Hugo on the fly, as it were." I lowered my voice conspiratorially. "It's confidential—Palace business—and I don't want to cause him any problems with his Housemaster, if you see what I mean."

"Oh!" she trilled. "Well, it's a bit tricky, but you may have luck on your side. It's just gone two. The boys'll have finished their dinner, and the next class isn't until three so . . . I would say your best chance may be across the road, at the School Library. That's the octagonal building, by the Burning Bush."

"Burning Bush?"

"It's what they call that lamp standard over there."

"Really. Well, thank you so much."

I didn't have to wait too long. After some few minutes, young Etonians of various shapes and sizes began popping into the street peacocking in their black tailcoats, waistcoats and pin-striped trousers, looking like youthful extras in a period musical comedy, only somehow radiating more visible self-assurance and natural grace than any poor sap grateful to have made it to the chorus line. Life would require no auditioning from these boys, I thought. Leads had already been written for them.

Eventually—as predicted, hoped and expected—Hugo rounded the corner from Common Lane in tribal conversation with two other fellows, sandy undisciplined hair fallen in his eyes like a spaniel's.

"Hugo!" I called sharply.

He brushed back his hair with a careless gesture and

turned to look at me. His expression was sleepy. But he kept walking.

"I want to talk to you," I continued commandingly. Somehow sternness seemed the best attitude to strike with a fourteen-year-old, whether Etonian or inmate of a local comprehensive.

Hugo stopped. A dawning of understanding stirred lazily in his half-lidded eyes. His mates broke into silly grins and began a sniggery taunting that didn't take an anthology of Eton slang to recognize as the equivalent of "Hugo's got a girlfriend."

I put an end to that. "Piss off," I snarled. Their mouths fell open in expressions of mock horror.

I was beginning to enjoy this. I felt all hard-boiled. Damned if I hadn't forgotten my chewing gum, so I couldn't make punctuating snaps during interrogation. A pair of totally bitchin' stiletto heels would have done the trick, too. At fourteen, Hugo was already taller than I, and probably outweighed me by a stone as well. Physically, he looked a little more mature than the average fourteen-year-old.

"I'll catch you up," Hugo called to his friends in a reedy baritone. They shrugged and continued on their way. "What?" he asked of me, pouting. "You were in the Throne Room Monday morning after the—"

"After the murder, you mean?"

The pout deepened. "Aren't you really just some sort of . . . housemaid?"

"Ever heard of undercover, sonny?"

"Yeah," he responded slowly. Suspicion fought with awe in his features.

"Was I wearing a housemaid's uniform at Ascot yesterday?"

"No."

"I was in the Royal Box conferring with some very important people who want to get to the bottom of this Pettibon homicide."

Hugo stepped back involuntarily. "I thought it was . . ." He turned as if to move away.

"Solved? Don't go, Hugo. Either you talk to me here and now or we're going to have to take you in to help us with our inquiries. You understand me?"

"Aren't you an American?"

"I'm on secondment from Washington, D.C., to the Met." Is there an award for thinking fast? I nominate myself. "We're reviewing British security procedures for high-ranking officials, the Queen among them."

"But I already talked with someone about what happened Monday."

"There have been new developments. Views have changed." I took one step up the rank of wedding-cake steps the Burning Bush rested on. Being five foot three may not undercut Her Majesty's authority, but being the same height does nothing for *me*. "Let's review. Take me through that morning. Your cousin, St. John Leathley, accompanied you to the Upper Ward shortly after eight o'clock. You were already dressed in your livery, correct?"

"Yeah."

"And what time were you in the Throne Room?"

He pushed his hair away from his face. Mulishly he protested: "Isn't all this in some police report?"

"Of course. But I want *you* to tell *me* again."

He released a martyred sigh. "I was in the Throne Room about, oh, quarter to nine. We were having a . . . a sort of practice . . ."

"You were fooling around, you mean. With your swords."

Hugo shrugged. "I was with Nick—Nicholas Baines-Hamilton—one of the other Pages of Honour. And there was Wills and Harry, of course, and a few others . . ."

"And you left your sword behind."

"It gets in the way. Bloody thing tends to stick out, you know. And since I had it out of its scabbard already, and we were going downstairs to, er . . ."

". . . Rollerblade in the passageways?"

"Yeah." He cocked his head. "I don't remember telling the police that."

"There've been further inquiries."

"Oh." Worry flickered briefly in his face. "So, anyway, I took off the scabbard and left it and the sword behind."

"Were you the last to leave the Throne Room?"

He started, suggesting he hadn't been asked this before. "I . . . I don't know."

"Of course you do."

Hugo was silent a moment, looking away. I studied his profile, thus far unravaged by puberty's blackheads and assorted eruptions, lucky boy. He had a long straight nose, a wide mouth, and blue eyes with just about the longest eyelashes I'd ever seen. Attractive, I suppose, if you were a pubescent girl.

"I expect I must have been," he replied at last, airily, returning my gaze coolly. "Oh, yes, I remember now. I was having trouble with the scabbard fastening. The others couldn't wait, I guess, so they left without me."

"I see. So, for a time, you were in the Throne Room all by yourself."

"It was only for a moment or two," he declared with some heat.

"And the other boys can confirm this?"

"Um, sure. I guess." He cleared his throat.

"Mmm." He was less than convincing. The "moment or two" he was alone was, I was now certain, somewhat longer. I pressed on: "And then, around ten o'clock, you decided to retrieve your sword. That's somewhat in advance of the time for the Investiture."

"Someone complained about us Rollerblading, so—" He broke off, shrugging. "There wasn't much else to do. Rather boring. So I went back to the Throne Room."

". . . where you found your sword, stuck into Roger Pettibon, and raised the alarm. You did raise the alarm immediately?"

"Of course."

Across the road, a large touring coach had screeched noisily to a halt and disgorged a bevy of elderly day-trippers. One shambled across the road toward us, camera slung around his neck, avidly eyeing the Burning Bush and Hugo. "Stay where you be, lad," he shouted cheerily, raising his camera. Hugo met the intrusion with cold distaste.

"Stupid old bugger," he said under his breath as the camera clicked. "How would you like to be photographed every time you walked down the street?" he added defensively to my disapproving frown. "Or have pictures in the dailies of you passing out?" He pushed his hair back from his brow. "Are you done with me?"

"No, I'm not. I've got some more serious questions, Hugo, and I want you to take care how you answer them."

He warily eyed a couple of older boys passing by who flicked him an inquisitive glance.

"Did you know the deceased, Roger Pettibon?"

"No."

"No? Are you sure? After all, his home was in the castle precincts. You spend some of your holidays with your cousin St. John's family in the canons' cloister. And you were a . . . friend, I'm told, of Roger Pettibon's stepdaughter, Philippa Clair."

This last had a notable effect. Hugo reddened and shuffled from foot to foot. He stuffed one hand in his trousers pocket. "Yes, all right, I knew Pettibon a bit. I knew *of* him."

"*Of* him" echoed in my mind. Be gentle, I cautioned myself. You don't want Hugo to bolt. Not now.

"And from what you knew of Roger Pettibon," I asked, "did you like him?"

"I didn't give him much thought, really."

"Well, let me put it another way. Was there anything you *didn't* like about Mr. Pettibon?"

He shook his head and looked down at his shoes. A stubborn silence followed.

"Hugo," I said finally, "as you know, Pippa drowned at Easter. A terrible tragedy, just terrible. It was an accident—that's what the inquest said. But drugs were involved. There was a drug found in Pippa's system. Did you know she took Ecstasy, or any of that sort of stuff?"

"No," he replied, glaring at me.

"Eton pupils suspected of taking drugs are subject to compulsory tests. Isn't that right?"

"It's nothing to do with me. I don't use drugs!"

"No," I said, considering him, the angry flush, the direct gaze. "I suspect you don't. Thirteen or fourteen is pretty young to be into that kind of thing. Though it's hardly unheard of," I added.

"It must have been a one-off. I don't even know what Pippa was doing at Runnymede."

"Too young to be at a disco where these drugs are often around, and anyway there's no disco at Runnymede.

She wasn't with friends at the time of the accident," I added, remembering the details from the newspapers. Hugo shuffled his feet. "Of course, drugs are a way of escaping. If you're very unhappy, if your family life is just plain awful, you know . . . Do you think Pippa was unhappy?"

"I don't know," he snapped crossly, shifting his weight from one foot to the other.

"You were a friend—her boyfriend, I think it would be fair to say, no?"

He pushed his hair back once again and seemed to consider the question. "I guess," he mumbled.

"Pippa talked with you about things? Stuff that was troubling her, perhaps?"

He began to make kicking motions with his foot as if he were worrying a football at the practice at Agars Plough. "I don't know. Perhaps," he replied, concentrating on his footwork.

I sighed inwardly. You'd think an Eton pupil, even a fourteen-year-old one, might be more abundant in his replies. "Hugo," I pressed, trying (unsuccessfully) to dampen my impatience, "did you try it on with Pippa?"

Hugo continued his imaginary footie. I could see a blush racing to crimson his face. I said, "I think you did. Well, of course you did. Why wouldn't you? It's perfectly normal. Nothing wrong with it." The footwork became more intense, manic. "But I think something happened. Didn't it?"

No reply. My eyes grew dizzy.

"Hugo, stop it! *Stop it!*"

He gave one final kick. "What?" he snarled fiercely, his face blazing. "What does this have to do with stupid dead old Pettibon? *I* didn't kill him."

"No one says you did, Hugo," I countered gently. "I'm only interested—for the moment—in Pippa Clair. I think something may have been happening to her. Something frightening and confusing and nasty that she couldn't tell anyone about. Or didn't know *how* to tell anybody about."

"And you think she told me?"

"I doubt she intended to. Blurted it out, probably. Under a kind of provocation that her girlfriends, for instance, wouldn't cause."

Confusion, embarrassment, then anger rippled their way across Hugo's young features. "Since you seem to know already—" He stopped, shrugging, looking away again.

"But I . . . we need your help, Hugo. We need others to verify what we're beginning to learn about Roger Pettibon."

"Pippa swore me to silence."

"And you feel protective of her, and her memory. I understand."

"I told her to tell someone at school, or her mother."

"And did she?"

"I don't know," he replied miserably. "I never saw her again."

"I'm sorry."

Hugo looked an agony of indecision in the silence that followed. If only Pippa had acted on his sage advice, I thought sadly. How differently events might have played themselves out.

"I was staying with St. John for a few days at the beginning of the Long Leave," Hugo said. "Before I went to my grandfather's—"

"The Long Leave in the spring? Before Easter? Easter was late this year."

He nodded. "I was with Pippa early one Saturday afternoon in Salisbury Tower. Her mother and her stepfather were going to be away most of the day. They both taught something at the Windsor Cultural Centre Saturday mornings and Pippa said they had some errands in Maidenhead. The car was gone from the front of the Tower. So, since they were going to be away for a time, well, I thought . . . I mean . . ." He reddened. "She wouldn't let me . . . you know. She seemed to . . . sort of . . . freeze. And then, when I . . ."

"Pressed her?"

"I suppose. She became quite upset."

"Hysterical?"

"Mmm, yes. Rather."

"It frightened you."

He squirmed. "I didn't know what to do. She didn't

blurt it out, exactly," he explained, taking up my phrase. "But I knew something was terribly wrong. She told me . . . some of it, I suppose. About her stepfather, you know doing—" He grimaced. "The rest I could guess. I was . . ."

The sick look on his face said it all.

"She told me not to tell. And so I didn't."

"I'm glad you were able to be her friend, Hugo. I'm not sure many boys would have managed the situation as well as you did."

"Oh? Well . . . She was all right, Pippa. She lost her father—her real father—at about the same time I did."

"A special bond," I commented, wondering whether he believed his father disappeared or deceased.

"What a *bastard* her stepfather turned out to be!" he added with passion.

"Did you recognize him when you came across his body in the Throne Room?"

"No." He rubbed at his nose. "I mean, I'd never seen a dead person before," he hastened to explain. "I was too . . . shocked, really, to notice who it was."

"I see."

His second lie, I thought, again sighing inwardly. At least his second lie.

I let Hugo go a few moments later. He seemed enormously relieved.

A tiny antiquarian and secondhand bookshop I passed on Eton High Street recalled to me both Hugo's cryptic notion that his father was "lost," possibly dead, and the Duke of Cheshire's overheard assurance that his son was very much alive—a clear contradiction that gave birth somewhere in my frontal lobes to a bouncing baby suspicion with ten perfectly formed fingers and toes. Backtracking, I stepped into the shop and inhaled the bouquet of a thousand books, nay more, in the very early stages of becoming the dust that some future housemaid would vacuum with her cyberHoover.

A young red-haired woman in a white blouse stood behind a small counter between two crammed and jammed floor-to-ceiling shelves, herself flanked by two mountainous piles of books she was busy price-marking with a pencil.

"I'm looking for a certain book," I said.

She smiled at the novelty of my request.

"I don't have a title, I'm afraid. It probably came out about, oh—" I calculated hastily—"seven or eight years ago. It was about Rupert FitzJames, the Marquess of Graven, who disappeared after his wife died in suspicious circumstances."

"Ah, yes, I know the one you mean," she said. She had a slight French accent. *The* slipped into *ze*. "*Nowhere Man* is the title. I think . . ." Her brow crinkled. "I think a copy may have come in the last few weeks. Let me look for it."

She shouldered her way into a minuscule anteroom behind the counter. "It is comic—you know, funny?—you asking for this book," she continued conversationally, rummaging through books in one of several cardboard boxes on an old table. "We had two or three copies for a long, long time that nobody seemed to want, but for the last, oh, nearly two years now, the same man has come in every few months or so to buy a copy if we have one."

"Short but distinguished-looking?"

"Yes. Do you know him? I asked him once why he buys the same book over and over, but he was a little—how do you say?—abrupt with me." She laughed.

"I'm pretty sure your regular customer is the Duke of Cheshire."

"The Duke of Cheshire? Really?" She made a moue. "But why would he buy the same book again and again?"

"He's the Marquess of Graven's father, and his grandson is studying here at Eton."

"Ah."

"He doesn't want his grandson reading it. Doesn't care for the content, I gather."

"I've never read it. It always to me looks a little . . . ah! I've found it." She lifted a book and blew along the top edge. Dust billowed. ". . . looks a little, you know, trashy. Ooph!" She waved away the dust. "I shouldn't say that to you. You won't want to buy it."

"Actually," I said, grinning guiltily, "I don't want to buy it. I just want to look at it."

Her smile faltered briefly. Then she recovered. "It does not matter. We always have a customer for this title. Here . . ." She edged her way back to the counter and placed the book, a hardcover, in my hands.

The torn, bloodred dustcover, featured on the front an extreme close-up of a face taken from a newspaper photograph. The little dots coalesced only if you held the book at arm's length—ideal for book rack displays, I thought: cold dark eyes staring at you haughtily, the mouth leering like a less lip-endowed Mick Jagger.

Nowhere Man: The Search for Lord Graven, as it was subtitled, was a thin volume, but a set of photos gathered in the middle detailed a life in progress, or regress, depending on how you look at it: Graven as a little boy in a sweet little suit standing in a garden with his father and his mother, the late duchess, taller by six inches than her husband; Graven in his Eton kit, about Hugo's age, only darker and broodier, making an obscene gesture to the camera; Poppy (real name: Annabel) who became Lady Graven, a stunning blonde, posing as a model in a swimsuit; an infant picture of Hugo, held by his mother; then a picture of a very frightened-looking Hugo, about five years old, clutching his grandfather's coat in the middle of a press scrum; pictures of the Gravens in a fashionable London nightclub, on a yacht in the Mediterranean, in their drawing room, looking too rich and too thin; pictures of the exterior of their Knightsbridge flat, their street, and finally, on the last page . . .

"Oh, yuck," I gasped, startled. "No wonder the Duke of Cheshire doesn't want his grandson to see this book."

In the photograph, Hugo's mother, cruelly lit, lay nude from the waist up, her slender arms stretched over her head and bound at the wrist with a leather strap to a bedpost. Her face was bruised, her eyes open and staring, her neck mutilated by a dark twist mark, evidence of strangulation by a ligature. A police photo, surely.

The saleswoman recoiled. "How awful to publish that. The poor woman."

"I think perhaps I will buy it after all," I said, noting some other information on the cover I thought might prove interesting to one of my Castle colleagues.

"You change your mind?"

"Nothing to do with the pictures, believe me."

18

THE BRAIN, A kilo of gray goo, is a curious organ. While much of it seems immediately useful and responds rather well to demands for information, there are times when the brain processes data in its own sweet time, oblivious to your promptings, and then, suddenly, long after its importance to you has waned, clacketty clacketty clack—*ping!*—out pops the useful little factoid you'd forgotten to remember in the first place.

Hence a slightly jolted feeling on my part as I crossed Windsor Bridge on my way back to the Castle, book in hand. I looked around, wondering as you do in such cases if there was a sensory trigger, a sight, a sound, a smell. But there was only the Thames to either side, sparkling in the high sun, benches scattered with weary tourists, their ice-cream bars dripping, oars splashing on water, dogs barking, one passerby's vinegar on chips pinching my nostrils, the spires of

St. George's Chapel rising above the Castle walls, a mirage in the heat haze. Nothing suggested Shillington to me, but Shillington rose unbidden in my mind nonetheless. *Ping!* Cath had said the name in passing the evening before. I'd felt a little tickle then. Now I knew—thank you, brain!— where I'd heard it before: Lydia Street, the woman in the wheelchair I'd met at the Garter Procession had uttered the same name while talking on the phone to the whatsit chairperson of the Windsor Cultural Centre board. Her side of the conversation had had a pacifying tone, which now, as I recalled bits of it, made me come over all suspicious, laced with not a little anger.

Or was I making a meal out of half a banana? Shillington wasn't *such* an uncommon a name.

Across the Datchet Road I espied The Royal Oak, purveyor of victuals and firewater. And home, among other conveniences, to a public telephone. There was one way to find out.

Hell, I thought, as numerals flashed and pips pipped, warning me my first twenty-p coin was about to be gobbled up by the phone. I was on hold. Being on hold in the UK is costly business. From a fistful of coins I'd extracted from my change purse and scattered on the counter, I plucked a fifty-p coin and jammed it into the slot. Idly, as I waited, I flipped through a newspaper someone had left behind. The *Evening Gazette*, as it happened, only the front-and-back sheet was missing, leaving me to a full-frontal assault by the day's page-three Gazette Girl and her amazing gravity-defying endowments. On to page five.

Where there was a continuation (three paragraphs worth), of a story from page one (probably two paragraphs worth) about the Pettibon murder. Most was a regurgitated encapsulation of events earlier in the week. There was a hint, though, of some small change, no doubt recounted on page one.

"Do you have the front page of this?" I dangled the detritus before a passing barmaid.

"Like as not," she replied, "but I'll have a look around."

"Thanks."

"Jane." A voice, Lydia's, came through the phone line. "Sorry to have kept you waiting. What can I do for you?"

"Well," I began cautiously, "when I paid you a visit Tuesday, you took a call from the chairman of your board and the name Shillington came up. Would this person by any chance be a parent or relation of Elise Shillington?"

There was a slight pause followed by a curious querying, "Yes?" Then: "It was her father."

"I couldn't help overhearing, you understand, but it sounded as though Mr. Shillington was very unhappy about something. Could I ask you what the conversation was about?"

Lydia laughed indulgently. "No. Sorry, Jane, it's rather confidential."

"I thought you might say that." I lowered my voice. "Lydia, I don't want you to break any confidences, but I've learned something this week that I think sheds a different light on Roger Pettibon's death, and I was hoping you might be able to help."

I took a deep breath and barrelled on: "I was visiting last evening with a woman I know in town, a woman I work with at the Castle. She has a thirteen-year-old daughter who was enrolled in the kids' Saturday morning art class last winter. She—the daughter—happened to tell us that Roger . . . well, that Roger had tried to molest her and that she thought he had tried the same with this other girl, Elise."

The sharp intake of breath on the other end of the phone was all I needed to hear. "So I would be right in assuming it's the same story with Elise Shillington?"

There was another, longer, pause. In reluctant tones, Lydia replied: "Yes. I'm sorry to say it is."

"Did you know about this situation before?"

"Not at all. It came as a complete surprise. I only learned the afternoon you paid me the visit. It seems Mr. Shillington does some regular business with the Castle. Someone told him when he was up there Tuesday morning that Roger had been murdered, which Mr. Shillington then mentioned at lunch with his family. His daughter reacted rather violently to this news and then it all came out. Mr. Shillington was quickly on the phone to Ken Rowland, our chairman, who telephoned me." Lydia sighed. "I'm very distressed to hear from you that this has happened to another child. Mr. Shillington's is the only complaint we've had. The only we've *ever* had along these lines. I'm afraid we're in a bit of a muddle as to how to handle it, particularly since the perpetrator—*alleged* perpetrator I suppose is more proper—is dead. What is the girl's name, if you don't mind my asking?"

"Cath Aiken."

"Oh, yes, I do know her. A very self-possessed child, as I recall. How is she? Does she seem at all . . . ?"

"She seems to have taken it in her stride, if that's what you mean. But you never know, do you?"

"No. That's partially why we're not quite sure how to proceed with this: If we start making even discreet inquiries among the parents, we may be creating unnecessary panic. If we don't, we may be ignoring children left with some sort of psychological damage. We thought it might have been a single isolated incident focused on one child but, now that you've called . . . still, it's difficult to believe Roger was engaged in some epidemic of this sort of activity. He'd have been found out, surely." She paused. The sound of muffled typing came down the phone. "And he always seemed to me such a *nice* man . . . ."

"You said you thought him opaque—I think was the word—on Tuesday."

"Well, yes. He was a little hard to really get to know. But I'd never have dreamt of this!"

"There's more, though," I continued unhappily.

"I expect you're thinking of Pippa Clair," Lydia cut in.

"Yes, actually."

"I couldn't help wonder. Poor Pippa. After you left Tuesday, I tried to reach Joanna but she had her answerphone switched on, not surprisingly. So I dropped a note in the post instead."

"You didn't mention . . . ?"

"Heavens, no. I expressed my condolences only. I could hardly raise these ugly accusations at this time. I have no idea what Joanna knows, or suspects. And, of course, it would only be conjecture as far as Pippa is concerned."

"I'm afraid not."

There was a low moan. "Oh, my Lord . . . what? What have you found out?"

"Lydia, I talked with Hugo FitzJames this afternoon. Pippa had told him Roger had been abusing her . . ."

"Oh, no."

". . . and then swore him to secrecy. Which he's honoured, even in the face of Pippa's death. It's not easy to fathom a fourteen-year-old boy's behaviour, but I think Hugo feels somehow protective of her, of her memory at least."

"I know you believe this portrait painter isn't responsible for Roger's death, Jane. But you're surely not suggesting a boy Hugo FitzJames's age would be capable of murder, are you?" She sounded horrified.

"I think anything's possible these days, sorry to say. I've doubted since the beginning the killer was Victor Fabiani. But, until now, motives have been pretty scarce.

"Of course, I could be dead wrong." I glanced at the paper bag containing *Nowhere Man*, Canon Leathley's protecting his cousin's whereabouts coming to mind. "But I think an adult known to be sexually abusing a child could be easy prey for a blackmailer, don't you?"

"Yes, I suppose." A worried and reluctant tone came down the line.

"There's something else, too: Roger had a stepdaughter from his first marriage."

"Really? I didn't know that."

"Her name's Miranda Walter. She's now a member of one of the teams working on the fire-damaged parts of the Castle. Miranda was at the Castle Monday morning, and since then seems to have vanished."

"That doesn't mean she—"

"No," I cut her off, "but it's interesting, don't you think? Especially if you're looking for patterns. Men who do these sorts of things may have specific tastes, for all I know. What, for instance, does this Elise Shillington look like?"

"Mmm, let me think: petite, dark-haired, pretty, although not remarkably so; a certain seriousness, a bit shy, perhaps . . ."

"But for the shyness, that could describe Cath Aiken.

Miranda Walter, though I've never seen her, has been described to me physically along those lines. Thirteen or fifteen years ago, she might have been a dark pretty young teenager. And Pippa—I only saw her once, in her school uniform. But she seems to fit the physical description."

"And she was certainly a solemn kid," Lydia continued worriedly. "Oh, my poor Joanna! Does she know, I wonder?"

"Someone who's been through this suggested to me mothers are often the last to know, or at least to acknowledge what's happening right under their noses. Although . . ."

Turned away from the phone as I was, I failed to notice the money counting down. The eternally vexing warning pips sent me scrambling for another coin, distracting me from Lydia's response.

". . . to her."

"Sorry?"

"Oh, Jane, I must ring off now. My secretary's just informed me the chairman's on the other line again. I'm . . . I'm glad you called, and I hope you'll call me again if you think there's anything I can do. Sorry to be so abrupt."

The phone went dead.

And page one of the *Evening Gazette* was not to be found. "Someone must have pinched it for the football results on the back," the helpful barmaid offered.

At the newsagents across the road, however, there was a copy of the *Evening Gazette*. And the *Sun* and the *Daily Mail* and the *Daily Telegraph* and the *Guardian* and the *Times* and the *Independent* and all the rest, and each had a variation on the same theme: discontent among unnamed officials at certain (read: high) levels with the case against society portrait painter (as he was described) Victor Fabiani for the self-confessed murder of Royal Collection Trust curator Roger Pettibon.

How *frightfully* interesting, I thought.

"You intending to buy one of them papers?" the shopkeeper asked sourly.

"Er . . ." My change purse had pretty much been emptied on the telephone. Besides, I'd got the gist. "No."

Shortly after six o'clock I was back in my bolt hole in Clarence Tower having—reluctantly—changed back into my housemaid's duds and having—belatedly—completed the few remaining tasks left over from the morning's rota. I had just kicked off my shoes and was slipping *Nowhere Man* out of the bag when Davey Pye eased in through the door, black and white and red all over.

"Couldn't you knock?"

"Much more fun to catch you *en déshabillé*, darling."

"No such luck." I held up the book. "Look what I found."

"Mmm." He took it from my hands and scanned the cover. "Oh! Ah!" he exclaimed, enlightenment easing his brow. "Good gracious! I thought ten consecutive paragraphs would more than strain Andrew's capacity. Will wonders never cease?"

"In time, probably."

"His name's in smaller type, though. Who's the other chap, I wonder?"

"The real writer, I'll bet. Macgreevy probably did some of the legwork and connived for coauthorship. Read the back flap."

"And here was I assuming our favourite Windsor watcher had been spawned in Reuben Crush's dungeon laboratory," Davey commented, his eyes scanning the brief text. He handed the book back to me.

"Meanwhile, I think we might guess why Macgreevy's been hanging around Windsor," I said.

"Why?"

"Don't be a clot, Davey. Rupert FitzJames's father is here, his grandson is here, and his cousin is here. Macgreevy's snooping around."

"But this Graven business, like this book, is nearly as dead as last night's shepherd's pie."

"Oh, I don't think so."

"I'm not sure smugness becomes you, my dear." He sat next to me on the bed.

"No? Well, I just happen to know that Rupert

FitzJames, Marquess of Graven, is alive and well and living abroad—"

"Half of England concluded that eight years ago, you goose. The other half figured he'd snuffed it."

"—living abroad, I was going to say, Davey, in Malaysia . . . or Thailand—one of those countries, at any rate."

"Narrowed the odds of finding him to one in a hundred million? I say, you are a clever wench, Jane. I don't suppose you have a street address? A postbox number? The name of Graven's cunning cottage among the shady mango trees or whatever shrubbery is on offer in that part of the world?"

"No, you blithering twit. But I know who does." And I told him of yesterday's overheard conversation between the Duke of Cheshire and Canon Leathley, which effectively dewithered his withering witherings.

"My, my," Davey commented drily, "the good reverend Canon harbouring knowledge about a fugitive all these years? I'm shocked. And appalled, I might add. Shocked *and* appalled. It's not often I'm both. Or either."

"But why," I interrupted his prattling, "has Leathley suddenly decided it's time to bring his cousin Rupert in from the cold . . . or the warm, as the case may be? *That* is the great question, in my humble opinion."

"To which you have an answer, no doubt."

"Well, I have a hypothesis. Good as."

Davey sprang suddenly from the bed. "Oh, wherever is my poor head: All this missing-aristocrat chat has made me forget why I'm here. Mother wants you!"

"Good! Just the monarch I've been wanting to talk to. When?"

"Now!"

"Are the races over?"

"Yes!"

"Give me a minute to slip my shoes back on, Davey. Her Majesty's not going to have your head."

"I've still to give the corgis their tea—"

"Well, you are in for it, then." I chuckled, springing into action. "C'mon, race you to the bottom."

• • • •

"Wrong way," Davey shouted between gasps after we'd reached the passageway below Clarence Tower. I won.

"But the Private Apartments are this way," I called back, gesturing in the direction I'd been headed, southward. My voice echoed along the stone chamber.

"I'm to take you this way." Davey pointed north.

"Are you sure?"

"Yes. It's a surprise."

A surprise? I caught up with him. "I should point out it's not my birthday."

"Then happy *un*birthday. Come along!"

As we flew down the passage, up stairs, along a corridor, and up more stairs, our destination became clearer, but the surprise at the end remained elusive.

"Tell me!"

"No."

"I don't like surprises."

"Tosh! Of course you do. Everybody loves surprises. Unless they've got a dicky heart. You haven't got a dicky heart, have you?"

We paused before a familiar door on the top floor of the north side of the Upper Ward. A corridor officer from the Royalty Squad was in attendance. Davey brushed at his tailcoat, adjusted his collar, and regarded me inquiringly.

"Ready?"

"As I'll ever be. And don't be a smart-arse about it, either."

Davey tapped lightly on the door, pushed it open, and bobbed his head smartly. His back blocked my view.

"Your Majesty. Jane Bee."

He stepped aside and glanced away, suppressing a giggle as I entered the room, familiar with the redolent smells of paint and turpentine. There, in the middle, on an easel turned at an angle toward the window, sat Fabiani's unfinished portrait of the Queen in her Garter robes. To one side—no surprise—stood the Queen herself in a pale yellow dress, the usual three strands of pearls looped around her neck—the day's Ascot ensemble, I deduced, as I sank into a curtsy.

"Good, you're here at last," Her Majesty said and, smilingly, gestured toward the figure on the other side of the portrait.

"Oh!"

It was Victor Fabiani.

"They've let you out!" I exclaimed without thinking.

"Surprised?" Davey whispered.

"You have Jane to thank in part for your release, Mr. Fabiani," the Queen said. "It's she who believed you were innocent."

Fabiani gazed piercingly at me under heavy black brows. With a touch of belligerence he said: "I suppose I ought to thank you."

"Well, I was with you—here, in this room—for at least part of the critical time," I countered immediately, irked by the tone of his response. "And if you had been in the Throne Room earlier with Mr. Pettibon, you didn't look to me like a man who'd just killed someone."

His lips twitched, as if he'd intended a response then thought better of it.

The Queen interposed silkily: "David, have you given the dogs their meal?"

"Er . . . no, Ma'am. I shall do that now, shall I?"

"I think that would be a good idea."

Disappointment registered on Davey's face. I knew he was dying to stay. "Yes, Ma'am," he replied, slowly reaching for the doorknob.

"Your Majesty," I interjected, "I should point out that Davey—David—was also up here Monday morning, after I'd done posing for Mr. Fabiani."

"I came to fetch the Garter robes just after ten o'clock," Davey supplied, his face brightening considerably. "Mr. Fabiani was here then, too, looking as calm as you please."

"Yes . . . interesting," the Queen responded as Victor scowled. "Might this, too, be why one's Garter was not found Monday morning until quite late?"

"Ma'am, I dropped it by accident."

"One certainly had a unsettling moment there, seeing an extra Garter buckled around Mr. Pettibon's leg."

"My humble apologies, Ma'am."

"Well, you found it, so it doesn't matter now. Thank you, David. Do make sure there's enough water in the dogs' bowls. It's been an awfully hot day."

Effectively dismissed, Davey bowed and backed out the door with a tiny whimper I'm sure only I heard.

"I rather wish this weather would break," HM continued conversationally, as if trying to ease a certain tension that pervaded the room. "You'll be able to complete this portrait now." She cocked her head at her painted image, studying it. "It's quite good, I think." She smiled encouragingly at the sullen artist.

"Would Your Majesty sit for me one more time?" Fabiani asked, thawing slightly.

"Yes, of course, if you like. Let me see. Would tomorrow afternoon suit you? I could give you an hour after lunch."

"That would be fine, Ma'am."

"Now, shall we sit down? I have a few questions. And Jane is looking more than a little impatient, I think."

Fabiani shot me a look of surprise and annoyance as though I were an ant at his picnic.

"I'll sit here. Then you can study me, Mr. Fabiani. Perhaps you won't need tomorrow's sitting after all." The Queen took a straight-backed chair and tucked her handbag beside her. Victor pulled up a stool while I settled for an old ottoman.

"Jane has been rather diligent on your behalf, you know," the Queen began, but Fabiani cut her off:

"Well, I didn't ask her to!"

"Mr. Fabiani." the Queen's tones were rimed with frost. "I have great difficulty believing you were looking forward to a trial and a very long prison sentence for a murder of which you're entirely innocent."

"Is there assurance I am . . . Ma'am?"

"If either the police—or I—thought you genuinely were a murderer, Mr. Fabiani, then you wouldn't be sitting here with me, now would you?"

"No, ma'am, I suppose not."

"Good, now let's not have any more nonsense. Jane expressed her doubts to me Tuesday morning when she told me she'd been here in this room with you very near to the time Mr. Pettibon was killed. Since, for various reasons, I'm inclined to trust her sensibilities, one could only wonder what would drive you to declare yourself a murderer. I understand there are people who confess to crimes because they're disturbed individuals, but nothing in our conversations during my sittings at Easter suggested to me you were . . ." Her Majesty paused, seeming to grope for the right word.

". . . bonkers."

Found it.

". . . so, one could only conclude a sane man would do this insane thing for a very powerful reason."

Fabiani pressed his lips together as if determined to say nothing. Getting no response, HM queried: "Did the police not ask you what you thought you'd been up to when they released you from detention this afternoon?"

"Yes, Ma'am."

"And what did you tell them?"

"Nothing."

The Queen shook her head sadly. "You'll be charged with wasting their time, you know."

"They've said as much, Ma'am."

Her Majesty glanced out the window as if gathering her thoughts. The summer sun had settled into the northern sky and a few rays warmed the opalescent pearls, softening the lines around her eyes and mouth, silvering her gray hair.

Running her fingers absently along her pearls, she said thoughtfully: "One might confess to a minor crime one didn't commit if one were under duress of some nature, blackmail perhaps, or the expectation of some great sum after serving a jail sentence. But I can only think of one reason why someone would confess to a murder one didn't commit, and that's to protect someone, a loved one I should think.

"You have a daughter, I believe."

"Yes, Ma'am," Fabiani responded coolly, "But I think I can count a number of 'loved ones' among the people I know."

"And how many of them live at Windsor and work here at the Castle, I wonder?"

Fabiani fell into a stubborn silence.

"I expect, of course, you made no mention of your daughter to the police."

"No," he replied reluctantly.

"And they made no mention of her to you."

"They wouldn't know I had a daughter."

The Queen cast her eyes in my direction.

"They do know, though," I spoke up tentatively. "The police, that is. Or at least one of them. I ran into Chief Inspector Nightingale at Ascot yesterday and I told him about Miranda . . . among other things, that is."

Fabiani's dark eyes blazed. "Why the f—"

"Mr. Fabiani!" The Queen broke in. "The police would have found out soon enough. If they're satisfied you're not the killer then they will start looking elsewhere, and I daresay they will begin by looking for people with a connection to you. They're not stupid. They will assume, as we do, that you must be protecting someone."

"There is an assumption here, if I may say, Ma'am," Fabiani said angrily, "that my daughter is the one responsible for this death."

"Not necessarily. But your actions this week suggest that *you* think she may be."

Fabiani seemed to stifle himself with an effort of will. I watched his knuckles turn white as he gripped the edge of the stool.

"Mr. Fabiani," I said, "I've learned that despite the general leave granted for Ascot week, Miranda was in the castle precincts Monday morning. I've also learned she left Windsor later Monday morning in her car, with luggage, destination unknown. And despite the news of Roger Pettibon's murder and your arrest in all the newspapers and all over television and radio, she's made no attempt to contact the police, or come to your side, or make herself known in any way."

Victor's voice rose: "I can't believe this! Aren't you a housemaid?"

"I think you'll find Jane has other useful talents." The Queen was pushing her wedding ring around her finger with her thumb, a sure sign that underneath the surface she was vexed. "Jane also has, for someone her age—in this day and age—a reasonably well-developed sense of right and wrong, and what she's believed most of this week to be wrong is the idea that you've admitted to a crime you didn't commit. I daresay Jane doesn't care to be strenuously disbelieved by people in authority either," she added, glancing knowingly at me, while a blush of pleasure at her endorsement crept up my neck, "but that's beside the point.

"One shares her concerns, I might add. You must see, Mr. Fabiani, that work is being done in your interest," HM continued more mildly. "If the real killer isn't found, suspicion will naturally continue to hang over your head, whatever the police, or I, believe."

"Yes, Ma'am." Fabiani said it grudgingly.

"Had your daughter planned a week away from Windsor?"

Fabiani appeared to think about it. "Possibly, Ma'am," he replied at last. "I'm not sure what her plans for the week were."

"So you don't know where Miranda is now?"

"No."

"Are you quite sure?"

Fabiani didn't reply.

"Indications are she hasn't left England at any rate," I supplied.

"How do you know that?" he asked sharply.

The Queen gave me a cautioning glance.

"An informed source," I replied evasively.

Fabiani was beginning to have the look of a man whose options had narrowed. His eyes darted to the door, as if he sought escape. I supposed only the position of his royal inquisitor kept him put.

"One can very much understand the desire to protect a child, whatever she may have done," the Queen continued evenly. "There is an extra poignancy in your case, I think, because you have only just found Miranda—or she, you, rather—and now there is a fear you might lose her again. Unfortunately, both your admirable restraint and her apparent disappearance do little more than create suspicion. Your daughter was here at the Castle, too, that morning, which may have presented an opportunity. And, of course, a weapon was left lying about that I suppose anybody might have used."

"And what, Ma'am," Fabiani said with satisfaction, as if he'd at last found a way out, "might have been Miranda's motive?"

"One hopes, Mr. Fabiani, that your daughter had no motive at all, that she is innocent beyond any doubt. But can you assure me of that?"

"Ma'am," I said, raising my hand like an eager schoolgirl seeking the teacher's permission to speak. "I have some new information that may—" I caught Fabiani's eye and felt suddenly a rush of sorrow for him, and for the pain I was sure he would have to revisit. "—that may, um, shed some light on . . . things."

Her Majesty's eyebrows rose fractionally. "Go on, Jane."

"Roger Pettibon was, for a time, Miranda Walter's stepfather."

"Really," the Queen responded, her expression alert. "Did you know that, Mr. Fabiani?"

"It's something I learned recently, Ma'am," Victor said unhappily.

"There's more . . . I'm afraid." Having to present the gleanings of the last twenty-four hours filled me with dread. I wished I'd never been anywhere near the north side of the Upper Ward Monday morning, had never been tapped by Fabiani for the posing gig that made me doubt his guilt, was involved nohow nowhere at all. The thought struck me: Roger Pettibon richly deserved his bloody death. Who cares who stuck the sword in his back?

"Jane?" the Queen prompted.

"Oh, sorry, Ma'am." I took a deep breath and considered my words: "There is evidence, Ma'am, Mr. Fabiani, that Roger Pettibon had an unhealthy attraction to young girls, more specifically to girls in their early adolescence—"

"Ooph." The Queen made an uncharacteristic noise. Her hand went to her pearls, her lips pinched in distaste.

"I've learned of a couple of girls Mr. Pettibon touched in an inappropriate way, but today—I talked with someone who could confirm that Roger Pettibon was, well, more than just some sort of pathetic dirty old man."

"And?"

"I talked with your Page of Honour, Ma'am—Lord Lambourn."

"Hugo?"

"Some weeks before her death, Philippa Clair had confided to him that her stepfather had been . . ." I shuddered involuntarily, ". . . abusing her sexually for some time. And, of course, he—Roger, that is—had threatened Pippa if she told anybody. So it was pretty brave of her, I think, to even tell Hugo. Lord Lambourn, I mean."

I watched the Queen's hand, resting on the arm of her chair, slowly curl into a fist. She closed her eyes.

"And Pippa," I added, "was not Roger Pettibon's first stepdaughter."

The Queen opened her eyes, their cornflower blue sparkling with moisture. Victor's face, set in lines of strain, could disguise nothing now. Anger, revulsion, surrender. It was painful to watch.

"Mr. Fabiani," Her Majesty said gravely, "I am so very, very sorry."

Victor's head nodded almost imperceptibly, a tiny concession.

"When did you know?" the Queen asked him gently.

At first it seemed he would not answer. He looked dully toward the window, over the treetops toward distant Eton College Chapel, as if he were making up his mind about something.

"Sunday," he replied at last. "Five days ago. I could see she was upset about something . . . deeply upset." He sighed, his anger for the moment spent. "And so she told me, finally. Everything." He looked at me. "Exactly what you've been talking about. Possibly worse. He's a fiend. *Was* a fiend.

"She'd seen Pettibon, you see. A few days earlier. The sight of him had revived some very painful memories—"

"She had not seen Pettibon before?" I asked, "But—"

"Yes, I know what you're going to say," Fabiani cut in. "It does seem odd they never met before. They both live and work in Windsor, but it's a big enough town, and Miranda's only been here a year. If Pettibon ever visited the rooms Miranda was working on, she never saw him. And she'd no reason to go into the Royal Library where he works."

"But all the stuff in the papers at Easter about Pippa?"

"Miranda visited with her mother—her adoptive mother—in Malta over Easter, where she lives with her third husband. She missed the story, probably. And if I remember correctly, the papers referred to her as Pippa . . . Clair, wasn't it? Her natural father's name? Not Pettibon.

"Anyway, Miranda was working on some restorations in the Grand Reception Room Friday afternoon. She was up on some scaffolding, Pettibon happened to come in, and she saw him."

"She must have been deeply shocked," the Queen commented.

"Very, Ma'am. And horribly frightened, too. Seeing him again was like reliving a nightmare for her. His is a face she's tried to put out of her mind for the last fourteen years."

"I wonder if Pettibon saw her?" I mused.

"She says no. She left quickly. She told her supervisor she was ill and she went back to her flat."

"And yet she returned to the Castle Monday morning."

Fabiani regarded me with cold intensity. "So you say. But I didn't see her. She didn't come to see me."

"But the idea of your daughter coming back to the Castle Monday, frightened as she had been Friday, can't have seemed unusual or incredible to you," I argued. "Monday afternoon, you were ready to confess to a brutal murder you didn't commit. You thought Miranda did it. That she'd come to confront Pettibon and then . . ." I left the rest unsaid. "I think a frightened woman would have stayed at home. But an angry woman . . . ?"

"Mr. Fabiani," the Queen added, "one appreciates that Miranda was badly frightened by seeing her . . . her tormenter again. And one appreciates your attempts to protect your daughter, because that's what you're still doing, aren't you? You want us to believe Miranda was terrified, and in her terror, fled somewhere. Now that your 'confession' has been exposed as a ruse, you're still hoping to protect Miranda in another way. But the fact remains—on Monday you believed your daughter capable of murdering Roger Pettibon."

An angry flush darkened Fabiani's face. And then he exploded.

"All right!" His voice seemed to shake the room with its force. "Have it your way! *Yes*, I thought her capable! *Yes*, she was angry! *Yes*, when I heard Pettibon was dead, murdered, I thought she'd done it! I felt . . . I felt proud of her, you know? I was glad the little shit was dead! If that's what it took her to rid herself of her pain and her suffering, then bloody good job!"

Suddenly, there was a terrific crash as something hit the wall. The door, I realized as I jumped in my seat, gasping with surprise. Fabiani began coughing uncontrollably. A male voice called loudly with just a trace of anxiety: "Ma'am? Is everything all right?"

"Yes, Derek," the Queen replied quickly. The charged atmosphere had sent her hand to her throat in an unconscious protective gesture, and she released it as she tried to mollify the officer who burst upon us from behind the canvas. "We're fine, Derek. Mr. Fabiani is somewhat distressed, I'm afraid."

"Get the . . . bottle," Fabiani ordered, choking and gasping, his face purple. He pointed vaguely toward the other side of the room. "Whisky. Drawer. Get it. For Christ's sake, man, I need a drink."

Derek glanced at Fabiani with distaste, and then raised an inquiring eyebrow to the Queen. She responded with a nearly imperceptible nod.

"You may leave us," she said to the officer after he'd fetched a bottle of Scotch and poured Fabiani a generous shot.

"Are you quite sure, Ma'am?"

"Quite," she replied in a patient tone. "We're in no danger. Thank you."

"I'm sorry, Ma'am," Fabiani sputtered when the officer had gone. "I . . ."

"It's quite all right. I can understand you must be upset."

Fabiani glanced at his now empty glass. "Would Your Majesty care to join me? Miss Bee?"

"Not my tipple, I'm afraid," the Queen replied, amused. I shook my head. "But, please, do have another if you want."

He eyed the glass in his hand reluctantly. "No, I'd better not." He leaned over and placed the glass on a nearby table. "I'm sorry about the outburst," he said, "but you must understand my feelings. Men like Roger Pettibon are scum in my view, and the fact that my daughter was his victim enrages me. I can't say his death was undeserved. Can you say he didn't deserve this?" he challenged us.

He was echoing my thoughts. I had no reply. The Fount of Justice was herself curiously silent. After a moment, she said quietly: "I think everyone deserves a chance at redemption."

Fabiani's expression hardened. I piped up: "I think he might have been seeking some help from the Church. He'd been seen with Canon Leathley over the last few months."

"Really?" the Queen commented. Fabiani made a contemptuous noise.

"In any case," HM continued with a degree of impatience, "the court is the place where mitigating factors will be taken into account. The police, I'm afraid, are a blunter instrument. Their task is simply to find the offender. And one would like to be of some assistance, if possible. It's very disagreeable to have someone murdered in your own home, Mr. Fabiani, and if you've followed the papers the last few years, you'll know this isn't the first instance.

"One wonders, though, what assistance you're likely to give the authorities, Mr. Fabiani, given the bent you've shown this week for deception."

"Ma'am, I've already said more than I intended."

"You've said your daughter was angry, but being angry doesn't necessarily mean one will behave in a violent way."

"Unless, Ma'am," I said, for the thought had just come to me, "unless there's more." I looked at Victor. "Did Miranda make some sort of threat against Roger Pettibon? Is that why you reacted the way you did the next day?"

There was a painful silence. He glared as though his anger would flare again.

"Okay, all right, yes. She did," he said, sharply enunciating each word.

"And the threat was serious enough to worry you the next day."

"Miranda seemed a withdrawn young woman when I first met her, after she'd tracked me down. Much too serious for someone her own age, I thought. She didn't seem to have any friends in Windsor. No boyfriend in the picture that I knew of. Some of her interests seemed to lie in this New Age quackery that I've no use for. But on Sunday, she revealed a side to herself that endeared her to me in a new way. I'd grown fond of her, of course. I'd never expected to have a child, never thought about it much—too busy with my work, of course, and the women I've known . . . well, never mind. But when she showed up on my doorstep in London last winter I was . . . pleased, thrilled—once the shock had worn off."

"You're sure she *is* your daughter?" I asked. Rude of me, but Fabiani didn't, for once, take umbrage.

"She had all the right papers. She'd done her research. And she looks like me. I could see the resemblance right off. But nothing else about her seemed like me. Of course, she'd never been a part of my life, I never suspected her existence, and it's foolish to expect anything, and perhaps even narcissistic, but I found myself searching for other signs of myself in her—not just hair colour, or the curve of a nose, or the shape of one's eyes.

"And then, on Sunday she exploded with rage. And even in the midst of the horror of her story, I thought: God, the girl's got my damn temper. Does that sound mad? I don't know. But at that moment, for the first time, I truly felt like her father.

"And I could have killed Pettibon *myself* for what he'd done!"

A long silence followed this declaration. The Queen raised an eyebrow. "Interesting you should say that, Mr. Fabiani," she said, her voice pensive. "You see, I'm beginning to wonder if perhaps we haven't got you all wrong."

I stared at the Queen with surprise. But she was studying Fabiani the way I'm sure she must study a difficult guest granted a private Audience, trying to glean the truth from behind the mask of words and gestures. Fabiani's eyes drifted from the royal scrutiny.

Coolly, Her Majesty continued: "Whether you welcome Jane's intrusion or not, she ably discredited your professed motive for killing Mr. Pettibon—"

"As you say, Ma'am . . ." Victor repressed a frown.

"—but, unfortunately, Mr. Fabiani, what Jane seems to have done in the meantime is uncover another, much stronger, motive. You've just said you could have killed Mr. Pettibon yourself for what he did to your daughter. Perhaps Jane misread your demeanour Monday morning. You could have gone down to the Throne Room and then returned here, to this room, and composed yourself before calling her to pose for you. There was time. Not much. But sufficient."

Fabiani returned Her Majesty's gaze. "But, Ma'am, why would I concoct a phony confession? Why would I go to the police at all?"

"Why, indeed, Mr. Fabiani." The Queen rivetted him with her eyes. "Why, indeed."

19

BEING THAT IT was Friday evening and all, being that Ascot Week had essentially galloped to a finish for another year, and being that Ingrid, one of the other housemaids, was celebrating her twenty-first birthday, a whole crew of us from the lower orders went out for a bit of a bop to Stripes, a club just off Peascod Street that had decided to eschew the usual deep and funky spatial House, underground Techno, and Detroit grooves in favour of a time-tunnel experience back to the remote and distant 1980's. Which suited me fine since I was (selfishly) in want of a bit of nostalgic distraction anyway, and the poptastic tunes of my vaunted youth were just the tonic, given that the informational uncorkings of the last twenty-four hours hadn't exactly left me in a bubbly mood.

I was still reeling from the encounter only hours earlier with Fabiani. Could I have been so pigheadedly wrong? Had

294 ❖ C. C. Benison

I completely misread the artist's composure Monday when he called me into his rooms? It was true, as Her Majesty pointed out in conversation afterward, that I had no reason that workaday morning to be alert to the artist's mood shifts. Fabiani was a somewhat mercurial fellow at the best of times anyway. And there *was* opportunity, though barely. Perhaps a fifteen-minute opportunity if DCI Nightingale was scrupulous about the possible time of death, nine o'clock. And, of course, Fabiani did have a motive. A real one this time. And a damn good one at that.

"Considering what one now knows about Mr. Pettibon's . . . transgressions," Her Majesty had continued gravely as Victor shifted uncomfortably on his stool, "it's possible to see his murderer executing a kind of swift justice. Or *believing* himself to be executing swift justice. I think I'm reading you correctly, Mr. Fabiani, if you don't mind the observation, in saying you don't seem to me a methodical cold-blooded murderer—"

"Thank you, Ma'am." Victor regarded the Monarch sourly, his voice tinged with sarcasm.

The corners of the Queen's mouth turned up in a slight smile. "One does glean a thing or two about artists when sitting for one's portrait," she acknowledged dryly. "On the other hand, my experience of you suggests to me you might be capable of doing something . . . *imprudent* in the heat of the moment, Mr. Fabiani, then immediately regretting it. You do, I think, blow hot and cold from time to time."

Victor remained stonily silent.

"However," HM continued, "you do seem to me a man of some character and moral purpose. It's conceivable to me that remorse would drive you to admit to a crime of this nature—"

"Ma'am," Fabiani cut in strenuously, "to repeat my earlier question—why would I give the police a fish story?"

"For chivalrous reasons, in part, one might guess. And much fatherly concern, surely. You wouldn't want your daughter to suffer again—as Miranda most certainly would through a trial and public exposure—the agony of reliving this dreadful episode in her life. So you fabricated a plausible alternative motivation."

Victor paused. His expression was stormy. "Your Majesty, are you accusing me of murder?"

"No, Mr. Fabiani, I am merely making an hypothesis. The police have released you from detention, having satisfied themselves that your stated motive is false. But they are, as I understand it"—the Queen glanced my way for agreement—"quite in the dark about Mr. Pettibon's history with young girls, among them your daughter, of whose very existence they were also unaware. And I gather, too, there's very much a lack of physical evidence, at least to date, to place anyone in the Throne Room at the time of death. I believe the blood found on your smock, which was the same type as Roger Pettibon's, has been found, after further analysis, to be your own. Am I right?"

"Yes, Ma'am, I cut myself one day last week."

"Well, I suppose one could say, as the Americans might, that we're back to square one. Except for this: Roger Pettibon's secret life is secret no longer. At least a few people have admitted to knowing. A few others I can think of may be keeping the knowledge to themselves. But all, quite understandably, would bear strong feeling against Pettibon, unfortunately you among them, Mr. Fabiani."

"Then perhaps I should confess again," Victor said bitterly.

"I'm not sure the police would care to handle two confessions from you in one week," the Queen retorted calmly. "You'd be the boy who cried wolf, in their books." Then she paused and cocked her head at him, rather the way the Queen Mother does at certain moments. "Or might that have been the very idea—to throw the police off the scent? Send them on a goose chase over forged drawings, then have them dismiss you as a credible suspect."

Fabiani looked as if he were about to explode. He opened his mouth to speak but the Queen held up a cautioning hand.

"Again, Mr. Fabiani, I'm only exploring possibilities. As I've said before, I'm not pleased about people being murdered in my home, and I'm quite concerned that there be a resolution. And soon."

"Ma'am, I did not kill Pettibon," Victor insisted. "As Your Majesty suspected earlier, I was worried for Miranda.

That's all. On Monday I tried, without success, to telephone her at lunch, a time we'd arranged. And then, when I went to her flat, I learned from her neighbour she'd left in her car with luggage. This, after she'd told me she'd no plans for the week and we'd arranged to have dinner. So I . . . became worried. The confession was an impulse.''

"So you say. But how long did you really think you could sustain this notion that you forged Old Master drawings?''

Victor shrugged. "For a time, at least. I do happen to know it's difficult to prove a disputed drawing or painting to be genuine beyond doubt. I was talking about this, and about some of the techniques forgers have used, with Joanna Pettibon only last week. She told me, for instance, a story about Sir Peter Lely, court painter to Charles II, who was so captivated by a couple of the Leonardo drawings in the Royal Collection, he copied them himself and substituted his copies for the originals. So at least a couple of the hundreds of Leonardos in the collection may well be Lely's forgeries. But no one knows which ones. Or if the story is true at all. Or even if there are *other* forgeries in the collection.''

"How very interesting," said the Queen.

"So,'' Fabiani continued, "I expect this is what inspired my confession, if 'inspired' is the right word, Ma'am.'' He shrugged again. "I knew a little of the sorts of paper and inks a forger would need. My own art education naturally included study of the Old Masters, and we would make drawings after Leonardo or Michelangelo in class. I think, given the right materials, I could probably do a passable Old Master forgery. Given the suggestion there might be fakes in the Royal Collection and knowing that Roger Pettibon was a curator, it wasn't too implausible to suggest he'd been blackmailing me over forgeries I'd made in my foolish youth.''

"But you made one mistake, though," I piped up, having watched the recent exchange with growing dismay. "Leonardo's handedness.''

Fabiani regarded me with some distaste. "Yes, of course. Leonardo da Vinci was left-handed. Anyone with a knowledge of art history knows that! I'm implacably *right-*

handed. It's a great stumbling block if you've any intent of faking Leonardos. A simple test of my ability shading a drawing with my left hand would have convinced the police how weak was my claim to have faked Leonardo drawings. I kept waiting for the penny to drop. I don't know why it took them so bloody long to twig."

He looked off through the window. The Queen's eyes darted to her watch. "Well, Mr. Fabiani, this has been most interesting," she said, reaching for her handbag, the usual signal that an interview was at an end.

Thinking about the episode a little afterward, en route to Stripes, I wondered at HM's not voicing her concerns about Victor Fabiani to her detective, Derek Landerer. Did this mean she was satisfied he was innocent of Pettibon's murder despite her expressed doubts? Or was she simply recognizing that he was hardly some psycho killer likely to rampage through the Castle on a stabbing spree? For my part, I wondered how, Monday morning, Fabiani even knew Pettibon was in the Upper Ward at all. From his top-floor rooms, the artist could only look out windows high over the North Terrace. Or had Pettibon, as Fabiani had originally claimed, come up to the latter's rooms where they'd quarrelled with disastrous consequences? Had my ears really been numb to this?

So you can see I was feeling less than chipper by the time I changed into a frock and arrived at Stripes. I did, however, manage to lose myself in the music for a goodish time once I'd got inside and joined my mates. But then some bloke—a spotty-looking gardener from Windsor Great Park, no less—tried to sell me some drugs, which caused Pippa Clair to flash in my brain, which made me tell Pizza Face to sod off in an even more vehement tone than I might normally use. But the damage was done: the Pettibon murder had edged its way back into my brain. And it didn't help that a moment later I spotted Iain Scott (without the fair Amanda) materializing near the bar. He saw me, frowned slightly, then turned back to conversation with woman unknown. I wasn't keen to talk with him either.

I'd managed to reimmerse myself in Duran Duran for a while, shutting a mental door on Pettibon the (ugh) sexbeast, when the music stopped abruptly, a collective groan arose from the dance floor, and a disembodied voice called me to the telephone. I waited a second for the music to recommence, arose with a limp grin, and pretended to toddle off toward the loo, but made for the bar instead. There, a thin man in a zebra-striped shirt to match the zebra-striped decor was holding a phone receiver high in the air with a cheesed-off expression on his face.

"We don't normally take personal calls here, but this is *supposed*—" his tone was withering "—to be an emergency."

I felt a slight frisson of alarm. Emergency? Had my grandmother died? But who the hell knew I was here?

"Round this way," the man in the zebra-striped shirt shouted, gesturing impatiently to an alcove lined with wine bottles. He handed me the base of the phone. "You'll have some quiet."

Not much, but after I'd made a tentative hello I was relieved to be able to hear over the noise not a Canadian but an English accent. "I knew you'd be there," the voice said.

"Who is this?"

"Fleur. And you don't have to shout, Jane. I can hear you."

"Fleur! What's happened? Are you all right? The man said it was an emergency."

A short raspberry traveled down the wire. "Only way I could get him from ringing off. Look—"

"How'd you find me?"

"I knew Ingrid was having a birthday party and the lot of you were going out somewhere. Anyway, I was lying here watching the end of *Red Dwarf* on telly, and guess whose car should pull up?"

"Not—!"

"She's pulling her bags out right this minute."

"You're kidding! I'll be right there. Thanks, Fleur!"

I cradled the receiver, then paused to gather my wits. What would I say to her? The phone suddenly rang in my hands. Startled, I jumped, then peeked out of the alcove looking for someone to answer the insistent thing. But the staff were distributing drinks elsewhere and the sound of a phone ringing was drowned by the sound of music after five paces.

"Stripes," I answered the call.

"I want to speak to a woman named Jane Bee," a man's voice barked. "I know she's there. There's no good saying she isn't."

"Then I won't, Andrew."

Pause.

"What the hell are you doing answering the phone in a club?" Macgreevy snarled.

"I'm moonlighting. How did you know I was here?"

"That twit footman friend of yours said you were there clubbing. I rang up the footmen's lounge." Background cackle told me he was calling from his car.

"And how'd you get the number to the footmen's lounge?"

"In the gents', Riverside Station, where do you think? I don't know why I'm wasting my time calling you," he muttered. "Listen, Stella, as part of our bargain, I'm letting you know that I've found her."

"Found who?" I said coolly.

"Miranda, of course!"

"Well, *what* a co-inky-dink!"

"What? I can barely hear you with that bloody racket."

"I said: Where? Where did you find her?"

"She's been staying at some bloody ashram thing or whatever they call them now. Near Glastonbury. I'm on the M5. I'll be there in about half an hour."

"Then turn around."

"What?"

"I said: Turn around. Don't waste your petrol. Miranda's not there. She's here. In Windsor."

Another pause. I could sort of feel a cold blast through the receiver.

"You're having me on."

"No lie."

Another pause, this one punctuated by a screeching noise. He'd found a lay-by.

"What the hell are you playing at! You've bloody set me up!" he shouted. The nightclub din was no problem now. "You've had me chasing this woman over half of England just to keep me out of Windsor, you and your bloody swear-on-the-Bible—"

"Andrew, don't be ridiculous. I'd no idea Miranda was

here. She only just got back this minute. I never *expected* her back."

"Then her connection to this Pettibon murder is bogus. Was all along. Which you knew."

"I did not! And her connection's not bogus. Fabiani was released this afternoon. We've . . . *I've* talked with him. And Miranda *did* have a motive. A very strong one, as it happens.

"Now, if you step on it, Macgreevy, you just might get back here in time to get your scoop before the police get the wind up," I added hotly, feeling guilty at the same time, as if I'd shopped Miranda.

"So the cops are in the picture, are they? I see. I suppose they applied thumbscrews to Fabiani to make him tell."

"Well—"

"I thought not. You've wasted my time, Stella. Everybody'll have Miranda now. I think my angle's going to be the role of a certain busybody housemaid."

"You swore, Macgreevy!"

"I've gone over to the dark side."

"Fine!" I shouted into the phone. "Then I won't tell you what I know about Rupert FitzJames, the Nowhere Man! I know where FitzJames is, Macgreevy. And I'll bet you don't!"

There was a strangled noise in my ear. I slammed the phone down and angrily jerked at the cord.

A crash followed.

"Oh, my gosh, I'm so sorry." The waiter who'd handed me the phone lay in a heap on the floor behind the bar like a felled zebra, a tray's worth of spilled liquid and broken glassware strewn in a fan beyond his head. "Are you okay? Hello?"

"Please leave," he muttered into the floor. Iain and a few other chuckleheads at the bar leaned over to observe.

"Here. Let me help." Gingerly I picked at a couple of the larger pieces of broken glass.

"No. Please don't." He rose red-faced from the floor to a smattering of applause and brushed at his shirt.

"White vinegar'll get that stain out."

He scowled at me.

"I really am sorry. Thanks for letting me use the phone, by the way." I smiled sheepishly. "Emergency. Must run."

"Heather," I said a moment later, retrieving my handbag. "I'm off."

"But we haven't had Ingrid's cake yet."

"Something's come up."

"Jamie?"

"Don't I wish."

Not a sweet breath of wind stirred the air along lower Peascod Street, other than the air I was stirring by dashing down the cobbles. People spilling from pub doors to drink and canoodle in the sultry evening looked a blur as I passed, the dusk robbing them of colour and contour even the street lamps with their clouds of tiny fevered dancing insects could not restore. What, I wondered, my heart tripping as much from anticipation as exertion, was I going to say to Miranda Walter? As I clung by my toes to the edge of the pavement waiting impatiently for a break in the traffic along Clarence Road, I realized part of me—the emotional part—was rushing to warn Miranda off, to say to her: *I don't care if you did it, the creep deserved it, now get back in your car and head for the Chunnel, quick quick, hurry hurry. I'll drive you myself.* But some other part, some cooler reflective bit, I suppose, was asserting the need for a clear-cut resolution. HM's words came back to me: *Everyone deserves a chance at redemption.* Yes, I supposed reluctantly, even sad sick furtive people like the late R. Pettibon. And their deaths, too, warranted a kind of resolution.

As if to emphasize the point, as I turned the corner into St. Margaret Place, the heavens over St. Margaret Ward Church suddenly blazed in a lurid light that bleached the house fronts and flared the rooftops. And yet no thunder followed. A pale fuzzy sliver of a moon over the church steeple quickly reclaimed its place as the brightest object in the darkening blue of the sky, and I realized Windsor had been struck with summer lightning. Either that, I thought, or the gods shop at discount literary cliché warehouses.

Fleur waved to me from her second-floor window. She

was standing, a crutch under one arm (I was glad to see she'd got some medical attention), a dark outline against the ghostly flickering light of her television. I saw her glance up, and then her figure seemed to vanish as a greater light once again quicksilvered the sky. The silence following seemed ominous, as if thunder were biding its time. Fleur, restored by darkness, shrugged and pointed downward urgently toward the car, Miranda's car, the red-and-cream 2CV of description, parked in front of the house that contained her flat.

Light filtered through translucent sitting-room draperies of the top flat. The two flats below Miranda's were dark. I glanced into the car's interior—no luggage—then mounted the stairs and pressed the top button of the call box.

"Yes?" crackled a wary voice.

"Miranda, my name's Jane Bee. I work at the Castle. I was wondering if I could speak with you."

There was a brief silence filled by the metallic *whoosh* of the intercom. "It's rather late," she countered. "Couldn't you—?"

"It's kind of important. Would you mind?"

A buzzer sounded; the door snapped open. Before entering I thought to look across the road. Still in her window, Fleur made an encouraging thumbs-up gesture.

"Has something happened at work?" Miranda stood outside the door to her flat as I climbed the last of the stairs.

"You could say that."

"Are you with one of the crews?" She cast her eyes over my dress. "Have we met?"

"No," I replied, but I thought I'd recognize her anywhere. Miranda Walter was, without a doubt, Victor Fabiani's daughter. Her hair, as black and thick as his, was gathered back in loose wings with a clip, her forehead was high and clear, her eyes dark and luminous. Only the slender nose and delicate chin suggested another, feminine, source. Her striking beauty reminded me of the faces I'd seen in pre-Raphaelite paintings at the National Gallery: remote, pale, a little sad. She even held herself as they did in the old paintings, with an arm held protectively around the chest.

"I'm a member of Staff," I explained, avoiding specificity. "May I come in?"

She ushered me through to the front sitting room, starkly white and sparsely furnished—a few pieces from Habitat, a couch, a couple of chairs. Most of the horizontal surfaces—a table, the mantlepiece a shelving unit—were given over to a startling and curious collection of objects: masks, busts, highly decorated (but empty) picture frames, religious paraphernalia. And on the floor lay highly decorated picture frames and sections of baroque moldings, the latter cuing me to the realization that these things were the fruits of the plaster modeller's craft. I recognized, too, over the stuffiness of an apartment closed up for a week, the faintly bitter odour of drying plaster.

"How can I help you?" she asked, pushing a loosening tendril of hair back over her ear.

"It's about the events of the past week," I replied, drawn from admiring her handiwork to her wan expression. Did she really not know?

"About your father," I added, putting a question into my voice.

There was a slight intake of breath. Her beautiful eyes widened. "My father? Victor? What's happened?"

"You've been away all week, haven't you? At some sort of ashram."

"Retreat," she countered. "How did you know?"

"And there were no newspapers? Television? Radio?"

"No. It's a *retreat*," she replied with a touch of impatience, as if such things were self-evident. "But what about my father?" she added worriedly.

"He's been held by police most of the week."

Her eyes widened further. "What! Whatever for?"

Beyond the conventional expressions of mild surprise and shock, I found her face essentially unreadable. Then the gauzy draperies suddenly exploded with light. Miranda cried: "What was that?"

"Just summer lightning," I explained soothingly. "Miranda, perhaps you'd better sit down."

Quite the wrong thing to say, I now know: so doomladen, like those telegrams from the War Office in films. Miranda hugged herself and brought one hand to her mouth as if to suppress a scream. She stayed rooted. With growing dismay, I continued:

"Your father was being held this week because of a murder, Miranda."

Her hand sagged slightly. She spoke through her fingers. Smooth and pale they were, but with bitten nails, I couldn't help but notice.

"A murder?"

"Roger Pettibon is dead. He was murdered. Stabbed."

There was an excrutiating stillness in the room. Miranda's eyes, huge in her strained white face, stared at me. Then the arm, wrapped around her body like a tourniquet, began to tremble, her hand fluttering before her mouth. Unsure what to do, I could only watch as she bent over in an apparent spasm of agony, her whole body shaking convulsively. And then, as quickly, she righted herself, dropped her arm and, to my astonishment, released a shriek of laughter, otherworldly in its effect. Transfixed, I stared at her as the laughing went on and on, rising hysterically to a fevered pitch until at last she tumbled backward into a chair and the laughter collapsed into great racking sobs.

It was some time before she was recovered enough to speak. I found a box of tissues in her loo in the meantime, the only thing I could think of to do. She seemed more like an injured forest creature spurning help than a woman in want of comfort.

"You must think my reaction strange," Miranda murmured, dabbing the tissue at her red and swollen lids.

"Well," I replied, considering her, "yes and no."

She regarded me curiously.

"I know Roger Pettibon was once your stepfather," I explained. "And . . . and I know what he did to you."

She stared, appalled.

"Your father—Victor—told us . . . me, I mean. He didn't talk about it willingly, if that's any comfort."

"But why?" she said beseechingly, having recovered her voice.

"I said he's been in police custody, Miranda—"

"Yes, sorry, it went out of my head. But you didn't say why . . . ." She blinked rapidly. Awareness dawned in her expression. "You don't mean they thought . . ."

"No. Not exactly." I hesitated, alert to the effect of my next words. "You see, Miranda, your father *confessed* to killing Roger Pettibon."

Her initial reaction to my announcing Roger Pettibon's murder had troubled me. Had it been shock and surprise compounded of relief that this hated man, a man she wished dead, *was* finally dead? Or had her reaction been the release of pent-up glee and triumph also compounded of relief that this hated man was dead, and dead by her own hand. Her response to the news that Victor Fabiani had confessed to Pettibon's murder was almost as troubling. I suppose I was expecting her to be stricken. But instead she calmly folded her hands around a tissue and asked almost clinically:

"And did he? Kill Roger?"

"Could he have?" I returned, surprised.

This brought a response. Her eyes flashed. Her lips twitched.

"He loves you. You're his daughter." I continued, "He hates what Roger did to you. And your father's a man with a terrible temper. Isn't it possible he took revenge on your behalf?"

You could almost follow Miranda's thoughts in the contortions of her face. "Yes" to my question condemned her father; "no" pointed a finger elsewhere, and it was surely dawning on her that she herself was an ideal suspect.

"But Victor's in police custody. You just said." She avoided my question. "They must think he did it."

"He was being detained. He's not now."

"They released him!"

"They had to. Your father supplied a motive that finally couldn't stand up to scrutiny."

"What? I don't understand."

"Your father told the police Pettibon was blackmailing him over forgeries of Old Master drawings he'd made when he was a young man."

"Which isn't true."

"No." I shook my head. Then I hesitated. "But I did sort of get the ball rolling, because I was with your father in his rooms for part of the period when Pettibon was supposed to have been killed. Posing in the Garter robes. I was working in that part of the Castle," I added hastily when her expression suddenly hardened to cold distaste. "I expressed some doubts in, um, certain quarters about Victor being responsible, but—"

Miranda buried her head in her hands.

"Oh, Victor . . ." she murmured sorrowfully to herself. Then she raised her head: "I should thank you, I suppose."

"I wouldn't be too hasty. Your father's not out of the woods, unfortunately. The police may very well reconsider when they learn Victor had a genuine motive. But, for the time being, Miranda—" I tried to hold her eyes. "—and more to the point, the police are going to be looking elsewhere for Roger Pettibon's killer. You understand, of course, why your father confessed to murdering your former stepfather?"

The curtains flared suddenly in a flash of lightning, drawing her dark eyes away. Her lack of response stretched between us thick as taffy. I took the silence as assent.

"Victor told you this?"

"He said you'd seen Roger Pettibon last Friday for the first time in years and that by the time he visited you Sunday you were in a state. Quite a state, actually."

"I can't believe he would discuss such . . . intimate things with a stranger!"

"You mustn't blame him. One way or another, he's gone to extreme measures to protect you—"

"But—"

"Miranda, as it happens, Her Majesty's taken a personal interest in this business. She's not too keen on people being murdered in her home, even the likes of a bastard like Pettibon. She questioned your father when he was released this afternoon but, try as he might, there were some things he couldn't hide. Her Majesty's sharper than you might think."

"You were there." More statement than question, it nonetheless held a tone of amazement.

"Fate dragged me into all this." I shrugged.

"And the Queen knows?"

"The Queen's not a gossip. And she's concerned. You're not the last little girl Pettibon abused, and you were probably not the first."

Her eyes blazed.

"Pippa Clair." I explained the circumstances.

"I didn't know," she said hollowly when I'd finished. "You were away at Easter. Your father said."

"And Joanna Pettibon works in the Royal Library as well?"

"She's the Curator of the Print Room."

"What does she look like?"

"Oh, she's quite slim, dark hair in a sort of bob, pretty, a sort of china-doll face. Why do you ask?"

"Just . . . curious." She shrugged and looked away. "I wondered . . . what kind of woman Roger would marry after my mother."

"Your adoptive mother."

"Of course. I've been less successful tracing my natural mother than my natural father. Victor's a well-known portraitist and lives in this country. I think my natural mother may be in America somewhere."

Miranda gazed off into the middle distance. Lightning once again flickered behind the curtains, but it failed to draw her attention. That, I realized unhappily, was going to be my task.

"You know, the police are going to be around to talk to you before long. I'm sure they finally figured out that Victor was protecting someone and—" I felt crummy saying the next bit: "—and they knew you were at the Castle Monday morning."

Her eyes alit on mine. She was quite still. "How do they know that?" she asked in a strained voice.

"The usual log of comings and goings."

She caught her breath. "But I just slipped in. There was no one at the desk." She had to know how surreptitious this made her activity seem.

"At Engine Court?"

"Yes."

"But you were remembered by an officer at Henry VIII Gate."

"I went to fetch something I'd left behind."

"What?"

"My car keys."

"Wouldn't they be on a ring with your flat keys and such?"

"No, I keep them separate. And they were in a rain-coat I'd left behind on Friday—"

"When you left so abruptly."

"Yes." Her glittering eyes sought my assurance.

Raincoat? "But it's been so hot—"

"Not last week. The clouds didn't clear until mid-Monday."

So they had.

"Okay, you needed your car keys because you were going away. But you never mentioned any such plan to your father. You told him you had the week free. He'd planned to phone you at lunch and come around for his dinner in the evening."

"I changed my mind."

Skepticism must have been dancing a jig on my face for she insisted: "I did. After Sunday, after I'd . . . talked with Victor about . . . everything, I knew I couldn't bear to be in town. I've been to the Reclaiming Collective before, I knew they'd take me, so . . . But I had to go back to the castle for my keys. It's perfectly simple!"

"Look, Miranda, it doesn't matter what I believe. But you're going to have to be prepared for the day they—the police—ask. I mean, do you have any proof there'd been a coat with car keys left behind in the Castle last Friday?"

"Do they have any proof that I did it?" she challenged hotly.

"They don't have much of anything," I replied, slightly taken aback. "There were no fingerprints on the sword. Bloodstains on Victor's smock, the same blood type as Roger's, turned out after analysis to be Victor's. But the police are not going to stop looking for physical evidence. Something will have been taken away from the scene. They're going to want to look at the clothes you were wearing on Monday."

"Then they're welcome to."

"What do you wear when you're working at the Castle?"

"A boiler suit."

"And you keep it there? Or bring it home?"

She pushed back a loose strand of hair. "Leave it there." She scowled and once again strongly resembled her father. "What are you getting at? That I went to the Castle, hopped into my boiler suit, killed that bloody bastard with a—what did you say?—a sword? and then . . . ?"

"Then took the boiler suit off, carried it out with your raincoat, and then destroyed it or threw it away. Listen," I added, holding up my hands as her face darkened, "I'm only giving you an idea of what they might think."

"And what do you think?"

"I don't know."

I didn't know. The last few minutes had given me a glimmer of what she could be like when aroused. And if she'd been repressing hateful feelings toward her onetime stepfather for a decade or more, her capacity for killing him didn't come as a complete surprise to me. Pettibon's murder had never appeared to have too much of an element of planning behind it. The weapon, the sword, had been left in the Throne Room by chance (unless the "chance" had been planned, of course) and the setting seemed rather peculiar— surely you wouldn't *plan* to murder someone in—of all places—the Throne Room? Had Miranda come to the Castle Monday morning not to get her raincoat and car keys, as she claimed, but to confront her onetime tormenter and then, in a hot rage, fatally stab him?

"Where had you left your coat?" I thought to ask.

She hesitated, regarding me warily: "You'll think me guilty if I tell you."

I shrugged.

"In the Grand Reception Room. It's—"

"Yes, I know where it is. It opens onto the Throne Room. There's a glass-panelled door that looks right through. But why would I necessarily think you guilty because you were in the Grand Reception Room?"

"Because—" Abruptly her face shuttered. "Oh, nothing."

"Because that's where Roger was stabbed," I supplied. And then it dawned on me: "But, Miranda, listen, I never told you *where* in the Castle Roger had been killed."

20

THE THIN CURTAINS in Miranda's sitting room once again surged with a glaring light. And then, as quickly, the fabric surged again. And then again.

"Hardly subtle, are they?" I commented as Miranda paled visibly to the sound of car doors slamming outside the window. "They've probably been keeping an eye on your place."

Miranda's hand fluttered before her face; her eyes cast about the room as if she were seeking a place to hide. Even though I knew she hadn't a chance of escaping police scrutiny in the long run, or even the short run, I still felt somehow like a snitch and felt a perfect shit for it.

"Listen, Miranda," I said, rising and moving to the window to gently lift the curtain and confirm my suspicions (as if they needed confirming). "If you did happen to stab Roger, I'm not sure if I blame you."

The doorbell sounding was hardly unexpected, but its loud obnoxious buzz made us both jump anyway.

"I mean it," I continued hurriedly. "I'm not sure I'd blame anyone whose trust he abused in that way."

There was a second impatient buzz, urgent in its demand.

"Do you want me to answer it?"

Miranda seemed paralyzed and then, as the buzzer sounded a third time, she shook her head. "No, I'll get it," she said sharply, as if her wits had been restored to her. She rose and moved quickly into the corridor. Even the entryphone's tinny drone couldn't disguise Chief Inspector Nightingale's barking.

Then she turned to me. "I didn't kill him, you know." Her magnificent eyes willed me to believe her.

"Then how did you know about the Throne Room?" I said urgently. The sound of footfalls on the stairs grew louder. How I wanted to believe her!

"Don't talk about it!" she hissed at me. Her face was grim, her eyes fevered. "And don't . . . don't even mention it if they ask you."

"I—"

There was a sharp knock on the door.

"—I can't promise that!" I whispered back.

"Then I read it in the papers, okay!?"

I stared at her, not comprehending. Something in the few minutes seemed to have pulled her together.

"Miss Walter!" The voice on the other side of the door was irritable. The knocking resumed.

"Do you want me to stay?" I watched her hand reach for the doorknob.

"No! Go!" Her hand hesitated. She turned to me, her voice low: "You've helped me. You have. Thank you."

"I don't see how. I feel . . . I feel terrible!"

"Here goes." She pushed a strand of black hair behind her ear with one hand and with the other pulled open the door to reveal Nightingale, warrant card in hand, his stolid features sickly in the stairwell's pale green light. He opened his mouth, but then his eyes skipped past Miranda to me.

"Bloody hell!"

"I'm just leaving, Inspector."

"*Chief* Inspector."

"I'm just leaving." He turned as I edged past him. "And I'm sorry," I said between my teeth, "that I ever spoke to you in the first place, *Chief* Inspector."

"What the hell do you mean by that!" he bellowed after me as I pushed past a uniformed officer and raced down the stairs.

Under a streetlamp, I glanced at my watch. The hour was well past eleven; the sun had finally sunk into the sea beyond the Irish coast. But the air remained close and warm, almost bloody wilfully oppressive, if you want the truth. I know weather doesn't possess intelligence, but it was almost like someone up there was cocking a snook at England's perennial wet-weather whingers, and a little cooling wet weather would have been nice right about now. Or perhaps I was just feeling, projecting as I was, all bothered and baffled over the events of the week, at once both exhausted and restless, and was finding the exceptional weather a convenient target. Fleur, I presumed from her darkened window, had given up and gone to bed in her back bedroom where police lights did not penetrate. I wouldn't have minded having a natter with her but I didn't want to wake her, or her kids. Meanwhile, returning to Stripes wasn't on, either. The throb and din of a nightclub had lost its allure.

Almost unthinkingly, as if solitude were my real need, I made my way through the narrow streets east of St. Leonard's Road, the pubs shut for the night, quiet but for a few scuttling feet and a car engine starting, and found myself drawn along Brook Street and into Windsor Great Park, mysterious in the dark, the trees lining the Long Walk soft purple-gray shapes in the fragile light of the waning moon. Entering, I felt at first a tiny fillip of anxiety: the agreeable openness of the park in daytime had been swallowed by the night; no lovers strolled the walk, no Crown Estate workers tended the grass. But for the chirrup of insects on nocturnal business, and the call of night-loving birds, I was alone, a shadow among shadows. I trod over the dewy silvered grass and stood on the Long Walk, undecided which direction to turn. The Copper Horse, the equestrian statue of King

George III, lay far to the elevated south end of the walk, an indistinct stain against an indistinct horizon. But the Castle, much nearer, its illuminated south front a radiant beacon, decided me. Solid, rooted, eternal—and home (for a time)— the Castle was the very symbol of protection and safety.

Alas, only a symbol, I thought as soon as I thought the initial thought. (How this thinking thing does go on ceaselessly!) The ancient keeps and battlements had afforded no protection to the likes of Philippa Clair; they hadn't exactly jumped between Roger Pettibon's back and a moving sword.

And whose hand, I wondered, as I stepped lightly up the Long Walk, the Castle floating ever before me like a great passenger ship on a dark sea, wielded that sword?

I thought about my exchange with Miranda Walter. Her surprise and shock at my news of Pettibon's death had seemed unaffected, but her subsequent manner hinted of prevarication. And her final reticence about the Throne Room was tantalizing. Quite simply: Had she done the deed herself?

Or had she been witness?

I could imagine Miranda looking through the glass-paneled doors of the Grand Reception Room down the length of the Throne Room and suddenly beholding Roger Pettibon enter from the door opposite. Had she burst through from the Grand Reception Room at that moment and snatched up the sword? Or had she seen someone else enter the Throne Room behind Pettibon? Hugo FitzJames, drowned Pippa's friend, mislayer of sword and finder of body? St. John Leathley, Hugo's cousin and guardian, hearer of confessions and keeper of secrets? Or Joanna Pettibon? Was it not curious that the Curator of the Print Room, acknowledged expert in Old Master drawings, had not herself been more readily sceptical of Victor Fabiani's claims? "I don't know why it took them so bloody long to twig," I could hear Victor saying. And, by her own admission, Joanna had been in the Upper Ward that morning, too.

Or—and I hated admitting this to myself—was it Victor Fabiani Miranda saw enter the Throne Room with Pettibon? If, by her circumspection, Miranda was protecting someone, who, above all, would she most want to protect?

Had the tables turned? Was it now daughter protecting father?

Or, in her loathing of her former stepfather, would Miranda shield the identity of *anyone* who might have killed Roger Pettibon?

Or—?

"Ah!" I caught my breath and stifled a cry, stopping in my tracks. My heart beat a tattoo as a dark figure materialized from behind a tree on the west side of the Long Walk and seemed almost to fly across to the east side some few meters in front of me, a weird blue-white phosphorescent afterglow streaming in its wake. It made a peculiar cry, like an owl's hoot. I blinked. It disappeared.

Impossible. My eyes strained in the darkness, my mind rushing to make sense of what I'd seen. It's just bloody impossible. Spectral beings do not exist. They are bogus. They have bogosity. We live in a material world. Everything is subject to reason. I am a rational being. I am in my right mind. The last drink I had was before nine o'clock. I do not take drugs.

But the resemblance to humanity of the being I'd just seen ended just past the legs, if legs they were. There'd been a trailing of dark cords, as if of tatters and tears around the body, and where the head should have been—and this was the part that sent my fancy to reeling—a kind of headpiece from which branched an enormous pair of antlers, a thorny silhouette sharpened against the shimmering gold of the Castle.

Herne the Hunter, England's most famous ghost? Who, saith legend, was wounded by a stag in Windsor Forest, lost his mind, strapped a stag's antlers to his head, ran through the forest naked, and finally hanged himself from an oak tree near the Castle?

Could it be?

?

Nah. It had to be some nutball on a midsummer lark. Or a refugee from a costume party. Or Falstaff's understudy in the Theatre Royal's production of *Merry Wives of Windsor*.

But the venerable Theatre Royal wasn't doing *Merry Wives*. And who holds costume parties on hot June evenings?

I quickened my pace. Oh, surely some nut.

And then I remembered that a sighting of Herne the Hunter is said to portend disaster.

Lightning bleached the sky as I emerged from St. Albans Street across from King Henry VIII Gate some few minutes later, throwing into stark and lurid relief the crenellations of the Castle, flaring the ramparts bright as noonday, then as quickly and soundlessly vanishing, leaving the ancient pile once again submerged in nighttime gloom, looking more like some abandoned, yet oddly intact, leaving of a vanished civilization. But one or two of the narrow loopholes in the dense gray curtain of stone glowed with light, jewellike, intimating life within, and of course the Round Tower, spotlit, blazed upon the darkened crest like a golden crown, and for that I revised my view: The Castle seemed to me now an enormous living creature—St. George's dragon, perhaps—recumbent, perhaps under some spell, waiting, vaguely threatening.

Mind your moods, Ms. Bee, I thought, giving myself a mental slap, crossing the cobbles where the drawbridge would have been in days of yore and wending my way through the police barrier to the sentry who stepped from the shadows of the gate and silently examined my Staff card. A decent night's sleep would dispel the creepily vague sense of pessimism that had attached itself to me over the past few hours.

I passed through the arches and into the Lower Ward, a hushed and shrouded stone glade, its shadows unconquered by the soft glow of St. George's Chapel's illumination. A few of the slit windows in the Guards' barracks emitted an opaque light, for guarding the Castle is the twenty-four-hour task of young men, but not a ray shone from the Military Knights' residences where the old boys were tucked up in slumber. No Guard inhabited the sentry box, I noted. All was silent but for the faint sound of someone whistling off in the distance, somewhere beyond the Middle Ward. My eyes travelled unbidden to Salisbury Tower, secluded in the deepest of shadows, the variegated shrubbery of daytime gathered about the gate at night like black lace. Through the half-drawn curtains of the sitting room window, I could make out a pale light. Joanna was up, I presumed, unable to find peace in sleep, and who couldn't understand why? Her brother was most likely still out clubbing at Stripes. Her sister, judging from the absent Ford car, had returned to Oxford and the demands of her husband and four children. Leaving, I could only assume, Joanna to bear her tragedy alone, as perhaps she wanted. I felt a slight temptation to enter that gate and knock on that door nevertheless. Had she been deliberately obtuse about Fabiani as art forger because his confession was her protection? Or had she merely been befuddled by grief? And what did she know—or allow herself to acknowledge—about her husband's nature? But the hour was late, and if that observation didn't need underscoring, the Castle clock tolled the hour of midnight. Tomorrow was another day. Or, rather, today was another day.

I continued up the hill instead, past the sturdy Military Knights residences and their tidy gardens, my ears increasingly alert to the phantom whistler. The tune was "Memory," one of my favourites from *Cats*, and the refrain grew louder. I could have almost sung along. A figure rounded the bend near King Henry III Tower, a man by height and shape. The hard heels of his shoes beat time to the whistled music, the white of his shirt front glowed in the pale moonlight. I would have passed the figure unacknowledged at the junction of the paths next to St. George's Chapel, but the skies again put on their light display and I saw to my astonishment, horror, and utter embarrassment in the thunderous cascade that the whistler was none other than Jamie Allan.

The whistling stopped in midnote. Jamie stared at me with, I assumed, equal astonishment and something, I thought (hoped!), akin to delight. He drew closer. He was wearing evening dress, the black tie punctuating the white collar below his handsome face. We both exclaimed:

"What are *you* doing here?"

And then we both began our replies at once:

"I'm—"

And then it happened.

There was a short deep muffled burst of sound, a rich velvety bang, like an explosion inside a jewel case.

"What was that?" I said, turning, for the noise seemed to come from behind me, somewhere deep in the Lower Ward.

"Almost sounded like . . . a bomb." Jamie's tone was worried. I could sense his alertness as we both scanned the thick high stone walls enclosing the Lower Ward. Always the fear was that someone somehow would secrete a bomb in the precincts of the Castle when Her Majesty was in residence, a terrorist coup of the most insidious kind. But nothing along the battlements and towers seemed out of order, nothing changed or moved but for a rustle of wings from the birds perched upon the Queen's beasts, the heraldic carvings high atop St. George's Chapel. Quiet settled back over the night.

And then, before either of us could speak again, I saw it. The light I'd noticed behind the window of Salisbury Tower, pale and yellow, now flickered brightly and seemed to grow in magnitude to a orange-red glow. Jamie saw it in the same breath.

It was no ordinary light. Salisbury Tower was on fire.

We raced down the path toward the dreaded beacon barely conscious that no one else was about, no one else had heard the soft explosion and raised an alarm. Arriving first, Jamie flung open the gate of the forecourt, almost tripping over a terracotta planter in the path, then drove his shoulder against the front door. But it was solid oak, shut and locked. He sprang toward the window and rammed his elbow again and again through the panes of glass while I, with my poor bare elbows, could only seize one of the earthenware pots and do likewise as valuable seconds sped by. The glass was not thick, but the glazing bars, though slender, were more resilient. Finally, grasping one side of the window frame, Jamie kicked fiercely. One whole frame collapsed inwards onto the three-legged table, shattering the vase and scattering the flowers I'd brought only two days before. The fire leapt and roared, racing greedily toward the fresh new air.

The back end of the sitting room was bathed in flame. Great orange tongues licked the wallpaper and curled, crackling and spluttering, around the picture-laden table and the chair in which the Queen had sat. The spectacle was stunning, incomprehensible, and for an instant I froze, viewing the growing inferno from outside as Jamie pushed his way through the window. And then, without thinking, I followed, aware as I entered the room of a terrible heat on my bare arms and legs, of dense smoke insinuating its way into my nose and throat. Jamie, hunched well over, raced toward the untouched door to the hall, but at that moment I shrieked.

He turned, the fair skin of his face seeming to reflect the fire's radiance, and looked at me aghast. "You fool!" he shouted at me above the roar. Soundlessly, I pointed at what I'd seen. Then he saw it, too. It was a human figure. I could see a pair of bare legs thrusting from between the couch and the Queen's chair. The rest of the body was hidden from me. But Jamie could see more. A look of horror and pity flashed in his face as he tore off his suit jacket, thrust himself forward, and fell to his knees.

And then, crawling forward, I saw, too. It was Joanna, motionless, lying awkwardly in a pool of fire, her thin night-clothes bathed in dancing flames, her dark hair a blazing halo. Shattered glass, gleaming in the lurid light, trailed from her hand toward the fireplace, now only a detail in a wall of ever-spreading fire. The sickening stench of burning flesh assailed my nostrils. My stomach heaved.

"A blanket or a coat—something! She'll be in shock!" Jamie shouted at me as he beat the flames about Joanna's body with his jacket, coughing as the smoke billowed.

But there was nothing with which to cover her. The ravenous fire, racing toward the window along the ceiling, had torched the draperies. No throw-rug graced the couch, only now beginning to burn. There were only the pillows I'd sat against the other day, and a book, the diary, I recognized, thrown against a cushion, its pink surface charred yet curiously unburned. And then I remembered the architectural staple of British homes: the closet under the stairs. As Jamie pulled Joanna from between the furniture and, gasping with effort, lifted her into his arms, I darted toward the door. The flames, drawing new energy from the fresh draughts of air, raced to intercept me. Quickly, in the hall's eerie half-light, I yanked from the closet the first thing my fingers encountered, a long coat. Through the enveloping smoke, coughing and hacking, my lungs seared with pain, I managed to reach the front door, stepping on Maggie the cat who scratched frantically at the barrier, mewing piteously. I fumbled with the lock and finally, just as Jamie staggered from the smoke with Joanna, her nightdress burnt to a blackened rag, I scooped up the panicked cat and flung the door open.

It felt as though we'd been in the blazing tower an agonizing eternity of time, but later I learned only a few minutes had passed. In those few minutes, the slumbering Castle had awakened to the crisis. Members of the Guard, in their night camouflage, had tumbled out of the barracks next door, a team of them swiftly unravelling a hose reel while others raced away into the darkness to hook the hose to the nearest wall hydrant. Other men and women in varying states of hastily arranged dress raced toward us at breakneck speed from the other towers and precincts in the Castle. The klaxon of the fire bell seemed everywhere, echoing off the stone walls. And in the distance, as I quickly followed Jamie with Joanna's limp body in his arms through the gate, fire engines sounded. The cat bolted from my arms and disappeared into the protective darkness around the Military Knights' lodgings.

There was nothing to do but lay Joanna down on the grass verge between Henry VIII Gate and St. George's Chapel, check that she was breathing (she was), then wait for the ambulances. I hardly paused to consider whether it was best to place a coat over her. In the glow of the Chapel's illuminated stone, Joanna's body appeared more sickeningly burnt than I'd imagined when Jamie had called for some cover. But she was so exposed and vulnerable to the cooling air that I thought she must be protected from the effects of shock above anything else. As Jamie sank to his knees and settled her, raising her feet along the verge's concrete abutment, I quickly and gently arranged the coat. I looked then at Jamie and would have laughed if I hadn't felt so numb, so stupefied. His eyebrows were gone, his blond hair singed, his face, like his shirt, streaked with black, almost as it might have been if he were on war games somewhere. He saw me looking at him. Improbably, he laughed.

"What the *hell* is so funny?" I scolded him sternly.

"You've lost your eyebrows, Jane."

My hand went automatically to my brow. He was right.

I could feel only smooth skin and a bit of the sort of stubble my legs evidence when they're in want of shaving. For some stupid maddening reason, at that moment I burst into tears.

"You're shivering," he said, ignoring my blubbering. "It's the shock. I'll let you have my . . . oh, I left my jacket behind, of course." He looked back at Salisbury Tower. Though the soldiers had got the pumps working, the flames, ravenously consuming the timber construction of the interior renovations, had already leapt a floor, the raging heat blasting the window from its frame, the crackling sound growing stronger and stronger. And still more people raced down the hill as lightning once again flashed in the sky.

"Here," Jamie said, coming around to my side. "Don't take this the wrong way, but . . ." And he wrapped his arms around me and pulled me to him. I turned my face and pressed it into his chest, almost biting the shirt fabric to stave fresh tears I was now fiercely determined not to shed. He smelled wonderful, of smoke and starch and Pear's soap, and I concentrated on that, feeling the terror of the last few minutes begin to subside.

"You were good in there." His voice came into my ear over the tumult of sirens and shouting voice and boots running on stone. "Sorry for ordering you about like that. I think I've done that more than once this week, haven't I?"

"S'alright," I murmured, loath to be released from his arms, even as my shivering quelled.

"Feeling better?"

"Much. Thanks."

A moment later he said: "Funny running into you here. I tried to get you at the Castle."

I raised my head above his shoulder to look at his face and tell him the truth—that he *had* got me at the Castle, Windsor Castle, that I worked as a housemaid, that I'd never served a cup of tea on an airplane in my life, that Heather didn't have a single allergy as far as I knew, that I'd made up this stupid stupid story because, well, who knows?

And found myself staring at the Queen, her face raised in postage-stamp profile as she ran toward the flaming Tower, in the dancing light her expression a study in uncomprehending sorrow. Without thinking, I pushed myself from Jamie's arms. The movement caught the Queen's notice.

Faint perplexity, then mild surprise modulated her features as she slowed, then stopped.

"What has happened?" she asked urgently, a little breathless, looking from our blackened faces to the insensate figure on the grass, as both Jamie and I rose to our feet with haste.

"Ma'am, it's Mrs. Pettibon," I tried explaining. "Her sitting room caught fire somehow."

The Queen looked down at Joanna. "Her hair . . ." she murmured, shocked, staring at the figure on the verge, her hand resting on her neck where pearls had probably been an hour before. She was still wearing the pale yellow dress. "How is she?"

"Ma'am, she's seriously burned," Jamie replied. "We're waiting on an ambulance."

"And you two . . . Jane? Jamie?"

"We were—" we both began, glancing at each other with, I'm sure, the same surprised thought in mind: How does the Queen know *you*? "I mean, I was," I continued. "That is, he was—"

". . . she was—"

Then Joanna groaned suddenly. A uniformed figure emerged from the dancing shadows and began speaking to her in low tones. Joanna groaned again, then opened her eyes and stared with a kind of fevered uncomprehending intensity at the night sky.

"Mrs. Pettibon—Joanna—someone will be here soon," I said, trying to keep my voice as soothing and calm as I could.

"Perhaps some water, too." I heard the Queen say urgently in aside to someone.

She crouched down next to Joanna and reached under the coat to take her hand. "The ambulance will be here any moment now," she said in her most reassuring tones. Joanna's mouth moved soundlessly, her eyes open and staring. She seemed unaware the Sovereign was addressing her.

"The bottle . . . I . . ." Joanna's voice was barely audible.

"There, there, never mind," the Queen murmured. Her Majesty glanced at us. I shrugged.

"There was some shattered glass nearby, Ma'am," Jamie said in low voice. "Perhaps a bottle containing some flammable liquid."

"She might have been trying to burn something," I added, recalling the partially burned book flung against the couch.

Joanna groaned again. Where was that bloody ambulance? With no casualty hospital at Windsor, assistance had to come from Slough or Ascot. I could only hope her shocked mind was somehow able to block the terrible pain in the meantime.

"With your permission, Ma'am, I'd like to see what other help I can lend." Jamie addressed the Queen.

"I think you've done more than your share already," she replied. The sound of fire engines racing through the Henry VIII Gate nearly drowned her words. "Both of you. I've just been told what you did. But, yes, go if you wish. We can deal with this."

I watched Jamie join the fray, into the living tableau of tiny black figures battling a fire that seemed to unravel like some starving fiery dragon crackling with hideous glee as it devoured its way up the tower. Flames had started to lick at the night sky, a roseate hue spread over old stone walls and intent faces. Fire crews raced to assemble their equipment before adjacent parts of the Castle were consumed. Volunteers removed things from the Lower Ward shop next to Salisbury Tower and from rooms next door, in Henry VIII Gate. A contingent of soldiers carried out pieces from the armoury collection in the barracks. Into this melee, Jamie disappeared.

I wanted at the moment to ask Her Majesty who he was, how she knew his name, why he was at the Castle in evening dress, but I couldn't. The sadness on her face as she, too, turned her attention to the scene, was all too evident. More important matters held the royal attention.

"My coat," Joanna whispered suddenly. She was staring downward, as if it were a thing of horror, at the coat that covered her. Some tiny sensibility seemed to have found a footing in her mind. Her eyes held a glimmer of recognition and she struggled upward, then fell back.

"It's your Burberry, Mrs. Pettibon," I said. "We just want to keep you warm."

"I forgot about the coat," she continued, unhearing, her voice straining as she carried on, her distress growing, reminding me, absurdly, of the White Rabbit and his lost handwear. "The gloves! My gloves! Oh, my gloves . . ."

"Joanna, calm yourself," the Queen said gently. "Whatever can she mean?" she added to me in a lower tone as Joanna began to fumble with what little strength was left her under the coat covering her body.

"It's all right, Mrs. Pettibon, I'll find your gloves," I said, running my hands into the coat's pockets in an attempt to mollify her. There were indeed gloves in the right-hand pocket, no big surprise. I could feel them crammed at the bottom and was able to pull them out just as a man arrived with a flask of water. Mercifully, several ambulances came racing through the gate at the same time, their piercing wail fading to a whisper.

"Here's your gloves, Mrs. Pettibon."

I held them up so she could see. But her eyes had closed. She seemed to have fallen back into unconsciousness, her body slack.

I looked at what I was holding. The gloves were thin, gauzy, white in the many lights now flashing and flickering over the Lower Ward. They were the standard gloves of archivists, used in handling old drawings, old documents, fine fragile works of art. But these gloves were also stained, splotched with dark smudges, the fabric in some places almost glued together so that the fingers failed to unfold daintily as a glove might if held by its cuff. I ran my own fingers over the stains and a terrible feeling seized me. The Queen, too, looked at the gloves as I held them in the air. Our eyes met.

"Oh, no."

It was all I could think to say.

21

THE SPELL OF torrid weather broke—finally—on Saturday. During the night, in the hour or two before sunrise, clouds rolled in from somewhere north or west of Windsor, thunder burst upon the dark skies like a herald of doom, and lightning, real lightning, forked, rattling the windows of my room, waking me from a fitful sleep. Gratefully, I flung back the few bedclothes and let the newly cooled air billowing the curtains wash over me until I began again to drift off. But some few atoms of an alien odour carried along by the rushing air tickled my nose and I reawoke with a start. Smoke! And then memories of the hours just past, hours that seemed days ago, came charging back.

The Lower Ward had almost resembled a film set when I was at last persuaded—*commanded*—to leave. Great arc lamps bathed the scene in a diamond white light that rivaled in intensity the pulsating clouds swirling over Salisbury Tower, making shadowy twins of the fire ladders pitched high into the air. The bailey of the Lower Ward was strewn with red fire trucks and emergency vehicles and ambulances that, from the air, from the helicopter that shortly appeared overhead (commandeered probably by some aggressive television news outfit), must have looked like some pyromaniacal child's playroom. An army of fire fighters, soldiers, police officers, Staff, guests, and members of the Royal Family clustered within Castle walls while outside, through the Henry VIII Gate, I could glimpse a gathering crowd behind police barriers, the sort of people drawn to tragedy no matter what the hour, among them, having bruised his way to the front no doubt, Andrew Macgreevy, who'd made it back to Windsor just in time, bloody hell.

The Queen stood by, watching forlornly as a part of her beloved home burned for a second time in a decade, as various officials and intimates circled toward her with their updates and sympathies. Her most obvious distress was for Joanna Pettibon. Even in the high drama of the Great Fire in 1992, in the raging furnace that destroyed the whole northeast section of the Castle and involved fire crews from five counties battling the blaze for fourteen hours, no one had been seriously injured. Now this lesser fire, within the first minutes of its inception, had yielded up a tragedy greater than a damaged portrait or sideboard or carpet, or even walls and roofs, all of which could be repaired or replaced. As the stretcher-bearers with the greatest of care lifted Joanna's ravaged body, you could only wonder if she would live, and if she lived, what suffering she would have to endure. If she lived, she would have, I knew, one more burden added to so many others.

"You must give them up," the Queen said to me after the ambulance had sped away. Her Majesty seemed to know what I was thinking. My impulse was to stuff the gloves somewhere about my person (not an easy task, as my dress offered no hiding places) and then later throw them in the Thames or add them to the mound of rubbish generated each day by the Castle populace. I must have hesitated, for the Queen cautioned: "I do understand, Jane. But if you don't, attention may be unfairly brought on other people—innocent people."

And still I hesitated, standing there in the glare of the fire and the shouting pandemonium, stubbornly gripping the gloves, having scrunched them into balls, hiding them like a magician hiding coins, hoping that, when I opened my hand, the gloves would have disappeared.

"You must get some first aid yourself," the Queen continued gently, gesturing to a waiting ambulance set up near the east side of Henry VIII Gate. "Now, perhaps you should give me the gloves and I'll pass them on. It's for the best.

"Jane. Jane!

"Jane, Mrs. Pettibon's coat will have traces of blood as well."

Of course, I thought miserably. Reluctantly, I unclenched my fists and handed the soiled gloves to Her Majesty. "Sorry, Ma'am," I said.

"Well," the Queen received the evidence into her own hands, making an admission I'm sure she makes only in rare instances, "I'm sorry, too."

From the ambulance, as I submitted myself to the ministrations of medical staff, I watched as Her Majesty held Derek Landerer, her PPO, in conversation, then dropped the gloves into his big hands. I then watched him as he passed me and disappeared through the gate, no doubt to transfer them, with explanation, to some other member of the police force. Perhaps that's why I became irritable with an imperious nurse who insisted I, too, go to hospital for a proper check-over. True, my lungs hurt a bit, but I didn't see the point of hanging about an emergency ward wasting doctors' time. It was an argument I lost, however, and I was shortly bundled into the ambulance and sped over the Thames to Slough and Wexham Park Hospital, where I found to my delight a battered-looking Jamie Allan in charred evening dress, among the chaos of the customers that end-of-workweek benders traditionally dispatch to emergency wards. My opportunity, I thought anxiously, to finally come clean and squash all this air-hostess malarky but, after only a frustratingly brief conversation, we were each whisked away to separate examination rooms. When I was released, with antiseptic ointment, a directive to soak inflamed areas around my face and arms with cool compresses, and an otherwise clean bill of health, Jamie had gone. A stolid police officer drove me in a panda car back to the Castle where the embers of the fire, now under control, still cast a ruby glow to the night sky. I was dead tired, but as I dragged myself into bed I turned over in my head something Jamie had said to me in the hospital waiting room. And then I conked out.

I awoke again late in the morning to the sound and sight of a downpour, a hard cold rain beating against glass and the stone. A sheer curtain of white shrouded the Home Park outside my window. My room seemed as gloomy as a winter's afternoon, and I had to switch on my bedside lamp to bring any cheer. I felt loath to get out of bed. The events of the night had taken their toll. Besides, when I'd returned to my room at two o'clock that morning, I'd glimpsed myself in the mirror. I didn't fancy the encounter again. I was about to turn over and doze a bit when there was a tap on the door and Davey swanned in carrying a large silver tray.

"I say, good timing."

"What's this?"

"Your brekkie, darling."

"Really? Breakfast in bed?"

"Special order for our heroine. Mother's wish, no less. Imagine, me serving a housemaid in her bed. How standards are falling! Anyway, up pillows. I've only got two hands. And don't tell the others, or breakfast-in-bed will be on the agenda at the next union meeting."

"Ooh. Full English!" I exclaimed, lifting the silver covers one by one. "And the good china! Ooh, kedgeree. Brilliant! But, Davey, can't I have a soft-boiled egg?"

"Don't be smart. Now, is it coffee? You're a coffee drinker in the mornings, aren't you? Hold out your cup. Black or white?

"You look a sight, you know," he added, pouring the coffee and the milk together showily, like a seasoned waiter. "Like you spent all day at the seaside then went and stuck your finger in an electric socket."

"Is it that bad?"

"Here," he said, putting the coffee pot on a corner of the bureau and rummaging through the clutter.

"Must you?" He handed me a mirror. "Oh, God . . ."

"I'd get myself down to the hairdresser's this afternoon if I were you. Your hair wants cutting."

"But my eyebrows! I look like I'm guesting on *Star Trek*! What if they don't grow back?"

"Have you a eyebrow pencil?"

"Might be one in my makeup bag." I ate steadily. The food was marvellous. I don't think I've ever felt so hungry.

"Push over, Jane. Mind you don't spill your coffee. There."

"What," I said between bites as Davey smoothed out the tails of his coat and settled on the edge of the bed, "are you waiting for?"

"I'm an artist, darling. I'm contemplating the blank canvas. Turn a bit to the light."

"Don't make me look like Groucho Marx."

"Let's see, who has nice eyebrows?"

"Cindy Crawford. Elizabeth Taylor."

"I could do you a mole, too."

"No, thanks. Eyebrows'll do fine."

I felt the dull point of a pencil running over the naked bumps in my skull normally covered by my eyebrows and tried to eat without jiggling Davey's hand.

"I must say, I do admire you for what you did last night. Helping to save poor Mrs. Pettibon and . . ."

"Oh, it was nothing."

". . . and then taking time out for a snog afterwards."

"I was not snogging!"

"Oh, look what you've made me do. Do you mind?" He dipped the edge of a napkin into the coffee and used the wet end to rub at my forehead.

"Ow, the skin's tender there. And I was not snogging," I repeated heatedly. "And how do you know, anyway? I didn't see you."

"I fancy you were a little preoccupied, sweetheart."

"I was shivering, that's all. Jamie didn't have a coat or anything so he just sort of . . . hugged me to warm me up."

"Jamie, is it now? How quickly we're on to Christian names. I suppose a blazing inferno can have that effect."

"What effect?"

"Of levelling the classes."

"What are you blathering on about?"

Davey leaned back and regarded his cosmetic handiwork. And then he looked down at my eyes. He started. "Oh, my goodness! You've been talking about a certain Jamie you met at a pub last Saturday. Was he, last night, the same . . . ?"

"Well, yes, of course."

"Jane, sweetie! Don't you know who he is?"

"His full name's Jamie Allan, and he's with the Guard. A lieutenant, I think. Short-service commission and such."

"But he's also the *Hon.* James Allen."

"*Honourable?*"

"His father is Gordon Allan, the Earl of Kinross."

I nearly overturned the entire tray. "You don't mean the Earl who has the estate next door to Balmoral?"

"The very one. The Earl and Countess were here for yesterday's house party."

"And he's their son?"

"Second son. He was here to dinner."

"Wow."

"Wow, indeed. A nice catch for some fair member of our declining aristocracy, I daresay."

The beautiful blonde with Jamie at the Riverview flitted through my jealous mind. "But not for me, I suppose you mean," I shot back, somewhat fuelled by the nosh. "May not a housemaid snog with the second son of an earl?"

"I thought you said you weren't snogging, Jane."

"I'm being hypothetical. Does it matter, in this day and age, Davey, that I'm a housemaid and he's the son of some stuck-up toffee-nosed dyed-in-the-wool reactionary whose ancestors probably cleared my mother's ancestors from their Highland home?"

"Stop squirming. Actually the Allans are quite down-to-earth, I've observed. Well, *she* is. Haven't you seen them at Balmoral? The Countess is originally Canadian, don't you know, a colonial just like yourself. That should please you enormously."

"You haven't answered my question."

"There, how's this?" Davey handed me the mirror instead.

I made a whimpering noise.

"Well! I don't know why I bothered."

"It's not the eyebrows, Davey. They're fine." Actually, they were drawn a little high on my forehead, giving me a fixed look of faint surprise, but I wasn't up to caring. Another thought had rammed its way into my consciousness. "It's me. I told Jamie this stupid tale—I don't know why—about Heather and me being Air Canada flight attendants on a layover and that we were staying at the Castle—the hotel. And now, after seeing me inside the Castle—this castle, the real castle—last night, he must know something's amiss. Wait till he finds out I'm a housemaid. He'll never call."

"Quoth the Bee: 'And may not a housemaid snog with the second son of an earl?'"

"It's got nothing to do with upstairs-downstairs stuff. I don't care if he's the second son of a dustman. It's to do with . . . deceiving someone about yourself."

"I see. But if you're not sensitive about your humble station here in Mother's service, darling, why make up this fairy story?"

"I don't know."

Davey shook his head, clucked sympathetically, and took my hand to pat it. "Sadly, Jane, you are a housemaid. I fear Cinderella shall not go to the ball."

I withdrew my hand sharply. "But you're dead wrong, Davey. Cinderella *did* go to the ball. Eventually."

I found a hairdresser who could take me on short notice on a Saturday afternoon, one in St. Leonard's Road. In the sodden gray of a rainy day, it was a shock, as I passed through the Lower Ward on my way into town, to see Salisbury Tower, the site of so much fevered activity twelve hours before, nearly abandoned but for a few men in raincoats trodding through muck and debris in the forecourt, the windows black holes, the stone scorched, the once green and decorative shrubs reduced to charred stumps. On the town side, the tower stood firmly anchoring its corner of Castle hill as it had since days of yore, but the flames, spiralling through the few windows, had scarred the shining stone with streaky black smudges. A crowd of tourists stood and stared, gesticulated, and snapped away with their cameras in that vacant fashion tourists have. Hood up on my jacket, I scuddled past and made my way to the hairdresser's shop, where the first unchatty hairdresser I'd ever encountered snipped silently and without curiosity at my singed locks.

It was when I was paying that I noticed a familiar face outside trying to peer through the spiky leaves of the tropical plants splayed against the window. I thought about asking if the place had a back door, but decided as I zipped my jacket and lifted the hood I might as well face the Muzak.

"Looking for me?" I said, stepping into the drizzle.

"They said you'd gone to the hairdressers. They didn't say which one, though."

"Then you've put your investigative journalist skills to good use once again, haven't you, Andrew?"

Macgreevy regarded me darkly from under the newspaper he was holding over his head.

"And before you get into a lather," I continued, "it's not my fault you weren't able to bag Miranda Walter. I didn't expect her to magically reappear here in Windsor."

"What the hell happened to your face?"

"I got a bit burned at Ascot on Thursday, that's all." I turned away to walk up the road. Macgreevy grabbed my shoulder.

"Wait a minute." He pulled me back and peered at my face.

"Do you mind!"

"There's something strange . . ." He recoiled slightly. "That's it! You've got no proper eyebrows."

"It's a new look."

"This may be flaming June but it's not *that* flaming. Unless you've been near a fire, of course. And—interesting—here you've been at a hairdressers, too . . ."

"I wanted something short and sassy for summer."

"Pull the other one, Stell."

"Well, what does it matter, Macgreevy? All right, I helped at the fire last night and got a bit closer than I should have. So what, big deal, end of story. And would you take your hairy mitts off me? Thank you so much."

"Unnamed Staff members are credited with pulling Joanna Pettibon from the fire."

"Half the Castle was down in the Lower Ward. And it was nighttime."

"The hero of such a heart-warming little drama would be front page."

"I thought you were on suspension?"

"And I seem to have been spending it at your bidding. And I've done it for nought, haven't I."

"I've got nothing to say about the fire. If the police or the fire brigade or the press office at the Palace have something to say, then they'll say it. In the meantime, I'm taking my Staff agreement to heart. Me no talkee. You no writee." I turned away again.

"The speculation is Joanna Pettibon botched a suicide attempt," he continued, following, as if he hadn't heard.

"A pretty grim way to commit suicide, don't you think?"

"Oh? Yeah? And you know differently, do you?"

I was beginning to have that slightly entrapped feeling that comes with the landscape around Macg. "I don't know anything about it." I quickened my pace.

"Fabiani's not being held any more."

"No kidding."

"And Miranda remains elusive, despite your claim she's back here at Windsor."

"She *is* back. Didn't you see her car outside her flat?"

"So you've talked to her."

I peeked around my hood. We were standing waiting for the light to change at busy Victoria Street. "Yes," I said with reluctance, "I talked to her."

"And?"

"She claims she didn't kill Pettibon."

"Did she have any idea why her father might have thought she did?"

"No," I lied.

"I don't believe it. There's some connection. Pettibon was her stepfather."

"Then *you* talk to her."

"Think I haven't tried? I've been outside her house in this bloody rain half the morning. Either she's hiding, or she's buggered off again. She must have told you where she went."

"She didn't." The traffic light made its peeping noise and we crossed. Where was Miranda, I wondered? Still being held by the police? But that didn't make sense, unless . . .

Macgreevy persisted. "You're holding back on me."

"I didn't know I owed you anything. The bargain was this: I tipped you to Miranda Walter as a possible suspect in Pettibon's murder, and you were to keep my involvement to yourself. It's not my fault if, so far, Miranda's managed to inadvertently outwit you. And I don't know why you're so bothered about this anyway, really. You're on suspension. It's not your story."

"It's my story if I get to the truth first, suspension or no suspension. Mr. Bloody Reuben Bloody Crush knows how to forgive and forget when there's a circulation war at stake."

"Well, I'm sorry I can't help you with your brilliant career and your attempts to fortify Mr. Bloody Reuben Bloody Crush's bloody newspaper empire!"

"All right," Macgreevy said after a second's squelching up Peascod Street. "Then I do the profile about a royal housemaid, a busy Bee, who's managed somehow to put herself at the heart of three murders at three of the stateliest stately homes in Britain. And I'll garnish it with some speculation about a certain monarch, who, I suspect, has had occasion, in these matters, to step beyond her proscribed constitutional role."

"Your editors would laugh you out of Wapping."

"Care to try me?"

"You made a promise to me on a Bible, Andrew."

"Hell, I made an arrangement with the devil yonks back. You should see the portrait in my attic. Now, let's see, there's a coffee bar up the street. Shall we discuss matters over a meal?"

"You're a prize, Andrew, you really are. You threaten me one minute, then invite me for a meal the next. In some places they call this abuse. I suspect your wife didn't go poof! from some spontaneous combustion, ha ha. A great bloody spark probably set her off, and I'm looking at him right now."

"Shall I take that as a 'no' then?"

I hurried on ahead.

"You owe me a story, Stell."

"And you made a promise."

"You still owe me a story."

"*All right, then!*" I exploded, grabbed Macgreevy by the arm, and yanked him into one of the narrow alleys off Peascod Street with all the strength that fury bestows. "Here's your damn story: *I know where Lord Graven is*. And you *don't!*"

"Oh!" Macgreevy said, startled into rare submission. "You did mutter something about that on the phone last night."

"That's why you've been here, isn't it? It's nothing to do with your usual Rat-Packing Windsor-watching habits. Something rekindled your interest in the Nowhere Man. I found your book, by the way. 'With Andrew Macgreevy' the credits said in teensy-weensy type under the main author's huge big name."

"Well, it got me out of the provincials to the national papers."

"Oh, hallelujah. What a great day for a free press."

"I'm waiting, Stella. Where is he then? Lord Graven?"

"Where do *you* think he is?"

"You tell me. You're the one who brought it up."

"I'm not telling you anything unless you tell me first, so I know you're not wasting my time. And . . . *and!* Macgreevy—you hold to your original promise."

He made an affirmative sort of grunt.

"I ought to make you open a vein and do something in writing."

"Get on with it."

"*You* get on with it. Where do you think Graven is?"

"Well, he could be anywhere." Macgreevy looked grim.

"That's no answer."

"Well, er, there's been reports that he's in Mexico . . . or Zimbabwe."

"Hmph. And what's your source?"

He gave me a hard stare. "None of your bloody business."

"What's your source?" I said again. "I won't tell. I promise. And *I* keep my promises."

He flicked a drop of rainwater that had landed on his chin. "I have an . . . acquaintance in the post office."

"Here at Windsor, I presume."

"He lets me know from time to time if there's any, well . . . interesting post going to the Castle. He tipped me a few weeks ago to some regular letters that have been coming to Canon Leathley from Mexico and from Zimbabwe, without return addresses on them. Not the usual C of E business. And so, since I wasn't busy otherwise . . ."

"I see. Well, Graven can't be two places at once. Has it occurred to you that he might have been using intermediaries in his correspondence to his cousin?"

"Of course it's bloody occurred to me! But that bugger at the post office won't open the letters or let me take a look at them, no matter what I offer."

"It *is* a crime, you idiot."

"Do you have any idea what it would mean for me to crack this Graven story?"

"I'm beginning to. That's why you were hanging around the Castle after evensong on Tuesday. Hoping to spring on the Canon, were you?"

He shrugged. "You and that twit footman were stuck to him like glue. And then I thought better of it the next day. Not enough to go on. I don't want to blow my chances." He narrowed his eyes: "So where is Graven?"

"Not in Mexico. Nor Zimbabwe. Nor Brazil nor Paraguay or wherever fugitives land up. Or even some remote part of England, if there are any remote parts here. Lord Graven's in—how 'bout a drumroll—?"

"Stuff it."

"He's in Thailand."

Macgreevy's eyes narrowed. "How do you know?"

"I know."

"Source?"

"Kin to the horse's mouth. That's all I'm saying."

"Lots of people in Thailand. Big country."

"He's a Caucasian among Asians, for one. And I know roughly where in Thailand. But I can only give it to you phonetically, as I heard it: either Pa Ki or Pa Ka."

"The moron's probably got himself in the drug trade."

He paused. "How do I know you're not making this up to get me out of the country."

"Look, Dorian Gray," I said, turning to go, "you may have a portrait in your attic, but I don't have one in mine. Hell, I don't even have an attic."

He took my shoulder once more. "Thanks, Stell," he said. His attempt at nonchalance fell flat to my ears.

"Think nothing of it," I replied hastily. I didn't mind shopping Rupert FitzJames, Marquess of Graven. If he had killed his wife, he should be back home to face the consequences. And if he hadn't, then he should come back anyway. He had a father and a son to come back to.

"Offer's still on about a meal. This evening? I know a place in Datchet."

"Thanks, Andrew, no. I've got a date." Hoped, rather.

"Not that blond bloke you nearly tripped over yourself to get to at the Riverview."

"Maybe," I said, suddenly grateful for the camouflaging properties of my fire-reddened skin. Had I appeared that eager? "Look, I've got to go. My shoes are soaked. It's my day off and I don't want to spend the rest of it standing in the rain."

"Well, buzz off then, Miss Bee."

And buzz off I did, feeling in some way that I'd been burned twice in twenty-four hours. But I had a visit to make before I returned to Clarence Tower, and the anticipation put old Andrew clean out of my head.

By the end of a long rainy Saturday, three things had happened:

(1) I had gone out with Jamie.

(2) I received an invitation to tea the next day.

(3) Joanna Scott Clair Pettibon died in hospital at eight o'clock in the evening.

22

ON THE EAST Terrace of Windsor Castle a table had been laid out under an awning. Only the faintest breeze stirred the linen tablecloth, which was no surprise because only the faintest breeze was in evidence. It was nearly a perfect day. The sun was shining, but not making the sort of nuisance of itself that it had been most of the week. The sky was blue, but not a throbbing electric blue. A nice Wedgwood blue, rather. Birds flew in exultation above the ornamental trees and shrubbery and statuary of the East Terrace's formal gardens. Insects droned lullingly. The grass, slaked by a day of rain, was restored to an emerald brilliance. A sweetness filled the air, of flowers and warm soil and of cooling waters from the terrace's central fountain. Nature was on a gentle hum.

It was five o'clock Sunday afternoon.

Teatime.

And the only thing marring the graciousness and civil-

ity of the setting were those bloody airplanes beginning
their descent into Heathrow. I glanced up. Conversation had
idled, as it had done about every ten minutes or so since the
first cuppa had been poured. The airplane twinkled on high,
like a tea tray in the sky, and then faded to gray and from
view.

Tea is not normally taken on the East Terrace. Sometimes the Queen and Prince Philip have lunch or dinner
there on warm summer weekends, but tea is usually served,
for one of those unaccountable reasons of tradition that mark
royal life, in the Oak Drawing Room. But as Her Majesty
said to us when we'd assembled before five in the Grand
Corridor, trying, as is her habit, to put us at our ease: "It's
such a lovely day. I thought it would be much nicer to break
with tradition and have tea outdoors."

And so it was. Much nicer.

Although, despite HM's knack at easing social inter-
course, with the Sovereign as your hostess, you're apt to
become acutely conscious of your table manners. No elbows
on the table. Don't slurp your tea. Don't pick wax from your
ears. No off-colour jokes. Etc.

And the pleasant setting couldn't quite distract from
the circumstances that had brought us together. We weren't
the usual crowd of modern-day worthies—heads of business
corporations and actors and charity organizers—the sort that
join the Queen for her Meet-the-People luncheons back at
Buck House. We were a rather more eclectic collection but
all linked in some way to the tragedies of Ascot Week. All,
that is, except for Sir Bernard Scrymgeour-Warburton, Secretary of the Central Chancery of the Orders of Knighthood,
who was seated on my left, and who, after beaming for a
while around the table as if this were quite the most delightful occasion he'd ever attended, looked to be nodding off.
Among the more alert, however, besides me and HM: the
FitzJames brood—the Duke of Cheshire, his grandson,
Hugo, and his nephew, the Reverend Canon St. John
Leathley; Victor Fabiani and his daughter, Miranda Walter;
as well as Iain Scott and his sister, Hillary Elliott. Lending
his usual tone was Davey Pye, back to his regular daily dress
of black tailcoat and trousers from his scarlet semi-State livery, flourishing trays of tiny sandwiches and scones and

sponge and gâteau and biscuits with exaggerated panache and using his most friggypoo voice, such that even the Queen, who is used to his airs, was shooting him looks. I knew why he was being so over the top: he was dead jealous that I was seated at table and he was but serving the goodies.

"First breakfast, and now tea," he hissed in my ear as he bent with a tray of quite scrummy thank-you cucumber and chicken sandwiches, crusts cut off and all. "The sun has well and truly set on the British Empire."

Clever rejoinders were proscribed, alas. Her Majesty was speaking.

". . . and so," she was saying, as she poured a fresh cup for the Duke and cast another sharpish glance at Davey, "there was decent opportunity. The State Apartments were largely barren of the customary security people because they were closed to the public for the Garter Investiture. The means, Hugo's sword, was at hand. Handily so, one might say."

She passed the cup to the Duke, who was seated at her right hand. "But the police investigating, I think, were rather confounded by the lack of physical evidence—no fingerprints on the sword, for instance. Blood found on Mr. Fabiani's smock seemed promising, a match to that found on the Throne Room carpet, which in turn seemed to bolster Mr. Fabiani's confession. But that, after a time, after further testing, proved unhelpful.

"And with due respect to my very good Staff," she added, nodding in my direction, "no amount of cleaning could rid the Throne Room of the sorts of hairs and fibers and such that scene-of-crime officers find so useful. After all, thousands of visitors go through the State Apartments on an average day, and on the evening before the Garter Investiture, Staff was busy arranging the Throne Room for the next day and there were Security people about and—more tea, Canon?—and even early in the morning in question, my grandsons had passed through, with you, I believe, Hugo. So, in brief, it was all rather a forensic nightmare. I think I can understand, Mr. Fabiani, why the police were so happy to entertain your confession as long as they did."

I glanced at Victor, seated at the end of the table opposite Her Majesty. I had heard the portrait-sitting the Queen had promised him for Saturday afternoon had been canceled (for reasons of general gloom, weatherwise and otherwise) and so he seemed to be taking the opportunity to soak in the Presence under other circumstances. His brows were knitted and he was tapping an eyetooth thoughtfully with one fingernail, his tea virtually untouched.

"And then, of course," Her Majesty continued, as she poured tea into the Canon's cup, "we come to the motive, the real motive, which remained rather elusive. Roger Pettibon, by all accounts, was a pleasant enough individual, not the sort to raise anyone's ire, one would have thought. However, it seems Mr. Pettibon was leading what one might call a double life." She frowned slightly as she handed Canon Leathley his cup. "I don't think we need dwell on Mr. Pettibon's proclivities. You all know, or have been told." She glanced at the Duke and at Sir Bernard. The latter I poked gently in the ribs. "Quite," he remarked to no one in particular.

"And I know he's already caused at least one person at this table enough distress," the Queen added sympathetically, acknowledging Miranda, who, across from me, appeared wan, her hands nervously caressing the handle of her teacup. "But Roger Pettibon's compulsion led to the destruction of two lives—at least two—in addition to his own, and so one would like to bring some resolution to this unhappy episode." She shook her head.

"Some of you here, I know, have felt yourselves at one time or another to be under suspicion—"

"What?" interrupted His Grace.

"Not you, Freddie," the Queen assured him. Airplane noise cut out Cheshire's response. "Under suspicion," she began again. "Miss Bee, whom most of you know by now, doubted the police had the right man in Mr. Fabiani—"

"Oh? Why?" queried the Duke.

"Because Jane was with Mr. Fabiani in his rooms very near to the time Mr. Pettibon was killed. It appeared to her Mr. Fabiani lacked opportunity, you see, Freddie. And there were other anomalies, too."

The Duke of Cheshire leaned his head forward and

looked down the table at me. Curiosity mixed with censure on his features.

"I was *posing*, Your Grace," I explained. Why do people leap to these silly conclusions? "Wearing robes," I added hastily, as Cheshire's eyebrows ratcheted upward. At the same time I felt something rub my leg. I looked sharply across the table at Iain Scott but he was staring with a faintly bored expression into the middle distance toward the East Lawn. And Sir Bernard, sleepily biting into a biscuit, didn't seem the footsie type.

"Jane persuaded me something was amiss," the Queen said as my leg was rubbed again. "Unfortunately, she had poor luck convincing anyone else. Nonetheless, I thought she ought to carry on."

I recoiled suddenly. Something wet now grazed my leg. Miranda glanced at me, her face a question.

"There were five people who've acknowledged being in the Upper Ward Monday morning who knew the truth about Mr. Pettibon. Sadly . . . Is something the matter, Jane?"

"No, Ma'am. I'm sorry. One of the dogs startled me." I glanced down. A wet nose had poked from under the cloth and a furry face was gazing up at me expectantly, all savage teeth and sausage tongue. Slip us a biscuit, her expression seemed to say. Or else.

"As I was saying," the Queen carried on, while I obligingly let a biscuit drop, "Of the five, one of them, Joanna Pettibon, as I'm sure you know by now, died in hospital last evening, which is very sad. This is, of course, a particular tragedy for Mrs. Elliott and Mr. Scott, who have very kindly obliged us with their presence this afternoon."

There was a murmur of concurrence around the table as faces turned with curiosity and concern to acknowledge the bereaved family members. Hillary Elliott, at my right, responded with a weak smile, then bent her head.

"As for the remaining four, Miss Walter has, of course, known for some time the truth about Roger Pettibon, as he was once her stepfather. Mr. Fabiani learned that same truth Sunday. Hugo, I understand, was Pippa Clair's confidant in this matter, which I think is rather much for a boy to handle at such an age. You're to be commended, Hugo."

"Thank you, Ma'am," Hugo responded, taking several sandwiches from the tray that Davey again proffered. Hugo's appetite for food seemed undampened by the adult seriousness under the awning. Miranda and Hillary had barely nibbled at their sandwiches. Victor, too, seemed indifferent to what was on his plate, as did Iain.

"And I daresay, Canon, you, too, knew something of Mr. Pettibon's other life," the Queen concluded, turning to the figure at her left.

Leathley flashed gleaming spectacles in my direction, his eyes and their expression obscured. He might well have guessed the source of this intelligence: yours truly, of course. Between luncheon and tea, after HM had completed her regular Sunday afternoon kingship lessons with her grandson, and after she'd had a brief private Audience with Iain Scott and Hillary Elliott, she and I had had a sombre tête-à-tête in the Oak Drawing Room while she inserted the final jigsaw pieces into what was revealed to be an African jungle.

"Only recently, Ma'am," Leathley replied evenly to HM's probing. "Roger was very troubled, it was apparent. His stepdaughter's death had affected him very deeply. Knowing what I now know, I can see that Pippa's tragic end had been, I suppose you could say, a turning point for him, but when he first came to me he was not precisely forthcoming about the nature of his . . . distress."

He sipped his tea, then continued. "I counseled him as best I could in his grief, but it was only in confession last Sunday that he fully declared himself. I—"

"So you *did* speak with Roger Sunday!" I interrupted.

"—was appalled, of course," the Canon continued, ignoring me. "Shocked. We had a long talk." He paused, replacing the cup in its saucer. "My office is to absolve, but there is—if I may put it this way—no cheap grace in the Church of England. Before absolution is given, the sinner must make some satisfying restitution with the individual he's harmed. So I urged Roger to do just that, to make restitution."

He frowned. "Of course, I doubt he had the opportunity to move forward on this, because the next morning he was dead."

"Was there any reason why he decided to open up to you about this last Sunday, as opposed to any other time since Easter?" I'd guessed at the answer but wanted a confirmation.

The Canon toyed with his fork. "You know, Miss Bee, I believe I talked with you earlier in the week about the seal of the confessional . . ."

"Yes, I know, but surely death . . ."

"It is only because Roger's wrongdoing is now public knowledge that I'm discussing this at all. Otherwise it would go to the grave with me. It certainly wasn't apparent to me Tuesday why I should ever discuss these things with a young woman who'd only just been introduced to me."

"You'll have to forgive Jane's zeal, Canon," the Queen interposed.

His mouth formed a thin line. "Yes, of course," he responded reluctantly. "To answer your question then, Miss Bee: Roger had apparently run into someone from his past he believed he had harmed. Which I now think must be you, Miss Walter," he added, looking down the table. "I'm very sorry for the pain he's caused you. If there's anything I can do . . ."

"Thank you, Canon." Miranda spoke quietly.

"However," Leathley continued, "At the time, Roger gave me no name. And I must say, for myself—and this is unforgivable, really—I was beginning to find I couldn't stomach any more detail than was necessary."

"Did he talk about Mrs. Pettibon?" the Queen asked.

"Do you mean, Ma'am, did Joanna know about Roger's abusing her daughter?"

"In effect, yes."

"He seemed to think she didn't. Which I know seems extraordinary, but I'm led to believe considerable secretiveness can attend this sort of thing."

"It's more often denial, Canon," Miranda interjected. "The mother knows but can't bring herself to face the truth." She studied Hillary, who responded by pursing her lips and looking beseechingly around the table.

"I . . . I . . ." Hillary faltered, her voice strained. She tried again: "You must . . . understand this has all been a terrible shock for me. I had no idea Roger was that sort of man. I suppose the last few years I haven't seen enough of Joanna. Hadn't seen," she amended sadly. "My life in Oxford has kept me so preoccupied . . . the children, you know . . . everything, my husband, so . . . Really, when I came down midweek, and Joanna told me all about this appalling business, I was simply . . . I didn't know what to think. I did ask her at one point: Did she suspect? Did she know? Had it been going on for months? *Years?* She said, no. She didn't know. She hadn't suspected a thing. Still, as you say, Miss Walter, perhaps . . ." Hillary shook her head helplessly.

The Canon interjected: "I paid a call on your sister Friday afternoon, Mrs. Elliott, after you'd returned to Oxford. I know your family's Roman Catholic and I wasn't sure I should interfere, but I thought I might be able to lend some help. After all, there were certain things I knew . . ." He ran a finger absently down the teacup's delicate handle. "I think, Ma'am," he turned to the Queen, "that Mrs. Elliott is probably right. Joanna had only lately pieced it together. I'm afraid she was somewhat incoherent when I arrived. It was plain she'd been drinking fairly heavily, but I managed to gather that she hadn't been able to deal with Pippa's things in the wake of her death and when she did, finally, she came across a journal of sorts tucked away somewhere—"

"The diary . . ." Hillary murmured.

"—yes, a diary with poems and such, little stories, dark imaginings, the sort of thing a girl in her fraught circumstances might find therapeutic to do. I believe it was this journal that tipped Joanna to the truth, although I do acknowledge Miss Walter's observation about denial."

"Did you see this diary, Mrs. Elliott?" The Queen received Hugo's teacup and began pouring more tea.

"Yes, Ma'am. Joanna showed it to me not long after I'd arrived Wednesday. I think it had been rather obsessing her."

"And you, Mr. Scott?"

"Ma'am, my sister showed it to me on Monday after the police had been around to break the news about Roger."

"You told me in the Star that Pettibon was evil," I addressed Iain.

"Was I wrong?" he snapped.

Before I could rejoinder the Queen broke in. "I understand from my private secretary that the men investigating the fire have determined the blaze started from Mrs. Pettibon's attempt to burn a book of some nature, using picture restorer's fluid." She handed the teacup to Davey to return to Hugo. "Unfortunately the container exploded."

"Ma'am," I piped up, "before we got Mrs. Pettibon out of her house, I saw a slightly charred pink book on her couch. It was the same one she had with her during Wednesday's visit."

"It did have a pink cover," Hillary confirmed.

"I see," the Queen murmured thoughtfully. She probably had the same thought as I did: Had Joanna, in her drunken emotional state, been destroying something hateful, or had she been destroying evidence?

Canon Leathley's spectacles turned to me with a cold steely look. "I don't quite understand why you were suspicious of me?"

"I wasn't really. But I'd heard from—" I flicked a glance at Davey, who was placing a pot of fresh hot water before the Queen, "—a source that Mr. Pettibon had been seen frequently at church and in your company, so I thought you might know something useful. I don't know much about Church of England practices so I wasn't aware of the role of confession. But you did seem sort of secretive, especially with that red herring story. And then, on Thursday at Ascot, when I overheard His Grace talking about letters you'd been receiving from . . ."

I faltered. Leathley was glaring at me fiercely, his spectacles in his hand. "What!" I heard the Duke explode. A chilling silence followed.

"Um . . ." I began again, "from . . . Thailand . . ." How was I to explain the complication of Lord Graven when I knew both men were trying to protect Hugo? "Perhaps we should talk about this later," I suggested hastily.

"Is this about my father?" Hugo interjected instead, his voice matter-of-fact, a biscuit hovering before his open mouth.

There was another silence, the longish sort that might

as well stand in for an affirmation. Somewhere a bird sang brightly.

"I've read the letters. I know all about it. I know where he is."

"Hugo, how dare you read my private correspondence!"

"I'm not a child, you know!" Hugo countered with the lament of teenagers everywhere, chomping down on the biscuit. "And I've read that stupid *Nowhere Man* book, too, Granddad."

There was a burst of harrumphing from the Duke. Silly old poops, I thought. The way to a child's curiosity is surely to keep things shrouded in mystery.

"More tea, anyone?" The Queen offered in a restoring-order sort of way as Cheshire continued to splutter.

"Yes, please," I said as if on cue, and handed my cup to Davey, who received it with embellishment and conveyed it to the head of the table.

"Perhaps," Her Majesty continued, "Jane could explain, as it seems the cat is out of the bag, so to speak. I understand, Freddie, you're urging Rupert to return home to England."

"I've been doing so all along, Ma'am," Canon Leathley answered instead. "As Your Majesty probably knows, my uncle and Rupert were estranged for some time before Rupert left the country."

"Yes, of course. I'd forgotten." The Queen glanced at Hugo, the object of the estrangement, as she poured tea into my cup.

"However, I think," Leathley continued, "it may be time for Rupert to be *brought* home, if he won't come on his own."

"You mean, you're going to grass on my father," Hugo said.

The Canon paused. "Yes, if you must put it that way, Hugo. But Rupert's not well. He must come home and get treatment."

Davey handed me my cup and saucer. "From what I overheard," I began, after taking a sip, "it seemed there was a sudden urgency to have Lord Graven return home, that someone had spotted him in Thailand, and I began to wonder if Pettibon, who had also been in Thailand, might have been the someone in question."

Leathley glanced impatiently at the sky, at another twinkling airplane. "Very clever," he replied when quiet was restored. "Yes, in fact, he was. When Roger more fully talked to me about his . . . problem Sunday, he mentioned among other things that he'd been to Bangkok on holiday last year, or perhaps it was a stopover, Bangkok being, it seems, a destination for—" He glanced unhappily at Hugo. He cleared his throat. "—pedophiles.

"By chance, when he was coming out of his hotel, he glimpsed Rupert and realized who he was. Roger merely mentioned this to me in passing, perhaps not realizing or caring that there were people here in England who would be extremely interested in such information. But I was rather stunned that Rupert was taking the risk of being seen, coming into a large city where there would be English travellers who might recognize him. He was either being frightfully overconfident or perhaps he wanted to be caught by this time, or he wasn't well. I didn't know. Thailand, unfortunately, has not only a reputation as a haven for people of Roger Pettibon's bent, it's also a drugs haven, and drugs have always been Rupert's problem, as I'm sure everyone here knows."

The Canon sighed deeply, removed his spectacles, and studied them as if trying to locate a smudge. Another airplane cracked the silence. Sir Bernard stirred.

"Do I take it, Miss Bee," Leathley asked, bringing forth a handkerchief from his pocket, "that you imagine I killed Roger to protect the secret of my cousin's whereabouts?"

I felt like a shrivelled raisin under his withering gaze. "Well," I began reluctantly, "it had crossed my mind. You see, there seemed to be no apparent motive. But you were in the Upper Ward Monday morning, and you'd been having a sort of association with Mr. Pettibon and so, when I overheard His Grace talking about his son, I thought, well, maybe . . ."

"Then why would I be campaigning within my family to get Rupert back?"

"You wanted to show yourself to have no apparent motive, in case the police came calling. If they didn't come calling, then you could change your mind again and leave Lord Graven be where he was. From what I understand, His Grace wasn't keen to have his son back in England, anyway."

"This is preposterous!"

The Duke interrupted: "St. John, it does seem rather odd that you decided to tell me this week of all weeks that you'd been secretly keeping a correspondence with Rupert."

"Really, Uncle! This is too much! I have always had enormous reservations about protecting Rupert and keeping everything I know from you and from Hugo, but that's what Rupert has insisted on, and I've given in to his wishes—foolishly, probably; out of love certainly. The only reason I changed my mind and decided to talk with you about Rupert this week, of all weeks, is—and Miss Bee is quite right—is because of Roger Pettibon. But it has nothing to do with some complex motives for a murder: it's simply because Roger so easily sighted Rupert; that, plus the fact that the content of Rupert's correspondence has become increasingly both incoherent and remorseful, made me realize that the status quo cannot prevail. You were, of course, coming down to Windsor for Ascot, so I thought this was the time to talk about Rupert, the great forbidden subject. What I didn't expect, Uncle, was that you would be *quite* so indiscreet."

"It was the shock, dear boy."

"Who were you talking to that Miss Bee overheard?"

"Dicky Easterbrook."

"You might just as well have told the correspondent for the *Evening Gazette*!" Leathley sighed and added testily, "Well, I suppose it doesn't matter now."

"No," Her Majesty interjected in her reasonable voice, throwing bread (and cakes and tea) on troubled water. "In one way at least, it doesn't matter."

"I apologize for my outburst, Ma'am."

"Quite all right, Canon. I'm afraid murder tends to high emotion." HM glanced at Davey who was hovering near her shoulder. "David, you may leave us for the time being."

"Yes, Ma'am." Davey quickly stuck out his tongue at

me, a gesture only I noted, and sloped off toward the Castle with an empty tray.

Her Majesty continued: "I must take some responsibility for allowing a speculative tone to emerge around this table about Mr. Pettibon. It certainly wasn't my original intention yesterday to invite all of you to tea this afternoon to root out his killer, as some characters in a mystery novel might. That would be most unsympathetic in view of the presence of Mrs. Elliott and Mr. Scott. However—"

"Oh, Ma'am," Hillary entreated the Sovereign, "we're so dreadfully sorry for the trouble that's been caused Your Majesty. I'm horrified by what Joanna did . . . and the fire—"

"It's nothing compared to your loss, Mrs. Elliott," the Queen responded firmly and sympathetically. "Salisbury Tower will be restored in time, just as Brunswick Tower and Prince of Wales's Tower will be restored." She nodded toward the northeast section of the Castle where scaffolding clung to the curtain of stone. "It's life, unfortunately, that can't be restored. Barring, if you will, Canon, a certain incident recorded in the Gospel of St. John."

Leathley smiled over the rim of his teacup. The Queen opened her mouth to continue but the Duke suddenly interrupted: "Ma'am, if I may—you said *original* intention. With all due respect to certain of Your Majesty's other guests present—I hope they won't mind—isn't Mrs. Pettibon responsible for her husband's death? That's the speculation in the papers."

"The police believe they've reached a satisfying conclusion, indeed, Freddie," the Queen replied neutrally. "And certainly everything supports that conclusion. I think one can safely say that by last Monday morning Mrs. Pettibon knew—or had at least finally acknowledged—what her husband had been doing to her daughter. And I'm sure she was in a dreadful state about it." HM dipped her knife into the dab of butter on her plate.

"Mrs. Pettibon herself admitted to being in the Upper Ward that morning," the Queen continued, spreading the butter over her scone. "Doing paperwork, I believe she said. She professed to me to be unaware her husband was in the Royal Library at the time, much less the Throne Room, but she speculated that perhaps Mr. Pettibon wished to examine in the Ante-Throne Room the copy of the painting, *George III at a Review*, with the idea of putting it into a travelling exhibition. It was only some time afterward I thought this a bit odd. 'George III at a Review' is a *painting*, not a drawing, and so quite outside either Pettibon's responsibility. And why would Mrs. Pettibon think of that painting, of all the paintings in the Windsor Castle? One so close to the Throne Room?" She took a small bite of her scone.

At the other end of the table, Victor Fabiani straightened himself in his chair. "I see now why the experts didn't twig sooner to my unsuitability as a forger of Leonardos."

"Do you?" HM said evenly, lowering her scone. It was less a question than a comment.

"Well, yes, Ma'am. I think so. The expert advice the police sought first was Joanna's. After talking with Your Majesty Friday evening I remembered that one day a month or two back, when I'd visited the Royal Library, Joanna and I had talked about the challenges facing a forger of Old Master drawings. At the time, she made an aside about 'handedness' in relation to Leonardo. Obviously, she knew Leonardo was left-handed. Joanna Pettibon is—was, rather—a recognized expert in Old Master drawings! But I'm sure she realized I was right-handed. I think I even made a little joke about it at the time."

"Your confession, Mr. Fabiani, must have been rather a godsend to Mrs. Pettibon." Sir Bernard spoke for the first time. "At least for a while."

"I'm not sure my sister would have been able to find relief in anything," Hillary said tartly.

Fabiani looked off, toward the formal gardens. "Perhaps if I'd said something on Friday, then something could have been done for Joanna. But . . ." he turned back to us ". . . the idea she was responsible only crossed my mind for a second because . . ." He left the rest unsaid.

"Because you still thought I might have done it," Miranda supplied quietly.

Victor put his hand over hers.

"Yes, well, as some of you may know," the Queen interposed, "gloves were found in the pocket of Joanna Pettibon's raincoat Friday night during the fire. This is the most damning piece of evidence of all. Indeed, the *only* piece of evidence, really. They were the gloves archivists wear when handling artworks, encrusted with dried blood. And one can attest that Mrs. Pettibon, even in her clouded state of mind, showed distress at their being discovered." HM frowned, adding cheerlessly: "The blood, we now know from analysis, was her husband's."

There was a brief contemplative silence. A gust of wind gently lifted a corner of the tablecloth and then as gently released it.

"Well, then," said the Duke in a tone that seemed wont to jolly us along, "there you go. The incident's closed. However unwelcome these tidings, particularly for Mrs. Elliott and Mr. Scott, it appears Mrs. Pettibon murdered her husband. And I must say, for myself, I'm not entirely unsympathetic."

Her Majesty lifted her teacup to her lips. She glanced at me then took a sip. "I'm not sure," she said thoughtfully to no one in particular, "that it's at all true that Mrs. Pettibon killed her husband. I'm not sure that's the case at all."

23

A SILVER FORK dropped onto a Minton dessert plate, the sudden pinging ringing shattering the silence that greeted Her Majesty's announcement, provoking a couple of corgis beneath the table to a fit of irksome yapping.

"I'm so sorry, Ma'am," a flustered Hillary said as the Queen reached one arm below the tablecloth and made cooing noises at the perturbed dogs.

"Their hearing's so very sensitive," HM explained. "The oddest noises will set them off. There, there," she continued as a common old ordinary airplane above droned its way into Heathrow.

"You say, Freddie, that you're not entirely unsympathetic to a woman murdering her husband—" the Queen continued, returning her hand to the table, canine order having been restored.

"Well! He was a blighter, Ma'am!" The Duke responded, incredulous.

"Yes, quite. Indeed, that at the very least seems to be the common view among those who knew the truth about Roger Pettibon's . . . habits. One tends to react to the knowledge with distaste, certainly; if not horror or anger or, in some cases, I should expect—" she nodded toward Miranda "—fear." She lifted her teacup, contemplated its contents, then added gravely: "I'm hard-pressed to think of anyone more abominated in our society than someone who victimizes a child." She glanced unhappily at Hugo, who remained concentrated on a piece of lemon gâteau. "And I wonder, would one be going too far in observing that the offender's death wouldn't be entirely *un*welcome among his victims, their families, or their friends?"

The question being rhetorical, and the questioner being the Sovereign, everyone remained silent.

"I had been thinking about this earlier this afternoon, after I was presented with some new information." Her Majesty continued, looking over at me as she sipped her tea. "Roger Pettibon's death seems, on the whole, to be unregretted. If one takes, for a moment, the view that Mrs. Pettibon is innocent of her husband's murder, who then is guilty? I think for several people here, the identity of the guilty party is not quite the most important thing in the world.

"What is important is that Mr. Pettibon is no longer free to continue in his ways, to hurt children, to ruin lives. Indeed, I shouldn't be surprised if some people mightn't feel a certain gratitude toward Roger Pettibon's murderer. Perhaps, I daresay, even seek to protect the guilty party. Shoo!" The Queen replaced her teacup and waved at a fat bumblebee hovering over the sugar bowl.

"Mr. Fabiani, for example," HM continued as the unperturbed insect buzzed down the table exploring the wares, "sought to protect someone he believed was guilty—his daughter, Miss Walter—inventing a ruse that, on the surface, looked like a scheme to allow Miss Walter time to flee the country or go into hiding or some such thing. And Miss Walter had, coincidently, left Windsor giving no forwarding address, which certainly seemed rather suspicious. However,

Miss Walter returned Friday claiming as I understand it, no knowledge of Mr. Pettibon's death."

"Ma'am," Miranda responded, one eye uneasily on the bumblebee which had settled into a small centrepiece of fresh-cut flowers. "I was at a retreat. There were no newspapers or television."

"Despite this, you gave a strong indication to Miss Bee moments after arriving back in Windsor that you knew where in the Castle your former stepfather had been killed. In the Throne Room. That seems to me rather inconsistent with your claim not to know Mr. Pettibon had been killed at all."

"It was a guess, Ma'am. An assumption. I . . ." She turned her dark eyes from the centerpiece and looked at me. "What I didn't tell you, Jane—and what I didn't tell the police—was that I saw Roger last Monday morning. Or, rather, I tried *not* to see him." She seemed to look through me, unseeing, as if replaying the events of the morning. The bee flew off. She was oblivious.

"I was in the Grand Reception Room retrieving my coat from where it had fallen behind a bench. I happened to look up, through the glass doors, and saw Roger coming through the Throne Room from the other end. He could see me. He was looking right at me. He seemed to be . . ." She shuddered slightly. ". . . fixed on me. I was horrified. He must have known somehow I was in the Castle. Perhaps he looked out a window, I don't know. I simply knew I didn't want to be anywhere near him.

"The doors between the Throne Room and the Grand Reception Room were closed, but I could see they weren't locked. So fast as I could I ran to the door and tried to turn the latch, but my hands were shaking so, I was fumbling, I thought I'd never get the handle turned properly. He was shouting something at me through the glass and trying to push against the doors. I only got them fastened in time. Then I ran to the other exit, to the stairs off the Waterloo Chamber. I was terrified he would follow me. I know I said to my father the night before that I wanted to kill Roger, but seeing him, on the other side of the glass, his face so close, after all these years, I just . . ." She close her eyes. "I just couldn't bear it."

There was a silence broken only by a chirrup of birds madly circling the water fountain.

"Perhaps, Miss Walter," Canon Leathley said, "he was seeking to make the restitution I talked about earlier."

"Well, I didn't know that!" Miranda responded bitterly, opening her eyes: "And it wouldn't have mattered anyway. I wasn't prepared to forgive him. I'm still not!" She reached for Victor's hand.

"But . . ." I said after a moment, perplexed, "I still don't quite understand. You saw Roger in the Throne Room. Did you see him *murdered* in the Throne Room?"

Miranda didn't reply immediately. She glanced at her father, then at Hillary. She seemed to be considering her response. Finally, with a little sigh, she said: "Do you remember me asking you for a description of Joanna Pettibon?"

"You said you wondered what kind of woman Roger would have married after your mother."

"As I was struggling to lock the door, I saw the sort of woman you described advancing into the Throne Room from the Ante-Throne Room at the other end. I only glimpsed her, really, but . . ."

"Yes . . . ?" I asked urgently.

"But, in that moment . . . she had a look on her face, a look of such concentrated fury that . . . well, when you explained to me on Friday that Roger had abused her daughter the way he had abused me, I thought . . . well, it just flashed in my mind: She killed him. *She* killed him."

Miranda looked off to the side, up toward the wall of trees on the north side of the Terrace. She added tonelessly, to no one in particular: "And I'm glad she did."

There was another silence, more deathly this time, around the table, mocked by the innocent noises of nature and the indifferent drone of another airplane. Finally, I said: "And you wouldn't tell me, or the police, any of this because you wanted to protect Joanna. Am I right?"

Again Miranda considered her response. "I didn't want to see her go to prison for what she did," she replied finally. "But if I'd known she was going to sacrifice herself in that horrible way . . ."

"The fire was an accident, Miss Walter," the Queen said mildly.

"And it happened so soon after I left you on Friday," I added to Miranda. "There was nothing you could have done, or I could have done, or anybody, really."

A gentle breeze wafted over the table, stirring the flowers in the centrepiece. No one spoke. The heedless happy sounds of birds flowed in and took possession of the conversational vacuum; somewhere off in the distance, toward the Long Walk, a muffled cheer could be heard, as if someone on his Sunday outing had realized some new joy.

Her Majesty reached down to pet one of the corgis that had appeared from under the table. "And so it would seem," she said contemplatively, "that poor Mrs. Pettibon did indeed kill her husband. Certainly, she had provocation. And Miss Walter has identified her as being in the Throne Room at the critical time. I, for one, don't for a minute believe that this death was planned. It was an act of passion, an act of anger, really. In the end, I daresay, an accident of sorts. Regrettable, in its way. And one might, as they say, close the books on this unhappy episode, but for one curiosity." The Queen lifted her hand and ran it over the pearls at her neck. "You see, one person at this table has given a disputable account of certain movements Monday morning."

HM paused. All eyes turned in her direction. But for a shrieking jet overhead, a chirruping of giddy birds and the discreet splashing of the East Terrace's central water fountain, you could have heard a pin drop.

The Queen continued thoughtfully: "There is a good deal of routine to life here at Windsor, if one thinks about it. People have regular jobs to go to within the Castle walls, or various assigned tasks that send them off to the certain places at certain times every day. The Guard changes on the clock. St. George's Chapel conducts services at the same hour. The shops in the three wards of the Castle open and close at times that vary only with the season. And so on.

"However, Monday last—Garter Monday—was not a typical day. It was a holiday for many of my Staff and others who work here. Routine was broken. Generally, fewer people were about. And, also, because it's one of the few days in

the year when the Castle is closed to the public, fewer people were expected—at least not until noon when guests invited to watch the Garter Procession began arriving. This
holiday atmosphere may account in part for the inattentive
security at Engine Court before nine o'clock that morning.
Certainly no one seated here was seen entering or leaving
the Upper Ward."

The Queen paused. "The situation was little different
in the Lower Ward. On an ordinary day, before nine o'clock,
well before visitors arrive at ten, the Lower Ward is, I expect, almost a haven of peace. The Lower Ward needs little
preparation for the Garter Procession. Only rope barriers
need to be erected to define the route and keep guests from
stepping into the Procession. Those are erected the evening
before. So I expect, as some of you can attest, the Lower
Ward was quite empty early Monday morning."

There were nods all around.

Her Majesty continued: "Sometime before nine
o'clock Monday morning, Joanna Pettibon walked through
the Lower Ward from her home at Salisbury Tower to her
office in the Royal Library. Canon Leathley and Hugo also
crossed the Lower Ward on the way to one's Private Apartments, at perhaps an earlier time. Around eight o'clock,
Canon?"

"About then, Ma'am," Leathley replied.

"But yourself returning to the Lower Ward in a round-
about fashion, through the north side of the Upper Ward, in
the vicinity of the State Apartments."

"I was curious to see the progress of the restoration,
Ma'am."

"Yes, I see." The Queen turned her attention farther
down the table. "Mr. Fabiani was, of course, already in the
Upper Ward that morning. He's been living temporarily
above the State Apartments while completing one's portrait.
As for those entering the Castle from outside the walls that
morning, Miss Walter, you were admitted to the Castle
through Henry VIII Gate at approximately eight forty-five.
Mr. Scott was admitted after eleven o'clock, well past the
time of Mr. Pettibon's death."

The Queen continued fingering her pearls.

"Did you return to Windsor from London by train, Mr. Scott?" she asked.

"Yes, Ma'am, I caught the train at Waterloo shortly after ten o'clock."

"Really?"

"Yes, Ma'am."

HM cocked her head slightly. "How very odd. Because someone in the Castle is quite sure he saw you in the Lower Ward before *nine* o'clock."

Faint consternation registered on Iain's face. "Well, Ma'am . . . I don't see how . . . I mean . . . Who, if I may ask—"

"One of the Military Knights saw you. Major Simms. I understand you're friends with his great-niece."

"Major Simms *is* quite elderly, Ma'am—"

"One's powers of observation do not necessarily decline with age, Mr. Scott," the Queen retorted. "Major Simms is a keen gardener and usually outdoors in the mornings tending his plants. He insists he saw you make your way past him. You *are* known to him, of course."

Iain frowned. "Major Simms must be mistaken."

The Queen began rubbing at her wedding rings. Always a dangerous sign. But she said evenly: "I understand Major Simm's great-niece is an attractive blond woman."

"Yes, Ma'am." Iain's voice was a question.

The Queen gave me an almost imperceptible nod.

"Did Amanda change her hair colour since last week?" I asked. Iain stared at me. "She must have," I continued, my faith in Jamie Allan's powers of observation. "If she was the woman who picked you up at hospital after the fight last Saturday, as she told me she did at Ascot. I've been told by someone else the woman who arrived at the hospital to get you had really dark hair."

Beside me, Hillary started. "Iain?" Her voice quavered.

"Be quiet, Hillary!"

"I think, Mr. Scott," the Queen interjected, "that the woman who came in her car to get you at Wexham Park Hospital was, in fact, your sister—"

"Ma'am, I was nowhere near—"

"I meant Joanna, Mrs. Elliott. The young officer who

pulled Mrs. Pettibon from the fire recognized her and later recalled where he'd seen her before."

"And he told me," I added.

Iain peered at me angrily. "And what does Amanda say?"

"To call her, for one thing," I answered, piqued. "She hasn't been able to get in touch with you."

"There was a fire. My home—temporary though it was—burnt down. I've been staying with Hillary. I haven't had time." His brow darkened. A worried look entered his eyes. "And what else did Amanda have to say?"

"I don't think Amanda's exactly sure where Wexham Park Hospital is," I replied. "But—" I groaned within. Amanda had turned out on the telephone to be much less insipid than she'd been at Ascot "—she insists you were with her the rest of the weekend. In London."

"Hmph." Iain regarded me with a modicum of triumph.

"However," I added, "the PC on duty at Henry VIII Gate last weekend recalls seeing Joanna drive up in her car and waving her through into the Castle around midnight. He believes there was another person with her, lying down in the backseat. But, given that he knew Joanna on sight, the PC didn't think to check the other figure's identity. He assumed it was Joanna's husband."

"Well, it likely was," Iain countered. "Joanna and Roger had been out somewhere."

"Roger lying in the backseat?"

"Perhaps he was legless." Iain shrugged.

I think a drinking problem is *your* side of the family, mate, but, feeling stalemated, I gave no voice to these thoughts. The others at the table were beginning to behave as those distinctly ill at ease. Hillary fussed nervously with a handkerchief she'd pulled from her handbag, wiping at her hands. Sir Bernard turned his head from side to side, his furry eyebrows raised in inquiry as though seeking a consensus for another line of conversation. But it was not to be.

"Nonetheless, Mr. Scott," the Queen proceeded, as Hugo stopped fueling himself with biscuits to study Iain's profile, "Major Simms is quite sure he saw you pass him in the Lower Ward Monday morning. And I expect, if an effort is made, someone else in the Lower Ward that morning may recall you as well. The sentry on duty, perhaps. The colour of your hair is not unremarkable, as I'm sure you're aware."

Iain lifted his teacup and said nothing.

"There are other aspects worth consideration," HM continued. "Mr. Pettibon's stab wound was on the left side of his back, for instance. There's one person here who's left-handed, and it isn't Mr. Fabiani. One can't help noticing, Mr. Scott, that, like Leonardo da Vinci—though perhaps only in this one regard—you are left-handed."

Iain abruptly dropped his cup into its saucer. "Ma'am, there could be a dozen reasons why a stab wound might be on the left side of someone's body."

"Yes, that's true," HM conceded. "But the stabbing was rather straight-on and quite forceful, as I understand it. Perhaps best achieved by someone standing directly behind the victim.

"It's interesting, too," the Queen carried on before Iain could say anything, "that Mr. Pettibon was lying arms outstretched, facing the Throne at the west end of the Throne Room. If, as Miss Walter describes the scene, Mr. Pettibon had been hurrying to reach the doors to the Grand Reception Room and Mrs. Pettibon had been in furious pursuit, one might imagine Mr. Pettibon falling at the east end of the room, nearer the Grand Reception Room. One has a sense, instead, that Mr. Pettibon may have been trying to elude someone, by heading back to the west doors to the Throne Room from whence he came."

"Perhaps Mrs. Pettibon was chasing him around the room, Ma'am," the Duke of Chester suggested.

"Yes, Freddie, that could very well be true as well."

"And I don't recall seeing Mrs. Pettibon with the sword Ma'am," Miranda added.

"That may be because none was ever in her hand!" I said. Rather too eagerly, I fear.

For the Queen gave me a cautioning glance. "There is another curiosity," she continued. "No sign of struggle was found on Mr. Pettibon's body. It appears as if he were killed quite suddenly. Without warning—"

"That doesn't seem all that curious, Ma'am," the Duke interrupted.

"No, I grant you, not on the surface. But is it not possible some sign of struggle, or at least of friction, might appear on the other of the two people in this tragedy?" She turned from the Duke toward Iain. "One wonders about the cut on your chin, Mr. Scott."

"Ma'am, I was in a fight a week ago," Iain replied with faint exasperation, his hand darting to his chin. He rubbed along the puckered surface of the cut, which was no longer a red line but a thin white slice of sickly hue. He would have a scar.

"And yet the hospital has records only of a concussed cheek and bruised ribs," the Queen said.

Iain blinked. "Then I must have cut it shaving."

"It looked pretty raw to me Monday evening when I talked with you at the Star," I added.

"Then I cut myself that morning!"

"That's no ordinary shaving nick," Fabiani observed. "You'd have to be using a straight razor to get that sort of cut."

"That's right. I do use a straight razor."

"That can be checked, Mr. Scott," the Queen warned.

Hillary, who had been silent and staring through his exchange, suddenly cried: "I . . . I don't understand—"

"I think Roger grabbed the sword Lord Lambourn left lying around first," I explained almost reluctantly. Hillary's distress was palpable. "And then he probably brandished it in your brother's face, to ward him off, cutting him—"

"Oh, Iain, no—!"

"Hillary, stop interfering."

"—and then Iain snatched the sword away from Roger."

"This is nonsense!" Iain exploded, his green eyes blazing.

"You are, you'll allow, Mr. Scott, the younger man, and much more fit than Mr. Pettibon was," the Queen interposed. "I'm sure, too, your training as a soldier would stand you in good stead, disarming anyone with a weapon."

"This is sheer conjecture! Even if Major Simms or whoever says I was in the Castle early Monday, there's no evidence I was in the Upper Ward! Or in the Royal Library! Or the Throne Room, for that matter!"

The outburst set the corgis off again.

"Miss Walter," the Queen said, after she'd calmed the beasties, "you said earlier you'd wanted to protect Mrs. Pettibon. That's why you said nothing to Jane or to police. Would one be correct in thinking you would do what you could to protect anyone you thought might have been responsible for Roger Pettibon's death?"

Miranda stiffened.

"You see, I wondered whether you might have seen someone else in the Throne Room with the Pettibons that morning?"

All eyes gravitated in Miranda's direction. Under our gaze, she seemed to sink into her seat, flushing slightly and pushing her teacup away as if needful of some distracting activity. She looked an agony of indecision.

"Come along, young woman," the Duke said impatiently. "Did you or did you not see anyone else in the Throne Room?"

Miranda glanced desperately toward her father. Victor opened his mouth to speak but nothing came out.

"Well, I think your expression's given the game away, my dear," the Duke commented, shaking his head with apparent regret.

Miranda's face crumpled. Her dark eyes were luminous. "I'm sorry," she whispered, looking down at her plate.

Iain snorted. He swiped at a bead of sweat that had gathered at the side of his brow. "Am I to believe you're referring to me?" he asked in a tone of feigned outrage.

"To be clear, Miss Walter, precisely who did you see?" the Queen asked gently.

Miranda looked up and toward the Queen, dismay written in her expression. "I saw a shock of red hair, Ma'am. And a face. Just for a moment. And then I ran. The face I saw—" She looked away, past her father, toward the gardens. "—was Mr. Scott's."

Iain was now breathing heavily, a bellows to his face which was roiling with angry blood. Miranda shrank from him. "All right!" he snapped, his voice barely under control. "I was in the bloody Throne Room! So what? There's no proof I killed Roger!"

"Oh, Iain!" Hillary exclaimed, aghast, twisting her

hands wretchedly. "You can't let Joanna be blamed for something she—"

"Joanna's *dead*, Hillary. I'm *alive*! There's no *proof*," he cut in, shouting. "Roger was an evil bastard. We both know that—"

"*When* did you know that?" The Queen asked, as Hillary began to sob quietly, lifting the linen napkin to her face with quivering hands.

Iain turned from his sister with disgust. He glowered at the Monarch, and then seemed to remember in whose presence he was. With an effort he composed his expression. "I always thought there was something queer about Roger . . . Ma'am." He jerked forward in his chair. "I could never put my finger on it. And then, early Monday morning, I overheard—" He lifted his head toward the East Lawn. "—I overheard Roger tell Joanna what he'd been doing to my niece."

"He *told* her?" I was startled.

"Your doing, probably, Canon," Iain remarked bitterly. "Part of the . . . restitution."

Leathley frowned deeply and opened his mouth to comment. But Iain quickly turned to me, cutting the cleric off. "Your . . . source was right," he snarled. "Joanna had picked me up at the hospital. I spent Sunday in bed. I didn't go out. Then Monday, in the corridor outside my room, I heard what Roger said. I was still a bit groggy. I'd taken a few painkillers the night before and wasn't absolutely sure I'd heard correctly. By the time I'd got out of bed, Roger had gone. *He* was the one who'd found Pippa's diary, Joanna said. The bastard had given it to her with this . . . this confession of his and then ran off, I suppose, to let her read its contents alone."

He paused. I'd been watching as his left hand had balled into a fist. The knuckles, still chafed from last weekend's fight, were pinched to white.

"And that's how I found her," he continued. "Joanna. In Pippa's bedroom. Reading what Pippa had written. I asked Joanna if what I'd heard was true. She said it was. She seemed very calm. She went downstairs, got her coat, and said she was going up to the library to have a talk with Roger. I was so—" His face suddenly reddened again, as if ignited by the memory of that morning. "She left the diary behind. I began to read some of it—" He stared, then put his fist over his mouth and chewed at the knuckle. "The words were a child's but the implications were . . . *disgusting*!"

The last word was virtually spat across the table. No one lifted a cup. Nor a fork. The only movement was of Hillary's silently shaking shoulders as she tried to contain her grief.

"I quickly put on some clothes," Iain resumed after a moment, "and went up to the Library myself. I found Joanna alone. She was . . . she was very nearly incoherent. She'd talked with Roger. Talked!" He snorted. "He'd gone off somewhere. Had seen something out the window in Engine Court—you, I suppose," he eyed Miranda coldly. "I don't know what Roger and Joanna said to each other. I've never seen my sister like that. Chalk white. Quaking. And then, suddenly, she went tearing off into the Library, toward the State Apartments." He looked around at us. "And the rest you know."

The Queen held him with her eyes. "Not quite, Mr. Scott," she said smoothly. "We don't know everything." She reached down to give an insistent corgi a biscuit. "We don't know why you went to the Upper Ward in the first place. Was it to comfort your sister? Did you think her capable of doing something rash? Or did you wish to confront Mr. Pettibon yourself?"

Iain appeared to consider the questions. "I was afraid for her," he replied obliquely. "And, yes, I hated him."

"Hated him enough to kill him?" Miranda interjected, a strange thrill in her voice that rivetted my attention.

Iain said nothing. He folded his arms once again over his chest.

"Why the elaborate alibi, then?" I asked, "I mean, if you're innocent."

He shrugged. His jaw remained stubbornly set.

"Major Simms says he didn't see you come back down into the Lower Ward," I continued, "though he saw Mrs. Pettibon hurrying past sometime around nine-thirty. Even though people aren't clocked going out of the Castle, I'm sure the PC at Henry VIII Gate would have noticed a red-headed guy leaving early by that exit, before people started arriving. And no one with your description left the Castle through the entrance at Henry III Tower either. I checked."

"Really?" He sneered at me.

"So how could you suddenly appear coming *into* the Castle after eleven o'clock?" I thought I knew. Jamie had been most helpful. "Did you jump over the North Terrace?"

Iain glared. "You never did tell me what it is you do here at the Castle."

"Jane's position in my Household is irrelevant," the Queen interjected.

Rebuked, Iain's expression turned sulky. "Yes, I went over the North Terrace and down the hill—"

"Eluding the various security devices because you knew where such things were, as a former member of the Scots Guard," I quickly supplied, knowing the regiments of the Foot Guard are much more than a scarlet-tunic'd day-time tourist attraction but a camouflaged nighttime genuine security force roaming the Castle grounds.

Ian nodded in response. "There's a secluded spot along the outer wall near the Datchet Road. I made my way over that and spent time walking along the Thames. There are some hidden places I know from my days at Eton."

"That you would concoct an alibi to your guilt, Mr. Scott," the Queen cautioned.

"Ma'am, you mentioned earlier the gloves that were found in the pocket of Joanna's raincoat." A cocky edge entered his voice. "Why would I have been wearing gloves?"

"I'd always found Mrs. Pettibon extremely conscientious," the Queen responded evenly. "She obliged anyone handling the valuable drawings in her care to wear gloves. Even one."

"But I wasn't handling the drawings, Ma'am. Joanna was wearing gloves. I don't know why. Force of habit perhaps. When she ran through to the State Apartments she was still wearing her raincoat. And those gloves."

I couldn't help leaping in. "I think maybe you took the gloves off your sister to wipe fingerprints from the hilt of the sword, and that's when they became soaked in blood. Then you put them in her pocket—"

Iain shrugged.

"—to implicate her."

"That's a lie!" he growled.

"Then why was the coat still in her closet at Salisbury Tower?"

Iain scowled at me. "The gloves were placed in Joanna's raincoat pocket," he began. (I couldn't help note the passive voice: *were placed,* indeed!) "Because there was nowhere else to put them. They couldn't very well be left behind in the Throne Room, because the source of those gloves is the Royal Library where Joanna works . . . worked, I mean. And I'd left Salisbury Tower in shirt and trousers. I'd been too . . ." I could see his jaw muscles working furiously. "Too . . . preoccupied to care about what I wore."

"And the coat?" I pressed on. "I would have assumed you'd have got rid of any clothing either of you had worn that morning. Burned it. Buried it. Threw it in the Thames. What about the coat?"

Iain grimaced. "Joanna had a number of coats of various sorts. I don't know women's clothes. I took the wrong coat. That's all. And then, when the weather changed, became so hot, there was no reason to go into that closet for anything. It was a bloody *stupid* mistake."

Off in the Windsor Home Park golf course, someone shouted "Fore!" only to be drowned out by an incoming airplane. The Queen fed the corgis another biscuit, then, when relative quiet was restored, remarked: "Despite your careful phrasing, Mr. Scott, there remains every indication you did this bloody deed."

"But, Ma'am, there is no proof."

"There may be something else in Salisbury Tower," I interjected. "Another piece of clothing you got wrong. They only need a speck of blood—"

"Salibury Tower has been gutted by fire," he cut in, a self-satisfied smile playing at the corners of his mouth. I immediately realized my mistake. "Virtually everything was destroyed. I had to buy new clothes yesterday." He indicated his crisp blue blazer and regimental tie.

"But the police have the gloves." The Queen's gaze

was glacial. "As Jane indicates, forensic science these days can achieve quite remarkable results."

"I don't deny being in the Throne Room, Ma'am. After all, I was witnessed, wasn't I? But even if forensics was to turn up evidence that I'd handled the gloves, that is still no proof that I wielded the knife."

"You are at least an accessory to a murder." Her Majesty's rings whizzed around her wedding finger.

"I am, Ma'am. It's true. But—" Iain paused. Almost, it seemed for effect. He looked up and down the table. "But," he said again, drawing us in, "need anyone ever know?"

24

"IAIN!" HILLARY STARED at him. She wiped at her eyes. Colour flooded back into her cheeks.

"Well, Hillary, *need* anyone ever know? *Does* anyone else know?" Iain glanced around the silent faces. "Her Majesty said earlier no one regrets Roger's passing. Knowing what you've learned this week, *do you?*" The ferocity of Iain's argument seemed to hit Hillary in the face. She recoiled. "Her Majesty also said she doesn't believe Roger's death was planned. Do you? Do you think either Joanna or I went up to the Library last Monday morning planning to push a sword through the stupid bastard's back? Well . . . ?"

Hillary blanched. "No," she replied in a strangled voice. "No, not really. But—"

"But what, Hillary?"

The professor's wife seemed to hesitate. "You always seem to be in want of money, Iain—"

"How dare you!" He cut her off, pounding the table with his fist. Hillary flinched. Teacups rattled. A corgi barked. "Money was *not* an issue! Money never entered my head when I—" He stopped short. "—when I went to the Upper Ward!"

"All right, Iain," she retorted with some recovery of spirit. "Don't shout at me so."

"Are you asking us to keep *shtum* about all this?" the Duke queried in a startled voice.

"Yes," Iain cried urgently. "Yes, I am, Your Grace. My sister is dead. My niece is dead. What is the point of bringing further grief to my remaining sisters, to my parents . . . to me! What good would it serve?"

"You realize, lad, you're asking your sovereign to break her own laws," the Duke added.

"I am asking no one to break the law, least of all Her Majesty—"

"You'd make us all accessories! It's shocking!"

"—I am merely asking everyone to keep what they've learned here to themselves."

"Well, I think it's damned cowardly," the Duke huffed. "And you so recently a member of the Guard."

"Iain, we've always had to pull you out of scrapes," Hillary said. "We spoiled you rotten as a boy and this is the result."

"Oh, Hillary, that has nothing to do with this! If something happens to me over this business with Roger, it will rebound on the family. Do you want more unhappiness? Roger is dead. One of us—Joanna or I—killed him. I admit it. It wasn't intended. You don't know what went on in the Throne Room that morning. What good would punishing me bring to the world? Her Majesty talked about resolution. Would my arrest really resolve anything?"

"Why don't you simply insist Joanna did it?" Fabiani asked coolly.

"Because . . . because *that* would be cowardly."

"I would say that's tantamount to a confession."

"I'm confessing to nothing more than being in the Throne Room with Joanna Monday morning, Mr. Fabiani."

"And if Joanna were alive today? What would you do then? The CID had dismissed my 'confession.' They would be casting a wider net today."

"But Joanna is *not* alive. Speculation is pointless."

The Queen tapped her plate with her knife." "You're asking much of a fourteen-year-old boy, Mr. Scott," she observed.

"I can keep a secret," Hugo declared.

"If it's a secret to be kept," Her Majesty demurred.

"I should like to see *you* keep a secret, Uncle," Leathley remarked.

"Mind your manners, St. John!"

"And this is certainly outside the seal of the confession," the Canon added drily, ignoring the Duke.

An uncomfortable silence ensued. I looked across the table at Iain, but he met no one's eyes. Rather, he rested his mouth on his crossed hands, almost prayerfully, as if he were awaiting our decision. He had put us in a pickle. Was there anything to be gained from shopping him to the authorities? Ought we to do our duty and adhere to the law? Or give Iain leave to put this unhappy episode behind him and carry on with his life?

Oy!

He was right. No one would likely be able to prove without a shadow of a doubt that he employed Hugo's sword. If he did. I imagined Iain that morning in the Throne Room snatching the sword from Roger and, in a fit of wrath, quickly dispatching his brother-in-law. But, then, perhaps, Iain had merely wrested the sword from Roger, only to have Joanna seize it and . . .

I watched a bird soar over the castle ramparts, free and unencumbered, and felt earthbound and confused. There was something unsavoury about Iain's refusing to come clean about the events of those critical moments. About his choosing expedience over the right or the just. And asking us to sanction it.

But, then, on the other hand . . .

The Queen cut into my thoughts, all our thoughts. "Mr. Scott, you'll have to weigh your sister's good name against your own. The world will believe she killed her husband."

"And the world will know she had just cause, Ma'am."

"Perhaps. Quite likely, I shouldn't wonder. But wouldn't it be more honourable to confess *your* role, whatever it was? The world may think you had just cause as well."

"Maybe my sister should decide. Hillary, which one of us—Joanna or me—would you prefer to bear the burden of guilt?"

"Iain!"

"That's very unfair, Mr. Scott."

Iain frowned at Her Majesty's censure. "I know what everyone must think of me. I'm not asking you to like me. Or to approve of me. I'm just asking that we put a stop to this family tragedy now."

"Oh, Iain . . ." Hillary moaned, shaking her head. "You can't talk your way out of this one—"

Miranda interrupted. "Well, I won't say anything, if that's what you want," she said with quiet force.

"And those are my sentiments," Fabiani added.

The Queen glanced around the table. Her mouth had been a grim line. "Well," she said, "You seem to have two votes, Mr. Scott. I expect, however, the rest of us will have to consult our own consciences on this matter." She turned her head toward the windows of the White Drawing Room and raised her hand. "We certainly can't promise you anything." She lowered her hand. A few seconds later Davey trotted out of the Castle.

"And," she continued, "I would urge you to give this matter your further consideration, too. Perhaps you ought to have a talk with your family."

"I was hoping Hillary would spare the rest of the family—"

"Oh, Iain, of course they must know!"

"Hillary—!"

"Perhaps," the Queen interjected, as Davey stepped to her side, curiosity fighting with solemnity on his face, "you would care to discuss this in private." She turned to her footman. "David, Mr. Scott and Mrs. Elliott will be leaving us now. Would you escort them, please."

Iain and Hillary rose from the table.

"One other curiosity," the Queen said, glancing at Sir

Bernard Scrymgeour-Warburton, then addressing Iain. "Mr. Pettibon was wearing a Garter when his body was found—"

"*The* Garter, Ma'am?"

"Ah! I think you've answered my question. Good day to you, Mr. Scott. Mrs. Elliott."

Hillary sank into a curtsey. Iain bowed sharply from the neck.

"And, David," the Queen said in a lower voice, beckoning him as the departing guests began to make their way up the steps to the Castle, "I think perhaps we could some of us use something a little stronger than tea."

"Oh!" Davey cast his eyes about the table. We must have all looked faintly gobsmacked from the afternoon's revelations. "Of course, Ma'am."

The Queen watched as one of her dogs scampered down the shaded lawn after a butterfly. She smiled, as if thinking of something else entirely; a childhood memory perhaps, of the War years spent at the Castle. The rest of us sat in silence, even Hugo, who had eaten just about all there was to eat on the table.

"The Garter on Mr. Pettibon's body *is* a curiosity." The Queen turned back to the subject. "Both Garters for use in the Investiture were untouched, laying on their velvet cushions in the Throne Room. So, it would seem there was a Garter surplus to requirements." Her Majesty paused and addressed Miranda: "I expect you didn't notice if Mr. Pettibon happened to be wearing a Garter when he came through the Throne Room."

"No, Ma'am, I didn't."

"Well, it would be a rather peculiar thing for him to do, but Mr. Pettibon, we now know, was nothing if not peculiar, to put it mildly," Her Majesty added drily. "Is it possible, Bernard, that a Garter may have passed down to Mr. Pettibon through a family connection?"

Finally called upon, the Secretary of the Central Chancery almost quivered with animation. "Unlikely, I think, Ma'am. It's *most* interesting . . ."

"But," I interjected, "I looked up a will at Somerset House a few days ago, a will of Roger Pettibon's aunt, and it seemed to indicate a gift of some family heirlooms that suggested . . ."

Sir Bernard was shaking his head vigorously. "We've no indication of a Pettibon family descended from any Garter Knight in the past. And I did seek the assistance of the College of Arms in this matter."

"I should explain," the Queen interjected. "I asked Sir Bernard if he might be able to trace the origin of this extra Garter, hoping it might help lead the police to Mr. Pettibon's killer. Of course, we now know both Mrs. Pettibon and Mr. Scott were involved in Mr. Pettibon's death, but this didn't quite explain the presence of the Garter on his body."

She nodded to Sir Bernard. He continued: "Unfortunately, as you might imagine, given the Order's six-hundred-year history, there is not a little inconsistency in the regulations concerning the return of Garter insignia. In the earliest days, Knights kept the insignia and handed them down as heirlooms. But King Charles I revised the rules in the seventeenth century. The custom today is that on the death of a Knight the Garter badge and star be returned to the Sovereign, and that the rest of the insignia, including the garter, be returned to the Central Chancery. However, in some cases, even into this century, some Knights made private arrangements for jewelled garters or jewelled copies of other Garter insignia, and these their families were permitted to keep. But, of course, despite the best of intentions, I'm sure, not all Garter insignia, of whatever manufacture, were retured to the Sovereign. Some have even shown up at auction. We do our utmost to have them returned to the Central Chancery."

He paused, raised his teacup, then thought better of it. The tea had gone cold.

"Of course, too," he continued, "records have not always been well kept, which adds, I daresay, to the confusion. The Chancery itself is not even a hundred years old, and the most accurate records matching specific insignia to particular Knights have only been kept since the War. So," he smiled and surveyed us all, "you can see that finding the ownership of a particular, apparently stray, Garter might be a rather daunting task.

"First, with the help of the College of Arms, I tried to find a Garter Knight ancestor of one of the people whose names were supplied to me by Her Majesty's assistant private secretary—names of, well, of some of you around this very table. The results were somewhat encouraging. I was most interested to find that Joanna Pettibon, or Joanna Scott as she was born, is a descendent of Charles II through a son born to his mistress Margaret de Carteret of Jersey, and who was a Knight of the Garter. But her family is descended from the fourth son of this illegitimate issue and so we might say, in layman's terms, that the connection is quite remote. It seemed to me not only unlikely the garter in question had been in Mrs. Pettibon's possession—even though it is, in fact, missing—but also impossible for a reason I'll get to in a moment.

"Of course the most obvious possessor of an ancestral Garter at this table would be yourself, Your Grace." He turned to the Duke. "The Dukes of Cheshire are direct descendants of James II's third son, Charles FitzJames, by his mistress Arabella Churchill. Charles FitzJames, the first Duke of Cheshire, was a member of the Order of the Garter."

"And I'm the first Duke since my ancestor to be invested," the eleventh Duke said, "but the first Duke's garter is at my home, Umbridge Trigoze." He paused and added, blusteringly: "I'm quite sure it is. It's in a case in the library. I haven't looked at it for some time, but . . ."

My eyes shifted from Davey, who had wheeled a drinks trolley out onto the stone porch above us, to Hugo, who seemed to be staring at his empty plate. It was hard to tell, of course: his hair so ably covered his eyes.

"Hugo?" His Grace said in a warning tone. "Hugo, that Garter *is* at Umbridge Trigoze, I trust."

"Um, I sort of borrowed it, Granddad," Hugo answered feebly, looking up, pushing his hair back. "I wanted to practice with it. It was going to be my first Garter ceremony."

"Really, Hugo! Why didn't you just ask me, rather than take something like that."

"Sorry, Granddad. I was very careful with it."

Canon Leathley broke in: "Do you mean, Sir Bernard,

that somehow Roger happened to be wearing the first Duke of Cheshire's Garter?" His tone was unbelieving.

"No." Sir Bernard was firm. "No, not at all. You see, I also took the opportunity to examine the garter. It was in police possession, but as it happened the police were rather interested in an expert opinion and so yesterday I was pleased to be able to provide one. There were no fingerprints on it, I gather, or any other useful information, but all Garters are not identical. Far from it."

He turned to the Duke. "Your ancestor's Garter at Umbridge Trigoze, Your Grace: what colour is it?"

"Oh, I think rather more of a lighter blue than the one Her Majesty presented to me on Monday."

"Exactly. During the Stuart reign, the favoured colour was a sky blue. But when the Stuarts were deposed, their successors, the Hanovers, changed the colour to a dark blue."

"Because the Stuart Pretenders continued to appoint new Knights to the Order, am I correct, Bernard?"

"You are indeed, Ma'am." Sir Bernard smiled. "Knights appointed by the true Sovereign need to be distinguished from those appointed by the Pretender. However, His late Majesty, King George VI, made yet another change, a very slight one, when he revived the Garter ceremony after the War. The colour was changed to a kingfisher blue, a colour favoured by Queen Victoria. It is, as I say, only a slight colour difference, but it is distinguishable. The garter in police possession is, without a doubt, from the post-War period. The question is: Whose garter is it?

"Now there are slight differences in material and manufacture even in these past fifty years, and of course, older garters bear some signs of wear. I examined the garter in question and could only conclude it came from the late 1940's or the very early 1950's."

I could see the Queen's brow furrow. "But," she said, "of those who were Knights' Companions in those days, I can't think that anyone is still living . . ."

"Except for *Royal* Knights Companions, Ma'am."

"Except for Royal Knights Companions," Her Majesty echoed, as Davey hovered at her elbow.

"One other observation, if I may interrupt, Ma'am. Because Ladies of the Garter wear their garters around the arm, rather than the knee, the wear on the buckle is rather different. The garter in police possession had clearly belonged to a Lady of the Garter. There are currently four Ladies of the Garter: Her Majesty Queen Elizabeth the Queen Mother, Her Royal Highness the Princess Royal, Lady Thatcher, and, as Sovereign of the Order, yourself, Ma'am."

"And my mother didn't attend this year," the Queen murmured.

"And both Her Royal Highness and Lady Thatcher are relatively recent appointments. The garter in question is rather older. So I venture to say, Ma'am—and I'm at pains to explain it—that the Garter Mr. Pettibon was wearing on Monday belonged to . . ." Sir Bernard paused for effect, almost seemed to be savoring it. ". . . belonged, quite simply . . . to Your Majesty."

There was a brief stunned silence, time enough for all of us to note a certain perplexity having its way with the Queen's features and then to jump in all our seats as a silver tray hit the East Terrace paving stones with a nasty metallic crash.

"You know, I was quite sure the Garter was mine," the Queen said as Davey bent over to pick up the tray he'd dropped. "But then . . ." She paused and looked at Davey questioningly.

"But it's im*poss*ible," Davey wailed, his face red from exertion and confusion. "Ma'am, I retraced my steps. I found Your Majesty's Garter just off the White Drawing Room."

"I'm quite sure the Garter I wore on Monday was not the one I normally wear," the Queen said firmly. "But there seemed no point in making a fuss. We'd already been delayed."

"Then who on earth strapped Your Majesty's Garter to that bloody man's leg!" the Duke thundered indignantly.

All eyes seemed to be on the Queen. But mine were on Hugo. He had paled slightly, I could see.

"I guess I did," he said quietly, seeming to sink into his chair.

"Hugo!" his grandfather barked. "What game is this?"

"Sorry, Granddad. I just . . . I found a Garter on my

way back to the Throne Room to get my sword. Below the Grand Vestibule. I . . . I didn't know whose it was. When I got into the Throne Room and saw . . . what I saw . . . I mean, I knew who he was, I knew what he'd done to Pippa, and the Garter motto sort of came to me. I mean, the words were right in my hands and I'd read it enough times when I was practicing. Shame on him who thinks this evil. *Honi soit qui mal y pense.* I didn't know who'd killed him but . . . well . . ." He shrugged. "I wasn't sorry and I didn't think anybody else should be sorry. If they knew what I knew, they wouldn't think this murder was evil.

"So I buckled the Garter onto his leg. And then I went for help."

The boy lifted his head, and looked around challengingly. One cool little Etonish dude, I thought. We all, HM included, simply looked at him with varying degrees of astonishment, mouths working with, one presumes, various responses. Finally Miranda spoke.

"Thanks," she said quietly.

Silence followed. Another bee hovered over the cut flowers of the centrepiece, then buzzed away.

The Queen moved her knife absently over her plate as if she were tapping the shoulders of a newly invested knight. "Well . . ." she said after a moment, "there you are, then."

"But, Ma'am," Davey interrupted, his face still a crimson balloon. "I don't understand. If Lord Lambourn picked up Your Majesty's Garter, the one I dropped on my way from Mr. Fabiani's rooms, then whose Garter did *I* pick up outside the White Drawing Room?"

Everybody's face around the table looked a blank.

"I'm not sure," Her Majesty said, taking the consensus. "It appears to be a mystery.

"Now, who would care for a drink?"

Epilogue

THERE ARE NO mysteries.

Some few weeks later, I was told, the granddaughter of Field-Marshal Viscount Jarrold, who was invested in the Order of the Garter in the early 1960's, wrote to the Central Chancery of the Orders of Knighthood with some embarrassment to say her grandfather's garter seemed to have gone missing, and, if it couldn't be found (for they had searched *everywhere!*) might they have another one? As I may have mentioned earlier in this chronicle, some of the Garter Knights are quite elderly, and none, it seems, more elderly than Viscount Jarrold, who has had the misfortune to lose some of his mental faculties along life's petal-strewn path. The Viscount was described to me by a certain source one day in July at the Palace of Holyroodhouse in Edinburgh where the Court was holding its annual rites, and I realized he'd been the confused-looking peer who'd toddled past

Lydia and me during the Garter Procession, the one who didn't seem to know where he was. "Bit gaga, that one," the man behind me had said. "He looks like he's missing something."

The Viscount *was* missing something. The man's comment was partly cruel and, I believe, partly perceptive. It wasn't so much gray matter Viscount Jarrold was missing. It were 'is bleedin' garter that were missin'. The man must have glimpsed the mantle opening to reveal a garterless knee while the rest of us were looking at faces.

At some point well before the Garter Investiture, we could only assume (because Viscount Jarrold couldn't remember), the Viscount dropped his garter (or his garter dropped from him) outside the White Drawing Room where Knights and guests were assembling. The Viscount didn't notice the loss because he wasn't up to noticing much of anything. This garter of the Viscount's Davey scooped up, believing it to be the one he'd dropped earlier, the one belonging to the Queen. It wasn't, of course. End of mystery. This garter was returned to the Viscount in due course with a pleasant note.

As for the Queen's garter: Being that it had spent some time wrapped around the knee of the very unchivalrous Roger Pettibon, it was quietly returned to the Central Chancery where it will probably sit under wraps until such time as the events of the late twentieth century are forgotten and the garter can be renovated for use by some future Garter Knight. The Queen now has a nice new garter.

As for other mysteries, I'm pleased to say I'm not a nut. The spectre of Herne the Hunter, glimpsed in Windsor Great Park one dark and not particularly stormy night, was not the very coinage of my brain. One day a few months later, in late September as it happened, I was flipping through *The Independent* when I came across a small item with a picture of a man wearing a pair of antlers. Face looks familiar, I thought. "Windsor man charged with mischief," the headline read. It was Geoffrey Gowerlock, Miranda Walter's neighbour, the fellow possessed of the secret teachings. According to the story, he'd been frightening people in the Great Park for years with his antics but had managed to elude capture until one Brain of Britain, a gardener on the

Crown Estates who'd been tallying the sightings, deduced that Gowerlock only made his appearances during equinoxes and solstices, all this being related to some amalgam of pagan, druidic, cabalistic, what-have-you beliefs. Gowerlock wasn't *that* frightening, I considered in retrospect. Why not just post signs in the Great Park on certain dates warning of sudden appearances by a man in antlers? No worse than the deer that sometimes cross your path on the Long Walk. Bit of fun, really.

The mystery of the purloined photo, the one of Victor Fabiani's half-finished portrait of the Queen, the one that had appeared unauthorized on the front page of the *Evening Gazette,* was solved shortly after Ascot Week. Relatively minor though the breach was, it nevertheless became a flashpoint in one of those occasional showdowns between press and Palace, with the gray men of the latter institution both undertaking a diligent leak inquiry among Household and Staff and applying pressure of various sorts on the denizens of the former institution. I suppose you could call it the jelly sandwich approach: If you keep squeezing something will eventually plop out the side. In this case, footman Nigel Stokoe plopped out. Not content to sulk over punishment for his latest misdemeanour, being caught *in flagrante delicto* with a member of the Household Cavalry, he'd decided to be vindictive, succumbing to the blandishments of a certain reporter at the *Gazette* by sneaking into Fabiani's rooms with a camera and snapping the picture himself. I suspect Nigel was shopped by the *Gazette* in exchange for some favour. Her Majesty may be forced to hold her nose and place the notorious proprietor of the *Gazette* on the next Birthday Honours List. Reuben Crush MBE, for servs. to . . . no, they couldn't say to journalism. For servs. to charity. That's always nice and vague. Meanwhile, rare as sackings are at the Palace, Nigel got the old sackeroo. Or got downsized, as we say these days. Violation of Staff agreement. I expect he's down the JobCentre these days looking at the vacancies postings for footmen.

However, the certain *Gazette* reporter who coaxed Nigel into disloyalty was not, you may be surprised to learn,

Andrew Macgreevy. Nigel had handed off the roll of film to
a Rat Pack temp covering the Windsor beat while Macg. was
on suspension. So Macgreevy was being straight with me
after all. (Perhaps there *are* mysteries.) He had little time to
pester me further, anyway, because, within days, he was off
to Thailand in his drip-dry safari suit on the trail of the
elusive Lord Graven to bring off, he hoped, the coup of the
decade. And he did bring it off (sort of), as chronicled in a
series of EXCLUSIVE(s)!!! in the *Evening Gazette:* picking
up the scent in Bangkok, following the leads into the dense
and dangerous countryside, surprising the Marquess in his
lair at Pa Kha, details of Rupert's Kurtzlike existence, the
flies, the drugs, the madness! And the picture! Rupert made
Keith Richards look like Little Mary Sunshine. And the interview! The self-righteousness. The pieties. The justifica-
tions. I was swept away. So was half of Britain. And so was
the Marquess who, realizing that less self-interested authorities weren't far behind the newspaper reporter, swept himself off, who-knows-where, just in the nick of time. Some
may think this cynical, but I half suspect Macgreevy of engi-
neering Lord Graven's second escape. Why? So he can find
him again, of course!

And what of Iain Scott? Well you may ask. A rumour floated
around in late summer that he'd been brought in for an
interview with DCI Nightingale & cohorts. I wondered, had
one of us at the tea table that June afternoon put a word the
right way? Or—depending on your views—the wrong way?
Had the disapproving Duke of Chester been unable to keep
shtum? Had the Canon weighed his conscience in the bal-
ance of church practices? Had Hugo been unable to resist
telling his friends? Sir Bernard for reasons of his own? Her
Majesty? Had the Queen, the Fount of Justice, felt duty-
bound? Or had the Queen, the woman, the wife, the mother,
the grandmother, the sister, settled for discretion?

It wasn't me who blabbed. I can say that. And, I suspect, it was neither Miranda Walter nor her father. My guess,
based on the reported outcome of the interview, is that
Amanda Simms remained steadfast as Iain's alibi and Miranda, the eyewitness to the occupants of the Throne Room

those few minutes that morning, kept her promise and denied seeing him. I suspect, too, the Scott family rallied around the favoured male child, the only son and heir, keeping the truth, as they perceived it, to themselves. So it appears Iain got off—you'll pardon the pun—scot-free. You may approve or disapprove, as you like.

Meanwhile, back in London, in the fall, Victor Fabiani's portrait of the Queen was previewed at the National Portrait Gallery to a storm of controversy. Well, a *breeze* of controversy. Rather than depict Her Majesty as a remote and mysterious icon, or as an upper-middle-class matron with a couple of corgis or, more lately, as a careworn wrinkled old woman, Fabiani had presented the Queen in the winter of her years with more than a suggestion of passion breaking through the reserve that is her public character, the china blue eyes steelier, the jaw more set, the stance hinting of vigour. The portrait was clearly dissimilar to the one Fabiani had started in the spring, the one in its partially finished state that had found its way to the pages of the *Evening Gazette*. That portrait had interpreted the Queen as she presented herself in pleasant conversation during the sittings at the Easter Court—human, decent, but solitary. The new finished portrait, the *re*interpretation, was drawn, I was sure, from the episode in Fabiani's rooms above the State Apartments after his release and from our Sunday gathering on the East Terrace. "Our 'Warrior Queen'?" one professional controversialist sniggered in one of the papers. The more withering critics believed the artist had veiled the Queen in attributes that were not hers by nature but were mythic, romantic, and, therefore, beyond the pale. Fabiani countered in the press that the truth about people is always hidden, yet vouchsafed, nonetheless, to the truly perceptive artist, implying his critics were a thick and dull lot. He had not veiled the Queen, he said in contemptuous fashion in a television interview, but had, rather, pierced the very veil that had long cloaked aspects of her personality from her subjects, and that furthermore certain critics could bloody well—But the interview ended just as the F-word was forming on his lips. At any rate, the public loved the portrait.

Record crowds were tallied at the National Portrait Gallery before the picture travelled to its home in Eton. As for those of us who have seen Her Majesty in some of these private moments, we could only say: Spot on, Fabbo!

And on a personal note, my eyebrows did grow back. And the Hon. James Allan called again. And then again. Despite earlier ruminations about my not-so-brilliant career, it turns out there are certain unexpected blessings to being a housemaid in Her Majesty's service. Davey was right: Windsor *is* the most roman*tique* castle that is in the world.

ABOUT THE AUTHOR

C. C. Benison is a Canadian writer.